Dark Blood

Dark Blood

John Meaney

To Paul McKenna, PhD,
Who truly changes lives –
a billion thanks

Copyright © John Meaney 2008
All rights reserved

The right of John Meaney to be identified as the author
of this work has been asserted by him in accordance with
the Copyright, Designs and Patents Act 1988.

First published in Great Britain in 2008 by
An imprint of the Orion Publishing Group
Orion House, 5 Upper St Martin's Lane,
London WC2H 9EA
An Hachette UK Company

This edition published in Great Britain in 2009
by Gollancz

1 3 5 7 9 10 8 6 4 2

A CIP catalogue record for this book
is available from the British Library

ISBN 978 0 575 08415 5

Printed and bound in the UK by
CPI Mackays, Chatham ME5 8TD

The Orion Publishing Group's policy is to use papers
that are natural, renewable and recyclable products and
made from wood grown in sustainable forests. The logging
and manufacturing processes are expected to conform to
the environmental regulations of the country of origin.

www.orionbooks.co.uk

One

Donal sat in the back of a police cruiser as it drove through the shadowed, broken streets of Lower Danklyn, past purplestone tenements that lay cracked and deserted. White lizards watched from the rubble. High overhead, a Tristopolis PD scanbat glided, observing.

I've seen men die before.

Not just men. His beautiful, lovely Laura, her head blown apart in a grey spray of brains and bone and zombie blood—

This one had better suffer.

But he could summon up no real joy. On some level of abstraction, Donal knew that Alderman Kinley Finross would take three hours to die. The bastard deserved every agonized second he was about to endure. Donal felt a sense of rightness – but only that.

There should be more.

Perhaps a living man, now, would feel his heart beat faster, his skin grow damp with perspiration, his stomach grow queasy.

More feeling.

In a living man, emotions would arise from masses of neurons in the bodily organs, and a flow of peptides almost as complex as the nerves themselves. But Donal was cold – would feel icy to another person, to a normal human touch – and his heart, Laura's heart, beat at the same unvarying pace inside his chest.

Laura. Oh, my Laura.

It hadn't been Finross who pulled the trigger. Senator Blanz had ripped Donal's Magnus from his grip, and used it to destroy Laura Steele, Donal's perfect lover, before swivelling to shoot Donal in the heart. After dying, Donal had awoken with his chest cavity split open, with paramedic mages working to install a beating black heart – Laura's zombie heart – inside him.

'Not long now.' Bud Brodowski, his massive shoulders convex with

1

muscle, turned the steering-wheel. 'Has weasel-face got his self supporters?'

There was a bend in the road. A group of people stood beneath billowing, floating banners: **Rending renders society cruel**. They opposed the death penalty as a matter of principle. Donal wondered if they spared a thought for the near-invisible wraiths they were using to hold the banners overhead. Perhaps those boundwraiths had their own opinions on dealing with murderers.

'Can we run over 'em?' Al Brodowski, hulking like his brother, was in the front passenger seat. 'Just a couple, please, Lieutenant?'

'Don't tempt me,' said Donal from the rear.

But he spoke on an inhalation, which gave his voice a strange resonance, as if he were Zurinese. He saw the shared glance between the Brodowskis.

Damn it. There's too much to remember.

So much changed when you had to consciously control the lungs, when breathing was no longer necessary. When, arguably, you were no longer a person but a *thing*, an abomination created by thaumaturgical intervention instead of allowing extinction to—

To provide bones for the reactor piles? Would that have been better?

Further back, Unity Party supporters glowered at the police car. Officially, their party did not condone this demonstration, not when their man Finross had been complicit in the death of Maria daLivnova, a very human Diva.

To either side in darkness, amber eyes glowed, disappeared as the deathwolves turned their attention elsewhere, then shone again as they followed the progress of Donal's car. They belonged to the prison pack, normally patrolling inside the grounds.

'You think they're expecting trouble?' said Bud.

'Nah.' Al shook his head, but still pulled his shotgun from its dashboard clip. 'Going to be a quiet day.'

'Not for Finross,' said Donal.

The prison gates looked like darkened pewter, two feet thick, on which the crossed axes of the Federal Prison Authority were embossed, overlaying a yin-yang whose dots were serpent's eyes. The gates swung inwards, and the cruiser passed through.

Gravel sprayed as Al turned the wheel, following the arc of the driveway.

'Sorry,' he said. 'Shit.'

'I hate this place,' muttered Bud.

The gravel was formed of knucklebones, taken from prisoners across the centuries. Mostly, it came from corpses, but some came from the excision of living fingers: a punishment for infringing prison discipline.

Near the main steps, where white runes glowed upon the flagstones, was parked Mayor Dancy's official limousine. The city's Tree Frog insignia glistened on the black doors.

'Probably his assistant,' said Donal. 'His Honour doesn't like these things, according to the *Gazette*.'

'Don't blame him.' Al drove past perhaps twenty parked cars. 'Here we go.'

'Got newspaper guys here.' Bud replaced the shotgun in its clip. 'Maybe they'll interview you, Lieutenant. You being a hero and all.'

'Huh.' Donal held out his hand palm up, fingers extended. 'You want to see my new heroic trick?'

Al halted the car, pulled up the handbrake, and switched the engine off. He and Bud turned in their seats.

'Like this,' added Donal.

Using neuromuscular control that he'd never possessed while living, Donal curled just his little finger tightly, while the others remained outstretched. Then, slowly, he curled the ring finger, then the forefinger, and finally the thumb. The middle finger remained outstretched.

Then he raised the middle finger horizontal to the vertical.

'Pretty neat, Lieutenant.'

'Ya gotta teach us that one.'

Donal slid out of the car, smiling. Then his shoes scrunched on knucklebones, and he looked up at the dark massive pile that was Wailing Towers, the city's largest prison. His smile had gone. If zombies could shiver, he would have.

It won't bring Laura back.

Still, Finross's death would count for something.

Someone had redecorated. The viewing chamber held rows of plush, dark-red upholstered benches, instead of the hard bonewood furniture that Donal remembered from four previous visits. In Tristopolis, unlike other cities, the arresting officer always witnessed the execution. It granted cops a sense of perspective on their work.

As always, the benches were arranged in tiers, sloping down to an armoured hexiglass barrier, floor to ceiling. Beyond it lay the execution chamber. Inside, a stone bier waited, with dangling, empty chains and straps.

Donal stopped in the aisle, deciding where to sit. Several journalists and bureaucrats glanced at him. Some noticed the pale complexion.

Others – Donal deduced, from the minutiae of widening eyes, a tiny rolling-forward of the shoulders – knew him for the lieutenant who had taken down Senator Blanz, dying in the process.

It's not me they're afraid of.

Choosing a near-empty row of seats high at the rear, Donal threaded his way past a down-at-heels journalist, then two men in grey suits. Each man wore a small black stud in his left lapel; inside the stud were superimposed a U and P, the symbol of the Unity Party. Neither man responded to a zombie detective lieutenant squeezing past them. Or perhaps they were fascinated – fearfully fascinated – by the waiting bier, the imminent reality of Finross's death.

It's the necrofusion piles that scare them. The thought of their own death.

Or perhaps they feared ending up like Donal, except that no Unity Party member would dream of taking out a life policy. As he sat down, he noticed both men flinch, just as he himself felt something cold from across the room.

Another one.

A black-coated doctor was entering with stethofork in hand. His skin was palest grey, almost white. He stopped, looked up at Donal, and nodded. His eyes were like chips of slate.

Donal nodded back.

Another of my kind.

The doctor paused at the front row, then ascended the aisle and made his way along the row below Donal's. Drawing close, he stopped. His hand, when he held it out, was long-fingered. Donal expected his handshake to be cold.

But when two zombies shake hands, their bodies are at the *same* temperature.

'I'm Thalveen,' said the doctor. 'Odom Thalveen.'

'Donal Riordan. Good to meet you.'

A faint scent of formaldehyde wafted from Thalveen's black coat.

'I guess you're here to make sure,' added Donal, 'that Finross lasts the course?'

The shock of rending would kill an unmedicated person within seconds. It took skilled medical care to ensure the vagus nerve and heart remained functioning. Anything less than two hours dying was considered 'easy and unusual kindness', prohibited by law.

'I *am* here to prepare Finross. Also the hookwraiths.' Thalveen's hair was lanky, and he brushed it back with one long finger. 'Why do people assume the wraiths enjoy their work? I try to minimize *their* suffering.'

'While maximizing the prisoner's, I hope.'

'Why, Lieutenant—' he gave a cold zombie smile, using Donal's rank, signalling that he knew who Donal was— 'that goes without saying.'

The grey-suited Unity Party men stiffened. Then they let out tense breaths, releasing their anger, and looked at each other.

Thalveen shook his head, saying loudly: 'Too bad Senator Blanz isn't here.'

Perhaps provoking the UP was unwise.

'He wouldn't see a thing,' said Donal, not caring. 'I know, because my hands were sticky when they resurrected me.'

'What do you mean, Lieutenant?'

'Isn't it called aqua humerus, or something? *I* think it's humorous.'

'Aqueous humour,' said Thalveen, 'is a liquid inside the eye.'

'Then that's what I had on my fingers, when I took out Blanz's eye-balls.'

Donal had raked with his hands like claws even as the shot took him in the heart. The memory endured, an undertone of terrible joy failing to offset the shock of seeing Laura's head explode.

One of the UP guys had grown so pale he looked almost zombie-like. Donal considered pointing that out; but Thalveen was offering his hand again.

'I have to take my place. It was good meeting you, Lieutenant.'

'Likewise, Doctor.' This time, it was no surprise that Thalveen's hand felt thermally neutral. 'I hope we meet again.'

'We will.'

Donal watched him make his way down to the front row. Ordinary living humans – prison guards, bureaucrats and journalists – paid special attention to the black-coated doctor. Some frowned, some looked away, while others deliberately forced down their squeamishness and nodded to Thalveen as an equal. No one ignored his zombie nature.

So it's always going to be like this.

Perhaps Donal would get used to it.

It was exactly nine minutes later – Donal somehow knew, without look-ing at his watch – that an old woman with cataract-milky eyes limped up the aisle. One of the grey-suited men rose, and went down to help. He led the woman to the seat he had been sitting in, sat her down, and took the place beside her. The other grey-suited man, on the other side of her, said something and patted her hand.

'Holy Mother of the Seven Blades,' she said. 'It isn't right. Not my Kinley.'

A zombie *could* feel icy cold, for Donal realized who the woman must be:

Alderman Finross's mother. A UP man was glaring at him, but Donal reacted in a way he could not have done when living. Consciously, he forced the guilt to recede towards an imaginary horizon, and into oblivion.

That was fine because Finross, ultimately, was the person responsible for his own execution.

Down below, Commissioner Vilnar was entering the chamber, along with Commander Bowman of Robbery-Haunting. Vilnar was blocky and shaven-headed, his suit expensive, his body overweight but muscular. He greeted one of the journalists, then the mayor's assistant who was sitting in the front row as far from Dr Thalveen as possible.

Bowman, maybe forty years old with cropped, receding red hair, was an unknown factor to Donal. But he glanced in Donal's direction and gave a minuscule nod, which was more recognition than Vilnar was granting him.

Politics? Or something else?

Commissioner Vilnar had attended Laura's funeral, against political advice. Grant him that much. There had been few mourners at the graveside. Commander Laura Steele was a cop who had died in the line of duty, in the Capitol building at the heart of Fortinium – but she had been a zombie.

Vilnar must have known Donal was here. Still, he took his seat, and folded his bulky arms, without looking around.

Meanwhile, on the same row as Donal, Finross's mother drew a prayer-chain from purse, and began to mutter the verses of a Septena. From his orphanage days, under the stern rule of the Sisters of Death, Donal remembered the prayers, and wondered if she was about to recite the entire forty-nine-verse sequence.

I'm not enjoying this.

Donal had made his guilt recede, but there was no joy to replace it. Conscious control of the emotions was a zombie's hallmark, wasn't it? So why couldn't he stop feeling empty?

Finross's mother faltered in her prayers.

Several seconds later, a door opened at the rear of the execution chamber, some fifty feet away and separated from the viewers by armoured hexiglass. Finross's mother had sensed the door's opening in advance. Donal wondered whether Kinley Finross's abilities as a minor mage – unlicensed and illegally trained – were inherited.

Or perhaps it was ordinary maternal awareness, raised to new heights of perception in this awful place. She resumed her prayers in a tense, rapid mutter. Donal wanted to tell her shut up. He wanted to tell her that everything would be all right; but it wouldn't be.

A gurney rolled into the execution chamber. On it, strapped naked in place, was Alderman Kinley Finross. He was gasping, hyperventilating, struggling against manticore-sinew cords that would never break. They left white marks on his soft, wobbling skin. As the gurney drew alongside the stone bier, Finross bucked, achieving nothing. Instead, the gurney seemed to shrug, and Finross rolled on to the bier. Then the gurney was backing away. Perhaps it rolled more easily now because of the lessened weight; perhaps it was glad to be leaving.

Several thin straps rose from the side of the bier, curled over Finross, descended, and tightened. As his movements were confined, his face bulged with pressure. He looked like someone about to have a coronary, but Thalveen would have made sure that such a premature ending could not happen. Not today.

Finross's mother prayed faster.

He was helpless when you brought him into the world.

Donal wondered what kind of awful symmetry was here, when a mother could see her son's ending in such a way. What childhood paths had led him to love power enough to ally himself with an illegal organization whose mages would eventually abandon him?

No. He's not the victim.

Remembering Laura's death was all it took to destroy that illusion. Finross deserved what was about to occur.

If only his mother weren't here, and praying.

Several minutes later, the flamesprites that lit the viewing chamber seemed to soften, to lower their illumination to a glimmer, while the execution chamber brightened. It was bizarrely akin to a stage show's beginning.

The hexiglass barrier did not transmit Finross's scream. Donal wondered why the audience needed insulation from the sounds but not the sight of agony. As he thought that, one of the bureaucrats, a fleshy man with oiled hair, brought a pair of burgundy-coloured opera glasses to his eyes, leaning forward.

Maybe they should serve beer. Make a real occasion of it.

Or perhaps notarised truthsayers should question any person intending to witness a state execution, and turn them away if they revealed a propensity for enjoying the occasion.

'— Mother of the Seven Blades deliver my enemies into my hands, and bring thy demon host upon their—'

As the old woman's prayer lowered in volume once more, Donal could see what had changed. A network of tiny holes had punctured the soft, bare soles of Finross's feet.

A fine fractal blossoming began.

It was a ghostly grey tree that formed, a spreading network of threads drawn from the skin by an ethereal hookwraith. Squinting, Donal could just make out the wraith's attenuated form. Then a second hookwraith flowed over Finross's fat white thighs, and bent to work on the soft inner flesh, not yet targeting the groin. Soon, fine threads sprouted here as well. Slender wraith talons drew Finross's nerves through his punctured skin, and spread them in the air.

Looked at in a certain way, it was a form of art.

But Kinley Finross was not destined to be the first person to die here today. Perhaps Donal was the first to hear the old woman cough, and the wheezing that enveloped her lungs. The grey-suited men on either side of her realized she was ill. One of them took out a clean handkerchief for her to use; then it became obvious this was more than a coughing fit.

'What are you doing?' One of the men glared as Donal moved near. 'Haven't you caused enough harm?'

'I'm trained in—'

But Donal stopped, because a black-coated figure was ascending in the fastest way possible: using his long legs to leap from bench to bench, up the tiers. In seconds Dr Thalveen was crouched over Finross's mother.

One of the UP men reached down towards Thalveen's lapel.

Donal moved faster, snapping a hold on the man's wrist, exquisitely aware of the joint's bony structure, of the angles of weakness.

'Let go of her,' the other man told Thalveen.

'Are you a doctor?'

'No, just—'

'Then let me work.'

A guard was running up the steps with an indigo case in hand. Donal guessed it was Thalveen's, retrieved from the chamber where he'd worked with Finross before the execution began, or the place where he'd prepared the hookwraiths for their task.

'Are you going to behave?' Donal said.

'Let go of— Yes.' The man looked at Donal's hand gripping his wrist. 'All right.'

'Good.'

Donal let go, and turned just as a large, florid man wearing a purple cravat reached him, standing on the next tier down. An obsidian stud, inscribed with an overlaid U and P, pinned the cravat in place.

'What are you doing with Mrs Finross?'

'Trying to save her life.'

Thalveen had worked on the old woman's acupressure points with his long fingers before the guard opened the medical bag for him. Now, Thalveen snapped open three bulbs containing fluids, and tipped one across Mrs Finross's chest – the orange fluid seeped into her skin as if her body were a sponge – and tipped another against her mouth, allowing drops to fall on her tongue. Vapour from the third drifted towards her nostrils, and entered.

Then Thalveen reached inside the bag for a quicksilver scarab with flailing insectile legs. But even as he brought the scarab close to the old woman's skin, she gave a bouncing kick against the floor. An awful hiss of escaping air was her final exhalation.

Donal had heard people die before. He recognized the sound.

'I think you should stop now,' said the florid man.

Thalveen sat back on his heels, struggling quicksilver scarab in hand.

'Yes,' he said. 'I don't sense her coming back.'

The grey-suited men looked at each other. Thalveen replaced the scarab in its jar inside the case. Then he stoppered the vials and put them in with the jar, and clicked the indigo bag shut.

He looked up as two of the guard's colleagues arrived with a stretcher.

'We've called an ambulance, Doctor.'

'Good.'

At that moment, a distant sound reached Donal even through the hexiglass: the empty howl of a man who had experienced the reality of a loved one's death during the process of his own.

Donal could find no joy in it. Not even for Laura's sake.

Outside, a black car rolled along the knucklebone-gravel drive, and stopped fifty yards from the steps that led into the main penitentiary pile of Wailing Towers. To the side of the car park was a long sidewalk where flamewraiths, in their minimized aspect, licked along the gaps between flagstones. On the steps and iron-bound doors, white runes glowed.

'Someone's late.' Al Brodowski, massive arms folded, stood in front of the cruiser he'd driven here. 'And I think they're *too* late.'

'Already?' Bud Brodowski checked his watch. 'But it's been an hour, is all.'

'Look.'

The white runes began to flicker red, then to strobe, alternating between white and red so fast they appeared pink.

'Oh, yeah. That's approaching death, all right.'

The black car stopped. From the licence plate, it was a rental. Al and Bud watched as the driver got out. He was narrow-bodied, dressed in a bluemole coat over a well-cut dark-blue suit. A black band of lizard skin encircled his blue fedora.

'Sharp dresser.'

'Ain't he? You make him for a cop, all the same?'

'Not from this city.'

The man reached inside the car, and drew out a grey box. Both Brodowskis found themselves resting one hand naturally on their guns. The thin man noticed them, grinned, and used his heel to slam the car door shut.

'Disregarding the rental company's property.'

'Has to be a cop.'

'What I said, ain't it?'

The man's pointed shoes scrunched on knucklebones as he neared the brothers. They could see the stubble on his long face, thicker over the upper lip. Perhaps he was growing a moustache.

'Am I too late for the big finale?' He nodded toward the runes, now shining a deeper colour, closer to solid red. 'I got a tender stomach, so it's just as well.'

'Uh-huh,' said Al.

'You got ID?' asked Bud.

'How I got through the gate.' The thin man touched the breast of his coat. 'Letter of authorization.'

'That's not exactly ID.'

'I wasn't exactly offering to show you ID.'

The brothers tensed. In the weight-lifting rooms at HQ, they were called the Barbarians. The sight of their swelling muscles and narrowing eyes had made more than one violent gang member grow weak and compliant. But the thin man merely shifted the weight of the grey box under one arm, and grinned again.

'See, guys – I'm not here, right?'

'Hey, Al. You think he looks kinda solid for an apparition?'

'I dunno, Bud. He looks kinda *brittle*, y'know?'

'Don't test me.' Then, with a grin: 'OK, I give up. Just arrest me and throw me in Commissioner Vilnar's car.'

'Say what?'

But Al's gaze had already flickered to a dark-green armoured limousine parked at the far end of the lot.

'That one, is it? Thanks, men. That's all I needed to know.'

Al and Bud stared at each other. They had the muscle to force the issue, but it was obvious that the stranger was no criminal. If he had been, he would never have passed through the outer gates.

But as the thin man walked on towards the commissioner's car, the brothers smiled.

'It's not like he hung around long enough for us to warn him, is it?'

'Nah. Shame, cos we'd have told him all about Lamis, we would.'

''Course we would. We aim to please, don't we?'

'Dunno about you, bro, but I usually aim for the centre of the body.'

'There is that.'

In the distance, high in the dark-purple sky, a tiny shape with bat-wings banked into a turn, straightening up as its nose pointed toward Wailing Towers.

'The ambulance is coming.'

'Guess the show's almost over.'

Two

Finross continued to die. His drawn-out nerves formed spreading branches, gauzy fractal trees that floated in the air. As the second hour began, his skin began to peel back in narrow, curling strips. The hookwraiths teased grey, glistening fat away from red-soaked, striated muscle tissue. Shimmering liquid highlights played across the revealed interior of Finross's body, as he continued to writhe and howl.

Someone – not the first – began to retch into a handkerchief, and rushed from the viewing chamber. Even the experienced journalists looked sweat-soaked and haggard, their complexions grey. Perhaps only Commissioner Vilnar, blocky and unmoving in his front-row seat, displayed no reaction to the ongoing suffering.

'The taxpayers got their money's worth,' he'd said to a reporter on a former occasion, after a senior figure in Bugs Lander's mob had paid the penalty for choking several competitors on their own intestines. The execution had lasted nearly five hours. *'Nice to see the underworld giving something back.'*

It had been a popular statement with the *Gazette*'s readership. The mayor's office had taken note. And perhaps the prison officials too, because today's hookwraiths were performing superbly, as the grey clouds of nerves around Finross's form were joined by spreading blue and red. The wraiths teased out capillaries first, then arteries and veins, so that the whole circulatory system fanned out alongside the nerves, hanging in the air like a delicate sculpture that had taken weeks to construct.

Surpassing themselves.

Call it a masterful performance.

Outside, the lightest of quicksilver rains was starting to fall, faintly hissing on the knucklebone gravel. The thin man was approaching the dark-green armoured limousine parked at the end of the row of cars. Before he reached it, the driver's door cracked open, and a tall figure climbed out. He was wearing a dark-grey chauffeur's uniform with a peaked cap, and heavy wraparound dark-blue glasses, despite the fact he was outdoors.

From the far end of the car park came a murmured, 'Lamis don't never get out of the car, does he, bro?'

'Not hardly. But there he is.'

Neither the thin man nor the tall chauffeur looked in the Brodowskis' direction.

'I'm Lamis.' The chauffeur's voice was sepulchral. 'You've brought a sample.'

'And now your boss owes my boss a favour.'

'If you say so, Inspector.'

'Uh-huh.' The thin man checked that the Brodowskis were standing too far away to overhear. 'So are you going to take the Death-damned thing or not?'

Lamis reached up and removed his shades just by an inch, until the thin man could see the darkness where Lamis's eyes should have been. Inside that darkness was—

'Shit. Impossible.'

'But you haven't.' Lamis replaced his heavy dark-blue shades. 'Excreted in your pants, I mean. Nor did you run from me, as most people would.'

'Got a sprained ankle.'

'And a strained humour, but good enough.' Lamis took the grey case from him. 'And my apologies. The resonance from this thing is ... unsettling.'

'Didn't make me feel too happy carrying it, and I'm not even a mage or anything.'

'You did a good job. You fly back home tonight?'

'Unless the border's closed, yeah. The old Transition Tempest has been wild lately. A lot of flights are delayed.'

'Thank you again, Inspector.'

The quicksilver rain was growing heavier, and the thin man hunched his shoulders.

'Any time,' he said. 'I love the weather here. Makes me feel welcome.'

But Lamis was staring at the red runes. If blood could glow, it would be that colour.

'I get it,' said the thin man. 'End of the show. I'm gone from here.'

He turned and headed back towards his rental car, tipping his fedora to the Brodowskis as he passed. Then he got inside, started the engine, and backed out too fast from the parking space, spraying knucklebone gravel that knocked against the bodywork of three cars.

He drove towards the main exit without looking back.

The Brodowskis watched him depart, noting the scanwraiths passing through the car, checking everything even on departure. This was a prison, after all, filled with inmates desperate to escape.

'Definitely a cop, bro.'

'You got it.'

They turned away, checking Commissioner Vilnar's limousine. The tall driver, Lamis, had climbed back inside. His curved dark glasses were in place as usual.

'You saw it, right?'

'What? When he nearly took off his shades?'

'Yeah. Then.'

'Uh ... Nope. Didn't see a thing.'

Inside the limo, Lamis's features might have moved fractionally, precursor to a non-existent smile.

After a moment: 'Me neither. Obviously.'

'Yeah. Obviously.'

Overhead, the bat-winged ambulance was gliding in an elliptical trajectory, looking for a place to land. Then it did something surprising – curving its wings, it dropped straight towards the roof of the main penitentiary pile.

'They'll never make it.'

'I dunno. That driver's good.'

'Pilot.'

'Huh?'

'They're flying, ain't they? So the guy's a pilot.'

'If you say so, bro.'

The black ambulance swivelled its afterburners downwards, and blue flames flared as it descended, braking. It lowered itself in the middle of a formation of five pointed towers, snapped its wings into its chassis at the last moment, and was gone from sight.

'Didn't hear a crash.'

'Got down OK. Sweet.'

'Who are you calling sweet?'

'In your— Now who's this?'

Another car was entering the ground of Wailing Towers. This one was long and darkest burgundy, almost black, its flared fins edged with obsidian. The windows and windshield were strips of polished darkness.

'I recognize the fancy limo.'

'So whose is—? Hades, bro.'

'Yeah. Exactly. You think the lieutenant knows?'

'Beats me. What do you reckon?'

'Haven't got a clue, bro.'

The limo pulled up alongside them. Then the driver's door opened, and a huge bearded man with a vast belly manoeuvred his legs from beneath the steering wheel. Puffing, he got to his feet, grimaced at the sea of knucklebones, then grinned at the Brodowskis.

'Hey, guys. Fancy seeing you here.'

'André. How's life?' said Al.

'See you got a job.' Bud nodded towards the rear. 'That who we think it is?'

'Probably. Give me a moment.'

He opened the rear door. What appeared first was a slender walking-stick formed of intricately carved bone. Then a frail ankle in expensive shoes. When the lady rose out of the limo, she stood straight, and flicked back a coil of white hair from her forehead.

'Hello, boys.'

'Uh, hello, ma'am.'

'Ma'am.'

'André,' she turned to her chauffeur, 'do you know my old friends, Aloysius and Boudreaux Brodowski?'

'Sure, ma'am.'

But André, like the rest of the world, knew them as Al and Bud, or simply the Barbarians. Now his mouth worked as he silently practised: *Alo-ysius. Bou-dreaux.*

The Brodowskis shook their heads, their muscular necks clenching and releasing.

'And who are you assigned to drive around?' The white-haired woman's face was lined, but her eyes were grey jewels, shining clear. 'Ah. Good. It was in fact Lieutenant Riordan that I wanted to see.'

The brothers tried not to look at each other. Both men knew that humming a tune would stop them subvocalising responses to questions they should not answer. But every song and ditty they knew had evaporated from memory. Their throats were dry.

Then the woman looked at the glowing red runes, before glancing up towards the roof. The ambulance was out of sight, but she said, 'The paramedics are here already. I don't ... Ah, you've a wait ahead of you, boys.'

'Ma'am?'

'It's not the alderman who's died. His execution is still in progress.' The woman's frown overlaid a momentary smile. 'Poor woman. I can sympathize.'

Then she looked up at the Brodowskis and added, 'So. You boys can rest – *now* – secure in remembering to forget that I was ever here.'

Each brother felt himself slide into a warm daydream, still standing upright, with perfect balance.

'Ma'am,' said André. 'Are we leaving?'

'Yes. This was a mistake. Because of him.'

Her nod was directed towards the far end of the parking area. For a moment, Bud had time to think: *Lamis. She's talking about Lamis, in the commissioner's car.*

Then he, like his brother, descended into soft, amnesiac sleep.

Donal was trying to tune out the suffering in front of him. What made it difficult was his new self-awareness, the unsettling realization that he could control his emotions – except that realization caused another emotional reaction. He had a strange sense of *architecture* in his mind, a form of internal perception he had never known.

Then again, I've never been dead before.

Down on the front row, Commissioner Vilnar touched his shaven temple, and bowed his head, as if listening to a phone conversation. He gave a tiny nod, then leaned toward Commander Bowman and murmured something, before getting to his feet.

Donal was glad that something had changed in the external world. Inside his own head was somewhere he didn't want to be. But he remained sitting, only his gaze following Commissioner Vilnar as he left.

He closed his eyes—

Laura. I miss you so much.

—and opened them. Even the sight of Finross dying was better than the inside of his mind.

Out in the parking area, Commissioner Vilnar stopped in front of the unmoving Brodowski brothers. Their eyes were open but unfocused, unaware of Vilnar's presence. He looked at them for a long moment, before snorting and shaking his head.

'Bloody woman.'

He left the entranced brothers standing by their cruiser, and headed for his limousine. The rear door opened as he neared, and he climbed inside. The rear seat was upholstered in soft grey scales. He moved into the centre, as the door closed and locked.

The partition slid down. In the front seat, Lamis spoke without turning.

'She's gone. But our friend from Silvex City came and went before her.'

'Temesin? Did she notice him?'

'Not that I could tell. It's Riordan she was thinking about.'

'She'd make a useful ally.'

'But she has no love for the department. Still, if you use Riordan for what you've in mind, perhaps she'll see her way clear' – Lamis used one long fingernail to tap his shades – 'to helping us.'

'Or maybe he's been through enough.'

'He's still a police officer, with a duty.'

'I know.' Vilnar rubbed a hand over his shaven scalp, then across his face. 'I do know that.'

'And I'm not going to mention how things are growing critical.'

'Good. I'm glad you didn't mention that.'

'Although of course they *are*.' Lamis reached for something. 'Take a look.'

He lifted a grey case high enough to balance it on the back of the seat.

'I'm getting a … sensation,' said Vilnar, 'across my skin. It's not a pleasant one.'

'And that's with heavy insulation.' Lamis lowered the case back on to the passenger seat, then slid it down into the floor well. 'You'd really feel it if I opened the thing.'

'Shit.' Vilnar hadn't been a street cop for a long time, but the vernacular remained. 'Is it weapons grade?'

'Definitely.'

'And what kind of weapon are the bastards building with it? Thousands of handhelds, or something singular and massive?'

'Impossible to tell, if the sample's not configured yet. And I don't think it is.'

'Balls.' Again, Vilnar rubbed his face. 'All right. Bowman was in the Westside Complex last week, but when he tried to sneak away from the initial meeting, his way was blocked by lifewards.'

'The complex where Finross's body is about to go.'

'Exactly.'

'And with the arresting officer being a zombie.' Lamis popped open a drawer in the dashboard, then drew out what looked like a pair of ordinary notepads. 'You might want to give him one of these.'

'All-time pads?'

17

'Correct.'

Vilnar took the pads from Lamis, and put them on the seat beside him. Then he took a fountain pen from his pocket – it was formed of polished quartz, a present from the mayor's office – unscrewed the cap, and pressed down on one pad, marking it. On its twin, an identical mark appeared.

'Good.' Vilnar looked at Lamis's reflection in the driving-mirror. 'I'll leave one with the Brodowskis. Excellent thinking, my friend.'

'It's what the city pays me for.'

'Actually, they pay you to drive me around.'

'Ha. So what do they know?'

Commissioner Vilnar stared out through the side window at the dark, massive penitentiary.

'Very, very little, as it turns out.'

Eventually, Finross died.

Magnesium-white flashbulbs popped as photographers recorded the aftermath: a dummy-like corpse, its nerves and arteries spilling out like lace. Tomorrow's *Tristopolitan Gazette* would doubtless feature a large blue-and-white photograph of Finross on page one. Other newspapers, from other cities, would run photos and reports of diminishing size, the farther away their readership was based. Across the northern border in Illurium, there might be a small paragraph, no picture. To the south, in Trilaxia and Shudderland, it was unlikely to make the news at all.

And the day after, Finross would be forgotten by nearly everybody.

So long as you're suffering somehow, you bastard. That'll be justice.

But there was no joy for Donal as he watched attendants remove the body, ready for transport to whichever Energy Authority complex had been designated to receive it. Usually that would be the Westside Complex, being the closest; but sometimes technical circumstances meant that workers at a more distant complex would be able to process the body more quickly. Donal knew the theory: the less delay between death and processing, the more the bones would howl with suffering inside the necrofusion pile.

It wasn't a theory widely discussed beyond legal circles. Ordinary citizens preferred to believe that they would pay no particular price beyond death for the comforts they had received in life. But cops could no more ignore the reality of the reactor piles than they could turn away from a terminal traffic accident. And processing their first TTA was a rite of passage for virtually every rookie of the Tristopolis PD.

'Lieutenant?' Dr Thalveen touched his arm.

'Huh? Sorry, I was dreaming.'

'It's self-awareness that's the danger.' Thalveen's eyes were stonily certain. 'Dreaming is very ... human.'

'You've lost me.'

'Thoughts becoming aware of thoughts. Most people would say that's what defines humanity, what makes us – them – different from animals. But thoughts can sense thoughts sensing thoughts ... and infinite self-recursion is a mortal danger. If you can call us mortal.'

'I'll bear that in mind.' Donal looked away, then back at Thalveen. 'Just how old are you, Doctor?'

'I was thirty-one when I died.'

'Yeah, but how long—?'

'All complex systems change.'

'I notice you didn't say living systems.'

'Very observant, Lieutenant. Were you always that sensitive to subtleties of language?'

Donal felt his expression tighten, consciously relaxed his facial muscles, then realized the fineness of his neuromuscular control, and felt a sick sense of wrongness.

'You'll get used to it,' added Thalveen. 'Given time.'

'That's comforting.'

The attendants had left with Finross's body. In the empty execution chamber, the stone bier looked unthreatening. Or perhaps that was Donal's subliminal awareness that the hookwraiths had sunk down inside the bier and carried on descending. The bier was an ordinary block of stone, and the chamber was an ordinary chamber. Finross's dying was over.

Laura. Can you somehow know that Finross is gone?

Thalveen hefted his indigo medical bag, and looked round at the departing journalists and bureaucrats.

'Looks like the show is over.' He cast his voice so that it would carry. 'Until the next time.'

No one turned to look. But the tension in shoulders and torsos, the tiny but visible shuddering of several men and women, were obvious enough for Donal to read. Thalveen's lips pulled back in something like a smile.

Then he murmured, 'Who says zombies have no sense of humour?'

Donal checked the expressions on the living humans, then turned and strode along the row of seats, away from Thalveen, not looking back.

You'll get used to it. Given time.

Walking away was one thing. Trying to forget Thalveen's words was something else.

The ambulance – unexpectedly, the second ambulance to depart from here today with a fresh corpse on board – had already taken off. Donal descended the steps on which runes continued to glow red, then stopped at the edge of the knucklebone gravel drive. The two grey-suited men stared up at the bat-winged shape gliding against the featureless indigo sky.

'Hades speed you,' said one.

His colleague made the Sign of the Axe, murmuring a prayer.

'Good riddance,' said Donal.

He walked past, hoping they would react by attacking him, knowing they wouldn't. He carried on, conscious of the knucklebones crunching beneath his shoes, until he processed the sight of the hulking Brodowski brothers, standing with their hands at their sides, their gazes unfocused.

Enscorcelled?

Donal's hand was inside his jacket, grasping the butt of his Magnus in its shoulder holster. He walked closer. He didn't draw, not yet.

'For ... you.' Al raised his left hand, still in trance. 'From the ... com-miss-ion-er.'

'Thanatos,' muttered Donal.

It was a small notepad that Al held out. Donal remained an arm's length away.

'Why would the Old Man give you that for me?'

'Can't be ... seen. With ... you ... today.'

Certainly, Commissioner Vilnar had not looked in Donal's direction during the execution, not even once. It had been a very public cold-shouldering.

'Hold the thing out, Al.'

Al's hand slowly rose.

I need to get him out of trance.

Donal had received trance-training at the police academy, but mostly defensive, to prevent falling under another's spell.

Didn't save the Diva, did it?

That was an old guilty thought that Donal pushed aside now. The question was whether to try talking Al back to a conscious, waking state, or to get help from someone inside the—

What the fuck?

Black cursive handwriting was growing across the notepad.

I'm assured you're reading this right n

Donal blinked as he took a step back. He whipped out his Magnus, centring on Al first, then swivelling, taking in Bud – who remained immobile – then the surroundings. No one was coming for him.

He glanced back at the pad.

I'm assured you're reading this right now, Lieutenant. You've heard of an all-time pad? This is one. It's like a hex-entangled warrant, but smarter.

Laura had used hex-entangled cross-border arrest warrants. Donal had been able to carry warrants that showed the suspects' details as blanks, waiting for a judge back in Tristopolis to later fill in the names – which would simultaneously appear on Donal's copies.

Then the writing scrubbed itself out of existence, blanking the pad before new words appeared.

I want you to

The writing stopped, then a line scored through the first four words, before the handwriting continued.

~~I want you to~~ Go to the Westside Complex, where I've authorized you to observe the forensic Bone Listener's work. I want you to make some excuse to leave the chamber, and go alone to find the minus-thirtieth floor. There, go to Director Braune's office. He's just resigned. His safe combination is 3-7- pentangle-5-talon-2-9-1. Retrieve contents. Bring to me.

Perhaps the pad worked both ways; but Donal had no intention of putting down his gun and taking his attention from the environment. In any case, what would he ask to verify the writer's identity? It wasn't as if he had a long, friendly past with the commissioner. He knew nothing of Vilnar's private life, neither his wife's name nor his pet's, nor even if he *had* a pet.

The words blanked out once more, then:

You'll have a chance to give me the papers in person. Sometime in the next few days. Until then, guard them.

'Maybe,' muttered Donal.

He scanned in every direction again, remembering to glance up at the blank indigo sky and down at the gravel beneath his feet – in case of wraith-hands reaching up through the knucklebones. Then Bud Brodowski began to sway.

Good luck.

And the notepad page was blank in Al's in grasp. Donal snatched it just as Al, too, began to blink rapidly.

'Are you two all right?' said Donal.

The brothers yawned and shrugged their massive shoulders.

'Huh? 'Course we are.'

'Why wouldn't we be?'

Donal tucked the notepad inside his jacket.

'Loot? You got a gun in your hand.'

'Me? Well, I don't need that.' He reholstered. 'I'm safe with you two around, don't you think?'

'Too right.'

'Freakin' A.'

Cars were filing from the parking area, with a magnified rustling from the knucklebone-sea they rolled across. Few vehicles were left. The dark piles of Wailing Towers were returning to their normal desolate state.

Donal tried to let out a calming breath, then realized his lungs had been empty since he spoke. He sucked in some air.

'We've got a mission,' he said. 'Before going back to HQ.'

'Doughnuts from Fat'n'Sugar?'

'Beers from Tentacle Sam's?'

'I was thinking we could see the place' – Donal decided not to smile – 'where they put the bones to work.'

The brothers looked at each other, hunched their shoulders like gloomy gorillas, and climbed inside the car without a word.

Three

Their route followed a black granite flyover, passing on splayed spider-legs a hundred feet above the banking district of Obsidian Spires, where security gargoyles launched themselves from ledges to glide in watchful arcs, hoping for a chance to use their venom. The flyover descended to the Arachnia Twistabout, where Al followed a helical route through a nine-spiral intersection, exiting via the westside ramp, three levels below ground.

They continued to the main tunnel of the Hypotown Expressway, its blood-red porcelain walls shimmering with the traffic's reflected headlights, echoing with the magnified sound of engines. Alongside them, in the next lane, travelled a black tanker bearing a silver Skull-and-Ouroboros logo. The vehicle belonged to the Energy Authority. Its cargo, whatever it was, caused a strange resonance in Donal: wet slugs sliding along his nerves.

'You sense that?'

'Huh?' said Bud.

'Never mind.' Donal glanced out at the walls, whose red surface glistened with scales. 'You ever heard that the Expressway was a real giant serpent, centuries ago? Turned inside-out by mages?'

'Heard a lot of things,' said Bud, 'when we were growing up. Like, how telling lies makes your dick shrink, which explains a lot about Al.'

'Hades, so *that's* the reason.' Al maintained watchful control, his attention mostly on the tunnel ahead, periodically checking the mirrors. 'You coulda told me sooner.'

Donal laughed. Perhaps this visit to the Westside Complex was all right, in the Brodowskis' company.

'You guys should be psych counsellors, you know that?'

'Say what?'

'Call it Barbarian Therapy.'

'Hey, I like that,' said Al. 'We could have a motto: "Get a grip, or we'll bust your teeth in."'

'That's just stupid.' Bud clicked his fingers. 'I got it. "We'll straighten your head out, or rip it right off."'

'It's a winner.' Donal smiled, ignoring the cold, slick sensation that the tunnel was inducing. 'You could open up a private practice. I'll invest, and make a fortune.'

'Yeah, if you had any money to—' Bud broke off. 'Shit.'

'Sorry,' said Al. 'I mean, Bud said it, but I'd forgotten too.'

'That's all right,' Donal told them. 'Really. I'm a poor boy from the orphanage, you know? I can't get used to it, either.'

Laura had named Donal her sole beneficiary, in a revised will drawn up some night while the still-living Donal had slept, as ordinary humans must. There had been only two restrictions. One was that he keep ownership of the apartment (occupying the entire 227th storey of the prestigious Darksan Tower) for as long as possible. The other was that he look after the Vixen, the car that was also – somehow – Laura's half-sister. How that could be possible was a mystery to Donal.

They drove on for a minute in silence. Then Al said, 'Is it true your new apartment is as big as a whorehouse?'

'Oh, yeah,' answered Donal. 'You'd feel right at home.'

Bud chuckled. 'That told you, bro.'

'Guess so.' But as Al took a downward-sloping exit, he added a comment that was disconcerting, coming from someone with a neck like a tree stump. 'Might be a wise thing to shift your money elsewhere, Lieutenant, way the city's going. I mean right out of the country.'

Looking across at his brother, Bud nodded.

'One a them Unity Party pricks was recruiting members,' he said, 'right there in the gym. Had to bounce him off the lockers a little, y'know? Just a bit of discouragement.'

'Wonderful, I don't think,' said Donal. 'But thanks for putting him straight.'

What am I, a spokesman for zombiekind?

'Any time.'

The tunnel here was shading into darkness. First the red walls deepened to burgundy, then purple, and finally black. No other vehicles were driving here. Al switched the headlights to main beam, slowing as he drove. Several minutes later, he stopped the car.

Ahead, the tunnel appeared to end in a solid, dark metal disc bearing a raised Skull-and-Ouroboros. Then a jagged vertical split appeared, pistons hissed, and the heavy half-doors ground their way into stonework, revealing an access tunnel to the Westside Complex proper. Blue flamewraiths – a hue Donal had seen nowhere else – drifted along the tunnel, on guard.

'Lovely place,' he said.

'A day-trip to the necrofusion piles.' Al put the cruiser back into gear. 'What could be better?'

'Can't think of anything,' muttered Bud. 'Not a Death-damned thing.'

Donal left the Brodowskis drinking coffee in a waiting-room, while he went through a succession of scanfields – including a billowing aurora that made his nerves whine as it passed through him – until finally two men in grey coveralls greeted him.

'Commissioner Vilnar,' said the larger man, 'arranged everything, Lieutenant.'

'The Bone Listener may have begun already.' The other man gestured toward a nine-sided door. 'But you can go straight in.'

Floating flames, an inch before the door, read: MORTISECTION – AUTHORIZED PERSONNEL ONLY.

'Very kind of you,' said Donal.

'The only thing is …'

'What's that?'

'…um, if you could be careful to stay in the chamber, it would be … safer.'

'Thank you.' Donal modulated his voice to sound pleasant. 'I'll do just that.'

But he was reading the movement of facial muscles that both men were trying to hide. Expecting a police lieutenant was one thing; expecting an *undead* detective was something else.

Was this why Vilnar had wanted Donal to be here?

Lifewards. They've got lifewards in place.

He remembered Laura, when she'd led the team that rescued him from ensorcelment. They'd broken through lifewards that he himself, in trance, had set in place.

'*The ward shield keeps out only living beings,*' she had said. And, when Donal had glanced at the hexlar-vested troopers, '*Oh, they're alive all right. It's me you didn't count on.*'

The thing was, he could also remember the Downtown Complex whose director, Malfax Cortindo, had turned out be the mage primarily responsible for the Diva's death. Cortindo was just one man – now a reanimated corpse, revenant rather than zombie – but what if there was further corruption within the Energy Authority?

Then the door to the mortisection chamber rolled open, and he saw a Bone Listener standing inside. The man looked to be in his early twenties, with the high forehead and moist deep-brown eyes of his kind.

'Bone Listener Pinderwin,' said Donal. 'May I come inside?'

'Lieutenant. Please do.'

An unpleasant resonance swept through Donal as he entered. Inside the chamber, he felt as if someone had just rinsed him through with dirty water.

'Please call me Lexar,' added the Bone Listener. 'And accept my sympathies about Commander Steele.'

'Thank you. I'm Donal. And I didn't get a chance to give you my condolences. Dr d'Alkernay was an amazing person.'

'The finest forensic Bone Listener for generations.' Lexar gestured toward Finross's nerve- and artery-draped corpse lying on a ceramic table. 'And this one had some kind of involvement in both their deaths.'

'Yes.'

'What a pity, for him. Even dead, he may experience regret.'

Donal did not want to ask what Lexar meant by that. Instead, he just watched as Lexar snapped open an instrument case, and drew out a short, dark-blue trident with an orange handle.

'I've never seen anything like that,' said Donal.

'You've only witnessed autopsies at the OCML, I take it.'

'Well, yes.'

The Office of the Chief Medical Listener was where forensic Bone Listeners carried out most of their work. That remained true, even though the establishment currently had no chief, no replacement for the murdered Wilhelmina d'Alkernay.

'You'll find things a little different here.' Lexar crossed to the wall, and pressed the heel of his palm against a raised green pentagonal button. 'The processing is much faster, for one thing.'

The ceiling, of flat pale grey stone, began to slide to one side. Revealed above it was a high, dark concave chamber; and in that chamber hung a black tree, suspended upside down as though growing toward the floor. Perched in that inverted tree was a several-hundred-strong flock of liquid metal quicksilver birds, small and shining with slender, hooked beaks.

A clanging sounded on the heavy metal door through which Donal had entered.

'That'll be the phone company knocking,' said Lexar. 'Getting impatient.'

'Excuse me?' Donal must have misheard. 'Did you say phone company?'

'The engineers, yes.' Lexar was heading for the door. 'You know how exchanges are wired, don't you?'

'Um ...'

But Lexar was already throwing the toggle switch that caused the metal door to grind open. A trio of plump workers in dark-green coveralls – two bearded men and one woman – crossed the threshold carrying what looked like picnic boxes.

'Not ready yet?' asked one of the men.

'Please take a seat.' Lexar pointed to a bench set against the stone wall. 'I'll be ten minutes, no more.'

'Fair enough.'

The three engineers sat down, and opened the boxes they carried. But Donal's attention was drawn to Lexar, who twisted the handle of his dark-blue trident, and held it extended. The fork vibrated, slowly at first, then with increasing frequency until the trident's end was a shimmering blur.

'This won't take long,' said Lexar.

Approaching Finross's supine corpse, he began to wave the pulsating trident over the dead man's skin. Where the trident passed, the flesh rose and fell in waves, like liquid. Lexar ran the device back and forth, three times from head to toe, then switched it off.

'— knows I don't like scarab-and-mayo,' one of the engineers was saying, peering inside his box. 'Dunno why she makes it.'

'Maybe that's why.'

'Huh?'

'Because she deliberately—'

Overhead, the quicksilver birds began to stir in their upside-down tree. Donal stared up at them, then noticed how Lexar had retreated from Finross's corpse. Taking the hint, Donal took several steps back, until his heel touched the wall.

The engineers were paying no attention.

'—chance of a trade?'

'Depends. You like lizard?'

'Yeah, a-course.'

'Here ya go, then.'

The trio were tucking in to their sandwiches when the first of the quicksilver birds dropped beak-first on to Finross's corpse, and got to work on the softened flesh. More birds descended, and then the whole flock was down, covering the body in a mass of shifting metal forms. An insectile rustling filled the air.

'They leave the nerves behind.' Lexar was almost shouting over the noise. 'Once they've finished, the guys can use the spindles to wrap everything neatly.'

He gestured toward a stack of white ceramic spindles standing on the floor.

Wonderful.

But Donal wasn't here to experience the processing of Finross's corpse, nor to form an opinion on how the Energy Authority treated executed prisoners. He pulled the all-time pad from his inside pocket, and checked. It remained blank. No more orders from Commissioner Vilnar.

'Sorry,' Donal said. 'But I'm not feeling very well. Which way's the bathroom?'

Lexar's eyes blinked moistly, then one corner of his wide mouth pulled back, and his chin dipped minutely. To Donal, it was as obvious as if Lexar had roared with laughter.

'Use the other door. Over there.'

'Thanks.'

It was a seven-sided hatchway that opened when Donal tugged down a small metal lever shaped like a bone. He stepped through, and felt a percussive wave of pressure behind him as the hatch closed by itself, muting the rustle of the liquid metal birds.

So which way now?

Donal passed the entrance to the bathrooms, and found himself at a five-way junction of shadowy corridors. As he turned in a circle, hand outstretched, one of the corridors caused his palm to prickle, while the others had no effect. So Donal tried that way and, perhaps ten feet in, found the air shivering and fluorescing around him.

Good job I'm not alive.

Then he was through the ward shield, heading deeper into the complex.

Donal kept alert, and was able to avoid passing Energy Authority employees in the corridors, by sensing them before they came into sight. He advanced in stages, checking potential hiding places as he went. It was slow progress, but he had no form of ID – or none that he wanted to show because, without a warrant, he should not be here.

Although he couldn't feel the presence of wraiths – a good thing, since they would report his presence – Donal found himself before a bank of open-door lifts. There was an external panel, and he pressed the button marked –*30*.

While he waited, Donal poked his head inside one of the empty cold shafts and looked down, then up. There was nothing to stop a careless person from taking a final, suicidal step into nothingness. Below him, a disc that filled the width of the shaft was rising.

Shit. That's fast.

Donal pulled himself back just as the lift shot past him. Solid steel – moving steel – now filled the doorway, and he realized the disc was merely the top surface of a gigantic column thrusting upwards in the vertical shaft.

A disc stopped in the next elevator to his right, and a bell softly dinged. Donal stepped on to the disc, and it began to descend. The downward acceleration was not quite enough to induce sickness. Then it slowed, and came to a soundless halt.

Here, arched corridors led off in three directions: two with blank stone floors, one carpeted. Donal remembered the instructions appearing on the all-time pad.

... go alone to find the minus-thirtieth floor. There, go to Director Braune's office ...

He followed the strip of carpet, slowing as he reached an open door. There was no sound of breathing from inside. Donal looked, saw stacks of both used and blank stationery, including internal memo envelopes formed of pale-pink wormskin. He took one, laid it on a desk, and pulled out his own fountain pen.

Guess I could buy a new one now.

It was scratched, a pressurised steel pen filled with jellysquid ink, as cops preferred. The ink let them write on damp brick walls as if on dry paper; the steel casing formed a useful weapon, held in the fist. Now, Donal used it to write *'Director Braune'* on the next blank addressee box. He scratched a line through the previous addressee's name.

He carried the envelope along the corridor, walking past occupied rooms with partly open doors. He stopped at a pentagonal ceramic door-way. A metal holder held a label reading: *Mrs Sally Pritchell, secretary to* followed by a blank space.

Donal pressed his palm against the door, and it slid sideways into the wall. Inside was a small room, with a grey-haired woman at a desk. Beyond lay the entrance to Director Braune's office.

'I've got a document' – Donal held up the envelope – 'which they said I had to leave in the director's office. I know he's resigned, but—'

He stopped as the woman – Sally Pritchell, according to the door tag – sniffed, then dabbed her eyes with a handkerchief that was already sodden.

'I'm sorry,' she said. 'But he didn't. It wasn't ...'

'Oh. You mean, it was a sudden resignation.'

'Yes. The board ... Dr Grayfell didn't ... I shouldn't say anything.'

'No.' Donal put the envelope on top of a black filing cabinet. 'You're not feeling well. I don't want to suggest ...' Pitching his voice low to form an imperative, he said, 'You're *sick* and very *upset*, and you need to *go home now*, Sally. Go on.'

'I ... Yes. Please.'

She was unsteady as she stood. Donal helped her, took her coat from a hook, and escorted her from the office. He led her to one of the occupied rooms, where three younger women looked up from their desks.

'Sally's unwell,' he told them. 'Could you call a taxi, please? I'm sending her home.'

'Oh. Of course—'

Donal left her among concerned colleagues. He closed the door on them, then loped back to Sally Pritchell's room and went inside.

Neat work. Like she wasn't upset enough already.

But feeling bad for the woman wasn't going to help. Donal moved fast, found the button for the inner door, pressed it, and stepped quickly into the director's office. Inside, Donal spotted a wall-safe standing open, its interior gleaming and empty.

'Shit.'

Beyond stood a wide black desk, and behind that, a wide strip of window looking out on to a system of immense shadowed caverns. There were rows of huge, dark-grey reactor piles, humming and pulsing with necrofusion power. Donal tried not to look.

Concentrate.

Perhaps there was a second, hidden safe. He scanned the room – as rich as Director Cortindo's place in the Downtown Complex, but without the exotic relics adorning the walls and display cases – seeing nothing obvious. Then it occurred to him that if ex-Director Braune had two safes, they'd almost certainly have different combinations.

So he went to the obvious safe, and checked the positions of the wheels. The topmost symbols were 3, then 8, pentangle, 5, talon (a hooked, stylized symbol), 2, 9, 1. It *nearly* matched the memorized combination, and when Donal moved the second wheel to 7, the lock loosened with a click. The code, the same as Donal had received from Commissioner Vilnar, had already worked for someone else.

'Thanatos damn it.'

The commissioner's orders had been to empty the safe; they said nothing about the nature of its contents. What should he look for? Casting around the room, he saw nothing obvious. Some textbooks, annual financial reports bound in pterashrike hide, a handmade card saying

Happy Birthday Grandad, a wall calendar, several—

He stopped. On the calendar, today's date, 35th Hcxtember, was marked with a blood-red cross, whereas other days bore small, neat annotations in purple ink. Was something extraordinary due to happen? Something Braune had objected to?

There was a phone on the desk, and Donal considered doing the obvious thing and making a call. But Commissioner Vilnar had used a private all-time pad, rather than normal channels. Perhaps there were reasons for keeping contact off the books.

So what should I do now?

He walked to the wide window, and stared out into the caverns. The air seemed to shiver with dark waves, filled with complex travelling webs of shadow, more obvious than the subtle shifting, just off the edge of vision, he had experienced in the Downtown Complex.

Pressing close to the glass, looking down, he could see a long pier-like walkway jutting into space. The walkway ended in a wide heptagonal platform, on which a group of people in expensive business suits had congregated around a complicated console. They were far below; there was no chance that Donal could see what they were up to.

He looked back at the doorway. There were no voices outside, but eventually someone would come, someone in a less fragile state of mind than the former director's secretary.

Whatever they're doing below, that's the event marked in the calendar.

Donal had no idea where the intuition had come from, yet he felt certain it was right. Turning to the window once more, he pressed the edges, looking for catches. Nothing. Then he touched a glass disc set into the ledge, and the window panel in front of him shivered, then grew liquid, shimmering like a soap bubble.

He pushed his hand through. The membranous window felt slick on his skin, remaining intact except for the circle enclosing his wrist.

'This is insane.'

Donal took hold, rolled sideways on to the ledge, and through the liquid barrier. There was a faint pop, and then he was clinging to rock-face, and the window to Braune's office was solid once more.

Suicidally insane.

He crimped his fingers around rough-edged holds, took one look down the vertical descent – perhaps seventy or eighty feet to the walkway – and began his descent.

Time was distorted. Donal felt only seconds had passed by the time he stopped climbing downwards and simply hung in place, level with the walkway some twenty feet to his left. Where it entered the rockface, a concave area held a tall, polished, dark-grey metal apparatus: a case studded with dials and connectors, the whole thing about the size of a truck. Several men and women were looking over the machinery.

'What is this reading here?' came a female voice from the other side of the apparatus.

'See, if you check the sum of these four outputs—'

Their attention was away from Donal's position.

Move now.

He used plenty of leanback as he traversed the rockface. Nearing the walkway's safety rail, Donal wanted to slow down and take care, but a footfall near the tall casing warned him of a woman's approach. He let go of both handholds, pushing hard with his foot—

Death.

—and caught the railing, grabbing tight. He swung forwards, knees bent as his feet struck the walkway's side. Using the springiness of his limbs to rebound upwards, he vaulted over the rail. He landed in a crouch, just as the woman rounded the corner of the big generator.

'Oh!'

'Excuse me.'

Donal tightened his shoelace, then straightened up, brushing his tie as he walked past her, heading for the wider platform where most of the people had gathered. There was a steel console, and grey-haired men in suits nodding as a younger man operated controls.

'—guaranteed full compatibility,' the operator was saying. 'As a backup to your own grid, you've then got one hundred per cent grid coverage, regardless of demand surges.'

'Very diplomatic,' said a large-bellied man whose golden tie-pin was formed from a Skull-and-Ouroboros. 'You make no mention of our recent brownouts.'

No one looked at Donal as he drew near.

'Let me answer that.' A man with cropped white hair gave a cough. 'If you'd like to talk to our R&D mages, Dr Grayfell, perhaps we can come up with an estimate. I mean, offer you assistance on failures within your current infrastructure.'

'I thought you were trying to sell us *alternative* power sources.'

'Naturally' – with a smile – 'that's our primary offer. Any consultancy would be speculative and require investigation. This technology, what you're seeing here, is proven and ready to ship.'

Observing the twenty or so men and women on the platform, Donal saw that they belonged to two groups, obviously part of a corporate negotiation. The reason no one noticed him, he realized, was that each group assumed Donal was a member of the other party. He took care to stand in a neutral position.

Glancing back along the walkway, to the concave area where the big apparatus sat – some kind of generator? – the woman was still looking at Donal. She was dressed in a dark olive skirt-suit, the kind of thing that Laura might have worn—

Damn it.

Donal turned his attention back to the senior business people.

'—amortize the equipment? Perhaps a lease-back arrangement on the pipeline plant?'

'That's what we need to cover in the boardroom afterwards.'

'Fair enough. I look forward to seeing your figures.'

It sounded civilized. But Donal, playing back the operator's words in his mind, *'As a backup to your own grid, you've then got one hundred per cent grid coverage'*, recognized the man's accent as Illurian. There were plenty of Illurian immigrants living within Federation borders so it meant nothing definite. But Donal stared back at the truck-sized container.

He had been in Silvex City. He knew how Illurian power centres operated; but perhaps that was not true of all the local Energy Authority people. One or two were frowning, shifting their weight every few seconds. *They* were in the know.

The massive cavern, filled with rows of reactor piles, was swept through with dark tidal waves of resonance that living humans sensed only as a feeling of vague dread. In the Downtown Complex, where Malfax Cortindo had given Donal the official tour, every fuel pile contained the bones of two thousand dead, in order to obtain critical mass. Here in the Westside Complex, each towering pile was four or five times the size of those downtown counterparts.

What was it Cortindo had said? He'd talked of resonance cavities in which standing waves of necroflux vibrated and strengthened. But the microstructure of living bones alters with the perceptions of body-and-mind as a whole. After death, necroflux passes through the bones, diffracted by the microstructure. The mixed-up chaos of fragmented thoughts, memories and emotions moans and howls inside the reactor.

'The conglomeration does not truly think or feel anything,' Malfax Cortindo had told Donal. And, *'That's what I'll tell anyone who asks me officially. You understand me, Lieutenant?'*

At the time, Donal had thought he understood perfectly. Now he realized how little he had imagined, how much worse the reality was. No wonder psychiatric problems were rife among Energy Authority workers.

'—time,' Grayfell was saying now, 'to repair to the boardroom? I believe we have a decanter of Pavelian '32 waiting, along with luncheon.'

'That sounds most pleasant,' answered one of the Illurian delegation. 'Do lead on.'

As the senior people headed back along the walkway, the more junior people – and Donal – moved aside. They fell in behind their superiors. Donal trailed the group, aware that the woman who'd noticed him earlier was still staring. She was clutching a clipboard now. Perhaps it held a list of visitors' names.

Behind her, the metallic grey generator rose up. It was the size of a truck, designed to move on necromagnetic strips, and fastened on the back of a large trailer. There was a series of massive clips across a vertical seam, and one large silver switch, pointing horizontally.

'Excuse me?' The woman advanced. 'Sir? Would you mind telling me your—?'

'Sorry.' Donal pretended to be startled, to spin on one heel, and trip. 'Oops.'

As he fell, he reached out for the silver handle, caught it, and stopped. Then he thrust down with one leg and heaved to the side, wrenching the switch.

'Accident,' he added. 'My apologies.'

'What the Hades have you done?' said a large man, red-faced and far too portly for physical violence. 'Are you insane?'

'Sorry.' Donal backed away. 'But what's that?'

The casing clicked.

Surprise.

Some of the delegation stopped. The most senior, well inside the concave area that led to the inner corridors and offices, were the last to turn around. The Illurians' expressions tightened. A soft whispering exhalation of air announced the breaching of some kind of seal.

One by one, the big clips snapped open. Then coldness washed over everyone nearby as the casing split along its vertical seam. Pale blue light shone from inside.

And one side of the casing shifted on extruded pistons, pushed back ten, then twelve feet from the remaining container, revealing what was inside.

'Oh, Thanatos,' said someone. 'Oh, no.'

'What the Hades are they doing?'

Inside the hollow generator, in slender steel frames, sat packed rows of shaven-headed children with closed eyes. Cables networked their skulls together, passing into an apparatus that formed the container's floor. The children's chests moved in slow, shallow synchrony.

'Power generation,' said Donal. 'The Illurian way.'

Beside him, the woman with the clipboard opened her mouth, but gave only a croak. Blood drained from her face. Donal took hold of her arm to steady her.

'I didn't—' She started to whisper, then stopped.

'Some people here did know,' Donal murmured.

But it wasn't just the most junior workers who looked astonished or sickened. Some of the older men – and one woman – with grey hair and costlier suits, stepped back from their colleagues, distancing themselves from the collaboration whose true nature they could no longer deny.

Now Dr Grayfell, scowling, was looking straight at Donal.

Time I was gone.

Beside him, the young woman wiped her face. Then, covering her mouth with her hand, she pitched her voice low.

'Out through those doors, and turn right. There's a lifeward blocking the way.'

Donal turned to look out at the caverns, the rows of reactor piles, so that no one could see his face as he said, 'Thanks. I'm sorry.'

Then he strode through the group of businessmen and women. One of the Illurians tried to grab Donal's arm, but Donal merely swung his forearm through an arc, breaking the grip as he walked. He went through a set of doors.

'I want to talk to that man,' came Dr Grayfell's voice.

The doors shut behind Donal.

Now. Fast.

Donal broke into a sprint, ran to the end of the corridor where it split into three – *no one here, good* – then threw himself to the right just as he heard the sound of doors opening. He accelerated, trusting the advice the young woman had given him – *faster* – and then the air was viscous and fluorescing coldly around him. He pushed on, and then he was through, taking the first turning he came to, then slowing down.

No living person could have come this way, through the ward shield. With luck, no one besides the young woman had recognized Donal for what he was.

He continued at a walk, slowing his pace but not his heartbeat, for his black zombie heart had pumped at the same rate while sprinting, while climbing, and while standing at rest. An undead body regulated energy production in other ways.

Laura, I love you. I miss you.

The universe gave no reply.

Four

Donal made it back to the mortisection chamber without tripping alarms or confronting any Energy Authority workers. When he entered, Finross's corpse still lay upon the ceramic bier, but the lacework of nerves and arteries was gone. The body looked shrunken, wrinkled, as though part of its bulk had been sucked out.

'—any trace at all of thaumatonic legendization,' Lexar was saying. 'This means . . .'

On a frame beside him, a vellum page, mostly filled with purple script, thumped up and down several times, like a drumskin struck by invisible sticks. It was an error message.

'Command: stet,' said Lexar. 'Explanation: "legendization" is a technical word in my domain. Command: add to vocabulary.'

Donal looked up at the ceiling. It was flat and pale grey, hiding the inverted tree and quicksilver flock that hung above it. Here in the chamber, it was only him and Lexar and the body. No sign of the engineers.

'Command: continue,' added Lexar. 'The uncovered memories are true representations of the deceased's filtered experiences. So testified by me, Lexar Pinderwin, Bone Listener Level Five, for the Office of the Chief Medical Listener, on this day, Quinday the 35th of Hextember 6607. Command: endit.'

A drop of blood leaked from Lexar's nostril. He wiped it away.

'You've finished?' asked Donal.

'Yes. The report's done.' Lexar nodded towards the vellum page, where his final words had been added to the purple script. 'But you won't find what you're looking for. *I* didn't find it, Listening to his bones.'

'Huh. What am I looking for?'

'A chain of links to follow. You call the conspirators the Black Circle. I didn't get their true name from Finross. He didn't know it.'

'So he was what, a junior member?'

'Practically a dumb tool,' said Lexar. 'He had a ... difficult childhood. It made him the kind of person Cortindo could manipulate.'

'That bastard. I've already killed him once.'

'I hope you get a chance to do it again, Lieut— Donal. Permanently.'

'Is a revenant mage more or less powerful than when he was living? Do you know?'

'You'd need to ask a mage, but my guess is' – Lexar's eyes blinked in their usual froglike fashion – 'he's stronger now, on balance.'

'Balls. That was my guess, too.'

Donal knew nothing about mage lore, or the differences between revenants and zombies, but he knew the changes he'd experienced in himself.

'Finross's body is ready for the reactors.' Lexar was putting his instruments into a case, ignoring the corpse. 'You want to see the process?'

'I can live without it.' Donal smiled. 'Or whatever you call what I'm doing now.'

'I'm sorry?' Lexar looked up, his trident device in hand. 'Oh, right. I see what you mean. Neither one of us is standard human issue.'

'Probably not.'

'So ... Did you need a lift back to Avenue of the Basilisks, Donal?'

'Thanks, but I've got chauffeurs waiting for me.'

'Chauffeurs?'

'A couple of charmers known as the Barbarians to their friends.' Donal walked towards the exit, then paused. 'Actually, they're good guys. The best.'

'You lead an interesting life. Or whatever you call what you're doing.'

'Yeah.' Donal pressed the door release. 'Take it easy, Lexar.'

'You too.'

It was late when the Brodowskis dropped him off at the front steps of police HQ. They drove on, while FenSeven and several other deathwolves watched.

'How are you doing, FenSeven?'

'All. Right. Do-nal.'

Donal passed up the steps, identified himself by stating his badge number, and waited for the massive doors to open. Entering, he waved to Eduardo, the sergeant whose upper body was permanently melded with the massive granite block that doubled as the duty desk.

'Hey, Lieutenant.'

'Everything going OK?'

'Ain't going nowhere. Same old.'

'Yeah.'

Donal passed along the length of the great foyer, and reached the lift shafts. There, he stepped inside number 7, and wraith limbs took hold of him.

How're you doing, lover?

'Fine, Gertie. Take me to minus twenty-seven, will ...? Hang on, do you happen to know if the commissioner is in?'

Yes.

Perhaps Vilnar would want to see Donal in person, finally.

'Take me to him, please.'

I can't. Sorry, honey.

'But you said—'

You asked if I knew something, and I said yes. Because I do.

'Say what?'

I know Arrhennius Vilnar is not in the building. See?

'Gertie ...'

So which way do you want to go? I like all ways myself.

'Thanatos. Just let me back out, all right?'

For a moment, he swung suspended above the vertical drop that went down for hundreds, maybe thousands of feet. Then he felt the pressure of part-materialized wraith hands upon his back.

Later, lover.

And she pushed him out into the foyer, very fast.

'Have a lovely evening, Gertie.'

As he walked back through the foyer, Eduardo called to him: 'Leaving so soon?'

'Yeah, I'm going home.'

'Have a nice one. Say, Lieutenant ...'

'Uh-huh?'

'Is it true your apartment looks like a whorehouse?'

'Um. Good night, Eduardo.'

'Good night, Lieutenant.'

Donal took a purple cab to Darksan Tower. Inside, three doormen in black coats bowed to him, and he touched his forehead in salute. He crossed the gold-chased floor and stopped before a bank of lifts. The centre doors opened, and Donal stepped inside a curved, brass-and-gold lift-car.

'Parking garage, please.' He pressed the button marked *PG*. 'How are you doing today?'

The panel rippled under his touch.

'Good.' Donal stood in place during the descent. 'Thanks. See you in a bit.'

He stepped through to the semi-lit garage, while brass doors slid shut behind him. Stretching to either side were rows of gleaming saloons and limousines. A uniformed driver was polishing the headlights of a Galaxia. He raised his hand, still holding the mantasuede cloth.

'How's life, Donal?'

'I swear I can't remember. How about you?'

'Can't complain. Well I could, but no one ever pays—'

'Sorry, did you say something?'

They both laughed.

'See you later, Rowan.'

'Later, pal.'

Donal walked past several large supporting pillars, and reached the farthest row. Finally he came to a streamlined Vixen, parked with an empty space to either side. Her fins were long, her green headlights slanted like eyes. Donal stopped in front of her.

'I know,' he said, 'that things are strange between us.'

There was no kind of reply. He reached out towards the bonnet, stopped, and withdrew his hand.

'Travelling by taxi is fine. Day to day driving is not what I need you to— Shit.' Donal rubbed his face. 'Look, I know you're grieving too. I promise I'll look after you.'

The car remained silent.

'So I'm going to carry on. The ones really responsible for Laura's ... For Laura. I'm going to get them.'

Donal waited for perhaps a minute without breathing. He could remain as still as the Vixen, if he needed to.

Finally he continued, 'There was Gelbthorne, in Silvex City, who got away. So did Malfax Cortindo. As for Blanz, I took the bastard's eyes out ... Last I heard, he was in a secure hospital in Fortinium, healing up to go to trial.'

I hope he dies.

But no one had given Donal an update on Blanz's condition.

'Anyway, that's it. I'm going to track them down. I promise you.'

Nothing from the car.

'Just ... Take care of yourself.'

Donal turned and headed back toward the lift.

It was perhaps two minutes later, when Donal had already ascended from sight, that a tiny drop of black oil sprang from the Vixen's right headlight. It rolled downwards along the curved chrome rim, paused, then dropped to the granite floor with a quiet *plop*.

The lift paused at ground level for a group of well-dressed residents to enter. From the tuxedos and gowns, they might have been at the opera. One of the men hitched a thumb inside his waistcoat, glanced at Donal, then turned to his companions.

'The City Council is about to see changes, my friends. Welcome changes.'

'Making the streets safer for ordinary folk, I hope.'

'Absolutely,' said another. 'In fact, the sooner they confiscate—'

One of the women touched the man's sleeve, then adjusted her white fur stole as she spoke.'Confidential matters, my dear, should *remain* confidential.'

The man she'd interrupted shook his head, then caught sight of Donal, and grew still. No one said anything until the lift stopped at the 129th floor, and the group stepped out into the richly carpeted hallway.

'Have a lovely evening,' Donal called out from the lift, as the doors slid shut, 'you perfect assholes.'

The lift's walls rippled with what might have been amusement.

'You have a great evening too,' said Donal to the lift, as it stopped on 227. 'But in your case, I mean it. Thanks.'

As he exited to a polished obsidian chamber, he caught the faintest, distant whisper behind him.

You're very welcome.

The lift doors closed, and then he was alone. The chamber was twenty feet high, ending in black steel double doors that swung open, sensing Donal. Beyond was a larger antechamber, furnished in steel and matte black, in which blue flames danced atop helical stands. A forbidding twelve-foot mask glowered from the wall.

'Home, sweet home,' muttered Donal.

The mask's mouth opened, and continued to open, forming a doorway through to the apartment proper. As Donal walked inside, he noted the tiny holes inside the mouth's metallic gums, where toxin-delivering fangs could extrude if necessary. Against physical threats, he was well-guarded.

And if the city confiscates all property from non-human beings?

It had been Senator Blanz who'd proposed the Vital Renewal Bill before the Senate in Fortinium. With his arrest as a murderer, Blanz had been discredited, disavowed by the Unity Party he had represented. But somehow the legal proposals, and the paranoia that drove them, continued with their own momentum.

Donal looked around the room. A floor of dark-blue glass, furnishings he could never have afforded in life, when he depended on his police pay. Inheriting all this—

'Laura,' he said out loud. 'Oh, Laura.'

From vents in the floors, flames rose and moved in slow motion, before disappearing. Donal nodded, then went through to the magnificent bedroom, and sat down in a glass chair. He picked up the book he'd been reading. It was brand-new, unlike the secondhand books he'd been used to buying at Peat's bookstore, and it was the last in the series. *Human: the Apocalypse* was rumoured to contain an explanation of why the fictitious parallel Earth featured a civilization with no knowledge of necroflux, where wraiths were unknown and mages existed only in secret.

He read for a time, then put the book down.

I wonder how many hours I've got remaining?

This was something he was getting better at estimating. He thought for a while, then spoke out loud.

'Two hours and seventy-five minutes.'

Donal had always, since his military days, worn his watch on the inside of his wrist. Now, when he turned his hand over, he didn't focus on the position of the hands, but on the grey disc of the watchface. Like a cake-slice, a sliver showed as black, taking up less than a twentieth of the full circle.

'Good guess,' he murmured.

If he held his hand still for long enough, he might even see the tiny decrement as the sliver shrank. Part of him wanted to know what would happen if he let it decrease to zero; but that would be an insult to Laura's memory.

Donal looked at the discarded book, shook his head, then began to take off his clothes and lay them on the steel four-poster bed. He stripped down to his shorts. Then he tapped the top drawer of the bedside cabinet, which slid open.

'Thank you.'

He withdrew the coiled black manticore-gut rope, and the drawer slid shut. It didn't respond to Donal's thanks, because it was ensorcelled but dumb, merely a device. Laura had not allowed boundwraiths to be trapped inside her apartment's furnishings.

Two hours and seventy-three minutes remaining.

'All right.'

His old boxing coach, Mal O'Brian, had insisted on fitness before technique, and aggression before fitness. The sawdust smell of the old gym came back to Donal as he began to jump rope, a simple double jump, just high enough for the black cord to pass beneath his feet. He kept the rhythm slow.

The cord flicked against the floor, a metronomic tick.

In his early days on patrol, with Fredrix Paulsen as his mentor, Donal had seen a zombie ex-firefighter called Manfred Rifftol, whose shambling form indicated the fate of anyone who failed to keep their resurrected body in shape. (His brain had remained sharp, though, which was why Sergeant Paulsen had used Manfred partly as a street snitch, mostly as a source of tips on lizard races. Manfred's primary income was from betting.)

Tick. Tick. Tick.

After a time, Donal switched to harder jumps, good for coordination and footwork. Again, he kept his new rhythm with inhuman precision, before returning to the basic two-foot jump, faster than before. He kept on going.

Tick. Tick.

And going. The first hour passed.

The thing was, while Manfred had survived as a disintegrating zombie, had he chosen to go the route of physical discipline, he would have held things together in a way no living human could.

Tick. Tick.

One hour and fifty minutes elapsed.

Tick ...

Two hours.

He kept going until two hours and seventy-two minutes had passed, before stopping with a suddenness that would have been dangerous had he been alive. He tossed the rope onto the bed.

One minute remaining.

Moving quickly, he crossed to the wall and sank cross-legged to the floor. A slender cable was already plugged in to the wall socket. Donal put both hands against his bare chest.

Thirty seconds remaining.

He pressed his fingertips against his skin, hard. A seam split open, and he hooked the skin back, opening a triangular flap.

Twenty seconds.

Then the pectoral muscle parted, exposing the beating black heart.

Ten.

I could stop. Just not do anything.

But that would be a betrayal of Laura, whose heart this truly was.

Oh, Laura.

Three.

He took hold of the cable, holding its free end just above the socket of his heart.

Two.

Decision.

One.

And he pushed the cable into place. The connection clicked softly.

Donal closed his eyes, rested his hands on his knees, feeling the charge build up in his heart once more.

In the morning, Donal walked to Avenue of the Basilisks. It took an hour, but it was early and he had the time to spare. Not needing to sleep had advantages.

Once inside HQ, he went to shaft 7, and waited for Gertie to take hold of him.

Arrhennius is in.

'You mean the commissioner.'

It hadn't occurred to Donal that Commissioner Vilnar might be on first-name terms with an elevator wraith. There was a lot about the Old Man that he didn't know.

I'll take you there, lover.

'Thank you, dearest.'

Maybe I'm not doing you a favour.

'What does that mean?'

But Gertie said no more as she slowly rose, taking Donal upwards at a leisurely rate, as though giving him time to reconsider. Before Laura's death and Senator Blanz's arrest, the Task Force had suspected Commissioner Vilnar of being a member of the Black Circle. There had been two separate indicators of guilt. First, it turned out to be an order from the commissioner's office that had resulted in Cortindo's being placed in stasis, instead of undergoing postmortem. Second, a thaumaturgical engineer called Kyushen Jyu had retrieved a telephone number from a live suspect's memories, indicating that illicit orders had come from the commissioner's office.

Yet Commissioner Vilnar's secretary, known as Eyes to every cop in the Department – because none had ever seen her except with cables attached to her eyes, linking her to the city's rooftop surveillance mirrors – had turned out to be Alderman Finross's niece, and the Black Circle's source within police HQ.

Laura had been impressed with how fast the commissioner moved when things came to a head. He'd led the escape from his office when Eyes – Marnie Finross – had trapped everyone inside; he'd directed Laura and the Vixen to hunt down Finross on the streets; and, somehow, he had uncovered the extra information which had led Laura and Donal to the Senate in Fortinium, where Blanz had assumed the form of another senator.

Hundredth floor. Last chance to change your mind.

'Why would I—?'

But she had already shoved him out into the vestibule.

'Later, Gertie.'

Good luck, lover.

Things had changed. Rows of desks filled the open office space. Each desk contained three or more surveillance screens – lens-fronted mirrors, linked by transparent cables to complex glass domes in the ceiling. Uniformed officers, mostly female, were watching the screens.

A handful of plainclothes guys were huddled around one desk, watching while the surveillance operator flicked stone switches, following some suspect's movement across crowded Hoardway, down into a Pneumetro station.

'Can I help you, Lieutenant?' asked a pretty young officer.

'I'm hoping to see the Old Man.'

'The commissioner's usually busy first thing in the' – she looked down at a wraith-written list – 'morning, but there's a note to say, if *you* turn up, you can go straight in.' Her smile was bright. 'Guess you're one of the privileged, sir.'

'I guess.' Donal gestured to the rows of monitors. 'How's all this working out?'

'Getting better every day. Don't know how one person managed it.'

She meant Eyes.

'And did she? Manage it?'

'Well … ' The young officer glanced toward the plainclothes team. 'We can surveil suspects without using scanbats. No one really thought of doing it before. Not systematically.'

'You guys know what happened to Eyes?'

'Sir?'

'I'm just asking what the scuttlebutt is.'

'Hard to know what's rumour and what's fact.' She tapped her desk. 'Word is, Eyes is in a catatonic trance inside a secure ward somewhere. And that she had something to do with Senator Blanz, and Dr d'Alkernay's murder. And what happened to Commander Steele.'

'That's all true,' said Donal.

'Oh.'

He smiled at her, and she smiled back. It should have been a light-hearted moment, except that Donal was micro-calibrating his body language to match hers. When the difference between unconscious action and conscious control was lost, was it possible ever to act naturally? Or must everything a zombie did become manipulation?

And yet, it might prove useful for Donal to have a friend inside the new Surveillance Department.

Laura. I wish I could ask you for advice.

'Take it easy,' he told the young officer.

'And you, sir.'

He walked past the surveillance desks, and stopped before a massive portal formed of black iron. This was new to him. The commissioner's previous office, which Eyes had attacked, remained inaccessible, sealed off from normal reality.

Iron doors pulled back, and Donal stepped into a short tunnel. The walls flexed, as though about to swallow him, the outer doors closed with a muted clang, then the inner doors parted. What remained was a circular opening – the word Donal thought of was *orifice* – around which a multitude of narrow, wriggling ciliaserpents moved. Their toxin, once injected, would take immediate effect, setting into motion a slow bio-chemical shutdown, a death as agonizing as rending by hookwraiths.

'Come inside, Lieutenant.' It was Commissioner Vilnar's voice.

'Sir.'

The ciliaserpents withheld their poison bites, allowing Donal through. A black iron chair – its arms, back and four legs formed of curved, pointed, dark metallic sheets – walked across the stone floor and stopped in front of him.

'Take a seat.'

It was more a matter of the seat taking him. Donal sat down, and the chair walked with mincing steps towards its master's desk, then stopped. The commissioner's huge scale-covered chair rotated until the commissioner faced Donal.

'Congratulations, Lieutenant.' His blocky face was expressionless. 'You and I are going to City Hall, the day after tomorrow.'

'City Hall?'

'So you can receive your commendation from His Honour, the Mayor.'

'Oh.'

'Don't fool yourself, Lieutenant. Once the publicity dies down, the knives are going to come out. And I won't be protecting you.'

Five

Tristopolis City Hall, huge and skull-shaped, formed of petrified bone, had existed for three millennia, maybe more. Scholars argued, but none had truly determined the construct's origins. It rose some three hundred and fifty feet above the grounds of Möbius Park, whose strange dark treescape was laid in interlocking twisted loops.

Inside those shadowed areas, translucent forms drifted, glowing crimson or lilac as their moods and hunger changed. They were ectoplasma wraiths, their bodies manifesting as the seventh state of matter, ravening with the need to subsume physical, living mass. Subsisting off a deep-buried power grid that existed only to feed them, they always wanted more.

Few intruders escaped the wraiths of Möbius Park.

Only the gravel roadways were protected from the wraiths, and venomous gargoyles drifted over those roads, on guard. Their perches were on the wings of City Hall, two arcing additions to the original skull, each of them nineteen storeys tall, filled with municipal offices and, some said, secret installations where only mage-adepts might enter and survive.

On the main driveway, a parkkeeper-janitor was raking the bonestones, while his non-ectoplasmic wraith companion drifted alongside.

What's the next event?

'Some presentation, day after tomorrow.' The man stopped, leaned on his rake. 'Usual kinda crap. Mayor and his cronies. Speeches. Newspaper guys.'

Maybe I should take a peek.

'Ya can't be that bored.'

Probably not.

Gargoyles were gathering above a roadway. Perhaps there was the sound of motors.

'Someone coming. Guess I'll get outta their way.'

Three dark saloons with silvered windows came slowly along the

46

gravel, tracked overhead by gargoyles. As the cars halted, flamewraiths rose on either side of the main steps: both an honour guard and a further layer of protection.

'Private security,' muttered the parkkeeper-janitor. 'Them guys.'

The men exited. Dark suits and cropped hair were enough to iden-tify them. At this distance, the tiepins and cufflinks, bearing the super-imposed U and P of the Unity Party, were impossible to make out.

I'm gone.

'You don't have to—'

The wraith was sinking down into the gravel.

Later.

'—go.'

With a long exhalation, the parkkeeper-janitor swung his rake, and returned to his endless task. He did not look up from the gravel as the visitors entered the main skull of City Hall. He already knew the hard-faced bastards would be scanning him, the flamewraiths, and everything in sight.

Freakin' . . . freaks.

But he said nothing as he continued to rake, only relaxing when the full complement of security men had disappeared inside the building.

Donal shifted his weight forward on to his feet. The black iron chair quivered, as though about to restrain him; but Commissioner Vilnar shook his head. The chair grew still, allowing Donal to stand up.

'Feeling restless?' The commissioner looked at him without expres-sion. 'Or were you hoping I'd look after you more?'

'Not what I was pinning my hopes on.'

Donal walked across the room, and stopped before the stone credenza. On top of it was something new: a large brass orrery, powered by clock-work. Small spheres representing the planets moved along rods bent into near-circular orbits.

'Prometheus.' Donal touched the innermost planet, then the next. 'Venus. Earth. Mars. Oberon.' The next two were surrounded with rings. 'Jupiter. Saturn.' And, far out from the others: 'Poseidon, and Hel.'

'Check out the rotation.'

It was a strange thing for Commissioner Vilnar to say. Donal focused on the brass Venus. It appeared to be a solid sphere running along a horizontal rod, but it was rotating on its north-south axis. The brass was liquid, ensorcelled.

'Is the whole thing to scale?' asked Donal.

'No. But the ratio of daily rotation to annual orbit is correct for every planet.'

'I can see that.' Donal turned back to face Vilnar. 'Nice toy.'

There was the tiniest movement of muscles around Vilnar's eyes. He was processing Donal's casual comment: that he could *see* the orrery was exactly correct. No living human could have made that judgement without a magnifying lens and several days' observation.

'And what else do you see, Lieutenant?'

'I see a police department with trouble brewing, if there are Unity Party recruiters inside the force as well as City Hall.'

'Hmm. And what if I said I agree with you?'

Donal thought back to Vilnar's words: *I won't be protecting you.* Meaning, he'd like to but he couldn't? Or just that Donal could go to Hades for all he cared?

'So what about the team?'

'The task force was federal.' Vilnar rubbed his temple, ran a hand across his shaved scalp. 'Without Commander Steele, I'm waiting for the federal liaison to make a decision. For the time being, Commander Bowman will assume command responsibility for you and your team members. But that does *not* mean the task force is operational, understand?'

'Sir? Commander Bowman has Robbery-Haunting to run, but we could still—'

'Do nothing until authorized.'

'Understood.'

'Hades, Donal.' Vilnar hadn't used Donal's first name before. 'You want Blanz to die for killing Laura, and you want to get Cortindo for setting the thing in motion. But Cortindo was in Illurium when he disappeared, and another country is about as out of our jurisdiction as it gets.'

'He might be back in Federation territory.'

'And he might not be. I've not even heard about Blanz's progress, about when he'll be able to stand trial.'

'I thought I'd killed him.' Donal remembered the rage as he clawed at Blanz's eyes. 'Can mages regrow eyeballs?'

'I don't know. Here's a more pertinent question. Can zombies testify before a supreme jury?'

'Of course—' Donal stopped. 'You think the law might be about to change?'

'See here.' Vilnar raised his bulky form out his chair. 'There's a moon missing from the orrery.'

He pointed into the brass model.

'All right.' Donal had never known the Old Man to take so long getting to the point. 'Is this some mystic thing?'

'Only to the mathematically challenged.' Vilnar's fingertip sketched a path around the tiny Poseidon. 'There's an irregular lumpy moon, not remotely spherical, that tumbles unpredictably, even though its orbit is predictable.'

'Excuse me? That doesn't hang together,'

'If the orrery included it, you could forecast where on its orbit the moon was, but not which way up it was pointing.'

Donal said nothing, fed up with prompting Vilnar.

'It can tumble in an instant,' Vilnar continued. 'Remember how Greater Alritel's inflation went to two thousand per cent in days? Or don't you read the foreign news section?'

'You're trying to tell me that things can change suddenly, is that it?'

'Hmm. And what else have you worked out?'

'That you haven't asked me what I found in the Westside Complex. So either you don't care, or you assume I found nothing. And you went to a lot of trouble for something you don't care about.'

Vilnar almost smiled.

'I expected you to find the safe empty, since Braune' – he meant the forcibly retired Energy Authority director – 'found his house had been burgled around the time I was writing you that note. I thought of rescinding the order, but I thought you might still find something of interest. *Did* you find anything?'

So it really had been Vilnar writing on the all-time pad. Donal had been almost certain – enough to follow the instructions – but he could have been wrong. The Black Circle included mages of high ability, Malfax Cortindo included.

'I did find an empty safe.' Donal tapped the tiny brass Poseidon in the model. 'I also found a bunch of businessmen from an Illurian power company demonstrating how they could hook their generators into the Tristopolis grid.'

'Illurian.'

'Yeah. You know how they generate power?'

'I read your report. All of it.'

'The Illurians had a portable generator here,' Donal said. 'With kids inside.'

'Thanatos.' Vilnar's blocky body seemed to expand, revealing the physical power he still possessed, despite the years that had passed since he'd worked the streets. 'How can an entire country close its eyes to what's going on?'

'Huh. The Illurian cop, Temesin. You know what he said to me? "At least we bury our dead." He maybe had a point.'

'Maybe. All right, Lieutenant. That's good work. Did the Energy Authority look like they were going for the deal?'

'Their Dr Grayfell was. Some of the others were a little shocked when they found out how the generator worked. I don't know if that'll make a difference.'

'I'm surprised the Illurians explained the mechanism.'

Donal smiled. 'It wasn't their idea, exactly. I accidentally tripped, and grabbed a switch to steady myself.'

'Ah. Too bad about your balance problem.'

'I'll write everything up and—'

'No need. Are there any other details you can think of?'

'None spring to mind.' Donal was fully alert again. 'If you wanted to communicate in secret before, why is it all right for me to be here now? But not to write up a report?'

'Because there's an overt reason for this meeting. You'll probably find an official letter on your desk, but in cases like this, I always see the officer involved in person.'

'Involved in what?'

'In receiving that commendation from Mayor Dancy himself. City Hall, day after tomorrow, at thirteen o'clock sharp. Rendezvous in the parking garage down below, two hours in advance. You'll travel with me.'

'Um, sure.'

'You don't look enthusiastic. I'm also accepting a posthumous award on behalf of Laura Steele.'

Laura. Oh, Hades.

'That's good, I guess.'

'It doesn't help.' Vilnar's voice went surprisingly soft. 'I know that. But they damn well ought to remember.'

'Remember that a zombie died in the line of duty? Half of the bastards there will probably say she died years ago. That what Blanz blew apart was some kind of *thing*.'

'So long as it's only half of them,' said Vilnar, 'we're winning the battle.'

Donal took a second to think about the meaning of *we* and *battle*. There was a political agenda here, taking him completely out of his depth.

So what am I going to do? Ignore it?

'I'll buy a new suit for the occasion.'

'Good. Perhaps we'll make a politician of you yet.'

'If you say so.'

'Get out of here, Riordan. See what you can do about keeping up your team's morale.'

'You mean Laura's team.'

'I mean the team that Commander Bowman's running pro tem. And you, I'll see on Sepday morning.'

'Sir.'

Donal looked at the orrery, thinking how odd it was that planetary positions could be predicted a million years ahead, while the events of the next two days appeared uncertain. Or perhaps that was Vilnar's point.

Then he walked to the door, and waited until it sucked open. At that point, perhaps a living human would have looked back at Vilnar. Donal stepped straight into the throat-like tunnel.

At the same time, a group of dark-suited men stood in the main atrium of City Hall. They looked at each other, saying nothing, then fanned out. They crossed the polished petrified-bone floor, walking over the inlaid iron pattern: the federal Salamander-and-Eagle. On seven sides, wide staircases rose up to the next level. At least one man ascended each staircase. Most were carrying fist-sized hex detectors: white-gold, egg-shaped miniature cages in which embryonic banshees lay quiescent. If they sensed malevolent ensorcelment beyond the normal security parameters of this place, they would wail an alarm no one could ignore.

Overhead, a flock of miniature white bats fluttered, keeping watch on these private security men who could afford banshees and other expensive gear. The bats were part of City Hall's own internal surveillance, passing their sensory information back to the three on-duty mages, sitting in a security chamber in the core of what would have been the gigantic skull's cerebellum, had a living brain occupied it.

Some of the bats followed each security man, including the solo individual on Ninth Corridor, where regimental banners and antique weapons of the Battling 303s were arranged in splendid layouts on the walls, and in glass-fronted display cases. Old spears and sniper rifles radiated from beaten helmets, like martial flowers in a weaponry garden.

The man – he looked chunky and muscular, his plain suit expensive, like his colleagues' – stopped to examine a banner, its dark stains a history of blood spilled and long-forgotten honour maintained or lost. He appeared not to notice the tiny white bats fluttering overhead.

But suddenly they wheeled away, responding to an ultrasonic alarm caused by somebody bumping into a Third Corridor scanport. As they departed, the lone man moved fast, pulling hex keys from his pocket as he approached a tall display case. It took seconds to open the ensorcelled locks. Opened, the case revealed a purple velvet drape laid across a shelf; and on the drape, polished antique weapons shone. The back of the cabinet was dark.

The big man pulled what looked like a black handkerchief from his pocket – and kept pulling, more and more fabric coming out, like a cheap conjuration on stage. Then the whole thing was free of his pocket, and the man carefully laid the shroud-like fabric behind the weapons.

He had perhaps twenty seconds before the bats returned.

The man began to shiver. He undid his tie and unbuttoned his shirt all the way, and pulled it open. He undid the front of his trousers, pushed them down. His skin was hairless, his chest devoid of nipples, his crotch smooth and featureless.

Fifteen seconds.

The next stages proceeded very fast. First, the man's face rippled like liquid. Then his face and torso split open vertically, from crown to crotch, then forking to open down the front of each bare leg like a seam, the entire opening forming an upturned Y. There was a wriggle inside, then a small lithe man in a hooded assassin's bodysuit stepped out of the larger body, accompanied by a soft popping sound.

The assassin's stretchweb bodysuit was saturated with shadowhex. The cocoon he had exited was of flesh-pink animaskin, already sealing itself up to conceal its hollow – now empty – interior.

Then the assassin pulled up the animaskin's trousers, while the animaskin's own fingers rebuttoned the shirt. A quick tucking-in and tie-knotting, and the animaskin looked like a functional human being once more.

It was already turning to walk away when the assassin, moving with a world-class gymnast's litheness, vaulted into the display case, and pulled the glass doors shut. For a moment, the assassin watched the bulky animaskin heading towards the staircase that led down to the atrium.

Three seconds.

Behind the displayed weapons, the assassin lay down on one side, curled up to fit into the narrow space, and pulled the shroud over himself. Something shifted, and multiple hues rippled across the shroud. Then the colours settled into place, matching the purple velvet beneath the weapons and the dark rear wall of the cabinet, as appropriate.

Zero.

And the bats wheeled in, exactly according to estimate, passed along the corridor. Everything looked normal. The bats turned back, forming an overhead escort to the animaskin – so like a functional human being – that was walking downstairs.

Meanwhile, under the chameleon shroud, the assassin let out a long, silent exhalation, descending deeply into trance. He would remain in this state for most of the next fifty-three hours, until it was time.

Donal avoided Gertie, and rode down with an elevator wraith who was nameless and rarely communicated. Impersonal hands pushed him on to the landing of minus twenty-seven, and then the wraith was gone.

Maybe I should go to the gun range.

Daily practice had been part of Donal's life for years. But really, he just wanted to avoid the empty office space, knowing that the rest of the team had probably found excuses to be elsewhere. It had been a pattern since Laura's death.

But when Donal stepped inside, he saw one person: neat white uniform shirt, chest ribbons, polished button-down holster. This was Commander Bowman, a fit man in his fifties with cropped red hair and unlined skin. Bowman smiled to Donal, but when he spoke, a strained harmonic caught Donal's attention.

'I don't suppose you've seen Commissioner Vilnar yet?'

'Actually, I have.'

'Well,' with the taut beginnings of a smile, 'you'll know you're going to be in City Hall, day after tomorrow. Hoo-hah and razmatazz.'

'I'm looking forward to it.' Donal was focusing on the tiny eye movements, the tension in Bowman's stance. 'What could be more fun?'

'Maybe bullshitting a superior officer?'

Donal produced a smile.

'As if I'd do that.'

'Huh.' Bowman gestured with a half-full coffee cup. 'You want some coffee?'

'No, thanks.'

'Really? Someone told me you always—'

'Well, you don't want to believe what people tell you, Commander. Especially,' Donal sniffed, 'that Alexa Ceerling.'

Anyone could see the tension clamping Bowman's shoulders.

'You have a problem with Detective Ceerling?'

'Me? No problem.' Donal turned towards an area of blank wall. 'Leastways, if you discount the body odour and the herpes, and the way she picks her nose. And did I mention she farts?'

In front of him, the wall began to waver.

'Hades,' said Bowman.

A section of wall faded away, revealing an alcove in which a young woman stood.

'I so do *not* fart, Lieutenant Riordan, sir.'

'Not even in the bath?'

'Never.' Alexa Ceerling turned to Bowman, wriggling her eyebrows. 'Is he good, or what?'

'Your evaluation is noted, Detective. Now get out of here.'

'Yes, sir.' She poked her tongue out at Donal. 'Lieutenant.'

Then she left the office, with fractionally more hip sway than she needed to use. She was no gym rat, but fit enough. Donal and Bowman watched until she was out of sight.

'Were you evaluating me?' asked Donal. 'Or Alexa?'

'Just gathering information.' Bowman turned to a desk and picked up a lilac sheet of paper, printed with blotchy dark-purple ink. 'You didn't catch anyone leaving this around here, did you?'

The leaflet read: *UNDEAD MEANS UNALIVE*, with a short rhetorical question underneath – *What are they doing while you're asleep?* Bowman screwed up the paper, and threw it aside.

'No.'

'Too bad. You might have straightened them out.'

'I didn't notice any group's name on that thing.'

'What the Unity Party's proposing is illegal, unless they succeed in getting the law changed. So forget those bastards, and tell me what you think of Detective Ceerling.'

'Young Alexa?'

'Yes, Lieutenant. Her.'

'I think she'll be the first female commissioner, if she puts her mind to it.'

'Ah.' Bowman looked at the glass cube that had been Laura's office. 'I think Commissioner Vilnar might agree with you.'

Was he implying a rift between himself and the commissioner?

'Has the Old Man been discussing an ordinary female D2' – Donal meant a Detective Grade Two – 'with senior officers?'

'No discussion.' Bowman gestured at the alcove that remained in the wall. 'But how do you think Alexa Ceerling got the resources to create a spy-hole right here in the building?'

'Good question.'

'And I don't exactly know the answer.' Bowman's smile was upturned and momentary. 'I think she's worth keeping an eye on, one way or the other.'

Trying to make me suspicious of Alexa?

That did not make sense. Donal looked again at the glass-walled inner office, whose door still bore the golden lettering: *Commander L. Steele*. The office was as empty as Donal's soul.

'Does the task force have a future, Commander?'

'I don't know,' said Bowman. 'Would it really be better for you if it did?'

'That's a strange question.'

'What would you do if you weren't a cop?'

'Hades. I haven't thought about it.'

'You're rich now.' Bowman's gaze travelled to the discarded leaflet. 'Assuming *they* don't get their way. But you don't need to work right now, any more than Commander Steele did.'

'There's your answer, then.'

'If you're trying to say there was no one more dedicated than her,' said Bowman, 'then I agree with you. But if you're counting on the feds to help you track down Cortindo and his pals, then you might have a long wait.'

'Why? Is there something you know that I'm not party to?'

'No. I probably know less than you.' Bowman propped himself against the desk that Viktor Harman – aka Big Viktor – usually used. 'But from what the commissioner has said, the ones you're after are likely to be the other side of the border. And the feds don't reach that far.'

'Which feds? Who runs the task force?' Donal felt a little stupid as he added, 'Who exactly did Laura report to? Or do I mean liaise with?'

'From Fortinium, a guy called Murgatrayle. The feds' local field office is not involved.'

This was more than anyone else had told Donal. He wondered what it meant about Bowman's intentions.

'If the task force continues' – Bowman pushed himself away from the desk – 'would you be willing to head it up? You understand ... *if* it continues. No guarantees.'

'I've less time on the team than any of the others. But I'll do it.'

'Good. That's what I needed to know.'

Donal laughed.

'Maybe we'll both be reporting to Alexa Ceerling,' he said. 'One of these days.'

'I hope so.' Bowman frowned, staring at the door Alexa had left by. 'I really hope so.'

It was a strange thing for him to say ... or perhaps just a strange tone of voice to say it in. But he nodded to Donal then, and headed out of the room.

Maybe I'll figure it out.

Donal stared around the task force office: unoccupied chairs, desktops bare of paperwork.

Empty. Just empty.

Three dark saloons rolled along the gravel roadway, slowing to a halt as they neared Tiger Mouth Gate, the northernmost exit from Möbius Park. From this position, the dark trees hid the giant rearing skull of City Hall. An ectoplasma wraith drifted among the boughs, was lost from sight.

Inside the three vehicles, no one spoke. In the back seat of the rear car, three men in dark suits sat unmoving, perhaps in meditation.

There was a gatehouse, but the security person – or team: you could argue the nomenclature either way, because the usual concepts failed to apply – remained inside. It was a wise move, because the air around the three stationary saloons grew chill and began to wobble, then darken. Just because the cars were leaving, not entering, did not excuse them from being scanned.

A large form that was mostly shadow manifested itself, curled over the lead vehicle, then passed down inside it. Reappearing, it moved on to the next car, and repeated the process. Then once more, checking the last car, failing to detect anything untoward.

As the iceghoul sank down into the ground, allowing its material form to fade, it left behind three cars covered in a thin, sparkling layer of frost. Each car's engine coughed before regaining power. Then the fanged gates opened, and one by one the vehicles rolled through.

Once out on the main road, in the rear seat of the final car, two men turned to look at each other, then at the unmoving figure that sat between them. It looked more like a clothing dummy now than a real man, for animaskins function only for minutes, and this one's hex had faded, all used up. Inert, it had caused no reaction from the iceghoul.

'Phase One accomplished,' said one of the men.

Up front, the driver thumbed a mike to transmit.

'Infiltration successful.'

'Good news. Return to Main Control.'

'Yes, sir.'

As the cars headed north along Talon Drive, their coating of frost began to evaporate. Behind them, no alarms sounded, no gargoyles rose into the sky, no wraiths burned with ectoplasmic fire. No police pteracopters came thundering down from above.

It was a solid beginning.

Six

She shouldn't have expected the guys to notice her clothes, at least not consciously. Or perhaps they *had* treated her with more respect than before. Hadn't she'd just been joking with Donal and Commander Bowman as equals? The thing was, she had dressed in this dark-grey skirt-suit and burgundy blouse for a reason.

When Laura had been alive, to copy her fashion style would have been too much like brown-nosing. Now, Alexa could think of nothing better than to emulate the dead commander's attitude towards work, maybe towards everything.

Eight days ago, Alexa had gone to visit the only other female team member, or ex-member, now living at the edge of the city with her parents. Her name was Sushana, and she was on extended sick leave, still attending rehab three times weekly, plus psych counselling from a local mage, helping her to overcome the trauma of being tortured and raped by Sally the Claw and his men.

'You're standing more like a commander, too,' Sushana had told Alexa.

That had brought back memories of Laura, sobering them both.

Now, Alexa walked through the Surveillance Department, noting the transparent cables that festooned the place, the rows of monitors and lenses and prisms that enabled officers to track suspects better than before. One of the men, Sergeant Rob Helborne, was in conversation with a group of AE detectives, but he noticed Alexa and gave her a wave. As she waved back, she wondered what Anti-Ensorcelment were up to.

Keeping track of other teams' assignments was unusual, but Alexa figured that Laura used to do it, and had friends in every team – witness the way Laura had been able to call on Robbery-Haunting for help on the day Mina d'Alkernay was murdered. In that regard, perhaps Commissioner Vilnar was an even better role model. He had managed the metamorphosis from street cop to tough politician in a way that Alexa found astounding.

The black iron doors opened. She traversed the threatening tunnel that could swallow a dozen people, and went through the inner doors where the ciliaserpents curled then extended, as if standing to attention. She was in Commissioner Vilnar's office.

'Alexa. How are you doing?'

'Fine, sir.'

A black iron chair skittered across the stone floor, and gave a little dance on its four legs.

'And how are *you* doing, Bert?' Alexa patted the chair's back.

The chair curled its arms in pleasure.

'Let's settle down.' Commissioner Vilnar sat in the big scale-covered chair behind his desk. 'And talk about a little assignment that's far too trivial for you.'

'Uh-huh.'

An assignment directly from the Commissioner of Police? Whatever it was, Alexa would consider it as non-trivial as possible, another upward step in her career.

When she sat down on the chair, Bert, it began to purr. She stroked its right arm, looking around the office. The orrery atop the stone credenza was new, but she was little interested in mechanical toys. A small bookcase on the other side of the room, containing black-covered volumes whose spines bore no titles, seemed to have acquired more books. She wondered if she would ever get permission to read them.

On the wall behind her, black drapes were drawn across, even though this was in the heart of the building, away from any exterior wall. Thinking about this, she remembered the deep vault where she had accompanied the commissioner on the day that Eyes – Marnie Finross – had broken from cover, and been chased by Laura through the streets of Tristopolis.

In that vault, Commissioner Vilnar had dealt with eldritch forces to uncover the whereabouts of Senator Blanz. Alexa's role had been to drag the unconscious commissioner away from the vault when his session was over, to force healing fluid into his mouth, and to keep her own mouth permanently shut about everything she'd seen that day.

'So.' Vilnar rubbed his bare scalp. 'You know we expanded Customer Relations a while back? Renamed it the Customer Relationship Bureau?'

'Um, yes.' Alexa didn't like the sound of this. 'The mayor's office wants to improve our image with the public.'

'Exactly.'

Many officers would say that increasing their powers to interrogate suspects would increase their resolution rate on open cases, and *that* was what would make the public love them. Or at least the victims, and the victims' families. But other cops were more thoughtful, Alexa included.

'You're not suggesting that detectives should take a rotation through the call desks? The Customer Relations call desks?'

'Not at all.'

'Oh. Good. Sorry, sir.'

'But I *am* suggesting that *you* spend some time there, Detective. On your own initiative, with no mention of me.'

'Um.'

'Just one shift, today. And another tomorrow, if you like, but no more. All right?'

Alexa couldn't imagine volunteering to sit with Customer Relations for a minute longer than she'd been ordered to.

'Of course, sir.'

'And you'll let me know afterwards what you think.'

So the commissioner wanted to talk to her again, to get her impressions and perhaps recommendations. Maybe this wasn't such a bad move after all. The task force was currently, well, task-less until reconfirmed by the feds. And the feds were taking their time.

'Absolutely. I'll get right to it.'

She patted the chair, Bert, once more. Then she stood up. The chair's arms drooped.

'I'll see you again soon, Bert.' And, to the commissioner: 'Thank you, sir.'

Then she left, with the ciliaserpents around the door waving in time, as though sorry to see her go.

Some ten minutes later, Commissioner Vilnar, who had been sitting like a carved block of stone, finally moved. He stood up, his blocky face serious, then he punched one fist into the opposite palm, and said, 'Thanatos *fuck* it.'

The visitor's chair – Bert – and several other items of furniture straightened up, unused to such language from Vilnar.

'My apologies.' Vilnar looked at the chair. 'And I know you're fond of her, but I may have just fed Alexa Ceerling to the demons. I'm talking figuratively, I think.'

Around the doorway, the ciliaserpents thrashed.

'Troy Gamarlov will debrief her, and deprogram her if necessary.'

Vilnar clenched his big fists, and his upper arms swelled inside the sleeves of his expensive suit. 'I don't like to do it, because she's sensitive. Insightful. But that's what makes her the best choice.'

The ciliaserpents quietened. The furniture relaxed to normal configuration.

'Shit.' Commissioner Vilnar stared at the black drapes on the wall. 'Shit. Shit. Shit.'

Donal stopped in the deep subterranean foyer and sniffed the air: cordite, a hint of noradrenalin overlaid with other pheromones. Gunshots banged nearby. Smiling, Donal realized he felt at home.

Shouldn't have left it so long.

Since Laura's— Since everything changed, he had avoided the firing range, just as he had stopped so many daily habits, including sleep. But he'd known straight away that fitness needed to be maintained. Perhaps combat shooting was second priority, on the short list of things he had to work at every day.

The counter in the reception room was carved from an off-white carapace, the shell of some long-dead giant scarab. Behind it, Brian, his skin pale-blue as always, was oiling a stripped-down Grauser.

'Loot! Bleeding Thanat— I mean, good to see you, Lieutenant.'

'Yeah. How're you doing, Brian?'

'Um, OK. Everything's still legit, and I mean totally.'

It was only a few weeks since Donal had called Internal Security to investigate, having warned Brian so he could get rid of the illegal target sheets – depicting real individuals – and subsequently threatened him, suspecting that he'd been selling ammunition privately. But it seemed long ago, like a memory of schooldays.

'I just want to practise.'

'Oh. Sure. Say, eight targets, eighty rounds?'

'How about thirteen targets, seven hundred rounds.' Donal wasn't quite sure why he'd specified such numbers. 'It's been a while. I'll probably miss the things completely for the first half hour.'

'If you say so.' Brian turned to the shelves, pulled out standard mansized paper silhouettes, and laid them on the counter. 'One moment, and I'll fetch the shells.'

More gunfire sounded, echoing along ancient stone tunnels.

'You seen Viktor Harman?' asked Donal.

'Say what?'

'Viktor Harman. Big guy, leather coat probably, round blue shades. Wears a Grauser under each arm.'

'Oh, yeah. Big Viktor. Cross-draw fiend.'

That was Viktor. In customized shoulder holsters, he wore stubby machine pistols as if they were ordinary handguns. He could rip the twin weapons from their holsters in an instant.

'He's the one I mean.'

'Haven't seen him for days.'

'Never mind. So gimme the shells.'

Brian disappeared round back, and returned with seven small boxes.

'Last time, Big Viktor blew every target into shreds.' Brian put the ammunition down on the counter. 'Have fun now, you hear?'

'I will,' said Donal.

He grabbed the targets and ammo, and headed down the corridor. It formed a long gallery, with the shooting lanes off to the right. Donal continued, wanting to go as far as he could, away from the few officers practising at this time.

A lean man with cropped grey hair, wearing a black T-shirt and combat trousers, stepped into Donal's path.

'Hey, Donal. Are you coping with everything?'

Eagle Dawkins was the rangemaster. He'd also been one of the handful of cops who'd attended Laura's funeral. A zombie burial was never high-profile.

'"Coping" is the right word.'

'You'll be able to remain calm. Commander Steele didn't practise much, but she knew how to keep control.'

Donal noted the implied command, realizing that Dawkins was professionally responsible for range safety. Dawkins had also known Laura in both aspects of her existence, as a living human and then a zombie. Donal wondered how Laura's shooting had changed after resurrection, but he killed the impulse to ask.

'I'll remember that,' he said.

'Let me walk with you.'

'Sure.'

It took a minute to reach the farthest shooting lane. Donal draped the paper targets over the waist-high partition, and placed the ammo boxes on the handy shelf. A target-clip was already overhead, so he picked the first sheet, fastened it in place, then pressed the button to send the target back along the lane. He let it go all the way to the end. Then he took an empty magazine clip from his pocket, and pushed in bullets, one at a time. The spring was particularly stiff, and Donal had to press down hard with his thumb. When it was full, he placed the magazine on the shelf. It was a spare.

Eagle Dawkins said nothing as Donal took out his Magnus, ejected the current clip, checked it, slammed it back in. It was only when Donal pulled the slide back that Dawkins spoke.

'You're not going to turn the lights on?'

'Huh?' Donal looked up. 'I hadn't realized.'

He flicked a switch, one of three on the wall beside him, so that low red bulbs glimmered.

'Commander Steele occasionally liked to make things difficult for herself. She was never the kind of shot you are, though.'

'Maybe she thought a commander has other skills to develop.'

'I agree. That wasn't a criticism.'

'All right,' said Donal.

Then he whipped up his pistol and pulled the trigger thirteen times – *crack, crack, crack* in exact metronomic progression – before lowering the weapon. Ignoring the spent casings, he ejected the magazine and slammed in the spare, bringing the weapon up to aim once more. Then he lowered it without firing.

'Good.' Dawkins nodded. 'Very good.'

In some precincts, rangemasters forced officers to pick up their shell casings when they shot. It made for tidy ranges. It also made for dead cops, when they reacted under mortal stress by reflex, and stopped to pocket discarded shells when they should have been returning fire.

Dawkins pressed the button which caused the target sheet to come whirring back. There was a single large hole in the silhouette's heart.

'Must have gone wide,' murmured Dawkins. 'Except that's an awful big hole. What kind of rounds are you shooting?'

'Same as these.' Donal pointed towards the bullets on the shelf. 'Chitin-piercing, standard load.'

'That's not ... I've never seen that before.'

Donal wondered how many zombie officers practised here.

'I'm just rusty,' he said.

'Huh. You might get away with that story, with other people.' Eagle Dawkins tapped his cheekbone. 'If you want me to peddle that tale to everyone else, then I'll do it.'

'Sorry,' said Donal. 'I've no idea what you're talking about.'

'Yeah, you do. No one can cluster their shots that closely, and I mean no one.'

'Things change.'

Like Laura dying.

Dawkins looked down the length of the firing lane. Then he nodded to Donal.

'Take care of yourself, Lieutenant. Call me if you need anything.'

He pointed to the black wall-mounted telephone.

'Yeah,' said Donal. 'Thanks.'

After Dawkins had left, Donal took the paper target down from the overhead clip. The hole was almost perfectly circular, and most observers would have concluded that Donal had hit the target once, and missed with his other twelve shots. But Eagle Dawkins wasn't most observers.

Had Laura not had this ability? Or had she chosen to hide what she could do, when she came down here for the mandated minimum practice sessions? Whatever her capabilities, what Donal had just demonstrated was startling ... except that a part of him took it for granted.

Constant practice had made him a good marksman. This wasn't the first time he'd drilled a target directly in the centre of the heart with his first shot. But no living human being could fire twelve subsequent rounds through exactly the same point, without deviation.

Perhaps I'm not human at all.

Donal fastened another target to the clip, and sent it whining back down the lane, wondering if he could do the same in darkness.

He switched the lights off, and raised his gun.

From time to time, Alexa experienced headaches, which very occasionally grew into fully fledged migraines. Usually, a lukewarm bath, a pot of helebore tea and a bar of blue chocolate were all she needed to make things right.

Something was thumping behind her right eye as she stared up at the floating sign. It consisted of ceramic letters rather than flamescript, held in place by necromagnetic induction. Alexa could see the faint outline of coils embedded in the ceiling.

~CUSTOMER RELATIONSHIP BUREAU~

Behind a reception desk, a pretty female officer stood up and held out her hand.

'Hi, I'm Cindy. How can I help?'

The department had been called Customer Relations. Was Customer Relationship Bureau supposed to sound more professional? Alexa wished she wasn't here.

'Detective Ceerling.' She opened her jacket to show the shield fastened to her waistband. 'I thought I might spend a short time here, see what you guys are up to.'

The commissioner had said to leave his name out of it.

'I'm curious,' she added. 'And my team's got a little downtime, so today's a good opportunity.'

'In that case' – Cindy's smile revealed beautiful teeth – 'please go right through. I'll call someone to show you around.'

She reached with one manicured hand for the indigo telephone on her desk.

'No need. I'll see you later, Cindy.'

'Great!' Her voice sounded thrilled. 'I look forward to it, Detective.'

Alexa's headache gave a thump as she walked through the internal door, and came out into an open office space. It was large, about the size of the Surveillance Department, but more brightly lit. Several coffee pots stood on a metal table beneath which flamesprites danced. Alexa helped herself to a cup, taking her time, looking.

The desks were polished. The telephone handsets – all of them coloured indigo, like Cindy's, rather than the usual black – also looked clean. Most of the staff were in plainclothes, all with laundered shirts, and smiles as bright as their clothing.

'Thanatos,' she murmured. 'What a place.'

Sometimes a street cop, after long years, would eat a bullet, putting their own weapon between their teeth and pulling the trigger. It happened particularly to those who'd experienced low-level ensorcelment over extended periods. But Alexa thought that if she had to work in a place like this, grinning all the time and being forever nice to people, then she'd probably go home and fire that final bullet herself.

'Uh, ma'am? May I assist you in any way?'

This was a male officer, as young and perfectly turned out as Cindy on the front desk.

'Detective Ceerling, just taking a look around.' Alexa sipped at her coffee, intending it as a covering gesture. 'Wow. That tastes really nice.'

'Thank you, Detective. We keep everything pleasant here, so that when we talk to people' – he gestured to the banks of phones, to the smiling officers talking on them – 'we don't need to play-act. "Sincerity is saintly," we like to say.'

Alexa lowered the coffee, and thought about pouring it over the guy's head. But that wasn't what Commissioner Vilnar had in mind.

Behind him, a phone rang, and the dark-skinned officer sitting at the desk picked it up.

'I'm Ted Chelton, Officer Ted Chelton. Can I help?' There was a pause, then Chelton said, 'Mrs Arrowsmith, if that had happened to me, I can tell you I'd be upset.' In fact, his tone was a little strident already. 'But you can rest assured,' with a lowering tonality, a slower rhythm, 'we'll look into evidence that someone might have dropped, that wasn't your son's.'

Alexa found herself fascinated by Chelton's changing voice. The other officer, smiling, murmured, 'I'll leave you to it.'

Nodding as he left, Alexa continued to listen to Chelton. Hearing just his side of the conversation, she could appreciate the man's skill. The caller had started off angry, but Chelton hadn't tried to use the kind of calm voice that an upset person would find infuriating. Instead, he'd grown annoyed on the caller's behalf – then slowly and subtly formed an alliance with her, before altering his tone until it became relaxing.

' ...and I hope your knee is much better soon. Yes. Bye-bye, Mrs Arrowsmith.'

He rang off.

Alexa stared for a moment, then remembered the coffee cup in her hand, and refreshed it from the nearest pot. Did the commissioner expect her to hone her public relation skills in this place, or was something else going on? For sure, even though every cop learned verbal de-escalation skills at the Academy, she was pretty sure not even the instructors could have handled an irate call as this Chelton had just done.

All around her, in the call centre, Chelton's colleagues appeared to be responding to equally challenging calls with equally exquisite skill.

Rubbing her forehead where the ache was beginning to intensify, Alexa wondered what she was supposed to do next.

'Hello there.' A nearby officer was holding out an indigo headset, like a radio operator's, which was attached to a telephone of the same colour. 'Would you like to listen in to a call? Hear both sides of what's going on?'

'Why ... yes. I'm pretty sure I would.'

'Take a seat, and we'll wait.'

Alexa sat down beside the man, getting the headset comfortable around her ears. She rubbed her forehead again, then waited. It took less than a minute before a switchboard operator put a call through.

'My name,' said the caller, 'is Eldred Colbridge, and I want to complain about the house next door, and my local precinct does nothing about it. Parties at all hours, and even though I'm a pensioner, I still need my sleep, don't I?'

'Absolutely right,' the officer beside Alexa answered. 'You do. My name's Zajal, by the way. So tell me about these neighbours.'

'They moved in a month ago—'

As the call continued, Alexa became aware of the real sympathy in Zajal's voice, the painstaking way in which he recorded the factual details on a lilac notepad, and the masterful fashion in which he mollified and then cheered up the caller, old Mr Colbridge, who rang off sounding as if he'd regained some zest in life.

Finally, Zajal put down the handset, and Alexa removed the earphones.

'That was amazing.' She reached up to her forehead, then lowered her hand, and gave a wide smile. 'I mean, really expert.'

'Thanks. Of course, when you're being sympathetic, you have to mean it, because—'

'"Sincerity is saintly," right?'

'That's exactly right.' Zajal grinned at her. 'And how do you feel? Because you were the tiniest bit peaky when you came in, weren't you?'

'Oh, did you notice?' Alexa held up both her hands. 'But I'm feeling wonderful now. You and your colleagues must be working miracles here.'

'We like to think so, Detective.'

The phone on Zajal's desk rang once more.

'Did you want to listen in again? Then maybe even answer a call yourself?'

Alexa stared at the indigo phone. She had a desk elsewhere, but that was empty, and not nearly as interesting. And the thought of what Zajal was suggesting—

'Do you really think I could?' she asked.

'Oh, yes,' said Zajal. 'You're a natural.'

Alexa blinked, and then began to blush.

Seven

The establishment was called Pies'n'Trolls, its name painted in curlicued script on a black panel above the window. It was a basic eatery, a greasy spoon on a nondescript street in Lower Halls, a working-class district whose inhabitants were mostly – but not all – standard human. The man who owned Pies'n'Trolls was called Jacko, and he was five feet tall but four feet wide, with scaled leathery skin and massive arms. Today he was wearing an apron splashed with yellow and blue, and holding a plate piled high with blossom salad, heavy on the saffronbells, edelschwartz, and purpledrops.

'Got your favourite, Sergeant.'

He was addressing a seated man who was slender, with white hair but the unlined skin of an eighteen-year old, and soft, gentle eyes that would have been appropriate for a twenty-year-old poetess. The man smiled.

'Thanks Jacko. You shouldn't have.'

'Yeah, I should.' Jacko put down the plate. 'So I don't suppose you remember Tweenie?'

The white-haired man was called Harald Hammersen. He was an ex-Marine, a member of Laura Steele's task force – if it still existed – and he possessed the largest network of informants of anyone in Tristopolis, perhaps of anyone in the country. Now, he blinked once as he mentally sifted through details of Jacko's family, including all twenty-three grandchildren.

'Of course I do,' he said. 'She'll be what, seven by now?'

'Exactly right.' Jacko's leathery face crinkled and folded as he smiled. 'She's the star of her junior flyball team, too. Wouldya credit that?'

'That's so hard to believe. Remember the night she was born?'

'Ha.' Jacko grinned at the few other occupied tables, and some of the regulars looked up and smiled back. 'Night the Barwell Spiders won the pennant. Like I'd forget.'

Then he used one great spatulate finger to tap the black folder that

Harald had placed on the table. On it was a logo, coloured indigo, in the form of a stylized telephone.

'You undercover, my friend?'

'Yeah, but nothing deep. Just—'

Harald broke off. From the rear of the diner, an unshaven man – not a regular – waved a hand, calling out: 'Waiter? If you would.'

'Where does he think he is?' muttered Jacko. 'The bleeding Five Seasons?'

'He's a customer.' Harald's voice was as mild as his appearance.

'Yeah, yeah.' Jacko raised his voice. 'Coming, ya buttwipe.'

The unshaven man swallowed as Jacko came lumbering towards his table.

'Um ... I was just wondering ...' His finger trembled as he pointed at the greasy menu. 'I'd like, er ...'

'Reptile eggs are off,' Jacko growled. 'So whaddya want?'

'Er ...'

Harald forked saffronbell petals into his mouth, closing his eyes briefly. The fragrant taste swelled in his mouth as he chewed. It was good to sit in his old pal's establishment, which seemed to be doing OK, despite Jacko's charming way with strangers. As Harald thought this, a tiny hovering sprite, chained to the doorway by a slender thread, sang a soft, clear note to indicate more customers were approaching.

Taking hold of the black folder, Harald shifted it from the table to his seat, leaving it beside him where others could not see. He had no idea how long the assignment was going to take, although Commander Bowman seemed to expect him to finish in a single day.

By the time Jacko returned to the table, Harald had cleared the plate except for one half petal that he left behind. Jacko nodded, understanding the discipline: you never clear the plate completely, unless you're on a mission and near starvation.

'I'll be back in a couple of hours,' said Harald. 'With a friend. Someone I've arranged to meet.'

'Whoa. What's she like?' Jacko's immense hands sketched an hour-glass shape. 'And does she go for older guys? A bit of rough?'

Jacko was married to an orange-skinned woman, heavier than him, and holder of the Tristopolitan ladies' bench press record in the over-40s age group. In twenty-five years, he had never been unfaithful. He and his wife laughed a lot.

'*He*,' said Harald, 'has stone eyes, my friend.'

'Ah.' Other people might have asked more questions, but for Jacko, if a man had sniper implants, that was all he needed to know. 'He's surely welcome.'

Harald slipped out of the booth, and grabbed the black folder with the indigo phone logo.

'Don't take no wooden florins, pal.'

Jacko saluted, one fingertip clacking against the hard skin of his brow.

'Beat it, Harald, ya bum.'

Smiling, Harald went.

In police HQ, Alexa put down her phone, smiling.

'How did I do, Zajal?'

The supervisor nodded, matching her smile.

'Superbly. You want to handle some more calls?'

'I've love to. And you know what?'

'Tell me.'

'There's some colleagues of mine I'd like to bring down here. You'll like them.'

Zajal looked at the rows of officers manning indigo phones.

'They're welcome to sit in, of course.'

'I'd like to start with my friend Donal. He's quite a guy.'

'Ah. Really.'

'We're not involved. Not ...'

'Not yet?'

Alexa shook her head, but she was blushing again.

'Bring him down,' said Zajal. 'We'd all love to meet him.'

'Then I will.' Alexa touched her cheek. 'Whew. I'll do just that.'

Harald, folder in hand, looked around the fourth-floor landing. Outside, in an alleyway, he'd watched three black lizards fight over the glistening remains of a rat. Here, things were clean enough. Someone had been using disinfectant spray, and the scent lingered. The dark-green linoleum was wrinkled, but frequent polishing had kept it free of cracks. The stairway treads and bannisters were formed from brown magnabeetle chitin, ugly but recently washed.

As he looked at the four apartment doors leading off the landing, Harald thought that there were worse places to live. He opened the folder, checked an entry on a typewritten list, then knocked on the door of apartment 19.

It took a while to open.

'Hello?' A sixty-something woman looked up at him. 'Who are you, then?'

'Morning, ma'am.' Harald shifted the folder so she could see the indigo-phone logo. 'I'm just conducting a quality check, to see how satisfied you've been with our service.'

'Well, you're a polite fellow. Come in and drink some coffee while you ask your questions.'

'There's no need to—'

But the woman was already heading inside, leaving the door open. Harald shook his head at her lack of security awareness. She'd not even asked to see ID.

He went inside, closing the door, and followed the short hallway to a small, tidy sitting room. Lace antimacassars were draped across the backs of two armchairs and a settee. Matching doilies decorated low tables on which traditional five-sided purple candles were burning.

'Here we are.' The woman came back in with a tray. 'Coffee, scarab cookies. Sit down, young man.'

'My name's Fred Harkin.' It was a cover name Harald had used before. 'Um, thank you.'

'And I'm Rita Westrason, but you probably knew that.' She put the tray down on a table, then pointed at Harald's folder. 'Probably got everything in there about me.'

'Not that much, ma'am.'

'Well.'

The next minute involved pouring, passing cups and plates, and getting settled. During that time, Harald noticed the blue-and-white photographs on the mantelpiece. One was old, of a young man in shirtsleeves; the other, less faded, of a similar-looking man in uniform.

'That was my Roberto.' Mrs Westrason pointed at the older photo. 'Not long after our wedding. He's been gone for fifteen years now.'

Gone to the necrofusion piles, she meant.

'I'm sorry. And is that your son?'

'Pietro. He's a chief petty officer in the Federal Navy, you know.'

'Good for him,' said Harald, meaning it.

'He's a good boy.' Mrs Westrason sipped her coffee. 'Ah. I used to have to take bicarbonate of soda every day, you know, or the heartburn would be something terrible. Now it's all cleared up. Isn't that great?'

'Um, absolutely, ma'am. Could you tell me if you're—'

'Call me Rita.'

'Yes, thank you.' Harald allowed himself a soft exhalation. 'So, Rita, how has the phone service been? Has it been, uh, reliable enough?'

70

It occurred to him that he could have prepared more detailed questions consistent with his cover. He should ask about the quality of signal, he guessed now, and how often a crossed line occurred. That kind of thing.

In the Marines, however, he'd learned not to plan in detail too far ahead of time. Because situations change, and planning too soon means having to plan twice over, or sink in the shit.

'Totally wonderful.' Mrs Westrason pointed to the indigo telephone. 'Clear as a bell, fast to connect, and cheaper than it was before. I mean the old black one, dear.'

'And never any problems, Rita?'

'Nary a one. And do you know, my old osteowhatsits has healed up, too. I know that's a coincidence, but a nice one, don't you think?'

'Um, sure. I certainly do.'

'So what do you do for the phone company, besides cheer up lonely old ladies?'

'Well, I also ...'

Harald spun a web of lies for the next quarter of an hour, embellishing more when he realized that Mrs Westrason wasn't showing belated signs of security consciousness. She should have confirmed that he worked for the company he appeared to represent, but she was just finding things to talk about, that was all.

Finally, he said, 'Sorry, Rita, but I have to check on some other customers. I hope they're half as nice as you.'

'Fred, you are a dear boy. You stay there a moment.'

'But—'

Mrs Westrason bustled into the kitchen, and came back carrying a small blue disposable snailskin bag.

'Greyberry cookies, and a couple of the scarabs,' she said. 'Because you're too thin.'

'No, I couldn't.'

'Of course you can. Unless you want me to phone your supervisor' – she pointed at the indigo handset – 'and simply insist.'

'All right, Rita. I give up. Thank you so much.'

It took another couple of polite minutes before Harald was out of the front door. He waved, Mrs Westrason shut the door, and he was alone on the landing, clutching his bag of cookies along with his folder.

'Nice to meet you,' he murmured to the closed door.

Then he headed for the stairs, head down and lost in thought.

The pretty young surveillance officer looked around the commissioner's office. She'd never been in here before. The furniture looked uncomfortable, but there were some interesting things on display, including a fascinating orrery. But her grandmother had come from Nulumbra, on the far side of the world, and she'd grown up on family legends about how things were different there. Perhaps that was why she found the orrery so striking.

'Do you like it?' The commissioner leaned back in his scale-covered chair. 'Being able to decorate your own office is a perk of the job that I've grown used to.'

'It's terrific, sir. I wish I could afford one.'

'Maybe someday. Hobnobbing with the rich and influential is hard work on the liver and digestion, if nothing else.'

'Sir.' The young officer smiled.

'And one of the people I've been schmoozing with is the managing director of Tristopolis City Zoo. He's also a city councillor, and a big supporter of the department when it comes to getting funding.'

'Oh.'

'So strictly on the QT, between you and me, if you should happen to pick up on any sighting of wolves ... Let me know first, all right?'

'Wolves?' The officer was puzzled. 'Not unlicensed deathwolves, sir?'

'Hades forbid. I mean low-sentience snow-wolves. Primitive cousins.'

'In the city? You mean, some have escaped?'

Commissioner Vilnar shook his head.

'The director didn't say so directly, and I might be reading between the lines and making up lies. So that's why I want you to come to me first.'

The young officer looked down at the floor, then up at Vilnar, her gaze clear.

'Absolutely, sir. I'm fine with that.'

'Good.' The commissioner knew that his reasoning didn't make entire rational sense, but that was all right. Let her think that there were confidential matters behind his request – or rather, behind his clear but off-the-record command. 'Very good. You can get back to work now.'

'Sir.'

She took a last look at the orrery, then the ciliaserpents were pulling aside to let her through the door, and she was gone.

The black chair stirred, tilting to one side.

'Don't ask me,' the commissioner said. 'But if it *is* about to happen, I'll tell you one thing now. We're not ready.'

The chair subsided into stillness.

'Nowhere near ready.'

At ground level, a stooped woman with a lined face, her hair as white as Harald's, was running a mop over the linoleum. Her bucket was beside her front door, which stood half open. On it, a thirteen-sided knotted-iron emblem hung, in the centre of which interwoven stiletto blades formed a star. This was the symbol of the Holy Reaver, and Harald guessed the woman was devout, hobbling to temple every day, nine days a week.

'I'm sorry.' He hefted his folder and the bag of cookies that Mrs Westrason had given him. 'I'm about to walk across your clean floor.'

'That's what it's for.'

'Thanks. Um, I don't suppose you know Rita Westrason upstairs?'

'What, that bitch?' The old woman stopped, and held her mop still. 'You know, she helped me bring my washing in from the yard, just yesterday. She *has* turned over a new leaf recently. But for years, she was the most miserable person in the block. Wrapped up in herself, in thorns of memory, like the scriptures say.'

Harald was fascinated, and knew that he broadcast that fascination. It was why people found it easy to talk to him.

'She changed suddenly, did she?'

'I don't know. Well, yes, but I couldn't say when.'

Thinking back to the notation in his black folder, and looking at the symbol on the old woman's door, Harald said, 'I don't suppose it would have been around St Lazlo's Day, would it?'

The saints' days weren't marked in Harald's folder. They were indelibly written in his mind, from childhood with a temple-going, ineffectual mother, and a father who was loving until the drink took over. At some time, Harald's father had brushed against the edge of a void-summoning field, and all the problems came from that accident. Harald had often wondered how Dad would have turned out otherwise.

'—right,' the old woman was saying. 'I had the Lanyard-and-Leash hanging on the door, so it *was* St Lazlo's Day. How did you know?'

'Um, I think Mrs Westrason had a kind of, what, conversion? Insight?'

'Huh.' Leaning on her mop, the old woman stared up the stairs, then turned back to Harald, and tapped her brow. 'Just as likely the brain sickness, like those old biddies get. You know what I mean?'

'Could be.' Harald began to chuckle.

'Go on, young man. Walk across my clean floor, if that's what you're going to do.'

'Well, I do have to go. Though it's hard tearing myself away from a beautiful woman.'

Lines deepened as the old woman smiled, and her eyes twinkled. There was truth in Harald's words, some kind of truth, because he could in fact see how she would have looked when young.

'Get the Hades out of here, with your glib tongue.'

But she was still smiling as she said it, and continued to smile as Harald leaped lightly over the clean area to the outer door. He waved, told her to take care, and left.

Outside on the street, as he walked on, he pulled a clear membranous evidence bag from his pocket, and wrapped it around the bag of cookies without slowing pace. The membrane sealed up. The cookies were *probably* harmless.

What he had certainly learned was that a personality change had come over Mrs Westrason on the day that her new telephone was installed. The phone outfit was a new one called CRS. Despite the details inside the fake folder, Harald knew very little about them, except that they were an established company but new to the Federation.

Commander Bowman had ordered him to check on the customers' well-being, whatever that was supposed to mean.

At the corner, Harald turned left, stopped at the second door on the row of tenements, and checked the next entry in his folder. A Mr Kelfeld lived here, aged seventy-one. He'd bought one of the new phones just two weeks ago. Harald closed the folder, climbed the stone steps to the door, and pressed the brass horned head affixed to the door.

When the door opened, the old man who looked out stood ramrod-straight.

'Good morning, sir.' Harald held up the folder, displaying its logo. 'I'm checking on the phone quality. You've had good service, since we installed the telephone?'

'Not a single hiss or crackle. Not like the old one.'

'That's good to hear. And how's your health been?'

'Do you know, I feel twenty years younger. The old aches and pains have gone the way of those hisses and crackles. Coincidence, of course.'

'Of course ...'

'Won't you come in, young man? I'm just making a pot of stabroot tea.'

Beyond Mr Kelfeld, in the hallway, stood a well-polished table. On it, Harald could just see the edge of an indigo handset.

'That's really kind of you, sir. I'd love to.'

Two hours later, when Harald returned to Pies'n'Trolls, he saw Kresham sitting at a corner table. Dark glasses hid Kresham's stone eyes. It was a habit of Federation military, and ex-military, to slip on a pair of shades whenever they went indoors, to keep their vision sharp when they returned to the dimmer world outside. Right now, the shades made Kresham look like an ex-soldier or perhaps a wannabe; but without the shades, the other customers would have known he was an ex-sniper. And retired snipers often became cops or freelance enforcers, although Harald knew of one highly decorated, long-serving retired sniper who was a music teacher in Deeper Southvale, and happy with it.

Jacko, remembering that Harald had promised to return at this time, had left a stone flask of tea with a clean cup. Kresham was drinking Blue Lizard beer from a bottle. He nodded as Harald came in.

'Hey,' said Harald. 'Where's Jacko?'

'Round back in the kitchen, with the missus.' Kresham pointed to a plate on which only two beans and a streak of sauce remained. 'They do kimodo sausages and liverbeans just right. Good protein.'

'Got to keep your strength up.' Harald slid into the seat opposite, and put down his folder. 'So how did you get on?'

Beside Kresham lay a folder identical to Harald's.

'Mainly old folk, taking up the early offer cos the rates are low, and they're at home all day so it's easy for the connection guys to come.'

'That's what I found,' said Harald. 'Anything else?'

Kresham looked round. There was a group of men in grease-stained coveralls, tucking in to purple omelettes and fried tubers. Two loners were drinking tea and reading newspapers.

'Pretty sprightly bunch,' he said, 'for a load of old folk. That was odd.'

'And did you notice that they got healthy recently?'

'Yeah, I picked up on that. One person,' said Kresham, 'seemed to have started being nice to her neighbours, for the first time in decades.'

Harald thought of Mrs Westrason.

'I had one exactly like that.'

'Huh. So the new phones,' Kresham lowered his voice as he tapped his folder, 'make people nicer and healthier. Bound to be a good thing.'

'Right. Bound to be.'

Neither one of them was smiling.

'You felt any desire to make a call yourself?'

'Not with those phones, no,' said Harald.

'Me neither.'

Both men stared at each other. Finally, Harald changed the subject.

'Tell me about Bowman. You've reported to him for what, two years now?'

'About that,' answered Kresham. 'He's a good guy. Closer to the commissioner than most people realize.'

'That's interesting.'

'Uh-huh. And he'd welcome you on board, man, if you wanna join Robbery-Haunting.'

'Maybe.' Harald sniffed the stone flask. 'Indigoberry tea. Not bad.'

'You're thinking the task force will continue, right?' Kresham tipped back his Blue Lizard, swallowed, and put the bottle down. 'Under Donal Riordan?'

'Hades, I don't know.' Harald poured himself some tea. 'First there's the question of what you might call our operational parameters, and then there's the question of team cohesion. Like what kind of leader would Donal be?'

'Oh. I see.'

Kresham's beer was finished, and he moved the empty bottle aside.

'Thing is,' said Harald, 'the chief suspects are probably outside city limits, maybe outside the country. So the feds will want a real federal team, that can take off anywhere they need to at a minute's notice, you know?'

'Uh-huh.' It wasn't just the shades that made Kresham's expression hard to read. 'And you were saying about Riordan?'

'Shit.' Harald exhaled, put down his tea. 'We've had our ... differences.'

'So he's not as good as I've heard?'

'Fuck it, Kresham. Maybe *I'm* not as good as you've heard.'

Kresham had not moved. He could remain motionless for a day or longer, if he had to.

'Tell me,' he said.

'When we were tracking down the bastards, after they'd killed Mina d'Alkernay and stolen Cortindo's body ... Look, it was obvious that somehow the Black Circle had inside knowledge, and the signs pointed to the commissioner being a mage, planted inside the department.'

'The Old Man?' Kresham whistled. 'You suspected the Old Man?'

'Yeah, and I was convinced that Donal Riordan was his spy inside our task force. Donal was the most recent recruit, and Xalia overheard him talking to the commissioner, and ... like that. He was the obvious suspect.'

'Obvious. Right.'

'Ninety per cent of the time, the obvious culprit is the real one.' Harald blinked his gentle eyes. 'But ninety per cent isn't *always*, and I should have remembered that.'

'I heard you pulled Riordan out of a tight spot in Silvex City.'

'And Cortindo and Gelbthorne and Blanz still got away. At least Laura and Donal took down Blanz, later.'

It cost Laura her life, but Harald didn't need to say so. The whole force knew what happened in Fortinium that day.

'Shit, Harald. There's no point in beating up on yourself.' Kresham raised his empty Blue Lizard bottle, and waved it so that Jacko, behind the counter, could see. 'If you want pain, we can get ourselves down the combat room and I'll give you a bruising, like the old days.'

'You and which regiment, exactly?'

'Dream on, buddy.'

Jacko arrived with two bottles of Blue Lizard. Kresham moved over, and Jacko sat down, giving him a bottle. The other, Jacko kept for himself.

'I propose a toast,' he said.

Harald refilled his cup from the stone flask, and raised it.

'Fuck 'em and die.'

Jacko and Kresham clinked their bottles against the cup. All three repeated the Marines' oath in unison.

'Fuck 'em and die.'

They drank.

At about the same time, two men wearing indigo coveralls exited a silver-windowed van, carrying equipment cases. They crossed the dirty sidewalk and entered an apartment block's lobby, tracking grime across the recently cleaned floor.

Climbing stairs, they reached the fourth storey, and stopped outside the door of number 19. One of the men knocked. After a minute, the door opened.

'Why, hello.'

'Good afternoon, Mrs Westrason.'

Both men blinked in exact synchronicity, pupils flickering into cross-slits like plus-signs, before regaining human appearance.

'Nice to see you boys again.'

'Can we come in?'

'I was hoping you would.'

They entered, and the door closed shut.

Eight

It was five a.m. Donal, in shirtsleeves with the cuffs rolled back, wearing an empty shoulder-holster rig, was sitting at his desk in the deserted office space. His jacket hung across the back of his chair. On the desktop, his Magnus lay disassembled. A bottle of strong-smelling moth-oil stood beside the gun, along with the thin brushes and spidercotton pads he used to clean it.

He was staring into space.

'Hey, big guy.' Alexa came into the room. 'How's it going?'

'You must be mistaking me for Viktor.'

'He's only a foot taller than you, Donal. Easy for a girl like me to get confused.'

'Uh-huh.' Donal looked down at his stripped weapon. It was perfectly clean. 'Give me a moment here.'

He snapped the Magnus back into wholeness, and replaced it in his shoulder holster. Then he wrapped up the cleaning kit, and placed it in the top drawer.

'Shouldn't you be at home asleep?' he added, checking the time on his watch.

Not just the time.

The watchface was mostly black, with maybe a quarter showing silver. Three-quarters charge remained: nearly three days before he needed to plug himself in to recharge.

'Not if you need cheering up, Lieutenant.'

'I'm happy. Have you ever seen a happier expression?'

'Not since I looked in the mirror when my lizard died and the house burned down.'

'Too bad.' Donal glanced at the glass door that still bore Laura's name. 'Honestly, I'm fine. Just thinking.'

'Uh-huh. You want some coffee?'

'No thanks.'

'Thanatos, Donal. You *have* changed.'

'Excuse me?'

'Refusing coffee, come on. What did you think I meant?'

Donal spread his hands, aware that they did not shake, not even the tiny tremor that a calm but living human would experience.

'I have no idea,' he said.

'You need to come with me.' Alexa folded her arms. 'Come on, Lieutenant.'

He'd jumped rope for most of the night here in the building, in a deserted gym, losing himself in the iterating, endless cadence of movement. Then he'd showered, and changed back into the same street clothes he'd worn yesterday, having brought nothing clean. He should go home himself, but Alexa wanted something, and she was part of the team – the team that he might have to lead.

Not as well as you did, Laura.

That was for sure.

'I'm coming.' He stood up, rolled down his cuffs and buttoned them, and pulled on his jacket. 'Where, exactly?'

'To make some phone calls, listen to people chatting. You'll like it. I did, and it was the commissioner's idea, now I come to think of it.'

'Phone calls.'

'You need to trust me on this one, Donal. Will you do that?'

He looked at her clear, open expression. She was young and intelligent and ambitious, and Laura had liked her a lot.

'Detective Ceerling, I am completely in your hands.'

'Well, that's good.' Her smile was like a schoolgirl's. 'That's very good.'

She led the way to the lift shafts and stopped. Donal walked past her until he reached number 7.

'You've got a preference?' Alexa asked. 'Fine by me.'

They stepped into the shaft together, and hung in place.

Which floor, lover?

Widening her eyes, Alexa looked at the insubstantial wraith surrounding them.

'I don't know,' said Donal. 'Where are we going?'

'Er, up to the second floor.'

There was a pause, while Gertie floated with Donal and Alexa in her grasp.

That's a cheery place.

Her tone lay somewhere between caution and irony.

'It's where we need to go,' said Alexa.

Still, Gertie hung there.

'Might as well take us up, dear.'

All right, lover. If that's what you want.

Donal said nothing as wraith limbs tightened around him and Alexa. Then the shaft walls appeared to slide downwards as Gertie flew up, carrying Donal and Alexa. Gertie might tease him out of habit, but this was the first time, as far as Donal could remember, she had genuinely hesitated to take him anywhere. With a subtle motion, he pulled his left arm close to his body, checking the feel of the loaded Magnus in his shoulder holster, sensing the balance of the weapon.

It was a strange thing to do in the heart of Police HQ.

Commissioner Vilnar picked up the handset of his black telephone, spun the combination wheels to a long-distance number, and waited while it rang. Spikewraiths sighed on the secure line.

'Arrhennius Vilnar here,' he said when an operator answered. 'Put me through to Agent Murgatrayle, please. And I am aware what time it is. I can wait.'

He covered the mouthpiece with one broad hand, and looked at the black chair, at other items of furniture around his office, but did not speak. Finally, a human voice sounded on the line.

'That's right,' Commissioner Vilnar replied after a moment. 'But no, Laura Steele did not give me your name, or your number.'

Again, a pause.

'All right,' said Vilnar. 'She made a mistake in suspecting me, but she *had* narrowed down the leak to my office. Overlooking Marnie Finross could have been disastrous, but it wasn't, and that's good enough.'

The black chair danced closer, unable to hear the other side of the conversation.

'No, you misunderstand. I don't want you to disband the task force. I want you to give command of it to Donal Riordan, and give the team every resource they ... Yes, I am completely serious.'

He listened for while, then shook his head.

'This is how it goes, Agent Murgatrayle. You don't know about me, but I know about you. We have certain friends in common. I swear this by the Void, and by the Seal of Shadow.'

There was total silence. Even the spikewraiths on the line were shocked into inactivity.

'Excellent,' said Vilnar after a time. 'We understand each other completely.'

In the office, the stone credenza took a shuffling step closer to the commissioner's desk.

'I don't know. Things are coming to a head but no, not a single sighting in the … Oh. You're sure? Then I'd like to make a request. If things go terminally wrong, place my wife under the protection of federal spellbinders, would you? Likewise the inhabitants of my office.'

The surrounding furniture grew absolutely still.

'Yes. And good luck to you, Agent Murgatrayle.'

After a few seconds, Vilnar replaced the handset.

'Three sightings of wolves in Fortinium,' he said. 'Sooner than we expected.'

The black chair curved its arms.

'No,' added Vilnar. 'Don't worry about me. This is what I signed up for, decades ago, didn't you know?'

The chair turned away.

Donal stopped beneath the floating sign. Several sarcastic remarks rose inside his mind.

~CUSTOMER RELATIONSHIP BUREAU~

Were the alkies in the drunk tank customers? Or were the customers the suffering family members turning up to bail them out? How about the wraith-whores pulled in by Hex Crimes and held in nine-dimensional cages until their pimps' lawyers sprung them?

But Alexa was exchanging bright girlish smiles with the young officer on reception, so Donal merely muttered, 'You've got to be kidding me,' and let it go.

They whispered, and the young officer giggled, then looked at Donal and said, 'I hope you have a nice time, Lieutenant.'

'Yeah. I'm sure I will.'

He let Alexa lead him through the partition door, into the call centre. Early though it was, the place looked busy. Several officers turned to smile at Alexa and nod at Donal. Alexa called out a greeting to someone named Zajal, and stopped at an empty desk with two chairs. Two indigo telephones stood on the desktop, one with an extra earpiece on a long cord, for listening in.

'—course, ma'am,' an officer with a restful baritone voice was saying nearby. 'And we'll talk to the guys for sure, seeing if they accidentally dropped evidence in your son's bedroom that came from elsewhere. Yes, of course we—'

Donal tuned out the sound as he sat. He focused on the dilation of Alexa's eyes, the shade of her skin, her fast shallow breathing, the subtle rushing of her voice.

'We can listen in on the other guys' calls,' she said, 'if Zajal connects us through. Or I tell you what, Donal. This sounds daft, but I'll ring you on that phone now, all right?'

He looked at the phone nearest him.

What's going on?

Alexa was already dialling, spinning the first four combination wheels for an internal number, leaving the remaining wheels pointing to null. The other phone rang immediately.

'Go on,' she said. 'Pick it up. Please?'

'Um ... All right.' Donal picked up the indigo receiver and held it to his ear. 'What am I supposed to do now?'

'Hear how clear the sound is, for a start.'

There was no delay that Donal could detect. It was odd to hear her voice coming from the receiver and her mouth at the same time.

Her smile was broad as she put the phone down.

'Keep holding the receiver.' She waved to the guy she'd called Zajal. 'And just listen.'

After a second, a two-sided conversation-in-progress sounded in Donal's ear.

'—third time little Tiddles has got stuck up there, and she's only a small lizard, so why won't anyone come to rescue her?'

'That's a disgrace, and I'll give you another number to call now. But I'll talk to them first myself.'

'She's up there scared, and she's perfectly safe if you wear acid-proof gloves to—'

Donal let the sound continue while he looked at the happy faces of the call centre officers, heard the energetic tone of their voices, noted the shining clarity of their eyes. Alexa was the same: happy and free of tension, so different from her recent stress.

It was ninety-eight minutes later, just shy of the full hour, when Donal finished listening in on his seventh call, and put the receiver down. He stared at Alexa.

'Well, Donal?'

A wide smile, a grin wider than he'd ever pulled before, stretched across Donal's face.

'This is wonderful, Alexa. Thank you.'

'Of course you're welcome. Sharing the joy, isn't that what it's about?'

Again, Donal looked around, seeing the happiness.

'It surely is. And you know what? I've an idea.'

'Do tell.' Alexa was like a schoolgirl hanging on her best friend's every word.

'The Old Man should come down here. He's supposed to be a politician' – Donal somehow grinned even more broadly – 'and customer
relations ought to be his thing.'

'You can't ring him directly, not any more. The Surveillance Department act like his secretary, the whole team.' Alexa looked at her phone.
'I know a guy called Rob. Why don't I call him now, see if the commissioner will see you?'

'Perfect.' Donal stood up. 'I'll go up, see if I can get the Old Man down
here, cheer him up. He could do with it.'

'Poor old guy. I'm sure he could.'

'See you in a bit, sweetheart.'

'Oh. See you, Donal.'

As Donal left via reception, the young officer returned his grin. The
happiness here was shared, not a selfish thing.

Donal stepped into an elevator shaft.

'Floor one hundred, please. And are *you* having a great day?'

The Surveillance Department was even busier than before, with officers
in front of every monitor, and prisms rotating as they switched between
views of Tristopolitan streets and buildings. The voices were low, serious
and business-like. There was a sense of focused concentration in the
room.

As Donal entered, a fit-looking older man stepped in his path, and
held out his hand.

'I'm Rob Helborne, Alexa's friend.'

'Donal Riordan.' He smiled, very wide. 'Call me Donal.'

'Right you are. And the commissioner will see you straight ... Um,
Donal?'

'Uh-huh?'

'Is everything all right, Lieutenant?'

'What do you mean? Don't I look happy?'

'Yeah, but you ... Excuse me. Mostly, people have kind of a worried
look when they go in to see the commissioner.'

'But the Old Man is just human, you know.'

Rob Helborne shrugged, not managing to match Donal's smile.

'If you say so. There you go, now.'

The black-iron portal was already opening.

'See you in a minute.' Donal touched Helborne's arm. 'And have fun,
watching the city.'

'If you ... say so.'

But Donal was already inside the short tunnel that led to Commissioner

Vilnar's office. As before, the tunnel walls pulsed as though gulping, perhaps thinking of swallowing this small intruder. Then the inner doors opened, ciliaserpents drawing back, and Donal stepped through.

'Hello, Commissioner.' He spread his arms. 'I've just had a lovely time in Customer Relations.'

The black chair took a step towards him, but Donal, smiling hard, walked to one side, past the brassy orrery on the credenza, rounding the commissioner's desk. Commissioner Vilnar was rising from his scaled chair.

'Riordan, why were you down in— *Mmph.*'

Donal's right hook took Vilnar in the side of the neck, hard, knocking him partway down. But Vilnar launched himself forward like a bull, the hard part of his forehead slamming into Donal's spleen.

'No.'

He slapped down at the back of Vilnar's neck. Vilnar's thick arms were encircling Donal's leg, trying for a takedown, but Donal sprawled back. Then Vilnar reared up, and something silver glinted in his hand.

'Fuck you. Stand down.'

The derringer was small-bore, but enough to blow Donal's head apart.

'No. Fuck—'

Donal leaped to one side, using the desk for cover as he ripped his Magnus out of his shoulder holster. Then a swift shadow flickered across his vision, and his gun hand was empty.

'—what?'

The black chair skittered away until it was at the wall, one pointed arm upraised, its extended corner neatly hooked inside the trigger guard of Donal's Magnus. It held the weapon aloft.

How the Hades did that happen?

Vilnar pointed his derringer at Donal's – therefore Laura's – heart.

'You,' he said to Donal. 'Are …. fucking …. *immune.*'

'Say what?'

Vilnar's face was slick with sweat, but his aim was almost as steady as Donal's would have been, had he managed to retain his weapon.

'The phones on the second floor are ensorcelled, as you so obviously worked out. Whatever the mechanism is, I know enough to realize zombies are immune. That means you.'

Then Vilnar looked at the chair, chuckled, and put away his derringer.

'Nice work, Bert. As for you, Riordan, you've just been disarmed by an item of furniture.'

'Er ...'

'Stand up and pay attention, while I sit down and talk.' Vilnar puffed as he returned to his big chair and lowered his weight. 'When I was your age, I'd ... Never mind. Look how much I'm sweating.'

'Sir, if I've made a—'

'Be attentive, Riordan, and we might let you have your gun back.' Vilnar looked at the chair. 'What do you think?'

The chair spread its free arm, the one not holding the Magnus. Its back raised and lowered.

'We're considering it,' Vilnar told Donal. 'Your team has a history of acting on untested suppositions, wouldn't you say?'

Donal clasped his hands behind his back. It was like standing at ease in the army, when the CO was fuming over something that might prove to be Donal's fault.

'We follow the evidence, sir.'

'And leap over the last few steps in logic.' Vilnar was rubbing his neck. 'Good punch, however. One of those pencil-necks in Accounts, you'd have killed them with that.'

Donal allowed himself to blink.

'You didn't go down, sir. And that was one Hades of a head-butt.'

He looked at the spare chairs at the far end of the office, shook his head, then folded his arms in front of him. He stood like a street cop, hands only loosely tucked in.

'Alexa Ceerling,' said Commissioner Vilnar, 'will attend a medical examination to get to the bottom of what's changed in her mind.'

'So you did send her in deliberately.'

'Into a section of this department, right here in Headquarters. You might want to consider the implications of that, Lieutenant.'

He's right.

Donal didn't like the thought, but he suspended his anger – just like that, *click*, it seemed to shift on to a shelf in his mind, deactivated – and thought about what he had seen.

'So I analysed the situation just fine. Something *is* changing everyone there.'

'Yeah. Too bad about the fisticuffs, Riordan, or you'd really have impressed me with how fast you spotted that. And no effect on yourself, of course.'

'None. How did you know that?'

'I've been reading a book.' Vilnar pointed to a thick black volume on his desk. 'It's a manual that a visiting engineer accidentally lost' – he half smiled – 'when he was installing additional phones.'

He pushed the book towards Donal. It looked imposing, *Field Operations Concepts, Vol. II*, and bore a tiny logo in the form of an indigo phone. Donal opened it to the table of contents.

'Multihex modulated encoding. Parasympathetic encryption algorithms. You understand this stuff?'

'Not enough.' Vilnar reached over, and turned the page back. 'You might want to check the copyright.'

Donal read it in silence.

This publication copyright © Central Resonator Systems, Exc., registered address: 2133a Karl Kastanza Drive, Outer Vitrinol, Plane 11-Q2, Silvex City, Illurium.

The remainder of the legal notice meant nothing.

'Illurium.' Donal thought back to the Westside Complex. 'Do they have anything to do with the power company making overtures to our Energy Authority?'

'"Making overtures"? You've been getting cultured, Riordan.'

'It was the opera-going that did it. Not that it helped the Diva much.'

'You didn't kill her. Malfax Cortindo did.'

'But I didn't stop—'

'And he ensorcelled you before that.' Vilnar's eyes seemed darker than normal. 'I shouldn't have sent you to see him alone.'

What?

Donal's mind, already icy cold, became an emotionless processor of logic and nuance.

'Are you saying, Commissioner, that you *knew* what he was going to do? Before you sent me there?'

Like sacrificing Alexa.

'I'm saying nothing except you're the right man for the job.' Vilnar took in a deep breath, expanding his heavy shoulders. 'CRS and the power company are separate legal entities, but they've a commercial alliance, and shared technologies.'

Donal remembered the Tristopolitan phone engineers waiting to remove the fresh nerves from Finross's corpse. Lexar, the Bone Listener, had said something like, *'Don't you know how telephone exchanges work?'*

'So what's going on? If this is an international industrial espionage thing, shouldn't we be bringing in the DIO?'

'We might, if we didn't stop to consider the recent involvement of a federal senator, the director of an Energy Authority complex, and a councillor in Silvex City.'

'You mean this' – he pointed to *Field Operations Concepts, Vol. II* – 'is connected to the Black Circle? To everything that Laura was working on?'

'I hope so,' said Commissioner Vilnar. 'Although I doubt that Black Circle is the name they actually use.'

'It's a codename that we ...' Donal fell silent. Then he remembered to breathe. 'What do you mean, you hope it's the Black Circle doing this?'

'The alternative is *two* organizations with the highest level of dark-mage expertise I've ever come across. Which would you prefer?'

'Huh. And calling in the DIO would alert the Black Circle?'

'It *might*. That possibility is enough to stop me.'

'Shit.' Donal looked at the thick manual again. 'Will you be able to decipher this fully? If you work at it?'

'It's incomplete, and there's a lot that— No. This stuff is technical in a major way.'

'I know a technical expert. He has a ThD.'

'Ah.' Vilnar sat back in his chair, which subtly curled around him. 'The man you got to interrogate the prisoner. The prisoner who went into Basilisk Trance.'

'Yeah, that's a problem. Kyushen was a bit traumatized himself, after causing that. But he did get us the information we needed.'

'The information that caused Laura to get Judge Prior to sign an arrest warrant with my name on it.'

'I know, but that was—'

'All right, Riordan. Who is this Kyushen, and where did you find him?'

'Kyushen Jyu, from St Jarl's, where I was a patient.'

'Ah. St Jarl.' Vilnar's gaze shifted left. 'That brings back memories.'

'You were there? At the hospital?'

'No, it's just that the Organists worshipped St Jarl, or claimed to. Before your time.'

'I've heard of them.'

'Uh-huh. They thought that the double meaning of "organ" was a sacred sign. Thirty-three people had disappeared before we found the Organists' vaults. They'd turned their victims into musical instruments, poor bastards. Arteries strung into webs of resonance tubes. Bones for structure and percussion. Keyboards formed from fingers.'

'Hades.'

'And the worst thing? When we entered, the music they were playing was *lovely*. Even the vocals coming through living skulls' open mouths.'

Donal nodded, saying nothing.

'So I understand something of what you went through.' Vilnar rubbed his face. 'With Cortindo, I mean. And here's another thing. That case, taking down the Organists, was what eventually got me this job.'

Further promotion was not something that Donal had dreamed of.

'I'm not a politician,' he said.

'Neither was Laura Steele, before her resurrection.'

Donal went absolutely still.

'People change,' added Vilnar. 'Sometimes they find new goals.'

'Before or after we take the Black Circle down?'

'Afterwards will do.' Vilnar's blocky face widened as he smiled. 'That will do.'

'So what's the first step?'

'You get your Dr Jyu to come in here and read this book.' Vilnar's gaze swept around the office, lingering on the black drapes at the rear, then on the chair that still held Donal's gun. 'I'd rather it didn't leave this room.'

'All right.' Donal checked his watch. 'It's still not six a.m. I'll ring him at nine.'

'Fair enough.'

'So why were you in the office this early, Commissioner?'

'Same reason as you.'

'I know, but ...'

If I had Laura, I'd be home with her as much as I could.

Vilnar's gaze seemed to age, becoming ancient.

'My Vera isn't safe if the city is in danger. Perhaps I should just ... But I made a choice. I'm going to do my job, protecting real people. The politics and conspiracies are just tools to achieve that.'

Donal stared at him, then held out his hand.

'It's my privilege to work for you, sir.'

Vilnar rose, shook his head with a tiny smile, then grasped Donal's hand.

'Likewise, Lieutenant. A privilege to work with you.'

They released their grip.

'And if you'll care to hang on to your weapon more tightly in the future' – Vilnar nodded towards the chair – 'you might even achieve what you're after.'

'I'll do that.'

'Good. Take it easy, Riordan.'

'And you, sir.'

The chair walked Donal to the door, then extended its arm. Donal thanked it, and retrieved his Magnus, which he holstered. The ciliaserpents were completely still as the door opened. Donal stepped through.

'Good man,' he heard Vilnar say.

Iron doors slid shut behind him.

Nine

Big Viktor leaned back in the hard seat, swaying with the hypotube train's motion, wishing he was in bed. The call had come in at four a.m., which was impressive in one way, because it meant that Commander Bowman had successfully made his arrangements with outlying precincts. Any phone call that mentioned white wolves was redirected to Bowman, Xalia or Viktor.

The hypotube carriage was almost deserted. It should be, given the hour.

Investigating the call, what Viktor had found was an unlicensed young witch, aged ten, whose nightmares manifested as glowing shapes that might look like wolves ... to someone with severe myopia and an alcohol problem. Viktor had quietened the neighbour who'd rung in, then followed an apparition as it flitted through grimy, litter-filled backyards, backtracking to the girl's house where she slept.

He'd served her parents with a summons to take her before a magistrate for registration within the month. They hadn't been happy, but faced with a seven-foot tall unshaven cop in a battered leather coat, they'd not objected either.

Now, Viktor was torn between heading back home or going straight to HQ. The problem with returning to his apartment was waking up after one hour's sleep, when the alarm went off. He decided not to decide until after Coldwell Node, four stops down the line.

At the front of the carriage, facing the rear, sat a slender young woman wearing a cheap, conservative blouse and skirt. Her knees were primly together, her jade-and-lemon eyes downcast. Her pale skin held a hint of scales.

Viktor looked away, aware that a man staring at a lone woman formed a threat, even if unintentional.

Several seats behind Viktor, a fat man farted, and said: 'Oops.'

'Welcome to my life,' muttered Viktor.

Outside the grime-streaked window, the tunnel darkness fell away, replaced by green-white eerie lighting in a near-deserted station. This was North 3009th Street, a long way from the investment banks and luxury department stores of downtown Tristopolis.

The area's shabbiness was matched by the torn clothes of four youths who stumbled on board.

'Morning, you fuckin' tossers!'

Laughing, they clattered their way along the carriage and sat down, bottles of spiderapple cider in hand. Viktor supposed it was a step up from antifreeze.

'Gimme fuckin' that.'

'Fuckin' what? You got your fuckin' own, ain't ya?'

The doors shut, and a bang sounded from the train's rear. The station slipped away as the initial pneumatic push caused the train to enter the tunnel proper, where necromagnetic windings induced further acceleration. Here, the tunnel corkscrewed downwards.

'You spilled it, you wanker!'

The train came out into what looked like open air, where the tunnel was transparent, supported by trellis-work two hundred feet above street level.

'Something's fishy in here, ain't it?'

In a minute, the train would be halting at a skyway station, midway between two old towers with worn, tired gargoyles who rarely flew. Perhaps the four idiots would get off there.

Viktor folded his arms, glanced at the young woman, then looked out the window at the architecture and the deep-purple sky.

'Bet something *tastes* fishy, if you lick the right spot. What you say, sweetheart?'

The young woman turned her head, staring at the cityscape as Viktor had. Her hands were clasped over her small handbag.

'Fuckin' A, right?' One of the youths, on his feet now, stumbled past Viktor. 'What *you* say, pal?'

Viktor said nothing.

The other three youths followed their friend's lead. One of them unzipped his trousers as he walked. Then he stopped in front of the young woman, his legs wide against the train's swaying, and reached into his crotch.

'You seen fish swallow?' he said. 'Gobble glub, gobble glub.'

'Hey, girl, we'll help you.'

'No, let her.' The one with his legs wide shook his head. 'Sweetheart, open up—'

Viktor rose up behind him, leg powering upwards with massive force, his shin smashing into the youth's coccyx, instep crushing the testicles. The youth snapped forward. Viktor dropped a hard elbow on to his spine, flattening the bastard.

Before the others could react, Viktor reached cross-handed beneath his coat, and ripped out a Grauser from under each arm, whipping them upwards in an X-shaped motion. Two of the youths staggered back, blood welling from lines cut open in their cheeks.

'You'll pick this idiot up, and haul him off at this stop. Got it?'

'Uh ...'

'Sir ...'

The train was already slowing for the skyway station.

'Take him home, or throw him over the edge. It's all the same to me. If I see you riding this line again, I'll kill you.'

Shaking, the trio dragged their companion – awkwardly, because they were in pitiful physical condition – to the carriage doors. From lowered eyelids, they glanced towards Viktor no higher than his shins. When the train stopped and doors slid open, they tugged their friend on to the platform.

For a moment, they stood there. Then one of them bolted for the stairs, the other two looked at each other, then followed, leaving their friend face-down on the platform.

Viktor shook his head as the train doors closed.

'Oh, damn.' He turned to the young woman. 'You hadn't intended to alight here?'

She answered with a small shake of her head.

'Good, then.' Viktor replaced his twin Grausers in the shoulder holsters. 'Sorry about all that.'

Farther back, the fat man was sitting with chin on chest, his eyes closed. Asleep, or pretending that what he couldn't see wasn't happening.

'Thank you.' When the young woman spoke, her teeth were revealed as a multitude of slender, curved needles. 'Although I could have coped.'

'I guess you could.' Viktor grinned at her. 'Good for you.'

He returned to his seat.

After the next stop, the hypoway descended underground once more, stopped at the next station, then continued on to Coldwell Node. Viktor and the young woman got off. She nodded to him, then headed for the Orange Line changeover.

'I'm going home,' Viktor said.

He made his way to the Blue Line platforms. As he walked, he decided what to do the minute he reached his apartment: switch off the alarm, then get into bed.

Donal, alone in the task force office, wondered where everybody was. It was too early for the guys to be here without an operation in progress. Recently, he'd seen very little of anyone.

Harald was doing something for Commander Bowman, Donal thought. He and Harald hadn't had much direct conversation since Laura's death.

He set me up to be killed in the Power Centre.

But afterwards, when Donal had been about to die in Gelbthorne's house, the armoured doors had blown inwards, and there was Harald, hexzooka on his shoulder, accompanied by his bone motorcycle, a Phantasm IV. The Phantasm had fought off the mansion's guardian daemosaur, while Illurian armoured police poured in to secure the place.

Donal had no problem with Harald; but perhaps Harald was still upset by his own earlier actions. He'd taken Xalia's suspicions as proof that Donal was a Black Circle snitch.

So, Xalia. Donal hadn't seen the wraith member of the team, either. His intuition was that she'd been more seriously injured than she'd let on, trying to penetrate the upper floors' defences here in HQ, attempting to get the goods on the commissioner whom she suspected.

I'll ask Gertie.

It wasn't just that Gertie was the friendliest wraith he knew. She seemed to have more knowledge than anyone else about what went on here.

And what of the other team members? Sushana was still out, recovering from her ordeal when Sally the Claw's organization had figured out she was an undercover cop, not the halfway-talented sorceress she'd pretended to be. She wasn't back on any kind of duty yet. If she ever returned, Donal suspected it would be to work behind a desk.

Alexa Ceerling ... Well, he knew what had happened to her. He supposed she was still in the Customer Relationship Bureau, engaged in bright conversation with civilians on the line, smiling hard.

Viktor Harman was the remaining team member. Good, dependable, and hard as a bastard. He'd almost rescued Sushana single-handed, clearing the defences so that when Laura and Xalia turned up, they'd been able to finish the job. It would be good to have him fully on board once more.

Donal realized he was thinking like a leader, although Commissioner Vilnar had not said anything specific about reviving the team. The thing was, if it were to continue as a federal operation, they would need authorisation from the guy that Bowman had mentioned, Special Agent Murgatrayle.

He checked his watch. Still not seven o'clock.

Too early.

But he picked up his desk phone anyway – his *black* telephone – and spun all the combination wheels to zero, connecting him with an operator.

Can I help you?

'Please put me through to St Jarl-the-Healer Hospital.'

To the main switchboard?

'Yes, please.' When the hospital switchboard answered, Donal gave his name. 'And could I speak with Dr Jyu, please? Kyushen Jyu, that's right.'

It was nearly three minutes before a familiar voice sounded on the line.

'Hello? Jyu here.'

'Hey, Dr Jyu. Kyushen. It's Donal Riordan.'

'Oh. Lieutenant.'

'How are things with you?'

'All ... right.'

Donal smiled. 'I could do with some technical advice.'

'Er, Lieutenant—'

'Call me Donal.'

'Donal, I can't do it again. I'm sorry.'

'There's no interrogation involved. I need you to take a look at a technical manual.'

There was a swirling silence.

'It's about multihex something, and parasympathetic algorithms. Top secret. Foreign.'

'You mean parasympathetic encryption algorithms? Like mind control?'

'Huh.' Donal laughed. 'You do understand this stuff.'

'What is this manual?'

'I'd rather not say what it's called. It can't leave Police HQ, I'm afraid. Which also means, you're going to be the only thaumaturgical engineer in the country to read it.'

'Oh. Hades.'

'What?'

'We're doing a major upgrade to the death support equipment in Terminal Ward One. I can't leave today.'

'So when can you come?'

'Tomorrow. First thing.'

'Good. Ask for me at the front desk.'

'Yes, I'll ... I still think about him. About Dilvox.'

'I know.'

'There was no excuse for me to ... Ah. I'll see you tomorrow, Lieutenant. Donal.'

'Tomorrow.'

Donal put the phone down.

I manipulated him well, didn't I?

Perhaps there were some things it was not good to be good at. What was it Commissioner Vilnar had said?

'People change. Sometimes they find new goals.'

No. Revenge was still his only objective.

I'm going to get them, Laura.

And now he had new tools and new abilities to help him take the bastards down.

Harald came into the office, followed by a bulky man who was in the process of removing his shades, revealing stone sniper's eyes. On the day Donal had joined the task force, he'd seen the man, but not since.

'I don't suppose you remember Kresham,' said Harald.

'Sure I do.' Donal shook Kresham's hand. 'But I don't know who you're with. Anti-Ensorcelment?'

'Robbery-Haunting. Pel Bowman's crew.'

'Commander Bowman's sort of in charge of us now, for the time being.'

'I heard.'

Harald was putting two black folders down on his desk. As he opened a drawer to put them inside, Donal noticed the small indigo logo, then snapped his gaze to Kresham's features, then Harald's. Neither man was grinning, not like Alexa.

'Have you two been making phone calls?'

Gentle eyes stared at stone eyes, then Harald and Kresham turned towards Donal.

'Why, have you?' asked Harald.

Donal could see the controlled tension building in Kresham's big hands.

'Yeah. The telephones in Customer Relations are that colour.' He pointed to the logo. 'I mean, right here in this building.'

'And you used one?'

'It doesn't affect people like me,' said Donal, deliberately staring at

Laura's name, still inscribed on the door to the empty commander's office. 'Although they appeared not to realize that. I smiled like an idiot until I left the room.'

'Balls,' said Kresham. 'Inside HQ? No wonder we're doing this hush-hush.'

Harald was still focused on Donal.

'You felt no effects?'

'No, but I saw what it did to everyone else. So where were you two? Another precinct?'

'Ordinary houses in Lower Halls, near where you used to live. Mostly older people, willing to try a new, cheaper service. And at home all day.'

'Easier to be there when the engineers call,' said Kresham.

'So was everyone grinning like a moron?'

'They were happy,' answered Harald. 'And very healthy. I mean, the usual old folks' ailments had cleared up. They all said it was a wonderful coincidence.'

'Coincidence,' muttered Kresham.

'Right.' Donal thought about Harald's history with the Marines. 'You had special forces trance training.'

'Yes, I did.'

'And—?'

'No, I did not try to entrance any of the victims. Something that powerful, when you don't understand how the changes were induced, you don't mess with on your own.' Harald sat on the edge of his desk. 'You want me to risk a civilian falling into Basilisk Trance? Under interrogation, I might trigger a fractal amnesia command, wiping out everything.'

Donal thought of Kyushen Jyu, and the Basilisk Trance he'd induced in the prisoner Dilvox because of the deep tracing tools he'd used. Such a trance was legally the same as death.

So do I tell them about Alexa?

'You did the right thing. I saw the commissioner' – Donal wanted to add that he'd punched Commissioner Vilnar in the side of the neck, but he stopped himself – 'in person. He's obviously running Bowman on this one.'

Harald nodded, which Donal took to be a good sign, indicating no more suspicion hanging over the commissioner.

I'll say nothing about Alexa.

If anyone on the team realized what had happened to Alexa, they might try to jolt her out of it, and in the process induce a Basilisk Trance or similar disastrous breakdown. Perhaps the Old Man had everything under control.

'We hear,' said Harald, 'that you and the commissioner are new best friends.'

'Excuse me?'

Perhaps Donal had underestimated Harald's suspicions.

'Aren't you both going to City Hall tomorrow? A little award, maybe? Some kind of commendation?'

'Um. Yeah. I'd almost forgotten.'

'Forgotten.'

'Yeah,' said Donal. 'I'm a poor boy from the orphanage, you know? What does City Hall mean to me?'

'You'll probably shake hands with the mayor his own self,' said Kresham. 'That makes you a VIP, Lieutenant.' His stone eyes dilated, then contracted. 'Shit. I don't know whether to salute or curtsy.'

'How about fucking off?'

'I could do that. Can I have your autograph first?'

'No.'

Harald smiled.

'I knew you two would get on fine.'

The early workers were already walking the corridors off City Hall, heading for their offices in the long wings either side of the main, central skull. Inside the atrium, and in the cranial corridors, the cleaners were finishing up, the carpets already swept, the glass cases polished, ready for the day's visitors.

Soon, the first party of schoolchildren arrived. It was still too early for normal opening, but these children were from Zurinam, flying back later today, and an administrator had arranged a special booking. Three teachers accompanied the twenty-seven kids, keeping watch, commenting on the weapon displays and other antiquities, talking about systems of government in terms that ten-year-olds might understand.

Eventually they reached Ninth Corridor, where the regimental flags and battered-then-renewed weapons of the Battling 303s were arranged in artful curves and blossom-patterns on the walls. There were several glass-fronted display cases, less interesting to the children – at least to the boys – than the wall-mounted lances and guns. But one young girl of quiet demeanour stopped before a case and stood fascinated.

Had she lived in Tristopolis and attended a normal school, an inspector would have picked out her potential as a matter of routine. As it was, her nascent witch sensibilities reacted to something in the display case, but she was too young – and overwhelmed by the sensations of visiting a new continent – to understand what she nearly perceived.

Then one of the teachers, a stern man whose own undeveloped mage potential tended more towards the giving of commands than sensitivity, uttered a gruff imperative sentence in Zurinese. The girl flinched, then rushed to rejoin her group, all doubts forgotten.

Perhaps that was a good thing.

Inside the case, lying still beneath his chameleon shroud, the assassin's eyes were open in darkness. His fingertips, sensitive through thin gloves, touched his black-on-black watch. Designed for blind people, it allowed him to check the time by feel.

He had come out of trance early, but there was no need to come fully awake into action, not yet. Nothing was due to happen until lunchtime tomorrow, nearly thirty hours away.

For a while, he kept his perceptions open, in case the youngster – he could tell it had been a child – returned. But nothing happened, and the feeling of being observed receded into nothingness. It was time to re-enter trance.

The assassin closed his eyes, and slowed his breathing down.

Ten

The grounds of St Jarl-the-Healer lay within Tristopolitan territory, but that was a legal technicality. Surrounding the hospital buildings and vast gardens and fortified walls, silver-grey woods stretched for hundreds of miles in most directions. Only by driving directly north could someone heading for the city proper – a returning visitor, or a patient on day release – pass through a mere twenty miles of sylvan environment, unchanged for three millennia.

In the centre of the hospital area, above the jagged towers and crenellated walls, floated iron creatures that looked too heavy to fly. In the ornate garden shrubbery, particularly in the tall fractal maze whose configuration tended to change when no one was looking, half-corporeal shapes drifted and watched, and moaned. On occasion, they laughed in an eerie, unnerving way that only the longest-serving nurses and doctors could ignore.

From the central mass of towers, a long extension formed of pterabone and black glass acted as a covered walkway, allowing access to a nine-sided, dark-grey windowless building that looked like the discarded battle helmet of some massive, brutish troll. It was a secure area, which meant that anyone approaching from outside the walkway would experience a blurring of vision, a disorientation which invariably resulted in their walking off into the grounds somewhere, however hard they tried to keep to a straight line. The closer one approached, the more unfocused and twisted reality became.

Sometimes, if the person had tried to push too hard beyond the critical boundary, the effects went deeper than disorientation. One such had been a medical commissioner called O'Driscoll, whose trance-shield training he'd considered protection against the vortex field. He'd awoken in the Acute Ensorcelment Ward. Granted, the number of medics attending him was due to his rank as much as the seriousness of his reaction to the defences.

But the Secure Unit for the Criminally Ensorcelled, known as the Sucker Wing among nurses when no outsiders were near, was protected for good reason – even at the risk of pissing off visiting dignitaries.

(And Commissioner O'Driscoll had eventually, after recovery, written a letter praising the hospital staff and their security arrangements. Whatever he felt in private, his public reaction was eloquent and positive.)

Now, although parts of the hospital were brightly lit as the establishment woke up, the Acute Ensorcelment Ward remained in semi-darkness. Low sensory input and extended sleep were part of the treatment. Seventeen of the twenty-one beds were occupied, but two of those beds had been pushed together to hold what looked like three teenagers huddled close, but were in fact one ternary being. Above each occupied bed, tiny monitor sprites hovered.

At the far end of the ward was a watch-station, where two nurses, both of them Night Sisters, were sitting at the long desk, drinking hele-bore tea and munching scarab cookies.

'Callie?' said one of them, keeping her voice low. 'You ever had a crush on a patient?'

'No. It was bad enough,' answered Sister Calico, 'falling for doctors in med school. Don't you remember?'

'I never did that.'

'Felice, you are such a liar.'

'Well.' Sister Felice's smile was elegant. 'Perhaps one. Or two.'

'And now you've fallen for a patient?' Sister Calico gestured to the rows of beds. 'Not one of them, I hope.'

'I was asking hypothetically.'

'Oh. Hypothetically.'

'Look, all I—'

'Bed seventeen. It's Mrs Jamieson.'

A monitor sprite had just flared yellow.

'Come on.'

The nurses moved with a fast flowing motion, their eyes wide in the shadowed environment, and in a second they were at the bed. Translucent tentacles were rising from the woman's body, as she moaned in her sleep without waking.

'We could wake her up.'

'Best if we solve the problem now.'

'All right.'

Phantom limb syndrome was easier to control when the patient was conscious. But if they could get Mrs Jamieson to a stage where even in her dreams the limbs failed to manifest, then she would be cured.

Her eyelids flickered.

'She's in REM sleep.'

'Fair enough.'

The two Night Sisters swung flexible metal arms into place, part of the equipment set beside the bed. Sister Calico worked the console, while Sister Felice directed the flexible extensions as they pulsed with light and invisible necromagnetic radiation. The Night Sisters' pupils narrowed into vertical slits against the brightness.

Soon, the sleeping woman quietened, and the spurious limbs retracted into her body.

'Nice work.'

'We're pretty good, don't you think?'

'Unbeatable.'

They put the equipment back in place, then walked together back to the watch-station.

'Kyushen Jyu,' said Sister Felice, 'has really optimized the gear, don't you think?'

'Oh-ho.' Sister Calico sat down, and picked up her tea. 'So it's not a patient you were thinking of hypothetically?'

'Actually it was.' Sister Felice's claws extended, then retracted. 'I was thinking of Lieutenant Donal Riordan.'

'Oh, him. Sister Lynkse *told* me you had a soft spot for that one.'

'That Lynnie has a big mouth.'

'She said your police lieutenant had a big— Now, what was it again?'

'He wasn't *my* lieutenant.'

'No?'

'No.' Sister Felice's claws were extending again, and her ears flattened.

'My mistake, then,' said Sister Calico. 'Hypothetically.'

'Shit.'

Sister Felice shook her head, retracting her claws once more. Then she picked up a cookie from the plate, as Sister Calico took a sip of helebore tea.

'Anyway,' she added. 'Lynnie never even saw his dick.'

Sister Calico sputtered, spraying drops of tea.

'You are such a *bad* person, Sister Felice.'

'I am that.'

But Sister Felice's expression grew harder, and she turned away.

'What is it?' asked Sister Calico.

'Two hundred yards in that direction' – Sister Felice pointed at the wall – 'there's a woman called Marnie Finross, in something like a

Basilisk Trance, but not quite. Even Kyushen can't bring her out of it.'

'You mean in the Sucker Wing?'

'Yeah. And if it hadn't been for her, my police lieutenant wouldn't be a zombie now. At least, that's what I gather from gossip and the *Gazette*.'

'Oh. That one.' Sister Calico put down her cup. 'I hadn't put the stories together. The shootout in Fortinium. That was the same guy, the one who died.'

'And got resurrected. Yeah, that was Donal.'

Sister Calico laid her hand on top of Sister Felice's.

'That changes things a bit.'

'It changes everything.'

At lunchtime, Donal left the building, and hailed a taxi on Avenue of the Basilisks. It took twenty minutes to reach the foot of Darksan Tower, where he paid the driver off with a decent tip, mostly for remaining silent during the drive.

The doormen bowed to him as usual. When he took the elevator to 227, he was the only person inside. Once inside the apartment, he stripped off his clothes, and pulled out his old black running-suit from a drawer.

I could afford something better now.

Once he'd changed into his running gear, he picked up his wallet, which included his detective's shield, but decided to leave the Magnus behind. This time, when he entered the elevator to descend, there was the faintest hint of spikes beginning to extrude from the walls, before they sank back inside, quietening. Donal wondered what it was about his demeanour that had started to trigger the security features. After all, Laura had made it clear that he was a friend, on his first night here.

He would never stop missing Laura.

Out on the street, a battered purple cab pulled over suddenly. Donal dropped his bodyweight, ready to run. But the driver was a man called Bilwin, whose daughter Donal had pulled out of some teenage scrapes, and who'd been grateful ever since.

'Hey, Lieutenant,' he called. 'You want a lift anywhere?'

'No, I'm just going out for a ...' Then Donal had a sudden impulse, generated by Harald's mentioning of Lower Halls earlier on, back in HQ. 'Were you headed back to the old neighbourhood, by any chance?'

'That's exactly where I was going. Hop in, Lieutenant.'

'Can I ride up front beside you?'

'Yeah, 'course you can.'

Bilwin moved a sandwich box off the seat – giving Donal a flashback to the Westside Complex, and the three phone engineers eating lunch while the quicksilver birds descended to strip Kinley Finross's body. Donal got in.

'You're looking pretty good,' said Bilwin, pulling away from the kerb. 'Maybe a bit pale?'

'Shoot, Lieutenant. I know what happened to you. Me 'n' some of the boys, we been drinking rounds to your health, down in the Nine-Sided Die.'

'Um, thanks. Nice of you.' As he spoke, Donal watched the people on the sidewalk outside. Well-dressed, serious, thinking about business, or perhaps the first martini of the evening. 'Your missus won't be pleased.'

'I don't spend *that* much time in the bar. Not nowadays.'

Donal turned to Bilwin. 'Nowadays?'

'Weird times in Lower Halls and the Nether Boroughs. Power brownouts. More ... street crime, y'know?'

'What kind of street crime?'

'Attacks and the like.'

Working in Police HQ, Donal should have picked up on this.

'You're looking a bit tired, Bilwin.' It was time to change the subject. 'Working long hours?'

'Yeah, and keeping away from the Boroughs, mostly. It's not as bad for me as some of the others, though. I'll grant you that.'

'What do you mean?'

'Er ...'

'Come on, Bilwin. How long have we known each other?'

'Hang on.' They were entering the thirteen-way intersection called Spasm Circus. Bilwin concentrated on shifting to the correct lane, then: 'I mean, what you might call non-standard humans. They're the victims, ain't they?'

'Are they?'

'Yeah. Drivers like Oxborn Spike – old Cactus, remember him? They're having a hard time of it.'

Donal recalled Oxborn, with his lilac skin studded with darker, abbreviated thorns. He looked fierce until he spoke in his hesitant, gulping voice.

'So you're personally making lots of money,' said Donal. 'Long hours, less competition.'

'Not really. People ain't travelling so much, see?'

Donal nodded. For a time, they followed the busy route of Helsink Freeway in silence.

'Anyway,' Bilwin said eventually, 'I gave a ride once, to one of those scary, brainy folk from the dark hospital, know what I mean?'

'You mean St Jarl's?' Donal thought about Kyushen Jyu.

'Nah, the real scary place. Mordanto. Creepier than Jarl's. Ever been there?'

'Never.'

'Well, they say that— Never mind. Anyway, this guy told me *mathematically*, like, what I should be doing. He said I should work long hours on busy days, get as much money as I could. On quiet days, give up and go home early.'

'OK ...' Donal wasn't sure how that constituted maths.

'No, see, what most of us do is, we work longer on the quiet days and knock off early on the busy ones, when we've made enough dough. In the long run, this guy said, that's more hours.'

'Oh. Sounds sensible.'

'Yeah.' Bilwin took a freeway exit, and turned on to a quiet, dilapidated street. 'Only he never said what to do if every day is a quiet day.'

There was a clunk. Donal realized that Bilwin had flicked on the central locking, so no one could pull open a door if the taxi halted, say at a red light.

'Look at those poor guys, Lieutenant.'

Donal saw a shambling group on the sidewalk. Five adults and three children with shabby clothes and pale skin—

Like me.

It was a family of zombies. Whether they'd been related in life, Donal could not tell. Resurrected children were something he'd not wanted to think about in the past.

Resonance washed through Donal's dark blood, and all eight zombies turned to look at him as the taxi passed. Then they were behind him, and Bilwin was taking a left turn. After they'd been out of sight for a few seconds, the feeling in Donal's arteries ebbed away.

'Probably homeless,' said Bilwin. 'There's been a lot of evictions.'

'What about the Anti-Discrimination statutes?'

'Landlords don't care these days. Word is, them statutes are gonna get revoked, is that what they call it?'

'I guess.'

Isolated in Darksan Tower, working in the task force, disoriented by Laura's death and his own resurrection ... it looked as if Donal was out of touch with the streets. Surely things couldn't change this quickly?

'That mage type,' said Bilwin, as if following Donal's reasoning. 'Him that told me what hours to work. He reckoned, in complicated systems like a city, stuff can become completely different overnight. That's what he said.'

He was cruising now, and Donal realized he'd specified no exact destination.

'I just wanted to check out the old neighbourhood.' Donal looked out. 'Maybe run the ... Uh, go for a run here.'

'Hey, it's all right, Lieutenant.' Bilwin grinned as he made another turn. 'You go jogging down in the catacombs. We know that. You've done it for years.'

'Not so much recently.'

'Guess it's quieter down there. Wouldn't fancy it myself.'

Donal doubted that Bilwin had run a step since his days in the schoolyard, but that wasn't what he meant, of course.

'I know, can we take a drive past Peat's Place?'

''Course. You looking to buy some books?'

'You never know.'

The last thing Donal had bought from Peat had been *Human: the Revenge*, whose sequel he'd finished the night before last. Being suddenly rich didn't prevent him from shopping at a secondhand bookstore, did it? And Peat, though short on conversation, was an observant being with deep philosophical views and knowledge of literature and verse.

'Oh, shit.' Bilwin slowed the taxi. 'Lieutenant ... This ain't good.'

'Hades.'

The front window consisted of two jagged fragment like teeth. The store's interior was blackened. The door had been smashed, then set alight. Charcoal and blistered paint were all that remained. The damage might have happened yesterday or a month ago.

'Drop me off here.' Donal opened his wallet, and pulled out florins. 'Here you go.'

'There's no need for—'

'Yeah, there is. Whatever went on here, it's not happening now. I'm going to poke around.'

'Hades, Lieutenant. Maybe you should just call it in.'

'Uh-huh. And you've been telling me about street crime rising. How quick have our guys been to respond?'

Bilwin shook his head.

'So I'll investigate,' Donal continued, 'which happens to be my job. Go on, Bilwin. Get on home, or wherever you're headed.'

'Downtown to get more fares, I reckon.' Bilwin stared at the ruined bookstore. 'Don't think I'll hang around here.'

'Probably best not to.' Donal opened the door, and slid out. 'Take it easy.'

'You too, Lieutenant.'

Bilwin put the taxi in gear, and moved off. For a hundred yards he drove slowly, as though hoping Donal would call him back. Then he sped up, and took the first turning left. Donal listened to the diminishing sound of the taxi's motor, then turned his attention to the remains of Peat's Place.

So many burned books.

'Hades.' Donal pressed his fingertips against the incinerated door, decided the whole thing might come crashing down if he pushed, then walked around to the smashed, empty window. 'Thanatos damn it.'

He stepped through the open gap, into the destroyed window display, then down on to the floor. Glass shards, grey and blackened with smoke, crunched beneath his running shoes. The bonfire stench was strong, but there was no sense of smouldering warmth.

Where was Peat when it all went up?

Donal moved into the dark interior, his black running-suit blending with shadow. Past bookcases that were half-charcoal, past spilled masses of books that were mostly ash, Donal moved slowly. If there were predators here, they wouldn't be looking for books, they'd be looking for the cash register – which lay toppled on the floor, empty.

He headed for the staircase at the rear.

'Ah, no.' There was another scent on the sooty air. 'No.'

Slowing down, aware that the staircase could fall, he wanted to run up and check what he suddenly knew, but disaster lay that way. He tested the treads, climbing close to the wall.

Careful.

It took time, and one tread crumbled, but then he was past it, nearly at the top. Once on the bare landing, Donal noticed the fire damage was less. There was a coldness in the air.

Then he was in the smoke-blackened bedroom, and the four-hundred-pound figure slumped on the floor was immediately recognizable. Donal went down on one knee to check, but it was unnecessary. Peat's corpse was at ambient temperature, and the woody smell that used to rise from his dark spongy skin was gone.

Noting the lack of fire damage, he wondered if smoke inhalation had suffocated Peat. Then he noticed the dark stain spread across the floor, and the gash in Peat's neck. It was a clean slit, probably from a knife.

'Peat. Ah, Peat.'

Donal guessed he hadn't fought back. Peat had possessed more-than-human strength, but with his gentle nature he could never have defended himself.

Stepping away, Donal retraced his tracks, trying to leave minimal disturbance. Scene-of-crime diviners, if they processed the scene, would appreciate his not disturbing the evidence. But he wondered, as he carefully descended the burned stairs, whether there would be a proper processing of this particular crime scene.

Back through the shop he went, exiting via the broken front window, and came out onto the sidewalk, trying to remember the location of the nearest phone booth.

There.

Two blocks away, beneath the rusted bridge that supported an elevated length of track, a dim light was glowing in a booth, somehow unvandalised. Donal jogged towards it.

He reached the booth and looked inside.

'For fuck's sake.'

The phone looked brand-new and functional – and it was coloured indigo.

Shit.

Trusting that he was immune, Donal forced himself to pick up the handset and ask for the emergency operator.

'Gimme Homicide,' he said, when a police wraith answered. 'This is Lieutenant Riordan, badge number two-three-omicron-nine, and I need a SOCD team' – he pronounced it *sock-dee* – 'in Lower Halls, stat. I have one homicide victim, male.'

At what location, Lieutenant?

'Peat's Place.' Donal gave her the address. 'It's a bookstore, or was. Someone burned it out.'

I'll inform the squad, sir.

Something in the wraith's tone had altered. Perhaps she already knew of the burning.

'You'll send someone straight away?'

I'll ask immediately, sir. How fast they respond is up to them.

'But—' Donal stopped, because the operator was no more standard-human than Peat or himself. 'I understand.'

I'll do my best.

'Thank you.'

The line went dead, and Donal replaced the phone. He walked slowly back to the ruined shop, then stood on the sidewalk, totally still, and waited without moving.

It took two hours for the investigation team to turn up.

Eleven

Perhaps 'investigation team' was too fancy a term for the semi-retired forensic officer and trainee scene-of-crime diviner who turned up. The diviner was pretty, and Donal watched as she tuned in to the environment. She winced, picking up a resonance of Peat's brutal death.

Good.

Donal knew that her fast reaction meant she would be able to identify the murder weapon. Perhaps she was good enough to identify whatever traces the killer – probably killers – had left. Then it would be house-to-house enquiries and listening to word on the street that would find the bastards.

Except that this wasn't Donal's case, and couldn't be, if he was to track down Cortindo and Gelbthorne.

'You taking this case, Lieutenant?' asked a young uniformed officer.

'That's just what I've been thinking about. I can't.'

'Huh. What happened, you were just jogging past?'

Donal looked down, realizing he was still wearing his black running-suit, and remembered his reason for leaving home. So much for a pleasant run.

'More or less. Look, gimme a ring on progress, will you? Let me know who's got the murder book. If you can't contact me directly, try Robbery-Haunting.'

'Got it, sir.'

But there was a glum undertone in the patrolman's voice that stayed with Donal as he made his way out of the ruined bookstore. It was the tone of disillusionment, of the knowledge that whatever the law said, some deaths were more important than others.

So what am I going to do? Walk away?

Donal forced himself to continue down the street. From a bar at the corner, music played. It was still afternoon, and people should be at work. But the Crossed Scimitars had some kind of clientele at any hour.

Donal stopped.

Then he headed straight inside.

There were glances of recognition and a couple of waves, but most of the customers ignored him. The place was rundown, but there was more than poverty and sleaze; there were thirty individuals here, each with his or her own life story filled with detail; and Donal knew some of the highlights. None of Peat's old friends were in here.

'Hey, Lieutenant,' said the hard-faced man behind the bar. 'What can I get you?'

'Nothing. I've just come from Peat's Place.'

'That was a shame.'

But an involuntary flicker of eye movement told Donal everything. In the corner, seven men were drinking. One of them looked up at Donal.

'You're looking good, Donal.' His expression, or perhaps subvocalisation, continued the sentence: *'for a zombie.'*

Donal sniffed the air. Had he been living, the general pungency would have masked any individual scent he might have tried to detect.

I can smell burned fuel.

'Uh-huh. I want to talk to Big Jag here.'

The big man in question smiled into his beer. Tattoos swirled across his face: motile, like black fern leaves circling a whirlpool. He'd been on the street less than a year, since his latest stretch in Wailing Towers. Inside, he'd been an eager member of the Human Brotherhood.

Mixed in with the faint stench of fuel was a trace of the woody scent that Donal had always associated with Peat.

''Course, you're an intelligent guy, Jag,' continued Donal. 'Like, if I went into your hovel right now – I mean apartment, no offence – there's no chance I'd find a murder weapon, or traces of whatever you used to burn the place. Right?'

Big Jag looked up, blood draining from his face. It made the tattoos appeared darker. He stared, then lowered his head. His massive shoulders slumped.

Then he began to cry.

Oh, Hades.

'You did it, Jag.'

'I don't want go back inside. It's not nice there.'

'Come on. Come with me.'

Two of Jag's companions looked at each other. One moved his hand towards his pocket.

'There's no need to *be afraid*,' added Donal, casting his voice.

The hand movement stopped.

'That's right.' Donal softened his tone as Big Jag pushed himself to his feet, and stood with his head hanging. 'This way.'

Donal left the bar with Big Jag right behind him.

Slowly, they walked down the street to Peat's Place. There were two cruisers and an unmarked parked out front. As Donal approached, a short, stocky Detective-One from the 53rd Precinct waved his notebook. It took a moment for Donal to recall his name.

'You're Kribble, right?'

'Sure, Lieutenant. Bit of a mess in there, huh?'

'Yeah.'

'Don't see much hope of catching the killers, myself.'

'Why do you say that?'

'Huh. Non-human, begging your pardon. Random hate crime. Happens all over.'

'Right.'

'So ...'

'So you can arrest Big Jag, or I can. It's your case, Kribble.'

Kribble blinked at the shambling hulk of a man behind Donal.

'You mean him?'

'That's the one.'

'Why? You don't think—'

But the young SOC diviner was just exiting through the broken window, stepping down to the sidewalk. She stared, then pointed.

'He's one.' Her voice was clear and carrying. 'One of them. The fuel and weapon resonances are really strong.'

Kribble's eyes narrowed. Then he reached for the handcuffs on his belt.

'OK, buddy. What made you think you could get away with this?'

'He hasn't even had a bath or changed his clothes,' said the diviner, 'since he did it.'

Big Jag was beginning to sob.

'Good work, Detective Kribble,' said Donal. 'Interrogate him properly, with a bit of gentleness and tact, and you'll get the lot of them. You'll want to retrieve the murder weapon from his apartment now, before his buddies get there.'

Kribble blinked.

'Feather in your cap,' added Donal, 'closing a case this fast.'

'Uh, sure—'

Behind Kribble, the uniformed patrolman who'd talked to Donal earlier was grinning.

'Let me know how you get on,' said Donal.

He turned and walked away.

Soon he came to a wide stone pillar set on a corner. There was a man-sized black iron door. To one side, was an indentation into which Donal's police badge would fit perfectly.

How did I know?

Donal stood still, allowing his awareness to descend into introspection.

Did I try the bar by chance?

He'd lived in the neighbourhood, and known the kind of people who frequented the Crossed Scimitars. But his intuition had grown stronger as he'd neared the saloon door.

No. Not chance.

Deeper into memory and awareness, Donal drifted down through the architecture of his mind, until he reached a place where the memory of subliminal sensations opened to his internal analysis. He had, at some level, smelled the trace molecules that led him to Big Jag. He could even, in memory, identify probable companions, men in the bar who'd been with Big Jag in Peat's Place.

Leave that to Kribble to sort out. With the young diviner's aid, he'd get the others.

Donal's awareness began to rise.

At the level of emotions, he made some kind of lateral drift, immersing his awareness in his grief for Peat, at the senseless fatal beating of that gentle being. Then he became curious, within his mind, about the structure of that grief, and he moved inside the awareness of motion, noting the pattern of feeling, and—

It was evaporating.

Shit.

Donal rose fast now, like a diver in a hurry, and surfaced back into normal awareness, snapping his eyes open. He sucked in a breath.

'Mister, are you all right?'

A boy aged maybe ten was staring at him.

'Yeah, I was just doing some breathing exercises, you know?'

'Um. OK.'

'You live round here?'

'Sure.' He pointed along the road. 'We live over Fozzy's Rags.'

It was a washeteria that Donal remembered well.

'Good. You like reading books?'

'Sure.'

'That's a good thing. You get on home now.'

'Yes, sir.'

Donal watched him go.

What about Peat?

No feeling of grief remained inside him. There was some old literary trilogy which supposedly expanded recollections sparked by tasting a scarab cookie – Donal had never fancied reading it, but Peat would have known the thing almost by heart. What Donal had just done was similar, but diving inward, going deeply inside himself. Except that he could not grieve for Peat, and from now on – he was sure – he never would. In examining that particular emotion-to-memory linkage, he had destroyed it.

Was this the kind of thing that zombies learned to avoid? The ones who wanted to remain approximately human?

'Fuck it.'

Donal pushed his badge into the opening, and the iron door ground open.

Down in the catacombs, Donal began to run. It took only seconds to reach his cruising pace, as though he no longer needed to gently warm up. Or perhaps the concept of a warmed-up zombie was an oxymoron.

Do you ...?

Here, the old sarcophagi were melded with the worn tunnel walls and floor, like geological features, their inscriptions long eroded into nothingness. Perhaps they even predated the reactor piles. In the newer tunnels, bronze and brass sarcophagi looked eternal, often under armed guard for the first few months, until the bones had degraded. Rich families could afford to save their dead from the reactors.

Since the day Donal had touched a dead artist's knucklebone and been lost in wondrous dreams, he *felt* the bones' thoughts inside himself, as though they were his own.

Do you hear the bones?

That was when he'd stopped running the catacombs. When Laura (and her hexlar-armoured troopers) had rescued him from his trance state, about to flense the dead Diva's flesh from her bones for himself ... then, things had changed once more. Entering the catacombs again, it seemed that the dead had grown afraid of him.

Do you feel the song?

He feels it.

Now, as he ran with a fluid integrity to his gait he'd never known before, Donal felt a grin spreading across his face. He was filled with creeping fear, but it was the bones' dread, not his own. He was enjoying it.

He ran faster.

There was a low opening to one side, and he ducked, leaped across an acrid puddle, his body horizontal, then he tucked into a ball, saw the ceiling pass overhead as he rolled on his shoulder, and he was on his feet and running once more.

Faster.

Insinuating whispers rose, grew in number, overlapped like breaking waves as he ran through a long cavern filled with a multitude of sarcophagi, some decorated and grotesque enough to form subterranean mausoleums in their own right. In the background, perhaps he felt or heard a whimpering, a deep harmonic of suffering, and he wondered if burial was not the escape that rich families hoped.

Leave.

The patterns of dread were altering, affected by Donal's passing, as if in torment they could sense his being here.

Leave us now.

Donal laughed and continued to run.

For three hours he ran, through labyrinthine complexes of subterranean aqueducts, then abandoned hypoway tunnels that had not been part of the Pneumetro network for a century, and then into more catacombs. He vaulted over a low sarcophagus. At an uneven stone pillar, he leaped high, kicked against the pillar to change his direction, spun around his vertical axis as he descended, and sprang into a fast run once more.

He became more adventurous, vaulting larger sarcophagi, scrambling over mausoleums, landing with a roll that brought him to his feet. Jumping across a gap, he struck the stone wall with hands and feet, using the compression of all four limbs to power his spinning jump on to another tomb, drop to his hands – an impromptu cartwheel, unplanned – and continue with the run, ignoring the background sea of whispers until he felt (or heard) something different.

Another one like him.

Donal cancelled the vault he'd been about to attempt, and ran around the worn sarcophagus instead. Could the bones sense other zombies here?

Where?

Up above, in the world.

But – he avoided a puddle – there were thousands of beings like him in the city overhead. Whatever the bones were sensing, it wasn't a zombie ... or not *just* a zombie.

Donal slowed, coming to a stop in a high, dark gallery. Some eighty

112

feet overhead, he estimated, was a stone balcony with what looked like the beginnings of steps leading up to the surface. Warped pillars formed from distorted blocks of stone supported the balcony.

Laughing, he leaped to the nearest one, fingertips and toes neatly landing in the gaps between stones, and crimped his fingers. Then he leaned back, using torque to press his feet against the surface – a combat school instructor used to shout: *'Only mugs hug rock. Soldiers are laid back'* – and then he began to climb, shifting his weight with a fluid action, spidering his way up the pillar.

Soon he was on the balcony, then ascending a helical sequence of cracked, crumbling steps, until he reached the hollow interior of a corner pillbox, much like the one he had entered by. From the inside, the doors required no validation of identity. Donal worked the mechanism, the black iron door swung open, and he stepped out on to the sidewalk.

Up here, the bones were silent.

As the door clanged shut behind him, Donal scanned the environment. He was at a crossroads with near-deserted streets. An unmanned street-cleaning truck, heavy with armour-like cladding, drove slowly with brushes rotating. Perhaps a block away, a siren started up, then cut off, as though someone had hit a switch by accident.

It was a big city and something happened every five minutes. But the bones down below had been disturbed by something – by someone like Donal, in some specific way. He jogged across the street. Bands of darkness swept rhythmically along the tall buildings.

Two blocks farther on, at the corner of 57th and 984th, he found an accident scene. Emergency vehicles had their black-light strobes going. A limousine was tilted at a strange angle, its roof and front end smashed, a lifeless, half-severed arm dangling through the driver's window. Across from it was a boxy van, its rear partly crumpled, whose side proclaimed *Bertelloni's Bakery*, above *Crunchy Scarab Cookies Like Your Grandma Used To Make*.

Was this what the bones had sensed?

A long black ambulance was driving up, its wings firmly tucked into its side. Behind the crashed limo stood a large purple golem, with uniformed cops around it. From the glass spilled across the tarmac, plus the crumpled roof, it looked as if the officers had used the golem to turn the car the right way up.

As Donal neared, the golem's blank face turned towards him. There was no other reaction.

'Police officer.' Conscious of his black running-suit, Donal held his badge high. 'Lieutenant Riordan.'

'Hey, Lieutenant,' said one of the uniforms. 'We're just clearing a TTA.'

'And I was just jogging past.'

A Terminal Traffic Accident was routine, unless you were a rookie – like the young-looking cop vomiting over a drain right now. A female officer was closing her notebook. She'd been talking to a white-uniformed zombie standing by the bakery van, presumably the driver.

Donal walked towards them.

Beside the woman, a large-bellied officer with buzz-cut grey hair said, 'Freakin' zombie. You believe all what he just said?'

'Yeah, Frank. Why not?'

'Because— Hey, who are you?'

'Lieutenant Riordan. What did the driver say?'

'Um.' The female cop, whose name badge read *Officer Cordoza*, opened her notebook, but didn't look at the pages as she said, 'The van driver reports a white wolf, a big one, running straight across the street. But it didn't make him swerve, he said. It was the limo that lost control.'

'A wolf,' said Donal. 'White.'

He knew FenSeven and the other deathwolves at HQ. Every one of them was dark.

'Yeah, exactly.' The pot-bellied cop spread his hands. 'Who's the icicle trying to kid?'

'Oh.' Donal looked at him. 'You mean, he's one of those freaking zombies?'

'That's just what I ...'

The cop's voice trailed off. He stared at Donal's face.

'Frank,' said the woman. 'You are such an asshole. Sorry, Lieutenant.'

'All right. So who was in the limo?'

Donal used the past tense. Neither Officer Cordoza nor her partner, whom Donal mentally labelled Potbelly Frank, tried to correct him. The wrecked limousine contained only corpses. That was why the black ambulance was cruising to a halt. Their role would be to remove the deceased, once the officer-in-charge gave permission.

'You taking over?' asked Cordoza.

'Not me. Who's in charge?'

'Sergeant Tsatslinx, sir.'

'How do you spell that? Never mind. Let's take a look.'

Common sense said this was an accident, therefore none of his business. But it was the most unusual sight around, and Donal was up here at street level only because the bones below had detected something.

'Hey, Lieutenant.'

'Sergeant. I was just out running, so don't mind me.'

'You want to take a look?' The sergeant beckoned to the golem. 'You. Command: remove the nearest rear door of the limo, now.'

Without a sound, the big purple shape moved forward, took hold of the door with its huge three-fingered hands, crumpling the metal further, then ripped the whole thing free. Then it stepped back and stood in place, arms hanging down, still holding the door in its right hand.

There was a small gash in its other hand, in which lilac fluid glimmered.

'One moment.' Cordoza made her way over to the ambulance, leaned inside the open driver window, then came back with a small packet in hand. 'Here we are.'

She ripped open the packet, pulled out a long strip of what looked like grey fabric. Several drops of viscous, fluorescing lilac blood dripped from the golem's hand. Then Cordoza laid the fabric strip across the wound. It immediately stopped bleeding.

'Another freakin' good deed.' The muttered words floated from the direction of Potbelly Frank. 'Who does she think she is?'

Cordoza's expression tightened, but she just checked the dressing, then turned to the limousine. Sergeant Tsatslinx was already peering inside. Donal kept back, not wanting to take charge.

'Nice suit,' murmured the sergeant. 'This guy was rich.'

He stepped back.

'I don't know, Sergeant.' Cordoza, hands on her hips, was frowning. 'I sort of recognize him, but I couldn't tell you his name.'

Donal stared at the corpse. The features had been stretched and twisted. The expensive suit and shirt were soaked in glistening crimson, and the smell of faeces and intestines was strong. Neither Cordoza nor Sergeant Tsatslinx appeared bothered.

But *something* was wrong.

'I'm just going to check.' Donal reached for the man's neck, as if to find a pulse. 'I know he's dead, but— Shit.'

'What did you do, Lieutenant?'

Donal had withdrawn his hand. Slowly, he reached forward again. When he touched the skin, the dead man's features seemed to flicker. This time, he understood.

'Illusion,' he said. 'It goes away when I make contact.'

'Huh. I recognize him now,' said Cordoza. 'Can't tell you his name, but … It's Hardieson, that's right. My brother works for one of his companies. I've seen him speak at some annual boring dinner.'

Donal stepped back. The handsomeness faded from the lined, dead face, and the hair appeared drier and devoid of lustre.

Like Blanz.

In Fortinium, Senator Blanz had assumed the appearance of an old politician called Will Sharping. But when Donal had grabbed hold of him, the illusion had dissipated.

'It's not really a disguise,' he said mostly to himself. 'More an enhancement, kind of thing.'

'Ensorcelment?' asked Cordoza. 'Cosmetic thaumaturgy?'

She showed no curiosity about the way Donal's touch negated the illusion. Probably, she assumed it was Donal's zombie nature that caused the effect; but Donal had still been alive when he confronted Blanz.

'I guess in business,' said Donal, 'you might want to look your best, if you can afford the thaumaturgy.'

But he had a feeling that perhaps the dead man had been a mage in his own right. Yet in that case, shouldn't the guy have been able to avoid an accident?

One of the paramedics – grey skinned and garbed in black – had stepped out of the ambulance, and was staring at the dead man.

'They gimme the creeps, them medics.' Potbelly Frank had drawn near. 'Wouldn't want one touching me.'

'Right.' Cordoza glanced at Donal. 'You get shot, Frank, and I'll just leaving you lying in the road. No big deal.'

'Huh?'

But Donal was scanning the tarmac now, ignoring the other cops. Perhaps over there—

'What's that, the Janaval?'

'Sure,' said Sergeant Tsatslinx. 'The Janaval Hotel.'

It was a big tower, as big as Darksan where Donal lived, and its gargoyles appeared centuries old, with eyes that glowered red. There might have been the faintest of scent-traces in the air, but it was hard to tell.

Then it occurred to him that he was as much an asshole as Potbelly Frank, ignoring the most obvious resource of all. He walked over to the bakery van – *Crunchy Scarab Cookies Like Your Grandma Used To Make* – where the white-uniformed zombie stood.

'You drive this van for the bakery?' said Donal. 'I mean, for a living?'

There was a tiny movement of the zombie's mouth at the word *living*.

'That's right, sir. I drop off bread and cakes and quality ingredients, like luxury flour, for those who like to carry out their own baking.'

Donal had no idea what the difference between luxury flour and the ordinary stuff might be.

'This evening,' the driver continued, 'I'd just left the Janaval when the – incident – occurred. Three of my colleagues are working the night shift in their kitchens. Plus they took delivery of various cakes and other desserts.'

'All right. What about—?'

'The accident? You've already noticed yourself, sir, unless I'm mistaken.'

'Noticed what?' said Donal.

'The paw prints on the road. Only a little damp, and almost evaporated. But add that to the lupine scent, and the traces are obvious.'

'Lupine.'

'Belonging to a wolf.' The zombie gave another nearly-smile. 'I was a languages professor before I died.'

'I—'

'Don't need to apologize. This job gives me time to read.' Then, with a bleak glance towards Potbelly Frank, 'While our kind still *have* jobs, that's all I need.'

'My name's Lieutenant Riordan. Anyone gives you any shit, get the female officer, Officer Cordoza, to contact me, if you can't do it yourself. Understand?'

'I understand. Good luck.'

'*You're* the one wishing *me* luck?'

'If you're hunting that wolf, you will in fact need it.'

'Huh.'

Donal turned away, then walked towards the Janaval, ignoring the looks that the uniformed cops gave him. The traces led this way—

Farther down the road, where traffic had stopped at a barrier, a car caught Donal's attention. Even as he looked up, the familiar finned, sporty silhouette moved, gunning its engine. The Vixen pulled out, hauled a U-turn, and drove away.

There's more than one Vixen in Tristopolis.

But not very many, that was the thing.

He rubbed his face, then returned his concentration to the fading spoor. *Lupine* spoor. The prints led to a brass-and-glass hatch set into the sidewalk. A quick route down to the basement levels?

But a uniformed doorman was already heading towards Donal, his gaze flickering, taking in Donal's frayed black running-suit.

'Sir? Can I help you?'

'Yeah.' Donal held up his badge. 'I need to get down there. Now.'

'Certainly, sir. Right away.'

Twelve

Two blocks over from the accident, on 59th, the Vixen pulled in to the kerb. She knew Donal had spotted her, but didn't think he could be certain it was her, and not some other Vixen.

On the sidewalk, a thirty-ish man in a good suit, looking dishevelled from drink, lurched towards the Vixen. At the tarmac's edge, violet steam rose from ground-level grilles.

'Nice car. I could ... do with ... one like you.'

Her headlights flicked on, glowing a dull, unsettling green that reflected oddly from the surrounding steam. From her engine box, a low subsonic growl enhanced the effect.

'Ugh.' The drunk staggered on. 'Shouldn't ... drink.'

The Vixen turned her headlights off and waited.

Five minutes passed before a faint, translucent outline of a hand rose up through a flagstone. Immediately, the Vixen's passenger door popped open, rising like a bird's wing to reveal the clean, unoccupied interior.

Sorry ...

Slowly, slowly, Xalia's head and shoulders rose through the sidewalk. Then, still mostly submerged below ground, she moved as if through quicksand, somehow broadcasting a sense of painful effort as she wavered, sometimes almost halting, then forcing herself onwards.

When her insubstantial hand touched the sill of the open door, Xalia's image grew denser. For a moment, she simply held on to the dark bodywork. Then she hauled herself out of the ground and into the car, where she lay curled on the floorwell.

Pushed ... too ... hard.

The Vixen's door descended and clicked shut.

You ... warned me. Should have ...

Xalia's form faded to a soft blue glow, scarcely visible to human eyes, had there been any humans to see. She said nothing more.

The Vixen put herself into gear, and pulled away from the kerb. Within seconds, she changed up to second, increased acceleration, and changed up again. She swerved past a boundwraith-driven garbage truck, wove between a purple taxi and a polished saloon, then floored it through an intersection as the lights went to red.

She hurtled through gaps no human driver could have seen, sped twice through crossroads against the lights, and within five minutes had a police cruiser on her tail. But that was irrelevant, because five blocks later she'd lost it, and three minutes after that she was turning on to Avenue of the Basilisks, accelerating hard towards Police HQ.

Screeching, smoke billowing from beneath her wheel arches, she came to a halt before the main steps, and howled her horn as she opened her passenger door.

Amber eyes glowed in the shadows near the steps. One pair, then five pairs became visible. The deathwolves padded towards the Vixen.

'Xal-i-a,' said the biggest wolf, FenSeven.

He turned towards his smaller companions, who nodded. They formed a semi-circle, guarding the car, as FenSeven turned away.

Then he loped up the steps. At the top, the big iron doors were already opening.

In the task force room, Viktor tossed aside the folder he'd been reading. His feet were up on his desk, his chair tilted back. When he turned to look at the clock, the chair creaked but did not give way.

'It's late,' he said. 'You want to go down to the range and let off a few? Or go get something to drink?'

'For *me*, it's late.' Harald looked up from the report he was typing one-handed, his steel-enclosed fingers looking like claws inside the compositor. 'On the other hand, *you* got in when everyone else had finished a day's work.'

'True. You want a hand with that? A bit of help with the commas and shit?'

'I can manage. Also, it's confidential.'

'Even the big words? Maybe use a colon or something?'

'A colon? What, you're selling a constipation cure?'

'See, that's where you go wrong, Harald. If you paid less attention to toilet humour and more to—'

That was when a big, dark shape with amber eyes flowed into the room. Viktor's feet were off the desk in an instant. Harald was already standing, as if he'd teleported from a seated position.

'Need,' the shape said. 'Help.'

'What is it, FenSeven?' said Harald.

119

'Huh.' Viktor could not have named the deathwolf. They all looked the same to him.

'Xal-i-a. Now.'

The last word was a growl. FenSeven turned and loped from the room, Harald right behind him, Viktor cursing as he kicked his chair aside and broke into a jog, following them.

At the lift shafts, FenSeven leaped straight into number 7 without even checking there was a wraith to catch him. Harald and Viktor looked at each other. Then they crossed to number 8, waited a second, and stepped inside together.

'Same floor as FenSeven,' said Harald.

Descending without another word, he and Viktor were already accelerating when they came out into the ground-level lobby. As they ran across the polished stone floor, FenSeven led the way ... accompanied by a glowing wraith-shape, Gertie, coasting at head-height.

'Hey ...' called Eduardo from the desk.

But they were already past him, through the open doors and running down the steps. On the sidewalk, deathwolves were guarding the open door of a stationary Vixen.

'Hades.'

Then Harald and Viktor were on the sidewalk, panting as they halted. Xalia's near-invisible form lay curled up inside the Vixen.

'Shit. What are we going to—?'

Gertie drifted over them, and passed through the Vixen's roof, semi-materializing inside.

Why did you let her go out?

Viktor said, 'She claimed she was all right.'

Harald looked at him.

She wasn't.

'We knew she was injured a few weeks ago.' Harald's voice was soft. 'But we thought she'd recovered.'

Stupid.

'Xalia was working on something with me.' Viktor rubbed his face. 'She— I'm sorry. It *was* stupid not to double-check.'

Not you. Her. Humans couldn't know.

'Ah, damn.'

'How soon,' said Harald, 'will she recover?'

Gertie billowed, rose up a little, then contracted and descended.

She won't.

'What?'

Xalia is dying.

120

Around them, the six deathwolves gave a low moan. Viktor shivered.

'Can't you help?' asked Harald.

Help her die easily?

'No. You know I meant—'

You've no idea what you're asking.

Harald ran a hand through his white hair. Beneath Gertie's glow, his unlined skin shone.

'Then there *is* something you can—'

Stand back. Out of my way.

As he retreated, Harald tugged Viktor's leather sleeve. They moved to one side, the deathwolves to the other, as Gertie's form brightened, pulsed, and brightened once more.

Still glowing strongly, she floated out of the Vixen, bearing the merest transparent outline that was Xalia – at least, all that remained of her in the human dimensions – and rose towards HQ.

Meanwhile, Donal had entered the Janaval Hotel the easy way, through the main doors and along plush corridors, accompanied by the doorman. Together, they stepped through a service entrance that looked like a section of wall, into a white ceramic stairwell. Donal went down first, followed by the doorman, and came out into the bright, white-brick expanse of the subterranean kitchens.

A chef was engaged in a discussion, or perhaps an argument, with his staff.

'—cinnamon in the cream, but less scarab dust in the dough next time, all right?'

'All right, chef.'

'Alexei and Jean-Pierre, you make the dessert for Professor Doubchon tonight. That's the order for Room 917.'

'Chef.'

They turned to look at Donal. He wondered if they could smell the burned-wood stench on his clothes.

'Police. You seen anything strange around here?'

'Um. No.' The chef looked at the others. 'You?'

'No, chef.'

Donal remembered the van driver saying he'd dropped off colleagues who were working here. None of these people were zombies.

'Have you got any—?' But then he felt something in his blood. Pointing to his left, he added: 'The bakers are in there, am I correct?'

'Absolutely, but there's nothing strange in that.'

'No, of course not.'

Donal made a complete turn, taking in the gleaming utensils and work surfaces, the scents of gourmet food: a pot of bubbling bouillabaisse, a block of jellysquid pudding from which waving tendrils extended. One of the staff had paused in the middle of preparing what looked like a breakfast tray of cruciform pastries and strong coffee, despite the late hour.

'The Janaval has guests from all the world.' The chef had noticed what Donal was looking at. 'Even Lightsiders, who find it impossible to synchronize their sleep patterns with, uh, people, who live ... here.'

His voice trailed off, as if he'd only just noticed the paleness of Donal's skin.

'Don't let me disturb you.' Donal turned away, then looked back. 'Maybe a pinch more salt in the fish stew.'

The doorman was standing there, waiting.

'What's your name?' asked Donal.

'Karlen, sir.'

'All right, Karlen. Can you hang around for a while? Just stay there.'

'Whatever you—'

Donal had already moved, rounding a corner of white-brick wall, finding himself before a steel door. He pushed down the handle and walked in, feeling the sensation – *people like me* – washing through his blood. Four zombies turned to look at him. All were wearing white.

Donal closed the door behind him.

'You work for Bertelloni's Bakery, right?' He held up his police badge. 'Lieutenant Riordan.'

'Right.' One of the bakers stepped forward. 'Has anything happened to Wilson?'

'He's the van driver? There's been an accident, but he's fine. A limousine went out of control, hit the van, then turned over. That's what it looks like.'

The four zombies looked at each other.

'I don't suppose,' added Donal, 'you guys have seen anything strange down here?'

'Strange, Lieutenant?'

'There might have been paw prints on the tiles.' No tell-tale flickering of eyes showed in any of the zombies' faces.

But then it wouldn't, would it?

Probably not.

'We saw nothing,' added the spokesman.

He's lying.

I know.

One of the zombies held up the power cord he'd been holding.

'Is it OK to carry on?'

'That depends on whether you've anything to tell me.'

'We don't.'

Perhaps Donal should have brought his Magnus. Then he could have threatened to shoot them.

'All right,' he said.

The spokesman remained where he was, but the other three undid their tunics, pulled them open, then inserted their fingertips into their own chests. With a soft, liquid sound, three zombie chests opened at once, revealing three beating, glistening black hearts.

'You don't have to wait' – the spokesman pointed to Donal's watch – 'until you're entirely depleted.'

'Thanks for telling me.'

The other three sat down cross-legged on the white-tiled floor. Now, as they played out the power cord, Donal saw that it branched, like the nine-tailed whip some of the nuns had used in the orphanage, back when Donal was young. The man nearest the wall plugged in one end, then inserted a lead into his heart, and closed his eyes. The next zombie plugged himself in, and then the next.

'That was an invitation, Lieutenant. Please join us.'

'Some other time.'

'Ah.'

From standing, the spokesman descended in a corkscrew motion to the floor, not using his hands, ending up in a cross-legged position like his colleagues. He unfastened his tunic.

I've offended them.

But the spokesman paused before looking up, and said, 'You've been near Chazley Hardieson, I can tell. His aftershave is unusual.'

Officer Cordoza had identified the dead man in the limo as Hardieson.

'Did *you* see him this evening?'

'Not today. But he's a regular at the hotel. Watch yourself with him, Lieutenant.'

'Why should I do that?'

'You've heard of the Unity Party. They have some rich sponsors.'

'And Hardieson's one of them?'

But the zombie was already plugging himself in, using the same branching cord as the others. Soon, all four were sitting with eyes closed, their black hearts beating in time, their bodies otherwise still.

Donal watched them for a moment, then another, before rousing himself and walking across the tiles to the faint outline he saw there. Paw prints, yes. But they led to a wall. Straight into a wall. And there was something else—

What's this?

At chest height, there was a – feeling? vibration? – that was familiar to Donal.

A wraith has been here.

Even living, Donal had got on with wraiths, just as he knew the name of every deathwolf at HQ. Perhaps it was simply his attitude, but by being sensitive to the presence of wraiths, there had been times when, if a wraith approached from behind, he knew who it was before they manifested themselves in front of him, or spoke inside his mind.

Now, he was almost sure he recognized whatever trace remained in the brickwork.

Xalia.

He hadn't even realized she'd been up to leaving HQ, not after what she'd been through.

She was tracking the wolf.

But Donal had no way of going through walls ... except to use the very ordinary door ten feet away. He went through, into a service corridor. Two, no, three paw prints showed on the floor. They headed straight into the opposite wall.

There was no trace of Xalia here. It was as though she'd started to follow through, then pulled back. As for the wall that the prints led to—

Donal put his hands against it.

Solid.

He would need to check the building plans to be sure, but his intuition told him that beyond this wall was nothing but impenetrable earth. Perhaps, if he called in help from HQ before the traces disappeared, he could get a sniffer wraith to follow.

When he looked down again, the paw prints had evaporated from the floor.

'Shit.'

No doubt, when he went back into the kitchen, the prints would have disappeared from there as well.

Donal went back out into the street. The ambulance had gone, and a lobster truck was using its claw to raise the wrecked limo from the tarmac. Officer Cordoza and Sergeant Tsatslinx approached him.

'Found anything, Lieutenant?' asked the sergeant.

'Nothing.'

'That's what we thought. Whatever the van driver thought he saw, maybe it was a firework or something that distracted Hardieson's man, turned the car over.'

'It didn't look like the van driver's fault.'

'No, it wasn't.' Sergeant Tsatslinx glanced towards Potbelly Frank. 'And that's how we're writing it up, Lieutenant. Just another TTA.'

'Yeah.' Donal realized that Cordoza was staring at him. 'Good work, Officer.'

'Thank you ... Sir.'

So she suspected he knew something. Too bad, because Donal wasn't about to share what he thought about traces that no longer existed, implicating an imaginary creature in the death of someone who thought zombiekind were undeserving of human rights.

It's task force business.

That was the other way of looking at it: not that he was betraying his badge, but that he was keeping secret the work of a federal task force whose remit extended deeper than investigating a possible traffic accident.

'D'you need a lift anywhere, Lieutenant?'

'That would be— No. Thanks.'

'You sure?'

'Thanks, but you guys need to clear the scene. Carry on keeping the streets safe.'

'We can do that.'

Donal watched from the sidewalk as the bakery van drove off, followed by the lumbering lobster truck, and finally the police cruisers. More pedestrians came on to the sidewalk. Soon, everyone would have forgotten what had occurred: just another Tristopolitan tale among millions.

He turned, and went back inside the Janaval Hotel. Karlen the door-man hurried over.

'Sir? Was there something else?'

'A couple of things. Do you know a Mr Hardieson?'

'Oh, yes. Dines here regularly. Used to come with a gentleman called, um, Doctor Carlendo, I think it was.'

For the second time since his resurrection, Donal discovered dark blood could run cold.

'Well dressed, silk cravat, grey hair, goatee?'

'That's the gentleman.'

Cortindo.

'And you've not seen this other guy recently?'

'Not for months, sir.'

Probably not since Donal had killed the bastard. He doubted whether Malfax Cortindo, since his resurrection as a revenant, had returned to any of his old public haunts. He probably hadn't come back to Tristopolis at all.

A pity.

Donal stared at the plush lobby and the corridor beyond, with its row of gleaming boutiques, right here in the hotel.

'You guys have a men's tailor here?'

'Um ... Certainly.' Karlen's eyes flickered towards Donal's running-suit. 'Um, everything's rather ... rarefied, sir.'

'I'll bet.'

Donal reached inside his wallet, and pulled out a white credit card. Until inheriting Laura's wealth, he'd had no idea such things existed. But a hotel doorman should know what the gleaming white card represented.

'Oh. I didn't ... Sir.'

In less than a minute, they were standing inside a hushed tailor's shop, and the proprietor was summoning a wraith to take Donal's measurements.

'And what is it that sir would like, exactly?'

'A new suit. Probably a shirt and tie, the whole works.'

'For what kind of occasion, might one ask?'

'Something suitable for City Hall.'

'City Hall?'

'Yeah. Tomorrow morning' – Donal checked his watch – 'I'll be shaking hands with Mayor Dancy.'

'Most excellent. The mayor buys *his* suits right here. Come, let me show you some fabrics.'

The wraith wrapped itself around Donal, measuring, then drifted off.

'Oh, about the cut of the suit ...' said Donal.

'I'd recommend a conservative style for City Hall.'

'Yeah, and it needs to a conceal a gun.'

'Certainly, a ... gun?'

'Big one. Magnus.' Donal held an imaginary firearm under his left arm. 'Fits right here.'

'Um ... Of course, sir. Splendid.'

'Maybe a special inside pocket for a spare clip.'

'A ... clip, sir?'

'Thing with bullets, you know?'

The tailor pulled out a silk handkerchief, and dabbed his forehead.

'Certainly. Any other special requirements, sir?'

126

'I was thinking it could be dark blue. Or should it be grey?'

'Perhaps sir could—'

'Maybe one of each.'

'Of course. Whatever sir would like.'

Thirteen

At one a.m., Kyushen Jyu decided he wasn't going back to sleep, at least not soon. He rolled from his low cot into a kneeling position on the floor, and stood up. Soft displays shone and moved inside the lab, along with the pervasive hum of working systems, a sound he normally found relaxing.

'It's the neural association,' he told himself. 'Nothing more.'

Police HQ was linked in his mind to feelings of overwhelming guilt, remembering the prisoner leaving the interrogation room on a stretcher. In that room, Kyushen's displays had contained a masterful excavation of the man's mind, with scrolling frameworks of golden script delineating thought-feeling-memory structures, within the modelling paradigm of Image-Inclined Hexing. Templates and metatemplates, instants conforming to adaptive patterns – all of it was perfect, and none of it mattered as they carried the man out.

'The lieutenant said I'll be reading a manual.' Kyushen's voice seemed to shiver in the shadows. 'Nothing more.'

He was wearing shorts and a T-shirt. Pulling on a lab coat, he went out barefoot, into a corridor that was deserted at this hour. There was a staircase, and Kyushen went up it slowly, climbing three floors, and coming out into the corridor that linked the Acute Ensorcelment Ward to Psychomantic Counselling. There would be Night Sisters on duty.

'Hello, Dr Jyu.' It was Sister Felice, one of the prettiest Night Sisters, who greeted him. 'Nice to see you at this time.'

'Just a small bout of sleeplessness, nothing more.'

'You want some tea?'

'I'm not sure. Yes, OK.'

She fetched a mug of tea from the nurses' station, and handed it to him. The mug bore the St Jarl's coat-of-arms.

'Tell me about it, if you like.'

'What? Oh. You treated Lieutenant Riordan, didn't you?'

Her colleague, Sister Lynkse, was suddenly standing nearby. Kyushen hadn't noticed her approach, but he wasn't startled. He was used to Night Sisters.

'Donal Riordan,' said Sister Felice. 'I was his primary nurse.'

'Uh-huh.' Sister Lynkse hummed softly, then: 'And she was a little smitten, as you doubtless realized.'

'Um.' Kyushen blinked. 'Sorry. I didn't—'

'Ignore Lynnie. What about Donal Riordan?'

'I did some . . . work for him. A few weeks back.'

'Prisoner interrogation,' said Sister Lynkse. 'Accidentally inducing Basilisk Trance. I heard about it.'

Sister Felice raised her fine eyebrows.

'He wants me to do more work.' Kyushen stared at the mug in his hands. 'Just technical advice, see. Translating jargon, explaining concepts. Should I have agreed to it?'

'You talked to him on the phone?'

'Yeah, and I'm seeing him tomorrow. Today, I mean. This morning.'

'How did he sound?' asked Sister Felice.

Sister Lynkse smiled.

'Like an integrated personality.' Kyushen took the question as a professional query. 'Strong, obviously different from before.'

'In what fashion?'

'Excuse me? You know what happened to him, don't you?'

'You mean the fact he's now a zombie?'

'With Commander Steele's heart inside him,' said Sister Lynkse.

'What a bitch.' Sister Felice's gaze swung back to Kyushen. 'His luck, I mean. Not the dead commander.'

Kyushen looked at her.

'Sure,' he said.

At two a.m., the assassin rose briefly to a shallow trance, checked his watch by feel, listened and opened his sensitivity to touch, to vibration, polling the environment for anomalies that might indicate his presence here was known.

Nothing manifested itself in his hypersensitive perceptions.

Motionless beneath his chameleon shroud, the assassin slowed his breathing once more to a level that would make him appear almost dead. A calming, silent automesmeric mantra caused his heart rate to decrease. He was deep inside trance.

In nine hours, it would be time to snap awake, filled with alertness and energy, with implacable resolution, and the desire to prove once again that he was among the best at what he did.

At three a.m., Viktor walked from Seven Blades, a Pneumetro station on the Purple Line, to the street where he lived. He'd stayed at HQ even longer than Harald, but finally – in the absence of news about Xalia – he'd decided to go home, half hoping that a gang of street youths, or perhaps even a more professional armed robber, would see him as a potential victim en route. But there had been no opportunities to vent his stress in the way he did best.

Here, though, in a street lined with old tenements where few cars were parked, a black – no, dark burgundy – limousine waited. Viktor shrugged inside his leather coat, loosening his shoulders, refreshing his neuromuscular memory of his holstered twin Grausers. Then he crossed the street, to the opposite side from his home.

The driver's door cracked open just as Viktor reached the cover of a rusted old Cosma Breeze. He ducked low, then threw himself into a sideways roll, coming up into a kneeling position with one Grauser drawn.

'Hey, is that you, Viktor?' The voice was slow, a little slurred, and half-familiar. 'It's me, André.'

'Huh.' Viktor rose far enough to see the bearded face. 'You're out of your neighbourhood.'

'Uh, well, we was waiting for you.'

'I'd never have guessed.'

'I know. Say, aren't you supposed to live on this side of the street?'

'You haven't changed,' muttered Viktor, stepping clear of the Cosma. 'You're not here by yourself, I wouldn't think.'

André had forced his bulk out, opening the door wide to do so, showing Viktor that there was no one else in the front of the limo. The solid black windows revealed nothing about who might be riding in back. But Viktor had heard rumours about André's new employer.

Then a window rolled down, revealing a lined face, and coiffed white hair in which several diamonds glinted. Her clear eyes focused on Viktor.

'You can relax, Detective Harman.'

'Yes, ma'am.' Reaching into his pocket, Viktor found his shades. 'Let me come over.'

He slipped on the round-lensed dark glasses as he neared the limo.

'I just wanted to talk to you for a spell,' the woman said.

Viktor's motion faltered.

'Sorry, Detective. Put it down to an old lady's sense of humour.'

'Ma'am.'

'You know what my interest is. How is he doing?'

130

'I don't know who ...' Viktor growled, then shrugged. 'All right. Look, your interest may be obvious. It's also a bit late, don't you think?'

'Viktor Harman.'

Shaking his head, Viktor took a step back, holding one hand up before his eyes, still with a Grauser in the other.

'Relax. I agree with you, Viktor. Even I can have regrets, you know.'

'Can you help a wraith in distress?'

'A wraith? That's somewhat ... outside my area of expertise.'

'Then you've nothing to bargain with, ma'am.'

'I just want to know how Lieutenant Riordan is doing. Nothing more.'

'The only person who knows that is Donal himself. Your – interest – is not in *his* best interests, is it?'

The old lady looked away.

'Damn you, Viktor Harman.'

'Ma'am, I don't think—'

'Don't worry, that wasn't a curse. You may be right. You also know where to contact me, if you find you need my help.'

'Help in what way?'

'You look big and scary, Viktor, but there's a mind behind that frightening face. You know what the Unity Party is up to. People like the lieutenant may soon need all sorts of help. That's when you pick up a phone and call me. Good enough?'

Viktor looked down at the Grauser in his hand, then tucked it into the shoulder holster where it belonged. He looked at the old lady through his dark lenses.

'Yeah. Good enough.'

'And good luck to you.' The dark window started to rise. 'André, I'd like to go home now.'

'Yes, missus. I mean ma'am.'

Viktor saw the beginnings of a smile on her face before the window closed, forming a curved black mirror in which his own reflection was distorted.

'You look after yourself, André.'

'Yeah, Viktor. You too.'

André ponderously climbed back inside the limo, started it up, and drove slowly down the street. Viktor watched it go, took off his shades and pocketed them, then headed for his front door. He took out his keys with his left hand, and held his right hand under his coat, on one of his Grausers. Nothing in the environment was triggering an alert in his subconscious, but these were weird times.

He entered without problem, and scanned every dark room in the house before using the bathroom, fetching a pint glass of squealberry juice from the old refrigerator, and carrying it into his bedroom. There, he lit three purple candles before undressing and climbing into bed. A fat volume lay atop the coverlet, and he opened it, laying aside the wormskin bookmark.

The book was called *Resurrection Code: Towards a Theory of the Undead Mind*, and it was written by Professor Blaustein of Donnerheim University. It was also required reading for several of the most prestigious doctorate programmes in the Federation.

Viktor took a sip of juice, turned back a few pages to check the chapter title – 'Recursive Metatemplates and their Boundary Conditions' – before returning to the place where he'd left off. He checked the time on his alarm clock, shrugged, and then commenced reading.

At four a.m., Donal was exploring a room in his apartment, a room that he'd scarcely been inside. In a small chest of drawers, he found bundles of soft, dyed mammoth wool in a dozen different colours, along with knitting-needles, a just-started scarf of burgundy and silver, and a knitting-algorithm, printed in purple on flimsy paper, that indicated how the scarf-knitting was to proceed.

Laura. I didn't know you could do this stuff.

It was nothing that Donal had ever watched or thought about, but the instructions were mathematical in a way that reminded him of his brief stint in Artillery School, and it wasn't as if he needed to sleep. There might be more useful ways for a zombie to pass the night-time hours, but what the Hades – no one could be serious twenty-five hours a day, nine days a week.

He picked up the needles and wool, read the algorithm through once more, and then tried to follow the instructions.

It took seventeen minutes to get the rhythm going, and two minutes more to decide that however much amusement he might get by taking his knitting in to the task force office, it wasn't for him. He threw everything back into the drawer.

Then he went back to his bedroom, pulled out the brushes and moth-oil from the bedside cabinet, and sat down on the bed with his Magnus in his lap. He stripped the weapon fast, and began the cleaning, treating it as a ritual to calm the mind, like a master carpenter maintaining his tools.

At five a.m., Harald came awake. He'd slept atop a thin mat placed on the hard, polished floor of his large, near-empty bedroom. Rolling to his feet, he padded to the bathroom, and came back drinking a tall glass of water. Then he reached into a bowl of flower blossoms, plucked one red petal, and placed it on his tongue. He stood still, eyes closed, allowing the petal to dissolve.

When it was done, he began to move. First moving his head through a complicated horizontal infinity-sign shape, like a Zurinese dancer, then a similar motion in the vertical plane, before moving to his shoulder joints which he likewise rotated with a complex, sophisticated movement. As he worked down his body, he loosened like a whip, perhaps a snake. Finally, he worked even his toes, ending the first phase of his routine.

During his time in the Marines, the High Command had brought in Zurinese meditation masters to improve the concentration of long-range penetration and sniper units. Those masters had taught, among other things, several series of static, difficult physical postures. Afterwards, the PT instructors had evolved their own dynamic forms, flowing from one posture to the other in continuous chains that took their troops to new levels of agility.

Not everyone followed the routines rigorously, but many did. Harald had continued on a daily basis since.

Exactly twenty-five minutes after beginning the flow, he had finished. Breathing normally, he carried his empty glass back to the bathroom, refilled it from the tap, and drank once more. Then he returned to his minimalist bedroom, carrying his telephone on a cord from the hallway, and placed it on the floor. He sat down beside it, folded his legs into lotus, and began to eat the remaining blossoms from the bowl.

At 5:50 exactly, the phone rang.

'Hello, Livitia.'

You knew it was me.

'You keep your word. You said half past, and it's fifty minutes past the hour, exactly.'

Livitia was a freewraith assigned to Anti-Ensorcelment, usually working out of the 77th but with authorization to enter HQ as necessary. Harald had known her for two years.

Xalia's unchanged.

'Damn. What's going on?'

Gertie took her to a deeper level still, into what you might call a ... cell, I suppose. Not a material cell, you understand.

'That's a bad sign, is it?'

There are strong healing capabilities, that's the good news.

'And the bad news?'

The fact that Xalia needs them. And using the deep places can be dangerous.

'Ah.'

Gertie allowed me to scan a little. Then she threw up thick barriers, shutting me out, along with any other nosy wraith.

'And Xalia's hurting?'

Yes.

Harald listened to the strange harmonies singing on the line, trying to interpolate among Livitia's words, parsing the meaning of what she *hadn't* said.

'Gertie's acting as healer, is that right?'

I didn't exactly rotate into this continuum yesterday. But even I don't know how many centuries old Gertie is.

'Uh-huh.'

Harald, I personally could not heal Xalia. Neither could my peers.

'But you think Gertie can.'

I don't know.

Again, Harald said nothing, as overflowing energies sang on the line.

What is it about a wolf, Harald?

'In what sense?'

Whatever she was working on.

'I wasn't working with her.' Harald thought about Viktor's guilt at allowing her to help him. But on what assignment? 'I hadn't realized it was important.'

Had something more than physical movement brought on Xalia's deterioration?

Perhaps it isn't important.

'Livitia, is there anything I can do? Me or any of the team?'

Again, the swirling, random songs filled the receiver's earpiece.

I'm sorry. There's nothing.

And then, all that sounded was the buzz of a disconnected line.

'Shit.'

With blinding speed, the back of Harald's hand cracked against the flower bowl, sent it spinning across the room, spilling petals, bouncing off the wall when it hit. It rolled on the floor, and came to a halt.

Harald, still in lotus, closed his eyes. He breathed slowly, concentrating on nothing else for twenty breaths. Then he opened his eyes, unfolded himself out of the lotus position, and moved forwards on hands and knees, picking up the flower blossoms from the polished floor.

Cleanliness and discipline. In the end, they were all you had when the world turned into a shit blizzard around your ears, collapsing on everyone you cared for.

At six a.m., Alexa sat down at her desk in the task force office. A clockwork disc rotated up out of her desktop, then unfolded its claws, offering an orange envelope: today's mail.

'Oh, is this for me?'

Her smile was bright as she took the envelope. The claws folded up and the disc twisted down into her desk.

'Well.' She put down the envelope and stared around the empty office. 'Just me. Guess I'll put the coffee on.'

She did that, waited until it was ready, then poured herself some. She used Donal's favourite mug. Or rather, what had been his favourite mug, before he—

For a moment, a frown clamped her forehead. Then she gave a big grin.

'Feeling good feels good,' she told herself.

She carried the mug back to her desk, and sat down.

'Looks like a memo.' She picked up the envelope. 'Shame. Not a card from Skinny-Ass Riordan. Oops.' She giggled. 'Tsk, tsk, Alexa. Bad girl.'

Then she undid the envelope, and pulled out the memo. It was dated yesterday.

TRISTOPOLIS P.D. MEMORANDUM
recipient eyes only

Sepday 37 Hextember 6607

To: Detective Alexa Ceerling badge # 78$\sum$2

Re: medical examination 38/06/6607

Please report to Dr T. Gamarlov in medical room 17 for a standard medical examination, at 10:00 hours on Octday, 38 Hextember. While it is two months before the next round of Sergeant's Qualifying Exams is due to start, I have a particular interest in knowing that you will check out.

Regards

A Vilnar

A. Vilnar, Commissioner of Police

'Signed by the commissioner himself.' Alexa folded up the memo, and placed it inside her handbag. 'Arrhennius Vilnar, you are such an old sweetie.'

Inside her desk, she had several textbooks from her home collection. She pulled out the one entitled *Three Stripes, First Time*, being a crammer for the sergeant's exam that had been written by one of the officers who devised the syllabus. Ignoring the coffee mug on her desk, she grabbed her handbag and the book, got up, took another look around the office, and walked out.

The first elevator was ready, and as she stepped inside the shaft, she said: 'Take me to the canteen, please. I've got some reading to do.'

No reply came from the wraith, but Alexa ascended to the canteen level, and semi-materialized hands pushed her out into the lobby.

'Thank you!' she called back.

Grinning hard, she headed for the hot drinks table, and poured herself a cup of hot blue chocolate. Then she walked through the big, noisy canteen until she found a small table behind a pillar, tucked out of general sight. There, she sat down.

Sipping her hot chocolate, she opened the book at page one.

At seven a.m., Harald was on his Phantasm IV, chin close to the handlebars as they took a howling turn into Hoardway. In half an hour, the traffic would be too heavy for fast manoeuvres; but now the motorbike, its bony carapace elongating slightly, drew closer to the road surface and poured on the speed.

They were nearing St Lee's Cross – long known as Sleaze Cross – where even now, with the night over, tired-looking prostitutes were standing at the corners, handbags at their feet. Here, Harald hooked a ninety-degree turn on to Behemoth Broadway, and sped up once more. Hoardway and BB formed an X over the mostly rectilinear grid of the city. A 135° turn took him into Third Avenue, where the traffic would be lighter than on First.

Knowing they were nearing the end of their run, Harald-and-Phantasm, acting as one joint organism, fully opened out, screaming at massive speed along the still-deserted canyon of Third, with the great dark towers on either side, and the always-purple sky forming a longitudinal strip overhead. The motorcycle roared with pleasure as they took a turn at maximum acceleration, hurtled onwards for two blocks, then screeched into First Avenue, forever called Avenue of the Basilisks.

Soon they were heading downwards on a ramp that led deep below ground, to the subterranean parking caverns that connected to the minus-fifteenth floor of Police HQ. Harald and Phantasm slowed, calming down as they navigated past the pillars, through scanfields guarded by sociopathic flamewraiths looking for any excuse to flare up, past a fluttering horde of venomous strikemoths, and into the parking levels proper.

They came to a halt in their usual bay, number 317, where Harald sat with his palms against the bony carapace that was still warm after their run. There was communion and comfort in sitting here, but Harald had work to do. He swung his leg over, dismounting.

'Take it easy.'

He touched the handlebars, and the bike quivered once, then grew still. Then Harald looked towards the walkway that led to HQ, where FenNine and several of his pack were on guard. Somewhere inside, but Hades-knew-how-many levels deeper, Xalia was undergoing an ordeal that no human could appreciate. He hoped to Thanatos that Gertie was going to be able to do something.

'I've no idea what's happening today,' he added. 'If I'm not back here by twenty o'clock, you might as well go home by yourself.'

The Phantasm gave a brief flicker of its headlight.

'All right.' Harald started towards the walkway. 'Let's hope today goes better than yesterday.'

At eight a.m., Sister Felice got into bed. Her room was on the third floor of the North-East Tower, and quiet enough. Like most Night Sisters, she could sleep even when there was noise. Now, she curled on her side, twitching her nose, then relaxed. Her breathing slowed.

After ten minutes, she sat up in bed, pulled her feet up close, turned around a full circle, then lay down on her side once more. For a moment she wondered whether she ought to live in the city, where she would have more opportunities to bump into interesting people, like a certain police lieutenant who worked out of Avenue of the Basilisks. But then there would be the twice-daily bus journey back and forth, and the ambient noise while she tried to sleep during the day. Night Sisters might be capable of sleeping anywhere, but here in St Jarl's, surrounded by forest, there was a sense of calm that was only occasionally broken by banshee howls, or the soft, haunting cries of pterafalcons overhead.

'Go to sleep,' she murmured.

From somewhere outside the building, gravel scrunched.

'Now what?'

It should have been a perfectly normal sound, nothing to prevent her relaxing into the refreshing sleep she deserved. But she sighed, rolled out of the bed, and padded to the window. She pulled open the heavy, dark-blue drape.

'Visitors,' she said. 'For some patient.'

There were three of them, dressed in suits and expensive moleskin overcoats, carrying briefcases as they left their car. Perhaps they were a legal team, visiting a patient to discuss litigation regarding an accident. Except that they appeared hard-faced in a way that reminded her of Donal Riordan, especially when he—

'Enough, already.'

She closed the drape, and returned to bed, climbing in and curling on her side.

'Sleep,' she told herself. 'Just sleep.'

Her eyes closed, and her breathing slowed.

At nine a.m., Donal was standing in the huge reception area of Police HQ. Beside him, Eduardo, his torso rising from the massive granite block as always, was reading today's list of visitors.

'Dr Jyu, is that who you're waiting for?'

'That's the man.'

'Oh, I thought it must be some broad.'

'Excuse me?'

'I mean the sharp suit, Lieutenant. How much did that set you back?'

'Hades.' Donal shook his head. 'I'm going to City Hall this morning. Today's my big day. I get to shake hands with the mayor, I think.'

'You're my hero, Lieutenant.'

Donal couldn't think of a fast reply to that.

'So where is Kyushen? I thought he'd be—'

The big doors swung open. Kyushen Jyu stood there gulping, surrounded by deathwolves. They growled, turned, and went back down the steps. The doors closed behind Kyushen.

'Er ... Morning, Lieutenant.'

'Sign in,' called Eduardo. 'Here.'

He lowered a clipboard by a length of black string. From his height above the granite block, he wasn't capable of leaning over far enough to hand things down directly.

'You're a hemimorph,' said Kyushen. 'Fantastic.'

'What?'

'The transition gradient is spectacular. The most interesting I've seen. Would you mind answering a few questions, maybe let me take a scan of—?'

'Nice to see you, Kyushen.' Donal tapped the clipboard. 'And the commissioner's dying to meet you.'

'The commissioner?'

'Just sign.'

While Kyushen wrote his signature on the list, Eduardo looked down at Donal.

'Hey, Lieutenant. Apparently I got a terrific gradient.'

'Everyone says so. I read it on the men's room wall.'

'They can kiss my block.'

'Uh-huh. Hang loose, Eduardo.'

'Yeah, you too.'

'Come on, Kyushen. You're going to love this techie manual.'

'It sounds exciting.' There was no irony in Kyushen's voice. 'I mean, really fascinating.'

From his granite block, Eduardo laughed.

'Have a lovely morning,' he said.

Fourteen

The big manual lay waiting on the desktop. Kyushen stared at it while Donal was introducing him to the commissioner.

'Take my chair, Dr Jyu,' Commissioner Vilnar said. 'There's coffee on the credenza, sandwiches, and if you ring 5999, someone will fetch anything else you need. And there's a private bathroom through that door on the side.'

Donal smiled, realizing that Kyushen was barely processing the commissioner's words.

'All right,' the commissioner continued. 'Lieutenant, let's go.'

'Sir?'

'I'd like to get to City Hall in plenty of time. You're travelling with me, remember.'

'Yes, sir.'

Donal looked around the office, nodded to the black visitor's chair – it tipped its back in return – at the brass orrery with the coffee tray beside it, at the other clutter. There must be confidential files in here, and the Old Man was planning to leave a talented civilian here for several hours; but it was obvious that Kyushen would not be alone. He would simply be the only human in the room.

'Let's go.' When Commissioner Vilnar reached the inner door, the ciliaserpents reached out to brush his skin – a gesture that normally accompanied the delivery of neurotoxin. 'Don't worry, I'll be fine.'

He stepped through, and Donal followed, happy that the ciliaserpents drew back from him. As they passed along the short exit tunnel, there was a sense of movement and preparation inside the walls, as though inner defences were arming themselves. The jagged-toothed doors opened, Donal followed the commissioner into the Surveillance Department, and the doors clamped shut behind him.

They walked past the monitors and out to the elevator shafts.

'Commissioner? Is everything OK?'

'That question already assumes things *aren't* OK. Which means I'm beginning to have hope for you, Lieutenant.' Commissioner Vilnar pointed to shaft 7, which was dark and therefore not in use. 'If you get back from City Hall before I do, check up on Gertie, will you?'

'Yeah. Of course.'

'And now, I'm going to see Commander Bowman for a brief chat. I'll join you down in the parking garage.'

The commissioner stepped into shaft 9, and descended from sight.

'Huh.' Donal waited for the next shaft to brighten, then stepped inside. 'Hey, Freda. How's it going?'

Good. Which floor?

'Parking garage, please.'

All right.

The wraith began the descent smoothly.

'What's up with Gertie, Freda? Do you know?'

Wraiths' problems.

'Excuse me?'

He was dropping faster now.

There are some things we don't like to discuss.

'Oh. I beg your pardon.'

Ask me again tomorrow.

'Right.'

The deceleration was harder than usual, for Freda. She propelled him out onto a grey landing.

'Thank—'

Freda was already gone.

'—you.'

Donal frowned at the lift shaft, then headed into the garage, where maintenance mechanics were working on several cruisers. Two purple golems were holding a car above their heads, while a human engineer inspected the exhaust.

A wraith swirled out of the chassis.

The suspension is shot as well.

'No surprise. Take a look at that.'

We'll need to replace the whole thing.

'You're telling me. What do these guys *do* with their vehicles?'

Part of Donal was tempted to tell them about life on the streets, but they probably already knew. Some people like to complain.

'Hey, Sam.' He stopped in front of the supervisor's office, with its open half-window that stretched from waist-height to the ceiling. 'How's life with you?'

'Great, Lieutenant.' The grey-skinned man looked up from the grease-stained manual he was reading. 'You need a cruiser to take you to City Hall?'

'How come you know everything that happens round here, Sam?'

'Need to have your finger on the pulse, don't ya? I keep telling these guys' – with a wave towards the engineers and golems – 'that it's *sensitivity* that keeps machinery working. But do they get it?'

'Could be you should read 'em poetry,' said Donal. 'Maybe paint the walls pink. Get a record player and have some opera playing. Like that.'

'Uh-huh. I'm glad you're taking my predicament seriously, Lieutenant Riordan. So, what about that car?'

'Don't need it, my good man. I am riding with the commissioner in his very own official limousine.'

'Oh.'

'Hades, Sam. Piss on my parade, why don't you?'

'Sorry. But have you met the Old Man's driver?'

'Can't say that I have.'

'Well, see, come and tell me afterwards what a bundle of laughs he is, and I'll tell you how lucky you were to spend time with him.'

'I'm not sure I understood that.'

'See? That's why I do what I do, and you're just a lowly lieutenant, sir.'

'No one in his right mind would have my job, for sure. Take things easy, Sam.'

'You too. And say hello to the mayor for me.'

'I'll be sure to do that.'

Donal went through the service area into the special-vehicles section, a part of the garage he had rarely been inside. Scanfields played across his skin, and he walked past two signs reading *Danger: High-Tension Hex,* and into a half-lit section of parking bays. There was only one car here: Commissioner Vilnar's limousine. It rode low on its suspension, as armoured vehicles do.

The driver got out. He was tall and wore a grey uniform, with unusual shades – heavy, curved and dark-blue – hiding his eyes.

He doesn't have any.

It was a strange thought to have.

Say what?

Yet Donal was absolutely certain.

Take off his glasses and you'll see something, but you won't see eyes.

There was a sense of presence about the man. Perhaps it was that, or perhaps it was the shadowed surroundings, that made Donal think of his confrontation with Malfax Cortindo among the subterranean reactor piles.

'My name is Lamis. Pleased to meet you, Donal Riordan.'

'Yeah. Likewise.'

'Have you ever seen a mountainous landscape, Lieutenant?'

'Uh ... Yes, I have. That's a strange question.'

'People talk about rising to a new peak, when they undergo personal change. But really, it's better to think of descending to a new valley. To a stable low-energy configuration.'

'Excuse me?'

'You must have studied basic thaumodynamics. Systems fall to the lowest energy configuration available to them in their current context.'

Donal stood in place, subtly lowering his centre of gravity, gathering himself.

'I also learned how to communicate with people. How about you, Lamis?'

'Ah. But I sense you're in an unstable equilibrium, that's the thing. As if you're on a mountain peak, and there are several different ways you could tumble down.'

'You're telling me life's uncertain?'

'Something like that. Also that you're changing inside, if you haven't already worked it out.'

'Very fucking funny. I've been a zombie for a matter of weeks. And you're a real bunch of laughs, Chuckles.'

'I *was* renowned for my sense of humour, Lieutenant.'

'You've got to be joking.'

'But not recently. I'm talking ancient history.'

'Now you *are* having a laugh.'

'Am I?' Lamis's face looked like stone: a statue with wraparound shades. 'As I said, it's been some time.'

Suddenly, there was movement behind Donal. He turned.

'Gentlemen.' The bulky figure of Commissioner Vilnar was standing there. 'Are you getting to know one another?'

'We're bosom pals already,' said Donal.

Lamis silently bowed his head, then climbed inside the limo and pulled the driver's door shut.

'Isn't he supposed to hold the door open for us?' Donal asked.

'Lamis?' A broad smile stretched across Commissioner Vilnar's face, and then he chuckled. 'No, not Lamis. He doesn't do that.'

'And what does he do?'

'That would be telling. Now, get inside, Lieutenant. We've a ceremony to go to.'

'Yes, sir.'

In the great skull building of City Hall, perhaps a third of the way up the cranial interior, Detective-Two Orla Gilarney was walking along an interior balcony, staring down at the near-deserted atrium, anticipating the swirling mass of bureaucrats and politicians and reporters who would soon infest the place.

She was carrying a small torch in her inside pocket. Her father had given it to her on making D-2. Proud of her promotion, he'd given her a practical present, one that could become a weapon, held in her fist. He'd told her that getting Grade Two was a big step up.

He hadn't said she'd be playing minder to a politicians' circus. City Hall was an interesting place, but Gilarney wanted real work, an actual case to grab hold of. Still, she brought logic and an eye for detail to everything she did, so she glanced over the wall-mounted weapons and banners, and checked the big, muscular uniformed officer who was watching over the entrance to Third Corridor.

'Hey, Brodowski.' She knew both brothers' names, but not how to tell them apart. 'You staying alert there?'

'Yes, Detective. Things are quiet.'

Behind Brodowski, a plainclothes man from the 83rd nodded.

'Nothing suspicious,' he said. 'Apart from maybe the food in the main hall. You seen those little squirmy things on sticks?'

Gilarney was amused but didn't smile.

'Forget the food. Keep alert.'

'Yes, ma'am.'

She walked past him, into the gloomy corridor he'd just exited. As she neared a large display case, she pulled the torch from her pocket and thumbed it on. The necrotonic battery should be almost fully charged; but when she directed the torch towards the display's interior, the bulb dimmed to a soft orange, then went out.

'Thanatos damn it.' She shook the torch. 'Cheap Illurian crap.'

Putting the torch away, she leaned close to the glass. Nothing suspicious was visible.

'Huh. All right.'

She returned to the corridor entrance, where Brodowski and the plainclothes were still standing.

'Where's your brother, Brodowski?'

'Pulled admin duty, poor bastard.'

'Maybe he's the lucky one,' murmured the plainclothes.

Gilarney shook her head, although she understood the guy's feelings. Soon enough, down in the foyer and inside the main hall, there would be a blossoming of egos, a hot-air fest with much mouthing of loud, calculating falsehoods and self-serving tales. The commissioner and that lieutenant – Riordan, that was it – would be in among the high-flying crowd, smiling and shaking hands, working the slimy politicians and lobbyists for their own gain.

There was nothing worse than politicians, apart maybe from has-been cops pretending to be politicians. Just the thought of it made her ass ache.

'Keep watching, guys.'

She touched the weapon holstered high on her hip. Then she headed for the stairs, determined to check out the main hall, and not just the buffet where the plainclothes had found squirmy things on sticks. She would be checking ways in and out – ingress and egress, as they drummed into her in the Academy – and firing random questions at anyone she saw, because she'd always been thorough.

The whole circus made her sick; but she had a job to do.

Donal sat straight-backed in the rear of Commissioner Vilnar's limousine. Up front, Lamis had a sure control of the heavy vehicle, taking it quickly along the dark helical tunnel that was pretty much the commissioner's private route into and out of HQ. Inside the tunnel, strange forms rotated in shadows, and Donal caught glimpses of twisted geometries beyond normal dimensions, as if he could almost see into the wraith continuum.

'There are more safeguards here,' said the commissioner, 'than you can sense.'

'Shame those safeguards don't extend to the officers who report to you.'

After a moment, the Commissioner said, 'You're thinking about Alexa Ceerling.'

'Yes.'

'You have my word, she's undergoing scans this morning. Whatever it takes to rehabituate her, the Department will make sure it happens.'

Donal remembered his own time in Rehabituation in St Jarl's: the painful re-knitting of mind and body, restoring old neural patterns as his injuries healed.

'Rehab isn't trivial.'

'I know.' Commissioner Vilnar flexed his right hand, and his voice grew distant. 'I *do* know.'

Outside, flat white sparks flew through the viscous air. Donal realized they were driving through some kind of hex field, but not a kind he was familiar with.

'The geodesic gets interesting,' added the commissioner. 'I mean the line of least resistance through the defences.'

'What do you—?' Donal stopped as he realized the car was upside down, hurtling along what should have been the ceiling. 'I see what you mean. But I've a different kind of question for you.'

'Really.' There was a faint smile on the commissioner's blocky face. 'I see you're not perturbed by sudden shifts in gravity.'

'Neither are you. What about the rest of the task force, Commissioner? What have you got them into?'

For a moment, no one could speak, as the hex-field howled inside the car as well as outside. Then Lamis had steered through the energy-maelstrom, and was directing the car up an ordinary straight ramp leading to the street.

'You mean, have I potentially sacrificed them, the way I did Alexa? The answer's no.'

'That's what I meant.'

'You don't sound reassured.'

'I'm not.' Donal stared at the commissioner's face. 'Because I can't tell whether you're telling the truth.'

'Ah.' The commissioner glanced at the partition separating them from Lamis. 'Despite your new abilities.'

In the driving mirror, Donal thought he saw Lamis's reflection shift, and an unsettling grin stretch across that sepulchral face.

'I haven't seen much of my colleagues recently,' said Donal. 'Until now, I assumed they were taking downtime by themselves, given the opportunity. But I suspect you have them working on something.'

'They're reporting to Commander Bowman, as are you, in theory.'

'And Pel Bowman does what you tell him to, sir.'

'So you're calling me "sir" again. It's nice to get some respect.'

'I'm not in the m—'

'My apologies, Riordan. With all the subterfuge, sometimes I get too hung up on playing games.' Again, the commissioner flexed his right hand. 'Life used to be simpler.'

'And I used to have one.'

'A life? Ha.' The commissioner gestured, and the driver's partition and all the windows grew solid black. 'So, consider this a form of briefing. What do you know about Mayor Dancy's policies and alliances?'

'Not much.'

'In your self-interest, you might want to change that. The City Council now has a lot of Unity Party members, some occupying key positions.'

'And the mayor's one of them?'

'Actually, he's the city's main chance of holding them back. So how good are you at memorizing names?'

'Try me.'

'All right. First, let me tell you the businessmen and women who still support Mayor Dancy. The richest is—'

Commissioner Vilnar continued to reel off a list of people, their attitudes and assets, their points of weakness, and their probable alliances. He briefed Donal on the good guys first, then the Unity Party activists, including several prominent industrialists who had made no public proclamation of their allegiance to the party. Donal wondered how he'd come by the information, but had no opportunity to ask as he tried to process the sequential auditory data into some kind of mental model he might remember.

At some point, he realized he'd constructed an imaginary castle in his mind, and the suits of armour and shields and other artefacts bore names – a moustachioed chess-piece called Alfredo King, an old sofa with curved arms labelled Sophie Armitage – so that he could imagine himself walking around, seeing the objects and touching them. It was a visual/tactile catalogue of everything the commissioner was telling him. A part of Donal's mind was astounded at what he himself was doing.

Then the limo's internal partition descended.

'It's ten minutes to ten, and we're nearly there.' Lamis's voice sounded right beside Donal's ear, although the man was still up front. 'Two blocks to Möbius Park.'

'You'll need to prepare yourself,' the commissioner told Donal. 'This is going to be an ordeal, but you're tough enough to take it.'

'The scanwraiths?'

'No, I mean the journalists. And remember, when a camera points at you, look happy. A big, cheesy grin is what we want.'

'Hades.'

In the front seat, Lamis chuckled, a sound like ice cubes spilling over knucklebones.

What am I doing here?

Donal placed his hand over his zombie heart. Under his left arm, the familiar Magnus was solid.

'And Riordan? Don't shoot any reporters.'

'I'll do my best not to.'

'Unless it's Carlsen from the *Gazette*. I've never liked his stuff.'

'I thought he was a sports writer.'

'He is. Did you see what he wrote about the Spiders losing last week's game?'

In a gallery inside City Hall, inside a display case, there was a subtle shifting of fabric. Under the chameleon shroud, the assassin's eyes were open. Now, still lying in place, he commenced a series of subtle exercises designed to lubricate the joints, awaken his tendons, and ready himself for fast, fluid motion.

Sections of narrow rod set into his skin-tight suit – one rod along the back of his right triceps, another along his forearm – and the narrow, hard rectangle set across his shoulder blades – did nothing to hamper the sophisticated biokinetic routine.

The assassin smiled.

Alexa was sitting with her legs crossed, her exam crammer in her handbag, her stare unfocused, not grinning. But she was wearing a soft smile, a relaxation of the facial muscles.

At three minutes to ten, a white door opened, and a grey-haired doctor beckoned. For a moment Alexa thought he meant her, and she uncrossed her legs, preparing to stand. But a heavyset man, a uniformed sergeant, was already on his feet, heading for the medical room.

'How have you been, Sergeant?'

'Much better, Doc. I did like you told me, and—'

The door closed on them.

'Never mind,' murmured Alexa. 'I'm happy just relaxing here.'

There was only one other patient sitting in the reception area, and he was a thin plainclothes guy who Alexa didn't recognize, reading a book he'd picked up from the low table. From here it looked like a cookbook, which made her smile because there were back-copies of *Ambush & Infiltrate* on the pile, which most cops would have reached for automatically.

Then the door to room 17 opened, and the doctor who looked out was slim and bearded, maybe a few years older than Alexa.

'Hello,' she said. 'Are you Dr Gamarlov?'

'Sure. And you're Alexa.' He glanced towards the plainclothes man, then winked at Alexa. 'I'm just guessing, you understand.'

'Good guess, Doctor. So where would you like me?'

'Come on inside.'

She entered a room filled with apparatus. There were several distinct brass frameworks, each big enough for a person to clamber inside. A bone-and-metal chair sat in the centre, its feet set into narrow rails laid in the floor, ready to move into any of the scanning frames.

'Cosy.'

'Not really. Perhaps I should get some tips from you on how to lighten the place up.'

'Why, yes.' Now Alexa's smile was brilliant. 'I'd love to help you, Doctor.'

'Um.' Dr Gamarlov rubbed his dark beard. 'Why don't you start by taking a seat?'

'Why not?'

She gave a giggle, put her handbag down, and then climbed onto the seat. She wriggled, aware of the tightness of her skirt as she sat.

'It's a little cold, Doctor.'

'Hmm.'

'I notice you're not married.'

'No.' He smiled, and held up his hand. 'Not married.'

Several certificates on the wall identified him as *T. Gamarlov, M.D.*

'And no nurse in the room to chaperone us, Doctor? I'll submit on one condition.'

'I'm not— All right. What condition?'

'You tell me what the T stands for.'

'Oh. It's Troy.'

Alexa liked that.

'Well, Troy. What are you going to do with me?'

'I'd like to start' – he gave a fake cough – 'with a highly sophisticated diagnostic technique. I've been working on this one for years.'

He reached for a tiny rubber-ended hammer.

'You've got to be kidding.'

'Uh-uh. It's a cliché, but it's still a real test, you know?'

'Do I have to cross my legs?'

'Yes, please.'

Alexa was conscious of the way her thigh stretched the fabric of her skirt as she moved.

'Um ...' Dr Gamarlov – Troy – tapped once, waited, then tapped again.

There was no reaction.

'Oops.' Alexa giggled. 'How would you like me to react?'

'Er, not everyone responds the same way. Perhaps we'll abandon that one, shall we?'

'All right.'

Troy took a metal wand that was connected by spiralling cord to a boxy silver apparatus inside which graph paper stretched between two rollers. He thumbed a button on the wand, and the graph paper began to move.

As he ran the wand over Alexa's torso, ink-needles inscribed jagged graphs on the moving paper. When the wand passed above her skull, the needles went crazy, swinging through ever wilder amplitudes until Troy ended the scan. Then he stared at the graph and blew out a breath.

'Is everything all right?' asked Alexa.

'It's widespread.' Troy shook his head. 'You've got apoptosis throughout your body.'

'Oh. Is that serious?'

'Millions of cells are dying.'

Alexa shivered.

'Are you sure?'

'The tests are accurate.' Troy grinned. 'Which is just as well, don't you think?'

'What do you mean? How long do I have to live?'

'Well, if your cells continue to commit suicide … Maybe sixty years, is my guess.'

'I— Did you say sixty *years*?'

'Sure. It's when your cells *stop* suiciding that you have to worry. That's when they form tumours, didn't you know?'

Alexa blinked.

'You mean I'm all right?'

'Full of health … and I'm sorry. Just a little doctor humour.'

'Thanatos.'

'So what I need you to do next, Alexa, is put your feet flat on the floor—'

'OK.'

'—and relax, because this is going to be fine.'

Anklets and bracelets snapped into place, fastening Alexa into the chair.

'Are you sure about this, Doctor?'

One of the brass frameworks began to hum.

'Perfectly.'

The chair gave a slight jerk, then began to move along the floor rail, heading for the apparatus. The hum became louder.

'I don't like this, Troy.' She had to raise her voice almost to a shout.

'It's going to be all right.'

And now the sound became an overwhelming vibration in her bones, her teeth, her nerves, her arteries. Even her vision blurred, as if her eyes were being shaken into jelly.

'No ...'

Her whimper was lost in the torrent of force.

Fifteen

The outer walls ringing Möbius Park were ancient and protective. Smooth gargoyles were etched against the outer battlements, faint outlines of entities that had not detached themselves and moved for centuries, perhaps millennia. Whether they were almost faded from existence, or might someday reconstitute themselves from the strange stone of the defences, no one knew.

The roadway that ringed the park was wide and rarely suffered traffic jams, for drivers preferred to find other routes through this part of Tristopolis. The old residential towers in the surrounding area were uniformly grey with black windows, occupied by ancient families with wealth. Inordinate levels of secrecy surrounded their occupations and their social circles.

As for the park itself, despite the warning notices set in the flagstones of the sidewalk beneath the outer walls, police cruisers still occasionally found melted puddles in which a few bones or teeth might remain, along with the untouched ladder or rope or other equipment they'd foolishly thought might help them scale the walls. There were rumours, never confirmed, that sometimes a lone person might be walking alongside the wall, *not* attempting to break in, yet suddenly disappear in a swirl of dark movement. Seconds later, a howl might sound from inside the grounds, accompanied by flashes of white and crimson light.

What Donal knew for sure was that ectoplasma wraiths did float among the trees, with licence to feed upon intruders. According to the rumours that he sometimes believed – and mostly didn't – the innocent people who disappeared were never identified, never reported missing by family or colleagues or neighbours. In his sceptical times, Donal considered this proof that the people had never existed; but at other times he wondered.

Lamis drove up to the forbidding mass of the North-North-East Gate, and stopped. In the back, neither Donal nor Commissioner Vilnar said anything. The air grew very cold inside the car. Then the faintest of wraith shapes passed through, and the temperature dropped further. Condensation gathered inside the windows, and the commissioner's breath steamed. Donal merely smiled, and perhaps even the commissioner's eyes revealed a flickering discomfort at Donal's amusement.

Then the gates rolled open, and the limousine moved forward.

'We drive along Widdershins Walk,' said Lamis, 'then take a sharp turn, back along Clockwise Crescent.'

Donal rubbed condensation from his window.

'You can hardly see out there. And we're driving on gravel.'

The trees were black. He could see no sign of the ectoplasma wraiths.

'I think I can find the way,' said Lamis.

'I've heard that the leaves of those trees can slice through metal.'

Lamis shook his head.

'If I drive off the road, the trees would be the least of our worries.'

'Welcome,' said the commissioner, 'to high society.'

Donal said nothing as they continued for five slow minutes through dark parkland, until they came out into the landscaped area before City Hall.

'It is quite something, isn't it?'

'Yeah,' said the commissioner. 'I get blasé, but it really is.'

Lamis took the car to a controlled stop.

'Have a nice time.'

'We will.' Commissioner Vilnar opened his door and stepped out. 'Riordan?'

'Yes, sir.'

Donal got out, and pushed his door shut, looking around. Given that they were an hour early, he hadn't expected many cars, but there were two dozen limousines and several sporty saloons.

He followed the commissioner to the foot of the broad, bonestone staircase leading up to the open maw of the great skull, the main entrance to City Hall. Flamewraiths danced in place along each side of the staircase, their orange glow failing to illuminate the dark parkland. Coloured light spilled from inside the great stained-glass windows of the skull's eyes. The noise level was rising as a group of men and women – mostly men with their ties loosened and top shirt-buttons open – approached Donal and Commissioner Vilnar.

'Remember what I said about not shooting them.'

'Hades,' said Donal. 'You won't change your mind?'

A magnesium-white flashbulb popped, and then another.

'Say, Lieutenant. How does it feel to get a commendation?'

'And what about having your colleague's heart inside your—'

'Is it true what they say about you and Commander Steele? Were you and she—?'

Donal felt a strong hand take hold of his elbow, and allowed the commissioner to steer him through the pack of reporters, and climb the steps at surprising speed, until they reached the entrance.

'Thank you, sir.'

'You're welcome.'

Perhaps three minutes later – even Donal's time-sense was disoriented – they were inside the main hall, having been announced by someone in a white-and-gold uniform: a major-domo or maître-d' or some such. Thinking about it, Donal wasn't sure he knew what a major-domo was.

Chandeliers with blazing flamesprites in diamond holders hung on bronze chains from the ornate ceiling. Rows of long tables with white tablecloths filled the place, gleaming with polished cutlery that bore the civic Tree Frog symbol. Black daffodils in crystal vases added a piquant tone to an atmosphere filled with expensive fragrances and aftershave. The buffet was at the rear, providing stand-up snacks for those who'd missed breakfast or needed a second. In an hour, formal lunch would be served directly at the banquet tables.

This is awful.

A press of bureaucrats separated Donal from Commissioner Vilnar. Donal took the opportunity, and moved sideways through the crowd until he came to a vacant area of floorspace. He wasn't sure what he hated most: the fishtank greed, or the appalling security context. The surrounding park made a terrific outer defence, but in here, the geometry was wide open, the crowd careless and unaware of the dangers of self-absorption.

Forget the dignitaries. Let's check the setup.

From the commissioner's briefing in the car, Donal had an idea of why so many people were here, and frantic to do some kind of business. This was the peak time for lobbying, with local elections imminent, and new budgets to negotiate for city departments, in particular for subcontracting work to local companies.

And check things better than the last time.

He remembered the Diva's corpse, splayed on a cold stone floor.

'Lieutenant Riordan?' Behind him, a woman spoke, her tone nicely modulated. 'So you're here.'

Closing his eyes, Donal tried to recognize the voice.

'Jo Serranto.' He turned to face her. 'Has the *TG* made you managing editor yet?'

Serranto's laugh was pleasant yet controlled.

'The *Tristopolitan Gazette*,' she said, 'needs all the good street reporters it can get. Even me. Even' – with a flickering glance towards a group of dark-suited men – 'in times like this, when unbiased reporting is so hard to achieve.'

'You mean, get past the advertisers.'

'That's very cynical, Lieutenant.' Serranto touched his sleeve. 'So, is there any juicy gossip from the Department that I should know about?'

Donal squinted, trying to identify the people Serranto had glanced at. He recognized no faces, but the black tiepins and lapel badges were familiar. The Unity Party were here.

Those bastards.

But here was another puzzle. Why was Serranto being so friendly? They'd met each other, but the personal warmth was new.

'No gossip,' he said. 'You don't seem to like the Unity Party.'

'They're spreading like a rash. That's what we wordsmiths call a simile. It's also' – a faint whiff of alcohol was on her breath – 'one of the nicer things I might say about them.'

'Say, but not write, is that it?'

'You're pretty sharp, aren't you?' Serranto stared at him. 'I'm not sure I'd realized that.'

'I've always had the highest opinion of you, Ms Serranto. So is there any street scuttlebutt that you know and I don't?'

'Off the record?' she said, and laughed.

'That really has to be my line. But whatever.'

'Well.' She touched his upper arm once more. 'Watch your back in the Department. Those UP bastards are everywhere.'

'Is there anything I should know specifically?'

'You think I wouldn't warn you if I knew details?'

Donal looked at her carefully, processing her stance – the centre of gravity too high up for a fighter, but just fine for a woman trying to look good – plus her fast, shallow respiration, and the splotches of colour on her skin.

'I think you're a good person,' he said. 'And probably courageous.'

Her eyes widened as she ducked her head back, just a little.

'Thanks.'

'Look, I'm going to take a walk around by myself. Just checking the security.'

'Aren't you supposed to be a guest? Mayor's commendation and all that?'

'I'm still a cop.'

'Hmm. I guess you are.'

Her lips remained slightly parted, and Donal didn't need zombie acuity to understand the signals she was sending.

A contact on the Gazette *could be good.*

Wondering whether he was manipulating her or being manipulated, he said, 'I'll call you next week. Maybe take supper in the Obsidian Gull?'

In his case, that meant picking at food, maybe taking one or two bites.

'The diner on 57th and 8th?'

'That's the one.'

'I'm sometimes in that neighbourhood.'

'Some time next week then. I'll ring you, and we'll have an omelette together.'

'You might have a deal, Lieutenant.'

She turned away before he did.

At the buffet, Donal saw plates of lizard legs, trays of still-moving segments of eel and foamworm, dark-blue pastries filled with white cheese, apples baked in tangwood resin, and sandwiches made with pink bread.

'Singularly unappetizing,' said a cold voice, 'even if you needed to eat.'

'Yes.' This time Donal didn't have to work at identifying the speaker. 'How are you doing, Dr Thalveen?'

'The same.' The black-coated medic gestured towards several men who were scarfing down lizard-salad sandwiches. 'The UP are out in force.'

'Someone's already pointed that out to me.'

'Ha. I noticed you talking to Jo Serranto. And was she friendlier than you expected?'

'Why should she be?'

'Well' – the curvature of Thalveen's lips was too unfriendly to be called a smile – 'I wonder if you've ever heard the term *zombiefucker*?'

Donal stared at him.

'Sorry,' Thalveen added. 'Was that offensive? I'll tell you what should offend you. Those manipulative bastards over there.'

Several UP men, glasses of Altrinian champagne in hand, were talking to a man who wore no tiepin or lapel badge.

'What about them?'

'See how they're persuading him to join them? Lower city taxes for corporations, the hint of a promise of a future contract. That's all it takes.'

'His arms are crossed,' said Donal. 'Defensive.'

'Don't believe what you learned about body language in police academy, Lieutenant. What matters is the dynamic, the ways in which the speakers match each other, or not.'

'Shit.' Donal could see that Thalveen was right. 'And they're doing it deliberately.'

'Now you're getting it.'

'Is that a compliment, Doctor?'

Donal could do without the cynical commentary. If he thought that all zombies invariably became like Thalveen, he'd be tempted to off himself right now.

At that moment, Thalveen turned around on his heel, with no word or change of expression, and walked away from Donal.

For Hades' sake.

It was enough to drive anyone into the arms of the Unity Party. Donal wondered what the reaction would be if he turned up at a UP office and tried to take out membership. Perhaps if he got bored, he might try it.

For now, he walked along the hall's perimeter, along the right hand wall as he stared at the stage with its empty podium, and the table of honour spanning most of the stage's width. White doors in the side wall obviously led to the kitchens. Donal could tell as much by the scents and faint sounds. Two uniformed cops stood at the doors, hands clasped behind their backs, watching the growing crowd of glad-handing politicos and business folk.

'All secure?' asked Donal.

'Yes, sir. Nothing interesting going on.'

The other cop nodded towards the civilians. 'I'll second that.'

'Me too.' Donal looked back to the rear of the hall. High overhead were ornate balconies, looking unoccupied. 'Someone checked them out?'

'Uh-huh. Got plainclothes guys in the corridors, too. I mean, at the balcony entrances.'

'And the kitchens?' Donal gestured to the white doors beside him. 'They been given the once-over?'

'Sure.'

In the crowd, Donal could see the pale, black-clad figure of Dr Thalveen heading this way.

'Perhaps I'll take a look myself.'

One of the cops glanced at the approaching doctor.

'Don't blame you, Lieutenant.'

'No civilians allowed through, except catering staff. Right?'

'You got it, sir.'

Donal went through. There was a long, curving corridor that he followed to its end, and came out into a white-tiled kitchen that reminded him of the Janaval Hotel. In an instant he knew that there were twenty-three people here.

Twenty-four.

It took a further three seconds for Donal to understand what he'd just experienced: the immediate knowledge that twenty-three zombies were present – *my own kind* – and then the visual confirmation of the living human who appeared to be the head chef. Two more living people came through from a back room. All of them, human and zombie, were dressed in white.

'Is there anything you need?' asked the nearest.

'Just checking. Everything's all right?'

'We're cool,' said a female zombie.

'Actually, we're cold,' another said.

The one who'd spoken first removed a shoe and pulled at its toe, so the sole began to part.

'Hey, what's this got in common with a zombie?'

'I give up,' said her colleague.

'They're both cold and soulless.'

All of them turned to look at Donal. He stared back.

Zombie humour.

'Thanks for the warmhearted welcome,' he said.

Several of the zombies mimed applause as he left via a side exit. Here, the floor was carpeted, and it came out into a polished corridor that led to the great atrium. Donal followed it, nodding to cops he knew, avoiding journalists, and reached a staircase that he began to climb.

From three floors up, a plainclothes female officer was watching him.

At least someone's alert.

He reached for his badge, but she called down, 'It's all right, Lieutenant Riordan. I know who you are.'

'Thanks.'

Half running up the steps, he reached the woman.

'I'm Gilarney,' she said. 'D-2.'

'Good to meet you, Detective. You in charge of the setup?'

'Yes, sir.'

'I need to walk around, get away from the politicians. I'm just curious, not checking up.'

'Of course.' Her facial muscles tightened. 'I understand.'

If Donal had remembered to inhale after speaking, he would have sighed. He breathed in now, and said, 'Honestly, I'm just heading for a men's room.'

Beyond Gilarney, two uniformed cops looked at each other. One leaned close to whisper, assuming Donal wouldn't be able to hear, *'I didn't know zombies gotta piss.'*

'Shit, no one knows what they do.'

'Dunno if they do that, either.'

'Do what?'

'Go for a—'

'Hey, guys.' Donal strode towards them. 'You keep things buttoned tight, OK?'

'Sure, Lieutenant.'

'Do that, and I'll keep my mouth shut about what you've been up to.'

'Er ...'

Both cops flushed slightly.

'Stay alert.'

As Donal continued past them, he wondered what exactly they *had* been up to. But they seemed competent enough in a gross sense – able to follow clear orders – and Gilarney appeared to have organized a decent setup. Each choke point had observers, so that when the crowd grew heavier just before the luncheon's start, and when the main hall was packed during the proceedings, no obvious outsider could make progress.

He walked along a gallery, half taking in the weapons displayed on the walls, the banners that formed a visual code for the values that soldiers had fought for, and so often died for. It was an interesting contrast to the self-serving manoeuvring taking place in the main hall, where the goals were self-interest and the weapons were false smiles and misused finances.

Past the gallery, to the right, there was a right-angled turn to a long corridor, its walls and carpets red. At intervals, there were dark drapes along the right-hand wall. He guessed that these were entrances to the guest boxes, set high up on the side wall of the main hall, looking down on the stage. During theatrical performances – he had a flashback to the Diva's singing, that aria that made him weep – there would be high-paying theatregoers seated here. For a political lunch, that was not a consideration.

'Lieutenant Riordan here. I'm holding out my badge.'

He pulled back the first curtain.

'Hey, Lieutenant.' A uniformed sergeant looked up, binoculars in hand.

He was sitting on a hard-backed chair. 'You're up for a commendation, right?'

'That's me.'

A rifle leaned against the balcony wall. The sniper-scope was polished.

'Looks like you're nicely set up here.'

'Me and the boys.' The sergeant – his name-badge read Parnell O'Doyle – gestured to the next two boxes. In each one, a young-looking cop with buzz-cut hair and a sharpshooter rifle was seated. 'They're fast, too. And pretty good at noticing anomalous behaviour.'

'Any particular threat you've been warned against?'

'Nah, just the usual. Elections coming, weird shit on the streets. Nothing that you might call specific.'

'Still.' Donal looked down at the glittering banquet tables, the small figures of the politicos and bureaucrats. 'Makes me feel better, you being here.'

'Uh-huh. I tell you what, Lieutenant. I'd rather be up here than down with that lot.'

Donal winked at him. 'That's why I'm talking a walk around. Security's not my problem. Not this time.'

'Yeah. That D-2, Gilarney. Seems to know what she's doing.'

'Pretty much what I was thinking.' Donal took another look down at the polished silverware, flamesprites dancing in candelabras, the gleaming dishes that waiters and waitresses were setting in place. 'Hades. I guess I need to get back down in the frenzy.'

'It's tough at the top.'

'Yeah.' He saw Commissioner Vilnar talking to Mayor Dancy, surrounded by well-dressed men who seemed to have a penchant for nodding in time whenever the mayor made an elaborate point. 'I'm so glad I'm nowhere near the top of the shit-pile.'

'Buried in the middle is better than underneath. I think.'

'Maybe. Take it easy, O'Doyle.'

'You too, sir.'

Donal glanced at the other two boxes before he left, but the sharpshooters were staring down at the increasing activity below, which was exactly what they were supposed to do.

Good enough.

He retraced his way to the end of the corridor, stopped and frowned, then carried on back to the main atrium. The uniformed cops made no attempt to talk to him as he descended the steps to the next level, where Detective Gilarney was checking the next floor down. He joined her.

'Good setup,' he told her. 'I might have put a man in the gallery, next floor up, but you work with what you have.'

Gilarney's face tightened.

'Thank you, sir.'

Donal nodded, then headed down to the ground level. On the atrium floor, he watched the civilians crushing their way into the main hall, then realized he could avoid it no longer. He was going to have to go back inside.

It could be worse. If he hadn't joined the cops, he might have ended up working with these people all the time. Hades, he might have become one of them.

That's a deeply awful thought.

He was almost smiling when he entered the viscous flow of people, made his way into the main hall, and heard Commissioner Vilnar's voice boom out: 'Ah, Lieutenant. Come and meet these good people.'

'My pleasure,' said Donal.

It was a lie worthy of a politician.

On the twenty-third floor of Police HQ, in the medical reception area, the door to room 10 opened. A female doctor poked her head out.

'Detective Dalk?' she said. 'I'm ready to—'

Her voice attenuated to a soft exhalation. The thin man she'd been addressing was sprawled back across several seats, a torn book clenched in his unmoving hand. The eyes that stared upwards were opaque, the transverse split across his throat took in both carotid arteries, and the blood spray had spattered the ceiling as well as the walls and furniture.

'Oh ...'

The doctor's gaze tracked the blood, a trail of crimson footprints leading towards the dead man, coming from room 17. It took her logical mind a moment to process the implications; then she walked slowly to the half-open door, and pushed it inwards.

'Dr Gamarlov? Troy? Are ... ?'

There was no point in continuing with the question.

'Oh, sweet Thanatos.'

Inside the room, geometric brass frameworks dripped with redness, were draped with gore, a scattering and spreading of parts that was the clearest expression she had ever seen of a medical school dictum, that the human body is mostly warm liquid. It was not a lesson she needed to learn.

And Dr Troy Gamarlov's head stood atop a groaning graph machine, now drenched in red, its needles struggling to scratch through viscous blood, recording information that no one, least of all Gamarlov, would ever read.

Sixteen

In City Hall, Detective Orla Gilarney stalked the third floor gallery.

'Where the fuck are you?'

Lieutenant Riordan, damn him, had said that he'd have placed a man in the gallery, as well as at the other choke points. But she had placed *two* men here, and if this turned out to be deliberate insubordination – being a woman in the Department could be tough – she was going to see Prigolin and Letharque before a disciplinary board.

'Shit. Shit.' Taking a right turn, she walked down the corridor, and called out: 'Gilarney here.'

When she pulled open the first curtain, only Sergeant O'Doyle was in the booth, which was where he was supposed to be.

'Everything OK here?'

'Absolutely.'

'You seen Prigolin or Letharque?'

'No ...'

'My problem. You carry on here.'

'Yes, ma'am.'

She went back to the gallery to look for the men's room. If she found them taking a piss at the same time, forget the disciplinary board. She was going to kick them so hard in the balls they'd be excreting through catheters for weeks, maybe for ever.

'Thanatos damn it.'

The man who held out his hand was pale for a living human. His chin was tilted up, as if he were sniffing the air and didn't like the results.

'—Assistant Mayor Van Linder,' the commissioner was saying.

'I'm honoured.' Donal shook the man's hand. 'Good to meet you.'

'Always a pleasure to meet an heroic officer.' Van Linder's eyes were as hard and shining as polished ore. 'Of any description, in these trying times.'

Behind Van Linder, two of his aides gave the tiniest of smirks.

'Very trying,' said Donal. 'I've heard of illegal evictions, even, that we're failing to resolve. So far.'

'It must be a constant struggle,' answered Van Linder, 'to ensure that *people's* rights remain inviolate.'

'The law is clear on everyone having rights.'

'Of course, dear fellow, just as legislation is subject to change. It's a human artefact, after all, not a force of nature.'

Donal started to reply, but Van Linder turned away then, as several businessmen approached. He'd definitely lost that one.

'Good,' murmured Commissioner Vilnar, leading Donal away. 'Well done, Riordan.'

'I didn't exactly convince him.'

'But you didn't punch him out. I'll live with that much victory for now. '

Donal walked with him for a bit, then noticed another press of people up ahead.

'Hades. Now who do I have to talk to?'

'Mayor Dancy. Don't worry. He approves of you.'

So Donal had a politician's approval.

Wonderful.

At least he could despise Van Linder with a clear conscience. What was he supposed to make of a slimeball who was on his side?

'Mr Mayor,' said the commissioner. 'Let me present—'

Back on the gallery, Detective Gilarney looked again at the places where Prigolin and Letharque should be standing. The men's room had been empty, which was no relief because it left her to wonder where in Hades they had—

'What's this?'

There was a glass display case, something she'd walked past a couple of dozen times today, but the interior was different. Artefacts were arranged on top of a velvet cloth that rose up behind to form a backdrop – but a lumpy, misshapen one. She tried the knob that opened the glass door, but it was locked.

For a second, she stared at the velvet.

'If I'm wrong . . .' Slowly, she pulled her handgun from her hip holster. 'Fuck it.'

Reversing the grip, she smashed the glass apart. Careful of the shards, she reached in and pushed aside a heavy silver plate, then grabbed hold of the velvet and pulled.

'No ...'

Still holding the velvet cloth, she took four paces backwards, and yanked hard.

'Fuck.'

The gun was the right way round in her hand, although she could not recall changing her grip. She stared for another second, and then another, and then she yelled out as loud as possible:

'Officers down!'

Broken and splayed, the two corpses were a tangle, impossibly contorted to fit into the space inside the display.

'Officers down!'

She sprinted to the atrium.

'Officers down!'

All around the building, silver and blue glinted as cops whipped out their guns.

A flashbulb popped as Donal shook hands with Mayor Dancy. They were standing next to the banquet table on the stage, and the mayor pulled out a chair.

'Please, Lieutenant. I'd like you to sit next to me.'

'Is that what the seating plan says?'

'Balls to the seating plan.' Mayor Dancy grinned, then winked at the commissioner. 'I learned a long time ago when to break the rules.'

'All right,' said Donal.

'Don't worry about eating the food. Everyone's so busy manoeuvring' – the mayor nodded towards the swirling crowds as they congregated around the tables – 'they'll get indigestion anyway.'

Mayor Dancy had what the orphanage nuns used to call a silver tongue.

Still, perhaps he's not all—

Donal dropped to a crouch and swivelled, staring towards the rear of the hall.

'Lieutenant? Is there a reason for—?'

But Donal could hear a distant, *'Officers down!'*

Without thought, his hand was inside his jacket, going for his Magnus.

From his balcony, Sergeant O'Doyle had his rifle to his shoulder, scanning for trouble through the scope, seeing nothing.

'What's going on?' called one of the sharpshooters to his left.

'Keep looking.'

O'Doyle kept his finger outside the trigger guard, knowing that an accidental discharge above a crowd of dignitaries would be disastrous. But the words that had yelled in the distance were replaying in his mind, causing an adrenaline surge to beat them all.

Officers down.

The assassin hung in a horizontal cruciform position, only inches beneath the main hall's ceiling, his feet pointed towards the marksmen in the boxes, his left hand pointing towards the stage. He tilted, so that his arm was at a descending angle. Then he made a subtle movement with his shoulders, and there was the softest of clicks.

His arms were now firmly in line, as the rifle components laid across the backs of his arms and shoulder blades snapped into place, creating one solid weapon. The barrel ran the length of his left arm, the firing chamber across his back, and the balancing rods that acted in lieu of a stock across the back of his right arm.

A harness held him in place, from gekkopads with a breaking strain approximately that of twenty heavy men. And the assassin was light.

He steadied himself.

Swirling panic was spreading below, pandemonium caused by a woman calling 'Officers down', but that was all right. His instructors had taught him that order is a faultline between areas of chaos; adaptation is the ability to flow along the cracks.

Steady.

The assassin looked down the length of his arm, using his left forefinger to aim. He'd intended to do this during the speeches and medal-giving, during the shaking of hands when the impact would be greatest; but this would do very well.

He exhaled.

Steady.

And curled the middle finger of his right hand.

The sound was a crack, triggering Donal's sprint towards Mayor Dancy, knowing that it meant—

No!

—the bullet had already struck, as arterial blood fountained from the mayor even as Donal's shoulder knocked him back, pushing him out of the—

Shit.

—way as two more impacts smashed blood from the mayor's ribs, then took away half the man's jaw as—

166

Shit. Shit. Shit.

—Donal brought his Magnus up, desperate to acquire the target, wondering where the Hades the shots were—

Vilnar!

—coming from, as the commissioner's temple exploded into pink mist.

The sharpshooters were swinging their rifles wildly, trying to find the incoming fire's origin, arcing left to right, sweeping from low elevation to high, looking for the outline of a rifleman.

One of them accidentally pulled his trigger, and a champagne bottle erupted on a table below. Men and women screamed, falling back, staggering as they tried to get away.

Donal was likewise swivelling back and forth, Magnus in a two-handed grip, looking for the killer, seeing nothing.

Two more shots ripped into the fallen commissioner.

It was appalling. There was no place a killer could be, not from the geometry of the shooting, unless—

Just as Donal started to look up toward the high ceiling, a hand grasped his ankle.

'Do ...nal.'

Commissioner Vilnar, his skull torn apart on both sides, was staring up at him.

'Oh, Hades.' Donal dropped to one knee. 'I can't—'

'Take ... this.'

The commissioner released Donal's ankle, moved his trembling hand towards his own face. Bullets did strange things when they bounced around inside living skulls, but this was a necrotonic sniper round that had gone straight through, and Donal had no idea how the man could still be moving.

Stunned, Donal had no way of understanding what happened next.

No.

The commissioner's fingers curved like claws.

Don't—

Claws that hooked around his own right eyeball.

Don't do—

Fingertips that pressed into the socket, and clenched.

That.

And ripped out his eye. His own eye.

'Take—'

The commissioner's hand fell to one side as a hissing breath left his mouth, the final exhalation of a corpse.

A corpse whose eyeball was in his hand.

On the ceiling, the assassin writhed through a series of twists that disassembled the weapon into disconnected segments across his back and arms, and turned him face-up to the ceiling with the harness looped around wrists and ankles, tight against the four gekkopads.

Then, one hand-plus-opposite-foot at a time, he rotated the gekkopads free, slid an arm's length along the ceiling, and repeated in fluid iterations, moving at a surprising speed.

Commissioner Vilnar's eyeball was in Donal's left hand, his Magnus in his right, as he jumped down from the stage and moved toward the hall's centre, in the midst of a growing space as the crowd seeped away, forming knots of panic at the exits. The other cops maintained their positions, searching for the shooter, except for half a dozen men now shielding Mayor Dancy's corpse, far too late.

Two men in dark suits were heading for the kitchen door. Donal didn't recognize them, but the two uniforms on guard simply nodded as the men drew near.

Not them. Somewhere else.

Then Donal caught the flicker of motion, high above the bright chandeliers.

Impossible.

A shadow that looked like a man was spidering across the ceiling.

'O'Doyle!' called Donal, but the panic-chaos of yells drowned him out.

Hades.

One of the sharpshooters might manage this shot, but from the floor, using a handgun with blazing chandeliers in the way—

Relax.

Donal slipped the slick eyeball inside his jacket pocket, and stood calmly erect, raising his right arm in the classic target-shooter's stance, so rarely appropriate for combat.

Exhale.

Emptying his lungs, calming his zombie metabolism, Donal's aim moved through a slow arc, ready for the—

Automatic gunfire exploded from Donal's left.

Hades.

He threw himself sideways to the floor, rolling, gun-hand rising as he acquired the targets of two white-garbed men – *zombies* – with machine-guns in hand, one spraying across the men trying to guard the mayor's corpse – the bodyguards screamed as rounds tore red chunks from their bodies – while the other zombie whirled, firing into the howling crowd, and he was the one that Donal took aim at.

And stopped.

In the high-speed turbulence of the moment, Donal was the only living being who was statue-still, finger on the trigger with his target in sight, but not firing.

He's ensorcelled.

But there were dozens of other cops in the hall. In the next second, crashing gunfire built to a crescendo as both zombies blew apart in grey sprays of dark blood, and then they were down and the threat was gone, and finally the shooting ceased.

Donal rolled to his feet and took a few paces towards the remains. Both uniform cops who'd been guarding the kitchen entrance were sprawled across the floor. They'd perhaps been the first to die.

Shit.

Whipping his head back and his weapon up, Donal took aim at the ceiling. But there was nothing there.

Shit. Shit. Shit.

He glanced back at the stage, now piled with bodies so that he could no longer see the dead commissioner. Touching his pocket, feeling the strange contents, he tried to work out what to do.

Curtains hung down beside the high boxes. The walls were covered with ornate decorations.

'Thanatos. I must be insane.'

But the civilians were still pressing and crushing each other at the entrances – lying flat would have been more sensible – and there was no way to move fast, not by any normal means, and Donal knew for sure that no one else had spotted the moving shadow.

Glimpsing Dr Thalveen, who stared from a crouching position beneath a table, Donal holstered his Magnus as he began to run. There were tables in the way, laid cross wise in his path, and Donal jumped and tucked his chin down, shoulder-rolling over the first table, across the cutlery and smashing plates, then striking the ground with his feet. A discarded chair stood in front of him and he used a jumping lunge, one foot on the chair-seat, launching himself to land on the tabletop, leaping to the next table, and from there to the wall, grabbing hold of a heavy purple curtain, and hanging for a second, to check it could bear his weight.

Then Donal began to scramble upwards.

The assassin sprinted along an empty corridor, came to a gallery, and ran straight through, knowing he had no time to—

'Stop!'

It was a female cop, her firearm trained on him, her grip two-handed, steady as she tracked his movement.

But the assassin twisted, rolled across the floor towards the cop, and came up whirling, slapping the weapon as he whipped a scything kick into the lower ribs – they cracked – and he brought his other hand up in what could have been a devastating palm-strike to the jaw, but stopped just before contact.

There was a tiny nozzle inside his wrist, and the vapour it sprayed was colourless.

As the woman toppled, the assassin was moving again, fast across the gallery, then leaping high to a stone window-sill. The window was tall and narrow, and he used counterpressure to ascend, fluidity and strength in perfect balance, until he reached the narrow, louvred opening at the top.

No normal person could slide through that opening.

Smiling, the assassin reached with one hand, twisting and writhing, using neuromuscular control to slither his way through, just as he had so many times in the practice gymnasium. He'd started his training aged five.

He was through, hanging by one hand, a hundred feet above the ground, at one side of the great skull. The administrative wing arced out, and he was close to the corner where it met the central skull. It took thirty seconds to reach that corner.

Then it was a simple matter of counterpressure, where the two walls formed a hollow angle, to control his descent.

As he climbed down, he was still smiling.

When Donal hauled himself on to the balcony, there was no sign of Sergeant O'Doyle, nor of the sharpshooters who'd been stationed in the next two boxes. They'd rushed outside to help, not realizing that their target had been above them all the time.

Donal rushed through to the corridor, then drew his weapon once more as he ran to the gallery, scanning in all directions, recognizing the fallen woman some twenty feet away.

Two uniformed cops were ascending steps from the atrium. One was bulbous-eyed with fear, but the other, huge and muscular, looked so calm he might have been about to doze off. It was one of the Brodowskis.

'Hey, Al,' called Donal.

'Lieutenant?'

'That's Detective Gilarney on the floor.'

'Shit.' Brodowski thumped his partner on the upper arm. 'Check her pulse, then call down for help.'

'Um, sure. What are—?'

'I'm going to help the lieutenant.'

Donal nodded as he jogged on, then came to a halt at a balustrade. Leaning over, all he could see was the swirling mass of well-dressed civilians in disarray, all he could hear was panicked shouts, and all he could smell was fear.

'There was a shooter,' he told Al Brodowski.

'I heard it was two zombies. Kitchen staff.'

'Shit.' Donal realized he'd missed a trick: the two dark-suited men heading for the kitchens. 'I think they were ensorcelled. The shooter who took down the commissioner was someone else.'

'They got the commissioner too?'

Donal was still scanning everywhere and seeing nothing that mattered.

'Yeah,' he said. 'Two for the price of one. Mayor Dancy went down first.'

Nothing.

'If some bastard got the commissioner, every cop on the force will ... Say, there's an open window.'

'Huh.' Donal looked up. 'A five-year old might get through there. It wasn't a child I saw.'

'You saw the shooter properly?'

'I wouldn't go that far.' Donal reholstered his Magnus, then stared down at the crowd. 'I saw a shadow. That was it.'

'So what do we do, Loot?'

'I haven't a fucking clue.'

The assassin crouched at the foot of the wall, observing the people who'd spilled out on to the gravelled roadways, waiting for the moment. When it came, he launched himself into a near-silent sprint across gravel, and in ten seconds reached the unbroken darkness of the trees.

Then he was inside, covered from sight by the black trunks and branches and leaves, moving fast, navigating through darkness. Within two minutes he'd already passed a floating ectoplasma wraith, its colours flaring white and crimson as it sensed the panic from beyond the trees, where it was forbidden to go. But it failed to sense the assassin sliding through the trees, and the assassin's smile returned as he realized his bodysuit's shadowhex protection was holding up.

In his tactical philosophy classes, the assassin had learned to think of fate as an ever-bifurcating waterfall to navigate by reflex-fast kinaesthetic feel in moments of danger. He had a choice now: to hole up or try for the perimeter of Möbius Park. But shadowhex protection faded over time, and he had been hidden inside City Hall for two days. He chose straightforward flight.

Beyond the darkness of the trees, the police would concentrate on the gravel roadways, or else assume the killers were already dead. Everyone knew the ectoplasma wraiths were deadly, and always hungry.

The assassin continued to run through darkness, among the trees. A white shadow, not a wraith, moved somewhere to the assassin's left, and was gone.

He accelerated.

Far off to the right, another patch of whiteness flicked through shadows.

Faster again, the assassin ran. He was no longer smiling.

A black root tripped him, and he went down rolling, but came up running, fluid once more. Increasing speed meant more risk.

There was another glimpse of whiteness, and he sped up once more.

And faster ...

Then whiteness burst from the undergrowth and *it was on him*, fangs into his thigh, tearing, and the assassin threw himself into a sideways roll, flinging the wolf free, and came up on to his feet. He had momentum still, enough to continue his run at speed. He was two paces forward before the other wolf hit him.

Snarling, the assassin smacked a palm-heel at its head – the neurotoxin spray would be useless – and attempted a knee-strike, but that was when the first white wolf recovered and thumped into him from behind. The choices of fate had narrowed down to one, for ever.

He was on his back and still fighting, knowing that he would dish out pain until the end, using his fingers to tear at one wolf's mouth, a thumb hooking at its eye, even as it snapped and bit and ripped and its mate did likewise. The assassin kicked, rolled, and tried to scissor his legs around the wolf, but there was a blur of movement and fangs tearing at the assassin's groin, pain exploding through his nervous system as his femoral arteries split and hot blood spurted into darkness, a darkness that grew bigger and enveloped him as vision faded before touch, and then sensation was a distant thing, soon to be gone, until the world was nothing but the sound of slavering and rending, of snarling and—

When the wolves were finished, they stepped back and looked at each other. One nodded. Then they loped off into the trees.

Behind them lay the assassin's blood-wet corpse from which the shadowhex-saturated bodysuit had been torn. It took perhaps five seconds for the first glimmer of white and crimson to show amid the darkness. Then a second ectoplasma wraith drifted overhead, then a third, and more were rising from the ground.

They congregated on the still-warm corpse.

Seventeen

Detective Alexa Ceerling stumbled into a walkway in the garage level. She was splashed with crimson, holding something in her right hand. As she entered the walkway, all four deathwolves stationed there looked up.

'Quick. Back there ... It's Sam.'

The biggest deathwolf, FenNine, growled. Then he ran past Alexa, followed two seconds later by his smaller pack comrades. Alexa watched them run, then reached for a yellow diamond-shaped button on the wall.

Inside the main garage, reserved for the maintenance of police vehicles only, a grey-skinned man lay face down in a widening pool of blood. FenNine reached the dead man first, then all four deathwolves were sniffing, tongues lolling. Suddenly, FenNine snarled, and his muzzle lifted up.

From the walkway, Alexa looked straight into his amber eyes.

'That's right,' she said.

Her fist, clenching a long scalpel, hammered against the yellow button. It took half a second for the defensive door to drop from the ceiling, blocking her off from the deathwolves inside.

Ten seconds later, she was jogging through the parking bays where cops left their private cars, looking for one she could— There.

In bay number 317, a familiar bone motorcycle waited. Quiescent, the Phantasm IV maintained a sense of heavy power, of massive speed and manoeuvrability.

'It's ... Harald,' said Alexa. 'He's in trouble.'

The Phantasm's headlight flicked on, green and bright.

'You know me, right? I'll take you to him, if you let me ride.'

A growl from the engine revving up was her answer.

'All right.' Alexa tossed the scalpel aside. It clattered on stone. 'All right.'

Then she swung her leg over the Phantasm's saddle, which altered shape to suit her. By the time she'd grasped the handlebars, the Phantasm

174

had already drawn its parking-stand up inside its body, and was rolling into motion.

It reached the upward-sloping exit ramp, already moving fast. As it shot up the slope, Alexa leaned forward, gripping hard.

'Fast as you can!' she shouted. 'To Shatterway Quay!'

In seconds, the Phantasm erupted on to Avenue of the Basilisks, wove between two swerving taxis, then straightened out, hammering along the straight boulevard, faster and faster, while Alexa crouched close to the bony fuel tank, eyes squinting against the slipstream, mouth pulled back into something that might have been a smile. The people on the sidewalks whipped past in a blur.

The Phantasm IV accelerated harder.

Sister Felice had been asleep for perhaps three hours when a percussive thump woke her. Immediately, as she sniffed the air, there was a suggestion of dust, perhaps the faintest tang of smoke. Then the banshee wails of emergency alarms split the air, and her ears twitched as she threw back the coverlet and rolled from the bed.

She pulled on her clothes very fast, and was still barefoot with shoes in hand when she pulled the door open, into a corridor where she could definitely smell dust. Then she was down the stairs, running towards the Acute Ensorcelment Ward. Suddenly Sister Lynkse was at her side, also running.

'Is it the new equipment?' she said. 'The stuff Kyushen put in?'

Sister Felice shook her head.

'Get back!' called someone from far ahead. 'No!'

There was a crunch, then a lumbering shape was visible inside a cloud of smoke, with a black-coated figure lying at his feet.

'Oh, shit.' Sister Felice grabbed Sister Lynkse's sleeve, pulling her to a halt. 'That's Gross Haughton.'

'Who?'

'Cannibal, rapist, you name it. He's supposed to be a secured patient.'

'Thanatos.'

The two Night Sisters backed away, just as one of the janitors came barrelling out of a side corridor, swinging a dark-grey fire extinguisher.

'No, Fred!' called Sister Lynkse. 'Stay back!'

But the big patient, Gross Haughton, had already dropped his heavy hand on Fred's shoulder, and elbowed him in the face.

'We can't allow that,' said Sister Felice.

'No, we can't,' said Sister Lynkse.

They extended their claws, and pulled back their lips from teeth that were longer and more pointed than they normally appeared. Both Night Sisters hissed, then ran towards the big figure, who was too focused on hitting Fred to realize the danger he was in.

Seconds later, they were upon him.

By the time a hospital security team arrived on the scene, Gross Haughton was down and still, his arteries torn but neatly bandaged after he'd lost sufficient blood to render him comatose. The two Night Sisters had propped Fred up against the wall, sitting, his expression bemused.

'Nice work, ladies,' said the security man. 'That's one less to worry about.'

'How many got out?' asked Sister Lynkse. 'How many from the Sucker Wing?'

She meant the Secure Unit for the Criminally Ensorcelled.

'All of them.'

'What?' Sister Felice, who had retracted her claws, now showed them again. 'How can equipment failure take out the whole wing? It's supposed to be—'

'This isn't equipment failure.' The security man gestured at the dust cloud thickening in the corridor. 'This is a jailbreak.'

Sister Lynkse hissed and spat.

'Is anyone else injured?' asked Sister Felice.

'I don't know,' said the security guard.

'Come on. Let's go and look.'

They checked that Fred was going to be all right, then set off towards the Sucker Wing, nostrils closing against the dust. Sister Lynkse grabbed a resuscitation kit from a wall hook as they walked.

'A jailbreak?' she said then. 'For which patient?'

'No idea.'

Sounds of groaning came from up ahead. Sister Felice had her own ideas about criminal patients being sprung from here, but right now there were people in trouble and this was her job: looking after the injured and making them well.

'Perhaps you'll get to talk to your police lieutenant,' said Sister Lynkse, stepping over a fallen cupboard. 'When they come to investigate, I mean.'

Sister Felice followed her.

'Yes,' she said. 'Perhaps I will.'

It was an orderly with a broken arm who was moaning, and they hurried towards him.

*

A young fleshy man with slicked-back hair, crying, followed the stretcher that bore Mayor Dancy's corpse. Donal figured the younger man for the mayor's son. He watched as they crossed the atrium, and uniformed cops pressed back, forming a clear route through.

'I want SOCD here now.' The man who spoke was Captain Craigsen, a uniformed senior officer. 'Screw the traffic. Ambulances and SOCD vehicles are priority one. Tell Despatch.'

'Yes, sir.'

'You. Zelashni.' Craigsen gestured to a bearded detective lieutenant. 'Tell me about the questioning.'

'I've got three truthseers up on the staircases.' Lieutenant Zelashni pointed. 'See? They've got line of sight on every conversation, while the interrogating officers are working there.'

Around the circumference of the atrium floor, uniformed and plain-clothes officers were questioning shocked-looking guests, some bloodied, their expensive tuxedos and gowns ripped and dirty. It was a neat setup, Donal realized: over twenty conversations taking place simultaneously, with only three truthseers watching from above, covering them all.

'Huh. All right.' Craigsen was giving no praise.

'That's a good arrangement.' Donal walked up to them. 'Process the civilians fast, get 'em clear, but make sure we learn everything we can.'

Zelashni nodded, but Craigsen's face hardened.

'You, Riordan, I mostly need to stay out of the way. You're a material witness.'

'So question me.'

'As if you've got anything to add beyond the obvious. Two – well, shall I call them resurrected persons? – opened fire on Mayor Dancy and then the crowd, and took out Hades knows how many of them, Commissioner Vilnar included. That about sum up what you might have said?'

'Sir, I'm pretty sure I saw—'

Behind Craigsen, Lieutenant Zelashni shook his head.

'Shut the fuck up,' said Craigsen. 'And get out of my sight, before I throw you in the wagon with the other icicles.'

'This was a professional hit.'

'I want you off this crime scene right now. That's a direct order, Riordan.'

Donal's voice went colder than a human's ever could.

'Then I'll do it. Sir.'

He turned and crossed the atrium floor, ignoring an attempted wave from Al Brodowski, and went out. The bonestone treads seemed to shiver beneath his feet as he descended to the gravel. A black ambulance was opening up, allowing the stretcher bearers to load sealed-up body-bags formed of slick membrane.

After a minute, Lieutenant Zelashni came down to stand beside Donal.

'This is a nightmare.'

'Yeah.'

'You need to get out of here.' Zelashni put his hands in his pockets. 'Let's take a walk.'

'Escorting me off the premises?'

'Fucking Hades, Riordan. Not everyone's like Craigsen.'

'My apologies.' Donal glanced back up at the rearing skull of City Hall. 'But it's his kind that are taking power, isn't it?'

'So let's walk. Politics is a little outside my scope.'

'Everything is politics. Vilnar told me that.'

'I never figured you for a politician.'

'I'm not.' Again Donal looked back. 'I think the Old Man thought I might be able to handle it. Bit of a switch for me.'

Zelashni set the pace, shoes crunching on the gravel roadway. They walked past the ambulance, where Mayor Dancy's sobbing son looked up at Donal, his mouth upturned into a trembling gesture of hatred. He was being comforted by several men in expensive suits. One, with a Unity Party pin in his lapel, was patting the younger Dancy's upper arm.

'Tell me what you saw, Riordan.'

'Call me Donal. And I saw a shadow on the ceiling, in the main hall.'

'On the *ceiling*?'

'A man in some kind of dark bodysuit, I think.'

'Thanatos, Rior— Donal. Every night, I read adventure stories to my son. I think we did that one last week.'

'You know SOCD are going to be here in strength. If you can get a diviner up there ...'

'On the ceiling. About what, eighty or ninety feet high?'

'There must be scaffolding or something. Unless they use wraiths to keep it clean, repaint it. Whatever.'

'Huh.'

The two men walked on, past stationary cruisers whose black-light strobes were flashing, past uniformed officers alertly looking in all directions without knowing what to expect, while their colleagues helped rich-looking people in shock to climb into their cars. Some of the limousines were acting as ambulances, hurtling off at high speed, spraying gravel, escorted by motorcycle cops on black, polished-chitin Panther 7s whose slit-shaped headlights shone purple.

'There were two dead cops on the third floor,' said Zelashni. 'Letharque and Prigolin. You know them?'

'Not really. Shit. They were the officers down?'

'Yeah. Gilarney found 'em inside a display case. Limbs broken, tangled up inside.'

'Ah, Thanatos. You got any idea how Gilarney is?'

'The medics were waking her up, last time I looked. Don't expect any sense from her.'

'Lethemist?'

Donal had come across its use before, and knew that it not only wiped out short-term memory, it also caused intermittent, excruciating migraines for months to come. Although non-lethal, its use by law enforcement officers was banned.

'That, or something like it. Knocked her out good, but at least she'll recover. Not like her guys.'

'Damn it, Zelashni. If the two men – zombies – in the kitchen did all the killing, why would they have killed someone on the third floor? And hidden the bodies.'

'Good question, and I know what Craigsen would say. Because their weapons must have been stashed, and maybe that display case was the hiding-place.'

'Shit.'

To retrieve the weapons, the two zombies would have had to deal with the cops watching over the gallery where the cache was hidden. It was perfectly logical, and perfectly wrong.

'Fuck,' muttered Zelashni.

He was looking behind him, and Donal turned to see. Three D-wagons were opening their carapaces, revealing the long horizontal bars that prisoners could be manacled to. Each detention wagon had a complement of seven armed officers with hexlar jackets, helmets, and shotgun with necroplosive rounds.

The kitchen staff, some twenty zombies, their wrists and ankles in chains, were shuffling towards the wagons.

'The two zombies with weapons,' said Donal, 'were ensorcelled. A couple of guys in dark suits went into the kitchens earlier ... Shit. I think they put the uniforms into trance as well. The officers guarding the door.'

'I'll talk to the uniforms. You know their names?'

Donal shook his head. 'They're dead. I'm pretty sure that one of the zombies shot them first, before anybody else.'

'That's what you might call convenient.'

'For my flimsy story, you mean?'

They stopped at the edge of the road. Beyond lay the dark trees. There was no sign of ectoplasma wraiths, but Donal knew better than to step off the gravelled roadway.

'I'll do what I can,' said Zelashni. 'You understand?'

'Yeah. Yeah, I get that. Thanks.'

Zelashni stared at him for a moment, then held out his hand.

'My first name's Elleston.'

'What's your son's name?'

'Uh, Martin. Why?'

'He's a lucky guy.'

They shook hands.

'Look after yourself, Donal.'

'You too, Elleston.'

Zelashni turned and headed back towards City Hall. Donal waited a moment, then continued along the darkened roadway that led through the shadows of Möbius Park.

He reached the North-North-East Gate, otherwise known as Deepwell Passing. Inside it was a lodge, where rarely glimpsed park-keepers lived and worked. Donal knocked on the door, and after a second it swung inwards.

A group of seven men, shoulder-to-shoulder, shuffled back.

'Er ... I'm Lieutenant Riordan.'

'You knocked, not hurrying—'

'—to get through. The—'

'—gate, I mean. Everyone's—'

'—in a hurry, but you don't—'

'—get things done that—'

'—way.'

The voice looped around, from man to man, but it was the same voice. Donal was facing a septune gestalt. Their torsos – *its* torsos – were connected by thick, short muscular trunks.

'You're a park-keeper, right?'

'Ha.'

'Ha.'

'Ha.'

'Ha.'

'Ha.'

'Ha.'

'Ha.'

After a moment, all seven said in unison, 'I am indeed *one* park-keeper.'

Donal thought about what to say next.

'You know there's been a multiple homicide in City Hall. What I'd like to ask is, for you to ring me if you find anything ... odd. Afterwards.'

'What—'

'—do—'

'—you—'

'—mean—'

'—by—'

'—odd—'

'—Lieutenant?'

Perhaps Zelashni believed only that Donal *thought* he had seen a shadow. Zelashni might not be convinced of the reality of a professional kill going far beyond the crudeness of a mob hit.

'There was an assassin involved. I'm the only one who thinks so.'

For a moment, all seven men – all seven parts of the one being – lowered their/his heads and closed their/his eyes, as if falling asleep standing up.

Probably has to sleep that way.

Then seven heads raised, seven pairs of eyes opened and focused on Donal.

'Yes,' came from seven mouths, followed by, 'I will—'

'—ring—'

'—you at—'

'—Avenue—'

'—of the—'

'—Basilisks—'

'—Lieutenant.'

Donal looked from face to face.

'Thank you, sir,' he said.

He turned and left, accompanied by a shuffling sound as the septune moved to close the lodge door. Then it clicked shut, and Donal was left staring into the blackness of Mobius Park.

Everything's gone to Hades.

Behind him, the heavy gates of Deepwell Passing opened. Donal walked through, putting his left hand into his jacket pocket for no conscious reason.

'Fuck!'

Then he was on the sidewalk outside, and the massive gates were closed.

I forgot. How could I?

He withdrew his now-sticky fingers from his pocket.

Ensorcelment. Has to be.

But who was it that had caused Donal to forget he had Commissioner Vilnar's eyeball in his pocket? The commissioner's driver, Lamis, was an interesting individual, but he'd not been present in the main hall when everything went to Hades.

Donal looked up.

'Commissioner Vilnar,' he said to the blank, deep-purple sky. 'You were an interesting man.'

What other abilities had Vilnar possessed? What secrets had he kept?

I'll find out.

If this was the doing of the Black Circle, of Gelbthorne or Cortindo, then it wasn't Mayor Dancy's death that Donal was going to avenge. It was Arrhennius Vilnar's, in addition to Laura Steele's.

'Whatever you started, Commissioner ...'

His voice dropped to a frigid bass.

'...I *will* finish it.'

The Phantasm IV leaned over, Alexa tight against the fuel tank, as it arced into an abandoned road, swerved past potholes, hurtled the length of the derelict street, and then began to slow. From the smashed skeletons of tenements on either side, white lizards were watching. A light quicksilver rain was beginning to fall; but the air was thick, and smelled of oil and salt.

'Quietly now,' said Alexa.

The bone motorcycle became almost silent, shifting to stealth. It avoided a clutter of fallen, rusted iron poles, and slowed further, to walking pace. Then it stopped at the edge of a great, rubble-strewn lot. Beyond was the darkness of Shatterway Sound, where a single long barge was moving in the black, thick waters.

'Harald's in that building.'

Alexa pointed to a shell with three walls standing, surrounded by a moat of concrete shards, sprinkled with broken glass, in which purple weeds were sprouting.

'You see the open doorway?'

The doors were long gone, taken by scavengers.

'We go through fast,' said Alexa. 'Very, very fast. You got it?'

As the Phantasm growled, she felt the power through her inner thighs.

'Good. Then we go.'

The motorcycle leaped forward.

'Faster.'

It accelerated up an angled slab of concrete, roared into the air, hitting the next slab just right and hurtling across the rubble, straight for the empty doorway. Alexa crouched lower, getting ready.

'Now.'

As the Phantasm howled through the doorway, Alexa threw herself off to the right, smashing her shoulder against a pile of bricks, rolling and then lying still, face down, one knee beneath her. After a second, she pushed herself up.

There was no sound.

Alexa limped across the broken floor, to the side of the darkened pit where the building's floor had once stood. Careful of the crumbling edge, she leaned over.

The Phantasm lay on its side, it bony carapace cracked across, its engine silent and its headlight dead, totally unmoving.

'Sorry,' said Alexa.

Then she dragged herself out of the empty building, step by painful step, until she could slump down against the broken outer wall. She sat on hard rubble, uncaring. The darkness of Shatterway Sound was a reminder of childhood, and as her head tipped forward, she fell into dreams about the past.

Dreams from which she did not intend to wake.

Eighteen

There was a diner, where several men in rolled-up shirtsleeves were tucking in to purple eggs and reptile rashers. Donal stopped, considered the state of his stomach – empty, yet without hunger – and went inside regardless. What he needed was a place where he could sit and think.

'What'll it be, pal?' The guy behind the counter was old, his apron white.

'Just coffee, black.' Donal looked around the place, noting that it was clean but not too busy. 'And you can bag me a dozen doughnuts to go. You choose the flavours.'

'Take a seat.'

Donal slid into a booth at the rear, reached into his pocket, and withdrew the sticky eye of Commissioner Vilnar. He held it in his palm, looking into the still-clear cornea. Soon, the protein structures within the eye would begin to unravel, and it would grow milky grey, quite opaque. Not that it would ever process vision again, since there was no living brain for the severed optic nerve to connect with.

'Ugh, what's that?'

The old man had fetched Donal's coffee without his noticing.

'It's a, er, novelty item. Kind of a joke, on the guys at work.'

'Huh. Not too realistic. You didn't want cream?'

'Excuse me?'

'With the coffee.'

'Oh. No, thanks.'

The old man returned behind the counter. Donal continued to stare at the eye, remembering how Sister Mary-Anne at the orphanage had used the human eyeball's structure as the quintessential proof of evolution by natural selection, as light-sensitive cells gave a simple jellyfish-like species an advantage, mutations that placed those cells within a concave hollow saw better, as did those that protected the proto-eye with clear membrane, and so on incrementally to achieve the imperfect but adequate stereoscopic vision of *homo sapiens sapiens*.

He put the eye back in his pocket.

There's a reason for this.

The coffee was growing cool. He took a sip.

I just need help figuring out what it is.

'Shit,' he muttered.

No one looked in his direction.

Dr Kyushen Jyu was still in the commissioner's office back at HQ, reading that damned manual, unaware that everything had gone to Hades. Maybe Kyushen could understand how a man might rip out his own eye, and not just give it to someone as he died, but also give that person temporary amnesia until he'd taken the eyeball from the scene.

Donal wondered what the scene-of-crime diviners were going to make of the commissioner's mutilated head.

Then he looked over at the counter, where the old man was carefully placing doughnuts inside a cardboard box. Perhaps Donal's unconscious intuition had asked for doughnuts not just to give the old man revenue, but to have something to take to the task force room.

Because the help he needed went beyond Kyushen's technical advice. It was Viktor and Harald and Xalia and Alexa who could help him nail the Black Circle bastards.

Good.

He had a start point. Now he could get to work.

Harald had spent over three hours going up and down between Robbery-Haunting and one of the deep levels, at the minus ninety-third floor, where little of the activity that took place was recognizably human. In R-H, he'd finished typing up his report on the happy, healthy phone customers with altered personalities, gone over it with Kresham, then handed it in to Commander Bowman. In the deep level, he'd talked to several wraiths that Livitia – his wraith-friend from the 77th Precinct – had persuaded to give reports on Xalia's progress.

But the wraiths who lived down here were a little ... different. Most of the conversations went like this:

The barriers have intensified.

'Is that a good sign?'

It indicates further rotation around the axes of this continuum.

'Meaning what?'

That Gertie is carrying out more work in other-dimensional space you cannot understand.

'And is that good or bad?'

If you think in such binary terms, then yes.

And then the wraith would sink down through the floor or into the solid wall, leaving Harald to parse what meaning he could from his memory of the conversation.

Finally, Harald decided to see if he could find Viktor, and ask him what the Hades he and Xalia had been working on. He hoped it was nothing trivial. And it occurred to him, as an elevator wraith carried him down to the firing-range level, that perhaps something had happened to Xalia as a result of what they working on, something beyond the wraith analogue of overexertion.

Stepping out into the lobby, he nodded to Brian who was behind the desk.

'How's it going?'

'Great, but—'

Thunderous automatic fire sounded from the far end of the range. Two Grausers, by the sound: almost certainly the Howler 50s that Viktor used. Harald wondered if anyone besides himself knew that the weapons had names: Betsie and Connie.

'I'll talk to you later, Brian. Excuse me.'

He headed along the half-lit corridor, to a gun-lane with low lighting where the shredded remains of targets lay at a tall figure's feet. Big Viktor was standing with his back to the lane, his chin down and his hands empty.

Harald knew better than to call out a greeting.

Then Viktor snapped into motion, spinning as his hands disappeared under his leather coat, then whipped up his Grausers and opened stuttering blasts from both weapons. Then he rotated away as if avoiding return fire, ducked back, and let loose once more.

Finally, the Grausers were holstered beneath his arms. He nodded to Harald.

'You found out anything about Xalia? I couldn't.'

'I talked to several wraiths.' Harald drew close, then stared down the range at the few tattered ribbons that hung at the far end. 'Can't say I learned much.'

'Yeah.' Viktor pressed the return button, and the target's remnants came whirring towards him. 'Those deep-wraiths are kind of ambiguous, or something.'

'I wanted to ask you something. About Xalia.'

'Fuck.' Viktor leaned his head back, staring at the ceiling, then puffed out a breath. 'I should've realized she wasn't recovered.'

'None us appreciated how badly she'd been hurt before. She should have told Bowman.'

'I guess.'

'So you *were* doing something for Bowman.'

'Huh.' Viktor rubbed his beard-stubble. 'You're a smart cookie, Sergeant Hammersen. Bowman briefed us, but I'd say we were doing it for the commissioner.'

'The same commissioner we thought might be a dark mage, just a few weeks ago?'

'Yeah, that's the one. Nuts. We were investigating sightings of white wolves.'

Harald's eyes rarely looked anything other than gentle. Now, when he blinked, they were liquid and soft.

'White wolves.'

'I don't know the significance. But we were investigating every sighting. Despatch are routing calls to us at any hour, from any precinct.'

'Us? Meaning you and Xalia?'

'And Bowman. Just the three of us, as far as I know. Oh, and there's one other thing. If I tell anyone, I'm supposed to kill 'em.'

'Quickly or slowly?'

'Not specified.'

'Well, you've been killing me slowly for, what, a couple of years now?' Harald slow-punched Viktor's arm. 'My assignment is, I've been talking to customers with new telephones. Me and Kresham.'

'Huh?'

'Some new kind of phone. Coloured indigo, not black. Might be ensorcelling their customers.'

'To do what? Make longer calls? Run up their bills?'

Harald almost laughed. 'Not specified, my friend.'

Viktor unclipped the remains of his target, looked at the fresh target-sheets, then turned back to Harald.

'You've got something in mind, haven't you?'

'Not really. I just wondered if Xalia got zapped or something.'

'In what way?'

'What was she up to? I mean, when she had her ... whatever. Breakdown.'

'Just another sighting, but none of the others have turned up anything.'

'And this one?'

'It was outside the Janaval Hotel, I know that much.'

'All right.' Harald knew the place. 'The street there will be busy. Bound to look normal.'

'Bound to. If we had anything better to do, there'd be no point in checking.'

'Exactly.'

'So, Harald. You got anything better to do?'

'No.'

'Me neither. Let's see if Sam'll give us an unmarked. Hopefully better than the last pile of shit.'

'I'll take the motorcycle.'

'Good enough.'

There were ten unused target sheets remaining.

'What are you going to do with those?' asked Harald.

'Just toss 'em,' said Viktor, taking hold of the sheets.

He threw them into the air.

'Fuck.' Harald was already backing off, smiling. 'You're nuts.'

Viktor launched himself into a shoulder roll, and came up spinning, Grausers in his hands, and the twin blasts tore apart the paper targets in the air, until it was thick with cordite and only shreds and ribbons of paper remained to float down to the floor.

'I've no idea what you're talking about,' he told Harald. 'I'm perfectly normal.'

Ten minutes later, they were on the garage level, standing in the midst of a busy crowd of cops, divided between those who were working the scene, and those who just had to take a look.

'An officer down,' muttered someone, 'in HQ.'

'That's just not ... right,' a female sergeant said. 'Hasn't happened for what, ten, maybe fifteen years? Longer?'

Then someone moved, and Harald caught a glimpse of Sam's corpse.

'Shit.'

Viktor was tall enough to see over most people's heads. He gestured with his unshaven chin.

'The deathwolves are over there. Talking to truthsayers.'

A uniform that Harald didn't recognize said, 'The deathwolves saw the killer, is what I heard.'

'Have they got the bastard?' asked Viktor.

'Naw. And it's one of our own. A cop. She did Sam, got out of the building, left the deathwolves chewing their nuts.'

'Say what? A cop did this?'

'Someone named Ceerling. Alexa Ceerling? You ever heard of—?'

But Harald was already heading for the walkway, and after a half-second delay, Viktor followed. Grim-faced, they strode through to the garage where cops parked their private vehicles.

'Where would she go?' asked Viktor, walking fast to keep up.

'I've no idea where she'd go to ground.'

'Shit. How do we find out what she's into? Her desk? Her locker?'

'Someone else will be going through her stuff already.' Harald increased the pace. 'But I do know her home address, from the time I gave her a lift to— Shit.'

Harald stopped in front of bay 317.

An empty bay.

'What is it?' said Viktor. 'Wait. Isn't this ...?'

'Yeah. Where I park the Phantasm.'

They looked at each other. Both of them knew that the motorcycle was capable of defending itself with lethal force. It wouldn't allow any person to ride it, unless it knew them.

'It *can* ride by itself, right?' said Viktor.

'Yeah, and I told it to go home by itself, if I hadn't come back, but not until twenty o'clock. It wouldn't go earlier, unless there was an emergency.'

'So either it's following Alexa, or—'

'Or she's riding it.'

Again, they looked at each other.

'Surveillance,' they said simultaneously.

They headed back towards the walkway.

There were no deathwolves around the steps of Police HQ. Donal thought about this, came to no conclusion, then held up his detective's shield and recited his badge number. The big doors ground open.

FenSeven was inside, with massive reinforcements. There must have been thirty or more deathwolves staring at him. Beyond stood troopers in hexlar vests.

'Come in, Lieutenant,' Eduardo called from the reception desk. 'I'll fill you in.'

'All right.'

The deathwolves parted to allow passage, and Donal walked up to the granite block from which Eduardo's torso rose.

'What's going on?'

'Alexa Ceerling killed two people, looks like. Right here in the building.'

'No.'

'Yes. Troy Gamarlov, he's a medic. She had an appointment with him, some kind of checkup, and now Gamarlov's body is in a dozen pieces all over the place, with everything covered in blood. Is what I hear, anyhow.'

'Hades, Eduardo.'

Donal knew that whatever Eduardo reported as rumour was usually true.

'Yeah. And the other stiff is Sam.'

'Sam?'

'In the garage.'

'No. Not Sam. Why would Alexa kill—?'

Donal's voice trailed off.

Because she was ensorcelled.

'You thought of something, Lieutenant?'

Ensorcelled by those fucking telephones.

'I don't know.' Donal could not disguise the grimness in his voice. 'Talk to you later.'

'Yeah. Later.'

Donal headed for the elevator wraiths.

Gertie's shaft was out of use, which was a minor mystery amid the confusion all around him. It was awful: Alexa committing murder inside HQ, the commissioner and Mayor Dancy killed in City Hall. Donal took the next shaft along.

'Minus twenty-seven. Please.'

The wraith took him down without communicating, then pushed him into the lobby area. He stopped there, looking in to the task force room, where eight large plainclothes guys, most in shirtsleeves, were tearing the desks apart. A couple were from Homicide, the rest from Internal Security, which was never a good sign.

Donal had been with Homicide for five years, before the Diva debacle and his reassignment to Laura's task force. Most of the Homicide guys were people he knew well; but these two had joined shortly before he left.

Not a coincidence.

Inside the glass-walled cube that had been Laura's office, a moustachioed man was scowling. Donal knew him, all right: Commander Seiyatch, whose refusal to work with wraiths or other non-human officers was a long-established fact, whatever regulations said.

This is going to be fun. Not.

'Riordan.' Seiyatch came into the open office area as Donal entered. 'They cut you loose from City Hall?'

'Took my statement, as a witness.'

'And look what you've come back to.'

Donal watched the IS investigators pulling apart drawers and filing-cabinets. One of the investigators glanced at Donal, raised eyebrows and shoulders in what looked like apology, then returned to his task.

'The paperwork's a mess,' added Seiyatch. 'Which I always consider a reflection on leadership.'

Anger started to blossom inside Donal. He stared at it in his mind's eye, deconstructing the emotion as being less than useful in the current context, and forced it aside.

'If you're interested in Alexa Ceerling's recent movements, she was working for the commissioner.'

'You mean Craigsen? Oh, no, he's not *officially* the commissioner yet.'

'Craigsen. You think he's got seniority enough for that?'

'I always thought being a commissioner is about politics.' Seiyatch smiled as one of the homicide guys tipped reports on to the floor. 'And Mayor Van Linder is going to want strong-willed leadership.'

That bastard. Maybe he had something to do with it.

It occurred to Donal that Assistant Mayor Van Linder had been standing far away from Mayor Dancy when the shooting started. Still, wouldn't Van Linder have been outside the main hall altogether, if he'd been complicit in the assassination?

But the shooter's timetable had been brought forward by Gilarney's discovery of the bodies in the display case. When she shouted *'Officers down,'* the shooter had to fire or lose his chance in the panicked evacuation.

'Alexa Ceerling,' said Donal. 'You want to know what happened to her.'

'To *her*? I know what happened to her victims. She's a cop-killer, and being a cop herself just makes that worse, wouldn't you say? It's time we cleaned up this department.'

Donal stood reptile-still, not even breathing. After half a minute, Seiyatch broke eye contact and stepped back.

'I agree with you, Seiyatch.'

'Uh, what?'

'It's time Tristopolis PD got rid of bad cops.'

Then he turned and left, peripherally noticing several smiles from the investigators, which disappeared as they resumed their work.

None of which was likely to help.

He stepped out on to the one-hundredth floor, and paused at the entrance to Surveillance. At the far end, close to the entrance to the commissioner's office – still Vilnar's office, as far as Donal was concerned – Viktor and Harald were talking to an officer in shirtsleeves. The guy was maybe fifty and fit-looking, and he'd introduced himself when Donal was here before.

The memory surfaced: Rob Helborne, Alexa's friend.

Donal wondered if Viktor and Harald – especially Harald, with his instinct for making contacts – had already known this was a friend of Alexa's. With the rows of monitors amid the transparent fibres hanging from the ceiling, it was surprising the surveillance officers hadn't tracked her down already.

If everyone felt like Seiyatch, they were likely to gun her down first, and let the Bone Listeners ask the questions on the autopsy table.

Not Viktor. Not Harald.

They were Alexa's friends, and would listen while Donal explained what must have happened. Already – he could tell from the way they'd taken Rob Helborne aside – they were trying to track her down by themselves.

'Hey.' Donal walked up. 'I know what's going on. Listen, um, Rob. You know there's still a visitor in there.'

He pointed towards the heavy portal of the commissioner's office.

'Thanatos. I forgot.'

'I need to see him. And you two,' he said to Viktor and Harald. 'Let's talk.'

'Yes.' Harald nodded to Helborne. 'All right? See you later.'

'OK. And I'll signal the office to open, Lieutenant.'

But the doors were already pulling apart.

'That's ... odd,' said Helborne.

Donal was already entering, with Viktor and Harald behind him. They hurried through the short tunnel, and the inner door opened. The surrounding fringe of ciliaserpents thrashed and whipped.

'Careful,' said Donal. 'They're not trying to harm us, but they're disturbed.'

He jumped through, then quickly moved further into the office, making room for Harald to follow, then Viktor.

'Oh.' From behind the desk, Kyushen looked up. 'Um, hi.'

He blinked. The manual was open to somewhere near the middle, and loose-leaf notes were scattered across the desktop. A pen was in Kyushen's hand, poised above a half-drawn diagram on his notepad.

'Dr Kyushen Jyu,' said Donal, 'this is Harald Hammersen and Viktor Harman, my colleagues. Also friends.'

'Nice to, um, meet you.'

Kyushen's gaze was already drifting back to the open manual.

'I've got bad news, everyone.' Donal swallowed as he looked around, not at the people but at the furnishings: the black iron chair whose name was Bert, the stone credenza, a convoluted light fitting that dangled from the ceiling, several other chairs and cabinets. And a tiny footstool, almost overlooked. 'I'm sorry.'

The chairs and cabinets swivelled to face him. Harald and Viktor took a step back, while Kyushen slowly put down his pen.

'Arrhennius Vilnar,' said Donal, 'died this morning.'

Shocked waves of silence seemed to pound through the room.

'It was a professional assassin.' Donal touched his jacket pocket. It still contained the dead commissioner's eye. 'Some scapegoats were gunned down, and I'm having difficulty persuading people that someone else did the shooting.'

'The commissioner?' Kyushen looked at the chair he was sitting in. A dead man's chair. 'Someone killed him?'

'Mayor Dancy was the prime target.'

Or maybe not.

That was something to consider.

'The mayor's dead, too?' said Viktor.

'Yeah.' Donal reached out to touch the black chair. 'I'm sorry.'

It shivered. Then the desk began to keen, and Kyushen stood up quickly.

'What—?'

The light-fitting twisted, the cabinets shifted their weight, and the orrery began to move faster. Donal wondered, as he watched and listened, what the commissioner's widow was doing right now.

She was a tough bitch, but she loved him.

It was a strange thought to have.

I never met her, did I?

Then he rubbed his face, and tried to concentrate on what Harald was saying.

'—supposed to have killed a doctor, as well as Sam.'

'I know,' said Donal.

The furniture's moans grew louder.

'She was ensorcelled,' Donal added. 'There are these phones in Customer Relations ...'

'Telephones?' said Harald.

'Yeah, these indigo things that—'

'Here? In HQ?'

193

'Yes. Alexa spent a lot of time in the place, and she persuaded me to go down there to—'

'You've used the phones?'

Donal said, 'Yes.'

Harald leaped forward, the heel of his palm heading for Donal's chin, but Donal was already rotating, slapping at the attack, circling away.

'It didn't affect me!'

Donal avoided a thrusting kick aimed at his knee.

'Stop!'

It was Kyushen, physically soft in a room with three combat-trained cops and surrounded by several tons of keening, animated furniture, who took command.

'No undead mind,' he said, 'can be affected by the command harmonics. Look, it says so right there.'

He pointed to a page full of dense equations.

'OK.' Harald stopped, in control of himself. 'Donal, I apologize.'

'You've seen the guys in Customer Relations?'

'No, their customers in the city, mostly folk living alone who are suddenly filled with health and free of illness. Me and Kresham, we both worked on it.'

'Huh.' A faint smile pulled at Donal's face. 'So the Old Man had you investigating, did he? Were you reporting directly to him?'

'To Bowman.'

'Close enough. The commissioner told me that he set Alexa up, but she was going to undergo detailed analysis – that was the reason for sending her in to Customer Relations, sorry, the Customer Relationship Bureau. Some expert was going to map the neural changes – and reverse the effect.'

'Didn't work out that way,' growled Viktor.

The furniture had grown silent.

'So it was the analysis session, with this Dr Gamarlov,' said Harald, 'that triggered Alexa's killing spree?'

'You know as much as I do now,' Donal told him. 'We need to figure out a way to help Alexa, right? Before some bunch of troopers guns her down.'

He hadn't told them everything. There was still the matter of the eyeball in his pocket.

'She's got the Phantasm.' Harald nodded towards Viktor. 'We just asked Surveillance to find it for us.'

'Good. So that's one possibility,' said Donal. 'What else can we do?'

'Go down to Customer Relations.' Viktor moved his huge shoulders beneath his leather coat. 'Bounce some heads off the walls.'

'They're victims,' said Harald. 'Just like Alexa.'

'Yeah, but ...'

'Which means,' Harald continued, 'that if we took one of them off by themselves, and then started to interrogate them ... Maybe we'll trigger the same reaction as in Alexa.'

'So you have an excuse to kill them?' asked Viktor. 'While they're trying to murder you?'

'No, Harald's right.' Donal pointed with his forefinger. 'She didn't just use violence. Alexa went to ground.'

'Maybe,' said Harald, 'to somewhere specific. Somewhere *programmed*.'

'So you get someone worked up,' muttered Viktor, 'then I can follow them. Try not to let them kill you first, buddy.'

'Good.' Harald was staring at Donal. 'But that's not everything, is it?'

'Not unless the phone company put out a hit on Mayor Dancy. Which maybe they did. Except that's nuts.' Donal leaned on the stone credenza, then took his weight off it. 'Sorry. So, Viktor, you've been working the phone gig as well?'

'Alexa's out there,' said Viktor. 'Have we got time for this?'

'We need to talk to each other.' Harald folded his arms. 'You know, like a team.'

Good man.

Donal was feeling better about this.

'What were you working on, Viktor?'

'Death-damned white wolves. Sightings from the public. I haven't caught a glimpse myself.'

'What? I just missed one,' said Donal, 'last night. Near a TTA.'

'You did? Me and Xalia and Bowman have—'

'I sensed traces of Xalia last night. I was out for a run, and I felt something. Maybe it was the wolf, maybe the traffic accident, I don't know. But when I was in the Janaval, I knew she'd been there.'

Viktor's lean face – men thought of him as ugly, women as sexy – hardened now.

'You were in the area when Xalia was injured? You happened to be there?'

'Injured?' Donal stared at him. 'Everything was over when I— Shit. I thought I saw the Vixen.'

'It was Laura's Vixen,' said Harald, 'that took her here. Injured.'

'Where is she?'

'In a deep level, with Gertie. Sealed off, since yesterday.'

'That doesn't sound good.'

All three cops looked at each other. Then they turned as Kyushen said: 'Gentlemen? I'm not much good at ... personal stuff. But I can draw up logic tables and deduction graphs. Sounds like you need—'

'Tables and diagrams,' said Viktor, 'aren't *action.*'

'Right.' Donal modulated his voice carefully. 'We need to do something. I'm going to ask one question before we make a move.'

'A fast question, I hope.'

'When Laura and I – arrested – Blanz in Fortinium, who told us he'd be there, and in disguise?'

'Hades, it was *your* job,' said Viktor. 'You were the one who got the briefing.'

'The commissioner.' Harald's tone was soft. 'I was there when he told you.'

'So how did he know?'

'Laura captured Eyes, Marnie Finross ... but she went catatonic, didn't she? So he didn't get the info from her.'

'That's a good question,' said Harald. 'Do you know the answer?'

'No.' Donal nodded to Kyushen. 'But we're going to work on it, while you two take on Customer Relations. If whatshisname in Surveillance, Helborne, tracks down the Phantasm, I'll let you know.'

There was a pause.

No one put me in charge.

For that matter, the task force probably no longer existed. That was something to—

'Yes,' said Harald.

'We're right on it,' said Viktor.

Their voices had gained strength.

Now we are a team.

Donal touched their shoulders.

'For Laura,' he said. 'And the Old Man.'

'Yes.'

'Yes.'

Harald and Viktor got moving.

Nineteen

Harald noticed the new sign. Everyone called the place Customer Relations (or Whinging Complaints, though not in writing) but the floating sign, held in place by necromagnetic induction, read:

~*CUSTOMER RELATIONSHIP BUREAU*~

And the receptionist's smile was very wide, as if her facial muscles could not help bunching up when she saw a stranger walk into her lobby.

'I'm Sergeant Hammersen.' He held up his shield. 'But call me Harald.'

'Of course ... Harald. I hope we can help you.'

'I think I need to see a supervisor. It's about arranging some training.'

'The supervisor on shift right now is Jack Capers. Isn't that a great name?'

'Uh, sure. So Mr Capers—'

'I'll call him now.' She picked up the indigo handset. 'Jack? Can Sergeant Harald Hammersen come in and talk to you? I've got him right here with me.' There was a pause, then: 'That's right.'

Harald noticed how her smile remained even while she was talking.

'Here.' She held out the indigo phone. 'You want a word with Jack now?'

Letting out a breath to calm himself, Harald tried not to spend too long staring at the handset.

'If he's free, I'll pop in now and chat in person. Seems friendlier, you know?'

'Of course.' And, into the phone: 'Can he come right in? He can? Wonderful.'

She put it down.

'You're very kind,' said Harald. 'Thank you so much.'

'And you are so welcome.'

Her smile looked wider than ever. It made Harald feel as if he should give her a tip. Then he nodded, and went past her desk, through the partition and into the call centre.

'Sergeant Hammersen?'

The man who spoke had a reddish goatee, and a grin as wide as the receptionist's.

'Call me Harald.'

'Delighted. I'm Jack. Jack Capers.'

They shook hands.

'And what can I do for you, Harald?'

'It's about your phone manner.' Looking around at the smiling officers, relaxed as they talked on their indigo phones, Harald felt cold. 'I hear good things about the way you guys work.'

'You want to listen in on a few calls? Even try answering some yourself?'

'I'd love to,' said Harald. 'But later. Right now, I've got a meeting. But my team's about to start a major enquiry that's all about ringing people, and I'd like them to get some additional training. Is that possible? They've had the usual academy stuff, but—'

'Oh, we can do better than that, Harald, I'm absolutely sure.'

'Yeah.' Harald looked around at the call handlers. 'Good atmosphere. You can see they're motivated.'

'I'm proud of them. You need motivation strategies for your guys,' said Capers, 'then we can provide that.'

'I'll bet. Um, they're the proof.' Harald continued to stare at the call centre. 'You know what? I have friends who are a bit more senior than me, just a group who hang out together, who are really interested in motivating their people.'

'Wonderful.'

'What time do you finish the shift?'

'Another twenty minutes. I started early.'

'Hmm. Could you make it to 251st Street later tonight, around nineteen o'clock?'

'Tonight? Sure.'

'There's a bar called Monazen Iona—'

'Oh, yeah,' said Capers. 'I've walked past the place. Looks a bit upmarket.'

It was very upmarket, as Harald knew, and therefore exactly the last type of place where someone would expect trouble.

'I'll meet you in the main bar at the front,' he told Capers, 'and we'll have a drink, then see what we can see. They're a friendly bunch, the guys.'

'It sounds great. Thanks, Harald.'

'You're welcome.'

They shook hands.

'Later.'

'Yeah. Later.'

Shortly after that, Viktor broke into Alexa's apartment, using the hex-keys he always carried. It was small, tidy, and had a lot of books. A set of dumbbells stood in one corner.

He knew immediately that the place was empty. Still, he went from room to room, looked inside the shower stall and under the iron bed. No one was hiding there.

Then he went back to the tiny lounge, and began a structured search. Perhaps he would find a note where she'd written down the contents of her dreams, of the mesmeric command buried inside her mind. Or perhaps this was wasting time, until he and Harald sorted out some other poor bastard from Customer Relations tonight, someone as screwed-up in the head as Alexa.

Fluid leaked from the Phantasm's cracked carapace. It lay on its side, atop sharp-edged rubble, at the bottom of a shadowed pit. Perhaps fifty feet above were the jagged edges of the hole that the motorcycle had plunged through. From down here, the ruined building at ground level was not visible. Having no roof, it did not obscure the patch of purple sky above.

The pale, blind lizards crept closer.

Neither of the motorcycles wheels had retained its shape. No sound emanated from its engine. No light shone from its headlamp.

Closer, the lizards moved, until one of them extruded a forked tongue to taste the spilled fluid. At that moment, the Phantasm's motor spasmed and coughed, and the lizards scuttled away in retreat.

The headlight glimmered a soft, eerie, steady green.

Donal tapped the commissioner's desk. Kyushen looked up from the manual, then checked the page number, and slowly closed it.

'I'm sorry,' he said. 'I'm not sure I can be much help.'

'You already were,' Donal told him, 'when you made Harald realize that the phones had no effect on me.'

'Oh. Good.'

'So can you figure out what else they're doing to people's minds?'

'Besides making them feel good?'

'And turning homicidal if someone tries to analyse them.'

'Yes, er, I can't figure that out.' Kyushen laid a hand on the manual. 'The resonant potentiation is effected by subharmonic signals that—'

'Feel free to translate that,' said Donal, 'into real words.'

'The manual tells me how the hidden commands are carried down the phone line. It doesn't specify the semantics – um, the signal contents – because it can be anything.'

'So you can't tell without analysing an actual call.'

'I guess. The good feelings that, um, what was the white-haired guy's name?'

'Harald.'

'The behaviour that Harald described, the happy customers, that's linked to some other goal in their mind, some deep association.'

'All right.' Donal rubbed his face. 'Aside from a tendency to go off the deep end, how is this a bad thing?'

'Over time, it might lead to some behaviour that could be triggered.' Kyushen stared at the closed manual. 'I'm not sure. Some of this, I could try to duplicate in the hospital lab, and use my own diagnostics to analyse.'

'All right.' Donal looked at the stone credenza, the brassy orrery, the black iron chair. 'Do you any of you' – he touched the desk – 'want to remain here, with Commissioner Vilnar gone? His replacement may well support the Unity Party.'

The chair shook one arm and stepped back.

'I'm guessing that's a no.' Donal thought about this. 'I'll have to talk to Eduardo, find out what paperwork needs to exist for you to leave the building. Kyushen, could you store this stuff in St Jarl's?'

'Um ... Maybe.'

'I've plenty of room at home, but if things are about to change,' said Donal, 'I may not be a legal person for much longer. Maybe the commissioner's widow would look after you.'

The chair flexed and bowed, as if nodding.

'All right, but let's not bother her immediately. Also, any documents that are official police information must remain here, inside inanimate furniture. I'll get some secure filing cabinets brought up.'

This was a surreal, one-sided conversation for Donal to be having. What he needed was action.

'All right, Kyushen, you take that manual back to St Jarl's now, and for Death's sake look after it.'

'You got it, Lieutenant.'

'Call me Donal.'

'Um— Right.'

'Good man.'

After Kyushen had left, the various cabinets and drawers began to disgorge piles of papers. Many bore additional security seals that Donal had no way of bypassing. Whether he should be reading the papers was another matter. Still, as he scanned through memos, he found nothing startling, apart perhaps from the budget figures. Donal had never realized how much it cost to run a police force.

So now what?

The gun range. He could go down and loose off a few, either before or after finding out whether Brian could keep the contents of Commissioner Vilnar's office in one of his storage rooms. If anyone knew how to smuggle fittings out of the building, it was Brian.

'Good. I'll be back later.' He walked to the exit, noting how listlessly the ciliaserpents drew back. 'I'm sorry.'

After he'd exited into Surveillance, he looked around. At one of the monitors, Rob Helborne stood up, then shook his head. Obviously, he'd failed to find the Phantasm or Alexa.

Donal gave a fingertip salute, then headed to the lift shafts, where he was glad to notice that number 7 was in use once more. He waited, then stepped into the shaft.

Hey, Donal.

There was something different. Gertie's tone was tired, her form scarcely visible, while above her hung another wraith-shape.

'Xalia?' Donal thought there might be a translucent ribbon or cord joining them. 'Is that really—?'

No!

This was Gertie, holding Donal in place.

What have you done? YOU'VE KILLED ARRHENNIUS!

Donal remembered the eyeball in his pocket, and the way that the commissioner's office had opened as he approached, without needing commands from the Surveillance officers.

'I didn't—'

And then he dropped.

Not Arrhennius ...

Donal fell.

No, Gertie. Donal would never—

He grabbed at the sill of a door opening, putting everything into the hooking of his fingers, reaching – *got it* – and swinging with massive impact against the wall – *hang on* – but the impact bounced him off and he was falling again, dropping down inside the vertical shaft, no longer able to reach the sides, understanding that finally he was going to die for real.

Laura. I'm sorry.

Don't be.

He twisted as he fell, tears in his eyes, and whether it was from slipstream or fear no longer mattered to anyone, because this was the end of—

Impact?

Light shining all around him, translucent blue, billowing and fluorescing ...

I've ... got ... you.

...and then hard darkness, hammering him from the world.

Brian looked up from the counter, where he had been examining a box of chitin-piercing rounds from a new manufacturer called Whamista. His blue skin grew paler as he tried to process the strange sight in front of him.

It was a large wraith, pulled into a strange configuration, dragging an unconscious pale-skinned man across the floor. The wraith – or was it two wraiths? – faded in and out of visibility.

'That's Lieutenant Riordan. Shit!' Brian pushed up a section of counter, and bent down to grab Donal's head as the wraith – or wraiths – let go. 'What's going on?'

Look ... after ... him.

'What? Are you injured?'

Yes ... Care for ... Donal.

'I will. He's been decent to me, though he probably doesn't— Hades! Come back.'

But the wraith had already sunk into the floor.

'Oh, Death. This isn't good.' Brian felt for a pulse in Donal's cold neck, and got it. 'Shit. Shit.'

Then he hooked his hands under Donal's armpits and dragged him through the counter opening. Brian's lower back was flaring with pain, but he grunted and pulled until Donal was at the entrance to the store rooms.

'Not good.'

Brian opened a door to a small room with a mattress, a flamesprite candle, and some stacked cartons of food, none of which were supposed to be here. Then he hauled at Donal again until he tipped him on to the mattress.

Donal's left hand flopped, revealing the watch worn inside his wrist, and the tiny sliver of black on silver. Whatever massive trauma had just struck, Donal was close to death.

'Shit. Oh, shit.'

Trembling, Brian rushed to another room, and came back more slowly, struggling with the weight of the industrial black battery in his hands. His back was in agony as he lowered it to the floor, limped out, and returned with a length of black cord that ended with silver connectors.

With shaking hands, he pulled open Donal's shirt – a button popped off, was lost – and dug his fingertips into the chest, failed to hit the spot, then tried again. This time the triangular skin flap came open, and the pectoral muscle pulled back.

The black heart was beating. Slick reflected highlights slid across its surface.

'Hades, Lieutenant. How did you get in this—? There.' The connector clicked home, inside Donal's chest cavity. 'All right. Almost done.'

With the other end fastened to the battery, Brian sank back, sitting on the stone floor, wiping his face. His shirt was soaked with sweat.

Donal lay unmoving, save for the rhythmic pulsing of his zombie heart.

Outside Monazen Iona, crimson flamewraiths, the exact hue of burning strontium, danced and blazed. Bronze sculptures, fanged, surrounded the doors. Although the sculptures never moved, they broadcast a potential for movement that kept troublemakers out, rare as they were. This was downtown and the clientele were business people, for the most part.

Sitting at the bar counter, the gentle-looking man with the white hair and thirtysomething features almost blended in. Harald was wearing his best suit, along with a dark-green tie that probably didn't match. He didn't look too much out of place, and that was good, because he didn't want anyone here to remember him.

Viktor, nearly seven feet tall, wearing his usual leather coat, with his ugly-handsome unshaven face that made women's knees go weak, was outside. He would stay outside unless something catastrophic happened here.

'Coldfire brandy, sir.' The bartender put down the drink Harald had ordered. 'Enjoy.'

'Thanks.'

Harald watched the flames play across the brandy's surface, then took a sip. As promised, while the brandy was hot, the coldfire was cool against his lips. He put the glass down and nodded.

'Hey.' A woman, three stools down, looked at him. Silver-and-black butterfly wings were painted mask-like around her eyes. 'Are you on your own?'

The bartender moved discreetly away.

'Sometimes' – Harald's voice went soft, and moved to a certain cadence and ambiguous syntax – 'it is good ... to be alone and ... resourceful, of confidence, remembering how it feels to be filled ... with strength ... Now, here ... to regain control. In. Your. Life. Now.'

The woman's eyelids were fluttering.

'Good.' Harald checked that the bartender wasn't watching. 'To have. Confidence.'

Then the woman sucked in a deep breath, her eyes opening wide. She stared at her glass, took one tiny sip, then put the rest down as she stood up.

She walked past Harald, not even glancing at him. Her expression, so disconnected before, was hardening with focus. She went out into the street, looking ready to face the rest of her life, and take control of it.

Harald smiled.

You miserable fuckers just love your hexzookas and wraith-propelled grenades, don't ya?' he remembered Psychmaster Lerdban yelling as the recruits began the penultimate phase of Marine Corps training. *'But there ain't no WPG or sniper round that compares with the weapon you got right in there.'*

It had been the young Harald Hammersen whose forehead Lerdban's finger jabbed into.

'When I've finished with you snotslime boogers, you'll be able to lock and load your brain faster than you can pull your trigger. Got that, you testosterone-soaked worms?'

'Yes, sir!' the class had responded, and Harald's voice had been as loud as anyone's.

As it turned out, Lerdban had not exaggerated.

Viktor Harman had a family history of law enforcement. More precisely, his father, mother, uncles and grandparents had all been gang enforcers, all in trouble with the law. As a police officer, he was on his own. He liked to think that he brought his family's finest traditions into the world of policing.

As for what Harald had learned in the Marines, Viktor wasn't entirely sure. He knew that Jack Capers was in for a rough evening, if he tried to get violent with Harald. Ideally, Harald would get out of the way of any attack, and allow Capers to make a bolt for it, so Viktor could track him.

Viktor's observation post was an alleyway half a block across from

Monazen Iona. Directly overhead was a stone ledge on which an old worn gargoyle perched. It shifted with a tiny creak, but made no move to pounce.

'Nice day for it,' muttered Viktor. 'You OK up there?'

The gargoyle was still.

Viktor rubbed his chin, conscious of the weight of the twin Grausers beneath his arms. This had the makings of a ruinous day: putting the frighteners on a fellow officer, possibly interrogating him. That was the kind of thing that Internal Security did, and everyone knew that IS were bastards.

In his left hand, he was holding a dull yellow callstone. Harald had one like it, and if either man pressed his, the other stone would light up. The real use was so that Harald could let Viktor know when Jack Capers was on the move. So far—

There. On the other side of the street, a man with a reddish goatee was standing outside Monazen Iona, looking up at the flamewraiths. He was an exact match for Harald's description.

Viktor pressed the callstone.

Inside the bar, the stone in Harald's grip glowed yellow, then faded. Harald slipped it into his pocket as he got off the stool. Then Jack Capers entered, grinned, and offered his hand. They shook.

'What do you want to drink, Jack?'

'Is that coldfire brandy?'

'Sure is.'

'I'll go for that, then.'

'I guess you heard the man,' Harald told the bartender. 'And I'll have another, please.'

'Sure thing.'

After the bartender brought the drinks, Harald pointed to an empty booth. 'Probably more comfortable in there. Easier to chat.' He picked up both glasses.

'Sure,' said Capers. 'These other guys, are they here yet?'

'Not yet. Let me give you the lowdown on 'em.'

As they slid into the booth, Harald kept an eye on the bartender and the few other drinkers here in the front bar. No one was watching as Capers sat and leaned towards the glass that Harald had set down. As Capers reached, Harald brought his fingertips gently down on Capers' eyelids and said one word.

'Sleep.'

Capers' chin dropped to his chest.

'That's right,' Harald continued. 'As you feel so comfortable ... relax-ing down ... time to slow ... down between heartbeats ...'

As the verbal induction continued, Capers breathed so shallowly he appeared comatose, already deep in trance. He dropped faster and deeper than almost anyone Harald had worked on.

'You're standing at the back of a theatre.' Harald had the poor bastard in deep trance; now it was time to make use of it. 'And you can see yourself sitting in a seat. And *that* Jack Capers is seeing himself on stage, talking to colleagues.'

In trance, hallucinations would be as compelling as reality. It was important to keep Capers dissociated from the imagined events about to unfold.

'One of the officers is asking about the indigo phones, and I'm won-dering, what do you say to him in reply?'

'Nothing,' mumbled Capers, eyes still closed.

'And they ask more questions, and what do you reply?'

'Nothing.'

'That's right,' said Harald, 'and then they bring out scanning appar-atus, and what do you do next?'

'Kill them.'

'That's ... right. And what then?'

'Run.'

'You run, Jack, and where do you run to?'

'Charcroft Depths. The old brewery.'

'And what then? Do you contact anybody?'

'No. Wait. Only wait.'

'Good.' Harald paused, let out a breath. 'That's very good. And you can relax now, and let the images fade, and remember a time when you were relaxed and felt good. That's it. Remember how it felt, intensify the feeling ... Good. And now, as I count backwards from nine to one, you can awaken ...'

As Harald counted, Capers breathed more deeply, slowly raised his chin, blinked as the count reached four, then took in a deep breath and opened his eyes wide.

Harald said, 'One, and how do you feel now?'

'Great. I almost nodded off for a moment, but I feel great.'

'Good.' Harald raised his glass. 'To Customer Relationships.'

'And motivation.'

They clinked glasses, and drank the coldfire brandy.

'It looks like the others have gone straight to the restaurant,' said Harald. 'Damn. Good brandy. Glad we had time for a drink first.'

'I thought you said the others would be here. Senior officers, right?'

'Uh-huh. We meet here first unless we're running late, but the real goal is going for a curry. There's a place round the corner called Fire In The Hole, which believe it or not is a trendy establishment.'

'I've heard of it.' Capers grinned, as he had in the call centre. 'Shall we go now?'

'Let's do that.'

As they passed the bar, Harald left a handful of florin coins, leaving a decent but not too-generous tip for the bartender. So far things could not have gone better, but there was no point in making himself memorable.

Capers held the door for him as they went out.

'Which way?' he asked.

'Right along here.'

Harald led the way, noting the way Capers matched pace but just behind him, and then Capers' hand disappeared inside his jacket—

'No!'

—and that was when the evening went to Hades.

Viktor watched Jack Capers reach towards his left hip, heard Harald's shout, knew that the ex-Marine could probably snatch the weapon before it went off, but also knew that *probably* wasn't good enough when your colleague's life was in danger, not to mention innocent civilians in the background.

He used his right hand only, employing his left to pull the jacket open, sacrificing the second Grauser's firepower for speed. The weapon came out smoothly from the holster.

Harald swept his right hand down towards the enemy's gun – in that instant in Harald's mind, Capers was a dehumanised *thing* that faced him, not a human being, because there could be no hesitation – and he was inside the arc of movement, beginning the throat punch with his left, when an explosion happened.

Blood and flesh and fragments of bone sprayed from Jack Capers' shoulder, and he dropped.

Twenty

They got clear as fast as possible. First, Harald grabbed a passer-by, a large man wearing a bright red and silver spidersilk tie, and led him to the prone Capers. Viktor was already kneeling there.

'Take over,' said Viktor. 'Press here.'

'P-Press ...?'

'Relax,' Harald told the man. 'Down. Press. Remain.'

'All ... right.'

'You.' Harald pointed at a couple, then zeroed in on the wife, who looked calmer. 'Dial threes, sixes and nines, ask for an ambulance. In there, that bar. Where the red flamewraiths are.'

'Yes.' The woman tugged her husband. 'Come on.'

Her accent was Tristopolitan. Good. Harald had once told a Zurinese tourist to call for the fire service, and he'd spun the dials to some weird number that wasn't 333-666-999.

Then Viktor backed off, and Harald simply crossed the street, away from the other spectators who looked incapable of moving. Harald moved faster when he reached a sidestreet, and came out on to 253rd where Viktor was already standing in a shop doorway.

'Harald. Did I made the right call?'

'Only if you wanted to save my life, buddy.'

'Yeah.'

They walked together, heading for the corner where an amber P sign indicated a Pneumetro station. No one called out as they descended the iron stairs to the grimy hypoway. Harald joined a short queue, handed over a 13-cental coin, and took his pentagonal pink ticket. Viktor waited, already possessing a nine-day pass.

Both men could have shown their badges and travelled free, but it was a right that applied only when on police business, and they wanted to pass through here anonymously.

As they waited on a platform, Harald murmured, 'It was my fault. He seemed to come out of trance fine, with amnesia about the experience.'

'You triggered something deep?'

'I guess. Shit. I hope he lives. The bleeding looked under control.'

'He already worked behind a desk,' said Viktor. 'He'll be able to carry on with that.'

They knew that a shoulder wound was likely to be permanently disabling, when the complex joint was smashed apart by a bullet.

Vibration shook the stonework all around. Then, behind the scratched, mostly clear hexiglass barrier, the train pulled in.

'So where are we going?' said Viktor. 'I mean, after we've changed lines a few times.'

They climbed on board the nearest ovoid carriage. Neither man saw anyone following them. Passengers got on, got off, none paying special attention or trying too hard to be unnoticeable.

'Capers said – in trance – that if questioned, he would kill his interrogators—'

'Thanatos.'

'—and run to Charcroft Depths, to the old brewery.'

'I don't know the neighbourhood well,' said Viktor, 'but isn't the brewery derelict?'

A massive pneumatic pulse pushed the carriages into motion.

Neither man spoke for the next four stops, as the carriages split from each other and took different branches off the Orange Line. The fifth station was a major nexus, and Harald and Viktor alighted together, not needing to discuss the decision. They took a Magenta Line train, rode it southbound for three stops, then changed lines once more. Several more changes, and they finally came to Blackweb Pentangle, an old station in need of repainting and retiling.

They climbed the exit steps, and came out at the edge of the small black spider-inhabited park the station was named for. The houses around the Pentangle's outer rim were five-storey, originally family homes for the well-to-do, long since divided into single-room bedsits with communal bathrooms.

'I think the brewery's that way,' said Viktor.

'All right.'

Ten minutes later, they were walking through the ruins of an old building that had once been proud to produce Farsight Ale. Now the big signs were grey and faded. One had fallen to the broken ground.

'You noticing anything with those highly trained Marine perceptions?'

'Yeah.'

'What?'

'Old bricks, dirt, smashed windows. Like that.'

'Uh-huh.' Viktor pointed to a plump woman, her head wrapped in a scarf, who was pushing a pram. 'Let's ask about Capers.'

The woman tensed as they walked over, then loosened a little as Harald gave his best good-cop smile.

'Hi, ma'am. We're just wondering if anyone knows a friend of ours, name of Jack Capers.'

'Sorry.'

'Never mind. I don't suppose you'd know who to ask?'

'There's a small store thataway, that's been there for— Oh, there's Mrs Hatchet. She's lived here for Death knows how long.'

'Thanks.'

They crossed the street to ask. When the old woman, Mrs Hatchet, heard Jack Capers' name, she shook her head.

'Young Jack,' she said. 'I haven't seen him in such a long time.'

'He'd be about thirty-five, ma'am.'

'Yes, Young Jack, that's right. Nice boy.'

'Does he live round here?'

'Number 27, next to the corner. Oh, but, it's over twenty years ago that his family moved away. Pleasant couple. They—'

'Thank you, ma'am,' said Harald. 'Thank you very much.'

They walked on, with Viktor leading the way. Rather than return to Blackweb Pentangle, they would make their way to the next station on foot, and pick up the hypoway there.

'We learned nothing,' muttered Viktor. 'Capers lived here as a kid. So what? There's no hideout for ensorcelled cops and dark mages. Nothing but ruins, and where the Hades is Alexa?'

'Maybe,' said Harald.

'What maybe?'

'Maybe we didn't learn nothing, excuse my double negative. Maybe Capers planned to come here, not because he'd been commanded to run to Charcroft Depths specifically, but to a place of safety, to a place he knew well.'

'Huh. Harald, you're a genius.'

'I know. Do *you* know where Alexa grew up?'

'Uh ... Shadebourne Yards, near the Groans?'

'I'm not sure. That sounds right, but Shadebourne's a large place. Time to get back to HQ, see if Surveillance can find anything with those monitors of theirs.'

'And check in with Donal. Maybe Bowman.'

210

'That too.'

They reached Dark-Green Place, a gloomy station built of greenish minerals, where they caught a Black Line train to Blamechurch Avenue. There, they walked up to street level. Viktor scanned the half-busy sidewalks, and looked back at the station.

'Still no one following.'

'I agree.'

'We can walk to Dingvale, catch the Dragonway bus to Avenue of the Basilisks.'

'Uh-huh. Might be better if we didn't ride back on the same bus.'

'Yeah. Good thinking.'

They'd be approaching HQ from the opposite direction to Monazen Iona, but there was no sense in making things easier for any potential witnesses to Capers' shooting. Harald considered suggesting that Viktor remove his leather coat, changing his image, but then every cop who knew Viktor would wonder what was going on.

As they walked the length of Blamechurch Avenue, the dark road leading from the eponymous Pneumetro station, Harald and Viktor automatically scanned the tall, old tenements. They noticed the lighted windows begin to flicker.

'Power brownout,' said Harald. 'We've had them in my neighbourhood, too.'

'Not in mine.'

Then, for a second, everything plunged into darkness. Harald and Viktor stopped. It was the middle of the day, but all the lights were out. Harald looked up at the dark-purple sky, wondering what it would be like to live somewhere that didn't rely on artificial lighting for people to see.

When the lights flicked back on, they were dimmer than before.

'That's a bit unsettling,' said Viktor, just as a baby began to cry in a nearby tenement.

'Looks like the Energy Authority have it under some kind of control.'

'I guess.'

At the end of the block, they stopped.

'What the crap is going on there?'

Across the way, a group of people stood at a bus stop, about to board. But the vehicle they were boarding had armoured windows, and an Engels County PD emblem on the side. The cops who were ushering them aboard wore white helmets and carried long staves.

All of the passengers had very pale skin.

'Rounding up zombies?'

211

'And taking them outside the city limits, to Engels.'

Ordinary citizens were walking past, looking down at the ground, as protective patterns executed in their minds, attempting to hallucinate normality instead of what was happening. Every cop knew the story of Mary Jo Gavin, stabbed to death in Horzahl Station in the middle of rush hour, and not a single witness among the hundreds of commuters that the police had questioned, in the presence of certified truthseers and truthsayers.

'We have to do something.'

'We have to think of Alexa.'

'Fuck.'

'Yeah.'

They turned and walked away, just like all the other citizens.

Harald entered HQ first, with Viktor due to follow in twenty minutes. Eduardo, on the desk, was trying to calm down a group of tourists bickering in what sounded liked Low Dalasien.

'Hey, Harald.'

'Eduardo. Sorry, I don't speak Dalasien.'

'Is *that* what they're jabbering in? Thanks, pal. At least now I know what kind of interpreter to ask for.'

He pointed to the phone on his desk. It was a still a black telephone.

'Good. I'll see you lat—'

'Need a word, Harald.'

'All right.'

'The lieutenant says you gotta practise more for the competition. Like there's money riding on us versus the 53rd, you know?'

'I wasn't ...' Harald patted the granite block. 'All right. I'll practise.'

'Good.' Eduardo winked. 'You're a good man.'

'And so are you.'

As Harald traversed the stone-floored lobby, he reflected that both Donal and Eduardo knew two things: that Harald practised his combat skills constantly, and that he had no intention of participating in any competition. He stepped inside the first available lift shaft.

'Gun range, please.'

Certainly.

The lift-wraith carried him down.

Once in the firing-range lobby, Harald could see Brian and Eagle Dawkins talking to a group of uniformed officers, far along the corridor that ran past the practice lanes. The uniforms were carrying targets and shotguns. For the moment, the place was quiet.

'All right.' Harald edged on to the counter, swivelled his legs over, and dropped to the other side. 'So let's see what we have back here.'

He went through a door into a passageway that opened to storerooms on either side. It took only seconds to find the one that featured a zombie sprawled across a dirty mattress, his heart exposed, a power cord ripped from it.

'Hades.'

It looked as though Donal had stirred during recharge-sleep, and pulled the cord from its socket.

Not every member of the Fighting Sevens, Harald's old unit, had been a living human. Well practised in emergency procedures, Harald picked up the cord, checked the battery it was connected to – not empty, but carrying a low charge – then looked up at the dim light bulb. That would work better.

There was a box of what might have been books. Harald dragged it under the light, and used it to stand on. He unscrewed the bulb, then took a careful grip on the cable and the black-resin bulb-holder, and used a sharp rip-and-twist to pull them apart.

In seconds, he had the raw ends of the live cable twisted in to the cord connector. Then he plugged the other end into Donal's chest.

As he stood up, a heavy shape barrelled into the room, knocking into Harald, grabbing for the cord and ripping it free by uncontrolled momentum.

'No! You don't—'

Harald hammered down, struck Brian's temple with the bottom of his fist, then caught the semi-conscious man before he smashed his face into the floor.

Donal gasped, his eyes still closed.

'What's going on?' said Harald. 'Brian, tell me.'

'The power ...' Brian pointed. 'Use the battery.'

There was a fully charged replacement in the doorway. He must have been carrying it when he saw Harald bent over Donal.

'All right.'

Harald pulled the cord away from the dangling ceiling wires, and snapped the connector into place on the new battery. Donal's face grew calm again.

'It's the   power,' Brian was sitting up on the floor. 'After brownouts, there's a change, for about an hour.'

'A change.'

'Gimme a hand here, will you?'

After a moment, Harald helped Brian to his feet.

'Watch,' added Brian, raising one hand towards the bare ends of dangling wire. 'See?'

As his pale-blue skin came almost in contact, dark-blue mottling appeared. Wincing, Brian pulled his hand back down.

'What the Hades is that?' said Harald.

'I don't know, but it hurts.' Brian pointed to Donal's black, beating heart. 'It makes folk like him sick, and right now he can't cope with that.'

'What happened to him?'

'That, you're going to have to find out from someone else.' Brian wobbled. 'Ah, you've got a hard fist, Sergeant. If that's what you hit me with.'

'Sit down. I'll get you some water.'

'Yeah. Thanks.'

By the time Harald had Brian comfortable on a chair, sipping water – and had handed over targets to three cops looking to practise – Viktor was in the storage room as well, having received a similar message from Eduardo on entering the building.

'So tell us,' Viktor said to Brian, 'exactly what happened to Donal.'

'Like I told Harald, you'll need to— Ask her.'

A glowing form was rising up through the floor.

Is Donal all right?

'Healing up, or seems to be,' said Harald. 'But who are you?'

Viktor frowned.

'That's Gertie from ... No.'

The big glowing wraith shifted form.

'Xalia?' added Viktor. 'But you don't ... No.'

Harald rubbed his face. This reminded him of something he'd heard of, one of many stories told late at night in some sergeants' mess. The trouble was, so many of those tales turned out to be true.

Call me Aggie.

'Oh,' said Harald. 'Hi. We haven't met. For a moment we thought—'

Short for Aggregate. Sort of a joke.

'Shit.'

Brian and Viktor stared from Harald to the wraith, Aggie, and back again.

'What's going on?'

I was both the beings you thought I was.

'Gertie?' asked Viktor. 'Or Xalia?'

'Not "or",' said Harald. 'Gertie *and* Xalia, am I right?'

As close as a human being can get.

214

'So Xalia was really injured. We thought she was getting better.'

We had an ... incident. After you left her here. There was only one way to save her.

Harald stared down at Donal's open chest cavity. The heart continued to beat, recharging normally now.

Events don't follow our plans, do they?

'Is this ...' Viktor tried to clear his throat, then growled: 'Are you permanently ... together?'

I don't know.

Viktor stared at Harald.

Besides, to reconstitute Gertie and Xalia, I would have to cease existing.

'Fuck,' said Viktor.

I haven't tried that, in this identity.

Harald held up his hand.

'Alexa is missing. She's ensorcelled, and she took the Phantasm. We think she might have been programmed to escape to childhood haunts, which in her case would be Shadebourne Yards.'

That's not good.

Aggie flared brightly. Whatever Xalia's condition had been, this aggregated wraith was powerful.

'Can you help us?'

What about Surveillance. Have you asked for their assistance?

'We're going to check back with them,' said Harald, 'but earlier they'd found nothing.'

'Alexa killed two people.' Viktor shrugged his massive shoulders, like a boxer loosening up before the first round. 'Everyone's looking for her, and they're more likely to shoot than arrest her.'

And if you find her? How can you avoid shooting?

'If there's a way, we'll find it. At least we're motivated.'

Yes.

'So can you think of anything?'

Yes.

Harald's mouth twitched. That was a touch of Gertie's sense of humour.

'Tell us,' he said.

Scanbats.

'That's not Surveillance. That's the City Mages. They don't owe us any personal favours.'

Are they the only ones who can merge with bats?

'Er ...'

Aggie's form brightened, as she extended a partially materialized limb towards Viktor.

He's got the touch of Mordanto upon him. They can help.

'Mordanto?' said Harald.

'Hades, *she* had a word with me. Was waiting outside my house, along with André. He's her driver now.'

'I heard.' Harald nodded towards Donal. 'Did you tell him?'

'No.'

'Will she help?'

'Your guess is exactly as good as mine.'

'That accurate, huh? Look, Aggie, what should we—?'

But the wraith was already drifting up towards the ceiling.

'Shit.'

And then she was gone.

Even the OCML gave people days off work. Even Bone Listeners needed hobbies. Some studied esoteric fields of scholarship, and contributed to journals that few people read. Some created intricate devices formed of bone, and delved into advanced perceptual and cognitive models, as if simply being a Bone Listener had not already immersed them in a rigorously arcane worldview.

Lexar Pinderwin lived on the seventeenth floor of a seventeen-sided tower. Like the other modest towers in the small enclave, it was coloured an appropriate bone-grey. Most of the residents were Bone Listeners, although none besides Lexar were forensic specialists or worked at the Office of the Chief Medical Listener.

A single cobalt-blue giant beetle clacked its way across the purple lawn that lay in the middle of the ring of towers. Benches were set all around, but today only one was occupied, by an old Bone Listener who sat watching the beetle.

'Master Pinderwin,' the old fellow said as Lexar approached. 'Come sit with me, if you have time.'

'I'd be delighted, sir.'

Lexar did not know Rakshun Aldrevun well, but Aldrevun's bulbous eyes still gleamed with the strength of a formidable Bone Listener. He was a professor of Lattice science, and several of the city's foremost Archivists had been his students.

'I can stay for a short while,' added Lexar. 'I'm not working today, but you know how it is.'

'Oh, I wonder if I do. There are so many paths available to us.'

'Yes, sir,' said Lexar, as if he understood what Aldrevun meant.

The bench was hard. How could Aldrevun spend so much time sitting on it?

'As one ages, though,' said Aldrevun, 'one has certain harsh realities to face. Still, if it's bad for us, imagine how it is for ordinary humans, who are not forced until old age to confront the simplest facts that we learn as infants.'

'I'm not sure I follow.'

'Humour an old man talking about his own death.'

'You have many years yet, sir.'

'Truth?'

'Well ... Years.' Lexar closed his eyes. 'The marrows remain strong.'

'Indeed. But my nephew died exactly one week ago. I've spent those nine days grieving.'

'Good passing. What happened?'

Bone Listeners rarely suffered illness, until the final weeks before the body's shutdown.

'He lived in Kalis. You heard about the riots in the Old Seventh?'

'Um, vaguely.'

The elegant old city of Kalis contained seven large wards, filled with pyramids and airy towers amid wide boulevards lined with cafés and restaurants. That was the popular image. But away from the city, in neighbouring Tourraine, there was a territory that Rialst and the Dankish Republic both claimed as theirs. And the wards of Kalis tended to be inhabited along ethnic lines, so that green-skinned Rialstan families often clashed with their grey Dankish neighbours, within a city that was supposed to be cosmopolitan.

'A rabble broke into our enclave, smashed homes, painted anti-Bone Listener slogans everywhere ... and took over twenty of our people out into the street, in order to beat them to death.'

'I didn't—'

'No, you didn't. Because that's not the kind of news the *Gazette* or the *Messenger* like to carry, not when they have advertisers. The *Gazette* mentioned "civil unease".'

Lexar rubbed his face. 'I'm not sure that's fair.'

'The violent, disgusting deaths of twenty-seven Bone Listeners were ignored by our local media. What does that tell you about the attitudes of mundanes towards those who are different?'

'The term "mundanes"—'

'Is far less insulting than what they've started calling us, or haven't you noticed? Tell me, how many more cases of non-mundane death are you investigating nowadays?'

'A few more zombicides than normal, perhaps.'

Aldrevun's lined face grew harder.

'Ask yourself whether the number of bodies reaching your autopsy tables reflects what's happening in the world.'

Lexar got up from the bench.

'Excuse me, but I must get home.'

'Of course. Forgive me for asking you to share my concerns.'

'That's all right, sir.'

'You should take downtime to look after yourself, while you can.' The old Bone Listener nodded. 'Disengage from the bones that haunt.'

Lexar gave a short bow, as if he understood what Aldrevun had been telling him, then turned towards the tower that contained his home, and began to walk.

And he continued to walk, right past the entrance, heading for an archway that led out of the Bone Listener enclave.

'Silly old bastard,' Lexar muttered.

But there had been a pogrom in Kalis, and the silly old bastard had known all about it while Lexar Pinderwin, promising young forensic Bone Listener, supposedly perceptive, had been going about his life in ignorance.

Could there be other zombie deaths, other *non-mundane* deaths, where the remains were somehow failing to reach the OCML? Could Tristopolis have changed so much, and so quickly?

'I'm not political. Never have been.'

Perhaps there were times when even the least political of beings must take a stand. If Dr d'Alkernay were still alive, he could ask her advice, ask what she knew. But she was dead, and Lexar had no idea who to even begin talking to.

'Lieutenant Riordan,' he muttered. 'Or Feoragh Carryn.'

Bone Listener Carryn was an Archivist, not a forensic specialist, and perhaps that was exactly the kind of person Lexar needed. Someone versed in the ways of the Lattice.

'Yes. Good.'

Lexar continued to walk for a long time, thinking about the overriding importance of his career, and how he might jeopardise that by talking to the wrong people. Forensic Bone Listeners were supposed to work in a world of their own.

Eventually, as he walked, he began to stare less at the sidewalk, and more at the people who were glancing at him from street corners. He was in a neighbourhood far from his own, where the inhabitants were standard human – mundane – and poor.

What he ought to do was flag down the first taxi he saw and get out of here. But there was a phone booth about a hundred yards ahead, so he overrode his rising unease.

The booth was new, surprising in this neighbourhood, and quite intact. Lexar picked up the indigo receiver – interesting colour – and spun the cogs to the number for the Archivists' switchboard, and put the receiver to his ear.

'Thanatos!'

He threw the receiver away from him. It bounced from the booth wall, and swung on its cord. Even then, he could hear the neural howl. Trembling, he placed it back on the hook, and the horrifying song cut off.

A song not of bones, but of nerves.

'Oh, sweet Hades.'

He stared out of the booth. Ordinary people lived here. People who could not detect what howled down the line. How many people had used this phone? And how many more devices like this were in the city?

'Aldrevun was right.'

He had to tell people what was happening.

'No. What I need is proof.'

And he was better placed than anyone to find it.

Twenty-one

Donal remained in coma, on the mattress in Brian's store room. Harald and Viktor continued to watch over him. Brian stayed with them when he could, leaving only when officers arrived at the counter looking for targets and ammunition.

When he came back from serving three detectives from Robbery-Haunting, Harald asked a question he'd been thinking about.

'Brian? How is it you have a mattress in here? And food supplies, and a moth-oil stove?'

'Um ...'

'You're not living here, are you?'

'I ... Shit.' Brian rubbed his pale-blue face. 'I had a bit of trouble with the landlord.'

'What kind of trouble?'

'The kind where he says he's evicting everyone, because he's selling the building, you know? Except that only me and the family above got notices. They also got "Fuck Off Greenies" written on their door, and I don't want to tell you what the bastards wrote it in.'

'I'm sorry.'

'Yeah. I don't know what happened to the family. You want to feel sorry for anyone, feel it for them.'

'Right.' Harald stared down at Donal, then at Brian. 'We've got a lot to deal with, but we will make sure you're all right.'

'I'm doing OK.'

'So's Donal,' said Viktor. 'He looks to be recharging just fine. Which gives me a really bad feeling.'

'Why's that?' asked Brian. 'I thought he was your friend.'

'He is. And that's why Sergeant Hammersen is about to ask me to do something I don't want to do. Am I right?'

'Not at all,' said Harald. 'As if I'd ever suggest that you ... really ... want ... to come to Mordanto with me.'

220

'Fuck off.' Viktor rubbed his eyes. 'Shit. All right.'

Brian pointed to Donal.

'I'll look after the lieutenant.'

'And I,' said Harald, 'will take this gentleman who's eager to take a drive, and we'll see what we can see.'

'Yeah. Great.'

Viktor touched Brian on the shoulder before leaving, and Harald did likewise. It was a gesture of friendship, or at least equality. Then the two men hurried out.

It was perhaps ten minutes later that the Robbery-Haunting guys returned to the counter, and called for Brian. He went out to see what they needed.

'You got any of those silver-crossed Cleaver rounds?'

'Hades,' said Brian. 'You know how much that stuff costs?'

'So we'll only take two boxes for practice. Or you want our boss should get authorisation from the commissioner?'

'Ain't you heard? The commissioner is dead.'

'The old one, sure. Rumour is, Craigsen's going to be the new man at the top.'

'Ugh,' said Brian.

'And what's that supposed to mean, Bluey?'

'I don't— Nothing. I'll get your ammo.'

'Good man. Or whatever.'

Brian fetched the rounds they wanted, and handed the boxes over without a word. Then he watched them head back to the firing lanes, feeling bleak. After a short while, he returned to the storage room that had been doubling as his bedroom, to see how Lieutenant Riordan was doing.

The mattress was empty. The power cord lay neatly coiled beside the necrotonic battery pack.

'I guess you got all the moves, Lieutenant.' Brian glanced at the wall, in the direction of the practice shots that were starting up. 'I hope it's enough.'

He pushed at the mattress with the toe of his shoe.

'Guys like you and me,' he added. 'We don't got it so good these days.'

Then he reached around to the small of his back, and drew a small shining automatic. It was a Silver Dragon, and surprisingly accurate given the shortness of its barrel. It contained only seven rounds, but if things went totally sour, that was more than enough.

Perhaps he would take out five of the Robbery-Haunting bastards before turning the gun on himself. With one round to spare, of course.

Brian had always been a careful man. Or careful ... whatever.

Donal hadn't known about the old shaft leading away from the storage rooms. After awakening, he had stood listening to Brian talking to the bigots from R-H, and reflecting on what he could remember hearing while in coma. Standing there, he had noticed the microcurrents of air as they played across his skin; and that was how he found a private way out.

There were no secret exits or entrances to HQ, of course. What he found was an old vertical shaft that allowed him to climb up five storeys within the building, before clambering out into an administrative level. From there he used a subterranean exit – actually a sequence of heavy portals guarded by deathwolves and bored-looking uniformed cops who made no comment about the stains on Donal's clothing from the climb – and passed through the semi-expensive stores of Kulring Mall, before riding to the surface.

He returned to Darksan Tower on foot. Once inside his apartment, as decorative flames rose from the floor grilles, he discarded his expensive, ruined suit, stripped down to his skivvies, fetched the manticore-gut skipping-rope, and began to jump. He found his rhythm, and kept it going.

As he jumped, he thought. His physiological processes appeared to have reset themselves. The earlier injuries might have been less due to the physical trauma of falling than to the side-effects of being caught by two part-conjoined wraiths: impacts not just on the surface but internally, where they might have partially materialized inside him, or allowed energy to spill through.

As if recalling a dream, he understood the new wraith Aggie's explanation of how she was the fusion of Gertie and Xalia. And he remembered that Harald and Viktor were going to Mordanto, without having made their reasons explicit.

He allowed himself to continue jumping for an hour, and then he stopped. Going on for longer would have been easy; but it was time to get the investigation moving once more. Let Harald and Viktor pursue whatever they were after. He would ring Kyushen first, find out whether he'd learned anything other than thaumaturgic engineering esoterica, then try to find out whether this Illurian phone company, Central Resonator Systems, had offices in Tristopolis. Someone had to install the damned phones.

Still in his shorts, he sat down on the bed next to the phone. Just as he was reaching for the handset, intending to ring St Jarl's, it rung. He picked up the receiver.

'Riordan.'

'This is St Jarl's-the-Healer Hospital. I have a call for you, sir.'

This was too weird.

'Thanks.' Then, as the background noise changed on the line: 'Hi, Kyushen. How's it going?'

'I'm disappointed, Lieutenant,' answered a feminine voice. *'I guess boys remember toys, and not the people with the healing touch.'*

'Uh-huh.' Donal gave a wide smile. 'Some people have claws, as I recall.'

'Ah, that we do.'

'So how are you doing, Sister Felice?'

'I'm quite uninjured in all the excitement, and of course Kyushen arrived after it was all over, so he's fine, too.'

'Excitement?'

'Or maybe you should think of it as a jailbreak, since it was the Sucker Wing they broke open. Civilians call it the Secure Unit for the Criminally Ensorcelled.'

'So you're not just calling to check up on me, Sister Felice?'

'Of course I am. And to let you know that Marnie Finross is no longer in our establishment.'

'Eyes?'

'I read about her nickname in the Gazette. *Yes. Me, I saw the guys who sprung her. I thought they were lawyers.'*

'What—?' He thought about the way she'd said she was uninjured. 'Were people hurt?'

'A few. They blew up the walkway, ruptured the defences, and all the dangerous psycho nutters – that's a medical term – got loose.'

'Damn it. I hadn't heard any of this.'

'Police HQ is a big place. And I hear you've a lot going on in the big city.'

'Yeah. Listen ... You and the other Night Sisters better stay in the hospital for now. Let ordinary human friends do the shopping for you.'

'We're healers.'

'I know.'

'Anyone can go crazy. I've not seen it happen with a whole city.'

'No, but it can. Maybe the whole of the Federation, for all I know.'

'Hades, Lieutenant. You know how to cheer a girl up.'

Donal, still sitting on the bed, turned to look at the pillows.

'I'm sorry,' he said. 'Sister Felice, I need you to do me two favours.'

'Two more favours? All right, what are they?'

'The first is, call me Donal.'

'*Ah, yes.*' There was a soft sound, partly laughter, partly something sibilant and less human. '*That I can do.*'

'And the second is to look after yourself. I mean, really watch out.'

Now there was a silence.

'*You do the same, Donal.*'

Then a click sounded, and the line buzzed. For a few moments, Donal continued to hold the receiver. Then he gently replaced it on the hook.

He rose to his feet, padded barefoot across the dark, polished floor, picked up his discarded suit jacket, and reached into the pocket. The eyeball that he drew out was less sticky now. It was still clear, although opacity should have long ago set in.

He placed it on the bedside cabinet, next to the phone.

'Friends,' he said.

After a moment, he walked out into the hallway and stopped. The walls were dark-grey and polished, decorated with inverted mirror-like shields that were more than twice Donal's height. Not knowing how he knew to do this, he picked a certain shield and tapped it, then spoke keywords he had never uttered before.

The shield swung back, revealing a small open hatchway. Inside was a dark, narrow vertical shaft. Donal poked his head through the gap. There was a ladder on the opposite wall, and it appeared to disappear downwards for ever, and to lead upwards to what must be the roof. Since the apartment was on the 227th floor, the roof was the only thing higher.

The rungs and struts of the ladder glowed a soft grey-green. Trying not to think too much about what he was doing, Donal swung himself on to it. Still dressed only in shorts, he clambered upwards.

Soon he came to a door that opened from the inside, and he stepped through, on to the roof. He was at the base of the complex, dark spire that rose from the building proper. On all sides, dark narrow cables hung in hypercosine curves, linking the city's towers, along with narrow stone channels no wider than a hand.

Donal walked to the very edge, feeling the cold winds against his cold skin, knowing that sudden turbulence was a constant danger here. He stared across the tower roofs and spires, the whole of Tristopolis laid out beneath a hemisphere of blank, dark-purple sky.

My city.

But not if the Unity Party had its way.

It's still my city.

He stopped breathing. After a moment, he raised his arms to either side, and stood like some cruciform statue. He allowed his thoughts to slow, distorting the physiological passage of time as he waited.

Waiting ...

Eventually, there was a scarlet glimmer. A pair of eyes, and then another. Then a hint of dark fluid movement among shadows on nearby towers.

Soon afterwards, they began to slink along the narrow cables and stone channels, eyes glowing stronger as they drew near.

The cats – Laura's cats – were coming.

The taxi dropped Lexar off on a narrow strip of sidewalk, at the edge of a seven-spiral intersection where people rarely walked. The traffic was heavy and the air smelled bad, but this was the way that Lexar usually came. He edged along a dark stone wall until he came to a massive round steel door bearing the Skull-and-Ouroboros insignia.

'Bone Listener Lexar Pinderwin,' he said loud enough to be heard over the traffic.

There was a grinding noise, and the disc-shaped door rolled into its groove. What it revealed was a stone tunnel inside which dim flame-wraiths barely flickered. Lexar stepped inside, waited for the outer door to shut, and waited for the inevitable scanfield to descend and pass through him. Then he continued to the inner door, which likewise ground open. He exited to an enclosed but roofless nine-sided courtyard.

Two men in uniform came out of a small guardhouse.

'Bone Listener, hey. How's things?'

'Doing OK. Listen, I'm not on the roster, but the other day, I left some of my instruments behind. Can I sign in, and go down and fetch them?'

'I'll have to ring down,' said the other guard. 'Hang on.'

He went into the guardhouse. His colleague and Lexar stared up at the sky from which a quicksilver rain was falling, then at the liquid metal puddles forming on the black, uneven ground of the courtyard.

After a minute, the other guard came back with a clipboard. *WESTSIDE COMPLEX – VISITORS' SIGN-IN* was printed across the top.

'Here you go, Bone Listener. Write "Pavel Layne" in the "Visiting" box, and sign as usual.'

'Nice of Pavel to take responsibility for me.' Lexar signed the sheet. 'There you go.'

'Have a good day.'

'You too.'

Lexar crossed the courtyard, passed through a short passage, and came out at the edge of a vast, stone-walled pit that seemed to descend for ever. Skulls decorated the walls, and the further that one descended, the odder (as well as more worn) the features appeared. He had never been able to determine whether the older skulls had been sculpted or represented individuals who had actually lived. On the one occasion he had asked Dr d'Alkernay about it, her answer had been a smile and a shake of her head, nothing more.

Iron tracks zigged and zagged their way down the walls, and into the depths.

Lexar waited.

After four or five minutes, a bone-and-iron open-sided coach came lurching up the vertical pit wall, clanking and shaking where the rail changed angle. When it reached the top, Lexar stepped in, sat down, and grabbed hold of the smooth-worn iron handles.

There was a jolt, and the small coach began its descent. It was a process that Lexar was used to, but not one that he ever expected to like. He occupied himself with a series of focus exercises, alternately opening and closing down his senses to the background resonance pervading this place. Finally, the coach lurched to a halt, and Lexar exited to a stone chamber where Pavel Layne was waiting.

'Lexar. Good to see you again, so soon.'

'Only because I'm forgetful. Will I be able to get into the exam room?'

'Sure. It's not been used for anyone since that alderman, uh, whatever his name was.'

'Finross,' said Lexar. 'Your guys are busy, though?'

'As always. You want to say hi to the grads?'

'Yeah, I'd love to.'

Lexar had helped out on the graduate training programming, for the new joiners whose abilities in osteoanalysis rarely matched their knowledge of thaumadynamic processes. No one expected them to be Bone Listeners; but they needed sensitivity far beyond that of ordinary humans. Among other responsibilities, osteoanalysts were supposed to pick out, from among the piles of corpses destined for the reactors, any deceased artists whose bones contained the interference pattern of their dreams.

'All right.' Pavel walked with Lexar as far as the trainees' workroom. 'I know I'm supposed to stay with you, but we really are busy. You'll be OK by yourself?'

'Sure. I think I know the way by now.'

'Then take it easy. I'll try to see you before you leave.'

'See you later.'

Lexar tapped on the door, and went inside. At benches and corpse examination tables, young men and women wearing pale-grey lab coats were sitting or standing. The lab coats bore the Skull-and-Ouroboros stitched on the breast.

'Hi, folks,' said Lexar. 'You all doing OK?'

'Hey, Lexar.'

Most of them were working on a single bone, set in a resonator cavity. Oscilloscopes and fluxometers traced the changing potentials of necro-magnetic fields.

'Lexar, you know you told me to read up about arthritis-mediated defects?'

'Uh, sure I do.'

'Well, I've been boning up on it ...'

There was a second's pause, before the other trainee analysts groaned.

'Oh, please.'

' ...but we need more people. I mean, we're working with a skeleton staff.'

'We so do not need this.'

'And you'll excuse me,' said Lexar, 'because I need to go off and be sick.'

He crossed the room, used the door at the far end, and headed towards the room where he had worked with Alderman Finross's corpse. He let himself in – the scanfield recognized him – and looked around the still, quiet chamber. Overhead was the inverted tree in which the quicksilver flock slept.

From his pocket, Lexar pulled a stethofork and several other instruments, including a small resonator blade. He could claim that he'd left them here, and had just picked them up. After preparing himself for sleight of hand while Pavel or one of his colleagues watched, it was almost disappointing to be here in the room by himself.

But to find the proof he needed, he would have to venture further. He used an exit he would not normally take, followed a short corridor, and came to what was supposed to be a secure door. A fossilized knuckle larger than a human hand lay on the floor, propping the door open. Half of the osteoanalysts used this route during their breaks.

Lexar went through, and descended a helical flight of ceramic steps to the Necrotonic Diffraction Analysis & Resource Classification Department, known to the workers as Sifting & Lifting. Here, osteoanalysts and their colleagues made the final checks and decided on which route the corpses would take, as secondary or primary grade material.

Here, the corridors were tiled in white, as were the processing chambers that opened off them. The first chamber was busy, and Lexar passed it by. Two doors later, he found a chamber in which corpses lay on three of the thirty-three white slabs, but no analysts were working. He went inside.

Lexar had sensitivity, allowing him to work without instruments even at times when other Bone Listeners, like his colleague Brixhan, deployed most of their detection devices. Even so, when he placed his hands atop the first cold corpse, it took a while before he could come to a conclusion. He shook his head.

Then he moved to the next body, repeated the procedure, before taking a small platinum rod from his pocket, forcing the needle-end through the hardened flesh, and closing his eyes to concentrate. Again he shook his head, and removed the rod. He looked at the next body, wondering if it was worth—

Voices sounded from outside, and he ducked behind a slab. His vision tunnelled inwards, as if someone were painting black around the periphery of his visual field, and a rushing sound filled his hearing. This was neurochemical stress, the side-effect of adrenaline dumping into his system, and part of his mind was interested in the phenomenon, even while the rest of him was panicking.

After the voices had faded as the people walked past, he became aware of the sweat layering his skin, now beginning to cool.

Abandoning the room, he checked the next chamber along the corridor – too many live people working inside – and the next – empty of corpses – and then the third, where the small shapes lying on the slabs looked promising. Two analysts were talking, leaving the room, and Lexar moved back out of sight. When they were gone, he entered.

Yes, the bodies were all of children. He should have thought of this before.

The first, when he scanned it, was obviously intact. Perhaps he should have stopped to think about the tragedy – the brain aneurysm was obvious to him, like a groan overlaying soft flute music – but he had to keep moving. He checked the next dead child and the next, until the fourth boy. This was it.

Quickly, he checked the bodies on the next two slabs, and they were in similar condition.

'Shit.'

He looked down at the pale, purple-bruised face. Then he lifted his resonator blade, and thumbed it on. The vibration was strong but without sound.

'Forgive me.'

It was obvious to his senses, but not to an ordinary human's. They would need proof, via dissection and an optical microscope. He lifted the dead boy's left hand, and swept the resonator down, just above the wrist.

The cut was clean.

In the pit, lying on its side, the motorcycle's engine growled. But its wheel, bent in half, squealed when it tried to turn. Undefeated, the motorcycle extruded its parking stand, slowly, slowly, trying to push itself upright. For several moments, it might have been succeeding, despite the fluids that gushed from its cracked carapace. Then the stand gave way, and the Phantasm crashed to its side once more.

Its headlight flickered, then resumed its green glow, weaker than before.

At ground level, propped against the ruin that surrounded the pit, Alexa Ceerling sat with her chin on her chest, her eyes closed, her ribcage scarcely moving. Even the mournful sound of oil tankers passing on Shatterway Sound could not penetrate the depths of the deep, final trance enveloping her.

A white lizard came close, sniffed at her leg, then backed off. But it did not go far. Its fellows stood motionless on the rubble, waiting without emotion.

When Lexar returned to the graduates' room, he was brandishing his instruments, the ones he'd supposedly left here two days before. No one paid attention to them, since they were accessories he had used in demonstrations and tutorials some weeks back, at the beginning of the training programme.

He crept up behind the trainee who'd made the smart remarks earlier.

'Is that a humerus you're analysing?'

'Shit! Oh. Sorry, Lexar. You startled me.'

'It's funny, but I think you're going out on a limb with that one.'

The other trainees shook their heads, smiling and wincing at the same time.

'You guys take it easy.'

'See you, Lexar.'

'Yeah, see you.'

Lexar was grinning when he left the room. Then he was alone in the corridor, and when he shrugged, he could feel what was in his inside pocket. The grin tightened into a grimace.

'Lexar!'

He almost let go with his bladder. Then he was in control, and turning around.

'Pavel. I thought you were busy.'

'I am. Are you going now?'

'Yeah, I must.'

'All right. I'll see you out.'

As they walked, Lexar was conscious of the heft of the instruments he was carrying. Swung hard, they might make useful weapons. But if Pavel knew what he'd been up to, it wouldn't be one soft-bodied analyst between Lexar and freedom, it would be the full complement of the Westside Complex security force.

'—progress?' Pavel was saying.

'I'm sorry? I missed that.'

'Have you got something on your mind? I was just wondering whether you had any further thoughts on the trainees' progress.'

'Um, sorry. Nothing beyond what I said before. They're all good.'

'They liked the training you gave. They've been talking about it.'

'Well, good. That's nice to hear.'

They stopped in the stone chamber that opened on to the great pit, where the open-sided stone-and-bone coach was waiting.

'Come back soon,' said Pavel.

They shook hands.

'As soon as I can.'

And then Lexar was inside the coach, and Pavel waved as the coach jolted and lurched upwards, beginning its ascent of the pit wall. It took thirty seconds to reach the first change in direction, from zig to zag, and for a moment Lexar wondered whether Security could deliberately cause the coach to disengage from the track and plunge downwards.

The coach groaned and continued its ascent.

Lexar thought there was a chance that Security somehow had him under observation right now. Even so, as the coach rose, he could not help opening his jacket and peering inside, at the small pale fingers that poked from his inside pocket. He stared for a moment, then pulled his jacket closed, and buttoned it up.

With a final jolt, the coach reached ground level and stopped.

Twenty-two

A purple taxi drew up before the tall, forbidding black gates. Above them, and above the great walls stretching to either side, a dark-grey shimmering manifested itself. Whether it rose and faded out higher up, or curved back to form a protective roof across the expanse of the grounds within the walls, it was impossible to tell from ground level.

Viktor and Harald alighted from the taxi. As soon as they closed the doors, the driver gunned the engine, and shot back into the road without checking for traffic. Neither Viktor nor Harald paid any attention. They were looking up at the bronze lettering that arced across the twin gates.

MORDANTO HOSPITAL

&

THAUMATURGICAL COLLEGE
CHRD. 6397

Archaic runes glowed black on the steel shields set on each gate, held in place by dragon claws that some people said were the real thing. Yet few people talked about Mordanto, and even now, the handful of pedestrians passing by looked anywhere but at the gates or the forbidding towers that rose beyond.

'Gentlemen.'

Viktor and Harald spun around. The white-haired woman was standing on the sidewalk only four feet away, leaning on her cane, looking as if she had been there for a long time.

'Shit,' said Viktor. 'I mean, hi, Professor.'

'Good to see you, ma'am.' Harald was more controlled. 'It's been some time.'

'Is that a diplomatic chastisement,' she asked, 'for my not attending the funeral?'

'Perhaps a sign of my puzzlement.'

'Can we just take it as read, that if I could have been there, I would have?'

'Ma'am.'

'And as for you, Viktor,' she waved her cane at him, 'I'm hoping you've realized that I can help you. It's all I want to do.'

'Er, sure. The thing is, maybe scanbat analysis will—'

'Well, gentlemen.' Her voice cut into Viktor's explanation. 'I see it's your colleague Alexa that you're most concerned for. I expected you to ask for help against what you call the Black Circle.'

'Maybe they're to blame,' said Harald. 'But in our world, you have to work with what immediately presents itself.'

'Especially during an official investigation ... which this isn't, is it?'

'Um ...'

Viktor shrugged inside his leather coat.

'*Can* you help us, Professor?'

'I want to see Lieutenant Riordan.'

'But at any time, you could have—'

'Ring him, get him to come here.' She closed her eyes, her mouth tightened, and the lines of her face etched darker. Then she opened her eyes once more. 'All right, I can see the urgency. Let's go inside, and you, Sergeant Hammersen, will promise to do everything you can to get him to come here immediately.'

'But he's a different person. He's not your—'

'Irrelevant. Those are my terms.'

'We agree,' said Viktor.

Harald shook his head, then blew out a breath.

'Yes. We agree.'

'Good. Walk with me, gentlemen. Lend me support.'

Viktor stood on her left, Harald on her right, and she took hold of their arms as they walked towards the gates. For a second, Harald wondered where her cane had gone, then they were almost touching the ironwork, but she wasn't slowing down before they—

'Hey.'

—were walking on flagstones that formed a path between black lawns, leading to the main towers of Mordanto Hospital. Harald and Viktor glanced back at the gates that stood behind them, still closed.

'It's kind of you two gentlemen to help an old lady like myself.'

'Our, er, honour, ma'am.'

'Yeah. Our honour.'

'So kind.'

Her face might have been lined, but there was something girlish about the old lady's smile as they reached the foot of the nearest tower.

Donal, dressed only in shorts, crouched on the roof of Darksan Tower, surrounded by cats. He thought deeply about Laura's death, about the Black Circle mages that he knew: Malfax Cortindo, now a revenant, and Gelbthorne. Blanz figured in the mental images too, but Donal made it clear that he was incarcerated in Fortinium, and therefore not a current danger.

The cats' eyes glowed.

One of them, scarcely more than a kitten, came forward and bumped his head against Donal's hand, and commenced to purr.

'Hey, Spike,' said Donal.

Then he closed his eyes, forming clear mental pictures of Gelbthorne and Cortindo once more. He remained that way as the cats began to slip away across the cables and connecting struts, back to other towers and buildings. Finally, only Spike was left. He buzzed, then walked away with tail held high, across a cable that hung over two hundred storeys above street level, safely reaching the far side.

Here and there on the highest ledges of the buildings, gargoyles blinked and stirred their stone wings, sensing the feline activity, then settled down once more.

Finally Donal opened his eyes and rose to his feet. He looked at the disappearing cats, then at the ornate spire that rose behind him, pointing into the dark-purple sky.

'Spike,' he said to the wind. 'How did I know his name?'

Then he went inside, and descended the grey-green luminescent ladder to his apartment, and returned to his bedroom, where Commissioner Vilnar's eye still rested on the bedside cabinet. This was something he could turn to his advantage, just as he had asked the cats to search for Cortindo and Gelbthorne in the city, although they might not even be in the country. But *how* to use the eyeball, that was a mystery.

He picked it up, held it on the palm of his hand, and stared at it, half expecting it to animate somehow. It remained dead. The only unnatural aspect was that it remained clear when it should have been cloudy, opaque with death.

'You knew something,' he said to the eye. 'I was in Illurium, and so was Harald, thank Death, or the bastards would've done for me. Laura and the rest of the team tried to arrest you, didn't they?'

All the signs had pointed to Commissioner Vilnar as being in collusion with the Black Circle. But it had been Marnie Finross, his secretary, who had been the problem – as the commissioner had already suspected.

'But something happened. Somehow you found out where Blanz was, so we could take him down.'

Whether Commissioner Vilnar had guessed at Blanz's membership in the Black Circle, Donal could not tell. But when Donal and Harald – reinforced by the Illurian cop, Inspector Temesin and a squad of his toughest officers – had faced down Cortindo, Gelbthorne and Blanz, the three mages had rotated out of existence, to reappear somewhere else.

'How did you find out where Blanz would be?'

There was no answer from the eyeball.

What was I expecting?

Donal sat down on the bed and closed his eyes, trying to recreate the scene in his imagination. Laura, Viktor and Alexa, along with officers from Robbery-Haunting, walked into the commissioner's office, and attempted the arrest, during which the office slammed shut, trapping them, while Marnie Finross escaped the building.

The team broke free, along with the furniture, who evacuated the office before it was sealed off from the normal human dimensions of geometry. That was why the commissioner had a new office now.

What happened next?

Laura and the Vixen had been the ones to spot Marnie Finross and gave chase, although it was the cats who had dealt with her. And the Commissioner—

'You stayed behind,' he said to the eyeball. 'You stayed … with Alexa.'

Alexa was – had been – so promising an officer. She'd already come to the commissioner's attention as someone who was capable. In his mind's eye, Donal imagined himself in the Vixen, looking back, seeing Alexa and the commissioner standing on the sidewalk, watching as the rest of the team took off after Marnie Finross … and then turning to re-enter Police HQ.

Yes. That was what happened.

Donal inhaled for the first time in several minutes, held it, then breathed out.

'Alexa was with you, wasn't she? When you tracked down Blanz.'

But they hadn't left HQ to do it. Donal was almost sure of that.

'So sacrificing Alexa wasn't your smartest move ever, I guess.'

None of this was helping. If the commissioner had ripped out his own eyeball for a logical reason, it didn't involve conversation in a zombie cop's bedroom.

The phone rang.

'Hello?'

'Donal, you're there.'

'Either that, or you're hallucinating me, Harald.'

'I'm glad I caught you.'

'It was sheer chance. I was about to return to HQ.'

'I've been trying this number over and over, along with every other place you might be.'

'Ah.'

He considered explaining that he'd been on the roof, either communing with cats or deceiving himself that he could. Not to mention talking to a dead eyeball.

'We've got someone helping us track Alexa.'

'Good. She's important.'

'Of course. But the thing is, Donal, we need you here.'

'Then I'm coming. Where are you?'

It couldn't be urgent physical danger, not if Harald had been making phone calls for ages.

'You know the Mordanto?'

'I've heard of it.'

'That's where we are.'

'See you in twenty.'

He put the phone down.

'You,' he said to the eyeball, 'are a problem. Do I take you with me, or leave you here?'

Gertie had sensed the eye in Donal's pocket, and almost dropped him to his death.

'You're staying here.'

He looked at his stained, discarded suit, considered wearing the other new one – since he'd bought two at the Janaval – then decided against it. He dressed in an old suit and shirt, the Magnus in his shoulder holster as usual, and left the apartment.

Once inside the elevator, he said: 'Lobby, please. Um ... No. Make that the parking garage.'

The elevator walls flexed inwards, in a gesture that Donal interpreted as something like a nod. When they reached the subterranean garage level, he thanked the elevator, and exited.

He'd half expected the parking slot to be empty, but the Vixen was there, gleaming and silent.

'I'm going to Mordanto. They can help us search for Alexa Ceerling, who's missing, also ensorcelled.'

There was no reaction from the car.

'I believe that Alexa might know how Commissioner Vilnar tracked down Blanz. If she does, and we can retrieve that information, maybe we can get the other fuckers, too.'

Donal touched the Vixen's front wing.

'Without you, Laura wouldn't have got Marnie Finross. It didn't matter that you weren't able to climb the wall. She knew you had a problem with ...'

He let his voice trail off.

What am I talking about?

There was no reaction from the Vixen.

'All right, I'm going. Look after yourself.'

He went back to the lift, which was still waiting, and entered it.

'Guess I should've just asked for the lobby, after all.'

The doors slid shut.

As the lift began its ascent, Donal thought he heard an engine starting up in the garage, but whether it was the Vixen or another car – or his imagination – he had no idea.

Alexa Ceerling.

At least he had an objective now.

Darksan Tower was a quite a place to live. Among other features, it had a minimum of three doormen on duty, twenty-five hours a day. One of them flagged down a purple taxi for Donal.

'Thanks, Kurt.'

'Take it easy, Donal.'

It was pretty certain that Donal was the only adult resident that the doormen addressed by first name. Even the children tended to be Master Albert or Mistress Lydia.

'Where to, sir?'

The driver had turned around in his seat to ask the question. If he was disappointed to notice Donal's pale skin and cheap suit, he hid his reaction.

'You know the Mordanto Hospital?'

'Um ... Not really.'

'Sure you do. Drive to Heptagon Pacifica, and I'll direct you from there.'

'Oh.' The driver rubbed his face. 'All right. You got it.'

'Good man.'

The driver took the Hoardway route, but the traffic was getting heavier, and after a time he took a shortcut, away from the main road and into the Iron Emporium. He slowed right down, passing along an alley normally used only by trucks, loading and unloading at the bays. On either side were black pavilions, tangled and ornate. There were warehouses filled with produce, the perishable foodstuffs that helped to feed the city: vegetables, live lizards, and catches from the West Sea – some cold and unmoving on ice, some squirming in crowded saltwater tanks.

'Good move,' Donal told the driver. 'Not many people come this—'

But as they passed a turning into another wide alley, he spotted a parked patrol car, and two uniformed officers – one unstrapping his long baton – walking towards a trio of suspects, who were standing by a warehouse loading bay.

The suspects had pale skin.

'Shit,' said Donal. 'Stop.'

The driver blinked.

'You sure?'

'Reverse back, and drive down that alley.'

'I don't—'

'Yes, you do.' Donal held up his detective's shield. 'Now.'

The driver reversed so that they passed the turning, then drove forwards and turned. As he turned, he did something that surprised Donal: he cut the engine and disengaged the clutch, coasting in neutral until pulling up almost silently behind the squad car.

'Thanks.'

Donal rolled out of the car, and strode forwards, badge held high.

'Officer!'

The bigger officer, the one with the baton, had his arm cocked, ready for a circular strike with plenty of follow-through. He whipped it towards the nearest zombie—

'I'm Lieutenant Riordan. Stop.'

—and pulled it downwards, unable to hold back the strike, directing it instead to the zombie's calf. There was a crack and the zombie fell.

The other officer said, 'They're only icicles, s-sir.'

Hefting the baton, the big officer scowled.

'They was acting suspicious. On these here commercial premises.'

Donal looked at the zombies. The fallen man was sitting now, holding his leg. The man and woman with him were looking scared.

'We did nothing,' said the woman.

Their clothes looked shabby, but had once been of good quality.

'Help him stand up,' said Donal.

They did so.

'You can walk?' he added.

'Yes. Thank you.'

'Then do it. Quickly.'

The three zombies looked at each other. Then they got moving.

'And you two,' continued Donal, 'can get back in your car and do your jobs.'

Both men's faces tightened.

'The suspects were—'

'I don't want to hear it.'

At the far end of the warehouse, the zombies turned right. One of the cops glanced at them, then stared at the waiting taxi.

'Beat it.' Donal climbed back into the rear. 'Go on.'

The driver reversed out of the alley, drove for twenty yards, then stopped. He watched in the mirror. Behind them, the patrol car pulled out of the alley and headed away from them, in the opposite direction, towards Hoardway.

'They ought to be OK,' he said.

Donal knew he meant the zombie trio.

'I hope so.'

'A year ago, you'd never have seen anything like that happening. Hades, not even a few months back.'

'Things change.'

'Not for the better. We'll probably be at war next.'

'Huh.' Donal looked out at the passers-by, as the taxi turned on to Umbral Prospect. 'Bad thought.'

'I know.'

They drove in silence to the twenty-one-way three-tiered intersection of Heptagon Pacifica, where Donal said: 'Third exit, then down one level, and take the second ramp.'

'Got it.'

The directions came naturally to Donal, although he had never been here before.

Ten minutes later, the driver stopped.

'Here.' Donal handed over a three-hundred florin note. 'Take it easy.'

'Oh, man. I can't possibly change—'

'You don't need to.'

Donal got out.

After a moment, the driver put his taxi in gear, and rolled away from the dark gates. Donal raised a hand, and saw the driver do likewise. When the taxi was just part of the distant traffic flow, Donal turned back to his destination.

'Mordanto Hospital,' he said. 'Not just for healing, though, are you?'

The gates looked heavy and strong. Beyond, the grounds seemed quiet, as though absorbing sound even as Donal could hear traffic passing behind him.

He took a step towards the gates, and then—

Hades.

—another, except that now he was walking on flagstones, already inside the grounds.

At the 157th Street corner of the Iron Emporium, the opposite end from Hoardway, three pale figures stopped in a black metal archway, staring at the street, wondering if they dared move out into the open. Just as they made their decision and stepped from the archway's shelter, a police cruiser squealed around the corner, the doors swept open on either side, and the same two officers as before came out.

This time, they had guns drawn.

The three zombies looked around for help, but the warehousemen were fading into the buildings, leaving half-unloaded crates. There was no one to watch as the officers stopped and raised their weapons.

'We did nothing to you,' said the woman.

'Fuckin' icicles.'

Both zombie men – one injured, the other bearing his friend's weight – closed their eyes. The woman stared straight at the bigger cop.

'Some day,' she said, 'your bones will feed the reactor piles.'

Behind them, from the alley they had fled along, an engine grumbled. It was like an ice tiger's purr: low yet promising swiftness and power. The male zombies opened their eyes and turned to look at the shining green headlights.

'Not today.' The big cop's trigger finger tightened. 'Say goodbye to your—'

And then the roar sounded.

'Hades!' The smaller cop opened fire, but not at the zombies. 'Go for the tyres!'

'What—?'

The bigger cop fired one round before the scream of brakes took the Vixen through an arcing turn, grey-blue smoke pouring from her wheel arches as the front tyres became the axis of rotation, and she swung sideways on, so that twin liquid crunches sounded simultaneously, and she dragged two wet, red smears across the tarmac.

She backed off, gunned her engine, and drove forward. There was a squelch, a thud, then nothing.

After a few moments, the Vixen gently rolled towards the three zombies, and popped open her doors. The trio stared at the empty seats inside.

The woman looked at her injured friend.

'We need the car's help.'

He nodded, then grimaced as the other two helped him into the rear. The man got in beside him, while the woman climbed in to the front passenger seat, looked at the crescent-shaped steering-wheel beside her, and shook her head.

Then the Vixen's doors closed, she moved into first, and rolled out on to 157th, merging with the traffic, giving the zombie woman just the briefest glimpse of an outflung hand and two glistening red streaks, before the crowded street obscured her view.

Foodstores predominated near the Iron Emporium. The shoppers were moving at their usual pace, intent on their business. Few of them were anything other than standard human; apart from that, it might have been any ordinary day from a week, a year or decades before.

None of the zombies spoke.

The taxi driver was a widower, though not old. As he drove on to the complicated intersection of Heptagon Pacifica, he thought about the cops rousting those zombies at the Iron Emporium, and muttered a short prayer to Saint Merlin for their safety.

He drove past the exit that would take him back that way.

'Been a while, bro.'

His brother and his brother's family lived in a lifeward-guarded cottage far out in the countryside, beyond the Jetshade Range. The driver had always been close to his brother, and welcome in his home.

He made a complete circuit of the intersection without exiting. The more he thought about it, the more he could not come up with a reason to go home, not even to pack. As he neared the turn-off for Greyville Zoomway for the second time, he changed lanes, indicated, and took the exit.

Progress would be slower than the Zoomway's name might indicate, but he would be out of Tristopolis proper within three hours, and among the Jetshade foothills by the early hours of morning.

'It'll be good to see you, bro.'

He settled in for a steady drive.

The Vixen drew to a halt before the Mordanto gates. From inside the car, the woman could see through the gates' bars. There were towers inside the grounds, and a lean, fit-looking man was ascending the steps of the nearest.

'That's the guy who helped us.'

'Interesting,' said the injured zombie in the rear. 'You know, I was resurrected here in Mordanto. I was a firefighter, and the department had resurrection policies as standard. Anyway, you can feel odd energies moving in this place, and sometimes the buildings howl.'

'When was that?'

'My resurrection? Nearly a century ago. Coming back here, I think I understand. The towers can feel pain, and that's not a metaphor.'

'Fancy talk for a firefighter.'

'I've had plenty of time to change.'

'Haven't we all?'

They watched the police lieutenant ascending to the tower's doorway.

'Shit.'

'Did you see that?'

The police lieutenant was gone, although none of them had seen the door open. After a moment, the woman laid her hand on the Vixen's steering wheel.

'Are you sure we ought to be here? It's a strange place, and it's not as if the gates look about to open.'

For a moment, there was no reaction from the Vixen. Then bright green light reflected back from the gates as her headlight beams intensified. They began to pulse in rapid, changing flashes. This continued for about a minute, during which the three zombies remained silent.

Then the Vixen's lights went dark.

'Whatever that was, it didn't—'

Black light strobed from the gates, then stopped. The Vixen gave a rapid series of pulses in reply. There were more black flashes from the iron gates, then the Vixen engaged first gear and leaped forwards, very fast, and in a second they were on the driveway inside the Mordanto grounds.

'The gates opened,' said the injured zombie from the rear. 'Really quickly.'

'No,' said the male zombie beside him. 'I watched, and they remained closed.'

In the front passenger seat, the woman turned.

'I agree with both of you.'

The Vixen gave a soft toot of her horn, and came to a halt.

Twenty-three

The hallway was long, lined with steel and decorated with diamond panes. At the far end was a doorway and, as before, Donal walked through it to find himself in a corridor overlooking the black lawns ... two storeys above ground level. Viktor was standing there, his big arms folded.

'This is a strange place to get help,' he said. 'And I'm sorry.'

'Where's Harald?'

'Up in the Eyries, with the professor who's helping us.' Viktor's already gravely voice deepened. 'Examining scanbat memories.'

'I thought that happens in the 99th Precinct, next to the Academy.' There was a tall nine-sided building solely for that purpose, visible from the trainees' exercise field. 'In Gestaltengram Tower.'

'That's the official way, with bureaucracy and court orders, like that.' Viktor began walking along the corridor. Donal matched his pace.

'Sounds like Harald's excelled himself.'

'Uh ... The professor's not exactly part of his network.'

'So who is he? Oh, crap. Aren't there any normal doors in this place?'

'Not—'

They were standing on the far side of the stationary door.

'—hardly.'

'Hades.'

Donal looked around, then up. He and Viktor were standing on a narrow horizontal ring that ran around the inside of a great hollow tower. The ring consisted of alternating translucent-blue and transparent treads. Similar rings lined the tower's interior all the way up, every fifteen feet or so, and likewise down into subterranean levels that were hidden in what might have been a dark-blue mist.

High up, gantries and platforms and a glistening steel sphere spanned the width of the tower. People were moving and talking up there.

'That's where we're headed,' said Viktor.

'So how do we get up there?'

'You're going to like this. Just keep on walking.'

'Is this is some new meaning of "like",' said Donal, 'that I haven't come across before?'

'Could be.'

The two men walked along the ring-shaped floor. After a while, it seemed to Donal that there were two people walking in parallel on the ring above.

'Keep walking,' Viktor told him, 'or it doesn't work.'

'What doesn't—'

Not again.

'—work?'

They were still walking, and for maybe half a second Donal thought there were two men on the level beneath, but then it was just him and Viktor continuing their perambulation. Except that they were now one level higher.

As they continued to walk, they passed ordinary windows set into the walls. After they had ascended four levels in the same fashion as before, Donal glanced out of a window overlooking the main driveway. A Vixen was parked there.

There's more than one Vixen in Tristopolis.

Either it was Laura's, or it was a different vehicle, and Donal had no way of working out which was the more likely. In this place everything seemed—

Shit. Another level.

—twisted in a way that made straight thinking impossible.

But as he continued to make circuits of the tower with Viktor beside him, each time he passed a corresponding window on the next level up, he got only a more elevated view of the same unmoving car. Finally, he scarcely glanced out at the Vixen, as the upper levels of the Eyrie were drawing closer.

On the last circuit, they walked on to a solid silver platform. Viktor stopped. Donal took one extra pace.

'What's going on?' he said.

There was a white-haired woman in an open, ankle-length lab coat worn over a plush turquoise gown. She was manipulating a polished console, though she paused for a moment to stare at Donal, and her eyes were startling.

She's . . .

Donal found himself unable to complete the thought.

Harald and a youngish-looking man, his head shaven, were watching as a third man, older and with a goatee, clutched the arms of the steel

243

chair he was sitting in. Vertical rods connected the chair to some contraption overhead, on which lay something that Donal had seen many times before, but always at a distance.

The scanbat's body was of steel and fur, its mandibles polished, each of its convex black eyes bigger than a man's head. The delta wings stretched out seven feet to either side. This close, it looked more like a moth than a bat.

Donal swallowed as he realized that the apparatus was lowering the scanbat, its head on a line with the goateed man's skull.

He's a mage.

This was Mordanto, after all.

And the young one with Harald. Another mage.

Then there was the old woman, whose eyes looked so compelling, her hands very practised as they manipulated the controls that caused the scanbat to continue descending.

'We supply your department's scanbats.' She kept her attention on her console. 'And attune the observer-mages who work in Gestaltengram Tower.'

'So you know what you're doing,' said Donal.

The lines of her face appeared to grow deeper, but it seemed that she had to concentrate on what she was doing. Donal rubbed his face and felt ashamed, not knowing why.

The scanbat continued to descend, lowered on shining rods. On the steel chair below, the goateed mage's eyes were fluttering, and his breathing was shallow.

What happened next was impossible.

It's illusion.

The rods lowered the scanbat.

Nothing physical.

And lowered it, until the scanbat's head reached the top of the mage's skull, and continued to descend for several seconds more, until the mage's features and the scanbat's head occupied the same small volume of space.

I am not seeing this.

It was a blur. It was a stereoscopic trick. The man's features were overlaid on the steel-and-black-glass head of the scanbat; or the scanbat's configuration overlaid the man.

Donal saw both things at the same time.

Impossible.

And then the mage's mouth opened.

'I've found her.'

The words echoed around the tower.

'Near Shatterway Sound, a three-sided ruin, off Conlanx Road.'

Then the scanbat was rising once more, hauled upwards by the apparatus that held it, and the mage was wiping sweat from his face. He blinked several times, then focused on Harald.

'You need to hurry,' he said.

His younger colleague, the shaven-headed mage, touched Harald's sleeve.

'I'll drive you,' he said.

But Harald was still looking at the mage who had merged with the scanbat.

'Was there a motorcycle in sight?'

'Maybe. Inside the ruin, the ground is dark, as if the floor has fallen in. Within the darkness' – the mage's eyelids fluttered, then opened wide – 'there is definitely something shining green.'

'The Phantasm.'

The younger mage turned to the white-haired woman, but her attention was on Donal.

'Professor Steele?' called the mage. 'I'll need authorization to take a golem to—'

He stopped and blanched as the woman's gaze focused on him.

Professor Steele?

Donal felt his muscles weakening, and he backed up against the wall.

Yes.

And when he opened his mouth, the words that came out were higher pitched than normal.

'M-Mother? It's ... you.'

'Oh, my Death,' said Professor Steele. 'Laura.'

'No.'

Donal shook his head.

It's Mother.

But he remembered the orphanage, the stern face of Sister Mary-Anne Styx who cared for him, the schoolyard taunting because he had no family, the leather strap whipping into his back because he had fought back. And the worn newspaper cutting that finally crumbled into dust when he was in the army, disintegrating the two brief paragraphs that described the auto accident and the cut-short lives of Mr and Mrs Riordan.

I have no mother.

Yet clearly he did, because when he looked at the old woman's eyes, at Professor Helena Steele's eyes – at Mother's eyes – all he could feel was love that gushed up warmly through his body. His zombie body. And the memories of a richly decorated home, and the smiles of Helena and Vladil Steele, when their marriage was still young and everything was fine.

I'm not …

Donal's knees gave way, and he fell on to the metal floor.

Not her.

I miss you, Laura.

He was pulling into a foetal position, his muscles contracting without volition.

I love you, Donal.

This was impossible.

You're dead.

And you're not?

He dropped into blackness.

Dangling over Viktor's shoulder, he became semi-consciousness. Directly below him were grey flagstones. They were outdoors.

'I can … stand.'

'Not by yourself.' Viktor bent forward, so that Donal's feet reached the ground. 'Keep steady.'

The massive strength of Viktor's arm held Donal upright.

Concentrate.

Professor Helena Steele, Harald and the shaven-headed mage were standing nearby. Beyond them stood a silver truck, its side door open to reveal a seated purple golem. But right beside Donal – and Viktor, supporting him – was a familiar Vixen, her headlights glowing strongly green as Donal gave a partial smile.

'Hey, Sis,' he said.

The Vixen tooted.

'You should let her take you,' said Professor Steele. 'And remember you are Donal Riordan.'

'If he stayed,' began the younger mage, 'we could treat him in the—'

'No,' said Harald.

'Sergeant Hammersen is right.' Professor Steele smiled, but her voice was sad. 'It would be better for the lieutenant to get away from here. With my regrets.'

Then the Vixen's doors opened, and a female zombie exited from the front, a man from the rear. A third zombie remained inside.

'Are you his friends?' asked Professor Steele.

'We hardly know him, but yes.'

'His heart belonged to another.'

The male zombie looked puzzled, but the woman said: 'Oh, shit.'

'Precisely.'

'We'll take care of him.'

Donal observed all this, without feeling the need to speak. Just watching, without descending back into coma, was all he could manage.

When Viktor spoke, Donal felt the words as a rumbling vibration.

'Tristopolis isn't safe. For any of you.'

Professor Steele took a step towards the Vixen, then stopped when the engine growled.

'You always had a problem with me, but that's all right. You are your father's daughter.'

The Vixen's headlights narrowed into horizontal slits. Perhaps the grille stretched wider.

'You know where to take them.' Professor Steele turned to the woman zombie. 'I'd appreciate a phone call when you're safe. And my young friend Kelvin' – she indicated the shaven-headed mage – 'can offer technical assistance over the phone, if you need it.'

'All right.' The woman helped Viktor walk Donal to the driver's door. 'You're Donal, right? In you get.'

Donal felt the hands manoeuvring him into place behind the crescent-shaped steering-wheel. He wanted to help, but his muscles felt soft, and his eyelids were pulling downwards, pulling his whole head forwards—

Stay awake.

He raised his chin.

'Drive fast,' said Professor Steele. 'And take care.'

Then the woman zombie was in the front passenger seat beside Donal, the man climbed in the back, and the doors closed by themselves. Harald, Viktor, Professor Steele and the young mage, Kelvin, all stepped back.

Donal's eyelids drooped, as the world appeared to grow dark grey.

I'm tired.

As the Vixen rolled into motion, he was vaguely aware of the surrounding grounds of Mordanto, of the exit gate they were heading towards. Then he allowed his chin to descend to his chest.

Rest.

His eyes closed.

'You have my daughter's heart, Donal Riordan.' Professor Helena Steele's voice was in his mind. *'I don't know whether to thank you or hate you for it.'*

He wanted to tell her to shut up.

'Whether you understand that remark is probably irrelevant.'

He wanted to tell her that he loved her.

Mother!

Sleep closed in, bringing no comfort.

When Viktor turned back from trying to watch the Vixen's departure through the gates – had they opened or not? – he saw Harald and the younger mage, Kelvin, but Professor Steele was gone.

'That went smoothly,' he said. 'Really magical.'

'I'm sorry.' Kelvin looked serious. 'You guys didn't mention her name, and I did.'

Harald was looking at the silver truck with the golem waiting inside.

'We need to get Alexa, and the Phantasm. We'd appreciate your help, Mage Kelvin.'

'You've got it.'

They climbed on board, then all the doors – including the side-door – fastened shut. Kelvin gestured, and the engine came to life. He used an ordinary-looking steering-wheel to direct the truck, and headed for the main gates.

'I've got a question,' said Viktor.

The solid-looking gates were growing closer, and the truck was gaining speed.

'What's that?'

'How does—?'

And then they were on the road, merging with the traffic.

'Never mind,' said Viktor.

Lexar Pinderwin stood surrounded by deathwolves inside the lobby of Police HQ. Facing him was the rearing granite block from which the duty sergeant's upper body grew.

'I need to see Lieutenant Riordan,' said Lexar.

'Someone will be right with you.' The sergeant gesture across the lobby. 'You want to wait over there?'

'Sure. Thank you.'

Two of the deathwolves accompanied him, while the others padded back outside. Lexar stood in place, conscious of what he was carrying inside his jacket. No wonder the deathwolves were sticking close – if Lexar had been anyone other than a forensic Bone Listener, they would have pounced already.

Two plainclothes detectives approached.

'Bone Listener Pinderwin? Please come with us.'

'Of course.'

With one detective on either side of him, Lexar walked towards the lift shafts. He looked back and saw the deathwolves staring.

The detectives descended with him, and came out on to a grey-painted landing, opposite a door labelled ROBBERY-HAUNTING.

'Has Lieutenant Riordan transferred to R-H?'

'This way, Bone Listener.'

They brought him to a glass-doored inner office. The lettering on this door read *Commander P. Bowman*. Inside, a lean man with cropped red hair stood up.

Lexar went in.

'I was hoping to see Lieutenant Riordan.'

'I'm Bowman. Riordan reports to me.'

The office door closed behind Lexar. It was just him and the commander.

'Does he work for Robbery-Haunting now?'

'No. The commissioner put me in charge of the task force, as a temporary measure.'

'Could he do that? It's a federal task force.'

'As I said, it's a temporary measure.'

Lexar was aware that he was in the heart of HQ, facing a man who was three decades older: a senior officer. But Lexar had already broken a multitude of rules today, without backing down.

'Commander, I would prefer to talk to Lieutenant Riordan.'

'My apologies, Bone Listener, but if I knew where he was, I'd escort you there in person.'

'He's missing?'

'We allow someone of Donal's rank a lot of latitude. He hasn't checked in, that's all.'

Lexar glanced back at the glass door, and the detectives outside.

'Perhaps I should just go.'

'Or perhaps you should trust me,' said Bowman. 'As Commissioner Vilnar did.'

'It's not a matter of—'

'There is a way, isn't there?' Bowman undid his cuff, and began to roll back his shirt sleeve. 'I wrote an essay on it, as part of my master's degree.'

'No. Please.'

'I know what's involved, Bone Listener Pinderwin.'

Bowman held out his hand.

'So Listen to me,' he added, 'while I tell you the truth.'

Lexar reached forward, and grasped Bowman's little finger. Bowman sucked in a breath, his teeth clenched hard, squeezing his eyes closed as the process continued.

As soon as possible, Lexar released him.

'You're on Lieutenant Riordan's side. Commissioner Vilnar trusted you.'

Bowman bit his lip, then withdrew his hand. Tears trickled from his eyes, but he ignored them. He examined his finger, now blackened to the second knuckle.

'Shit. The books were right.' He pulled his mouth into a brief grin. 'It does hurt.'

'I've never Listened to a living being. There are strict prohibitions.'

'And that has to be a good thing.' Bowman placed his hand on his lap, out of Lexar's sight. 'These are strange times, or I'd never have volunteered for that.'

'But you guessed I have something important to say, or you'd not have gone through the procedure.'

'I know the deathwolves were uneasy, and the scanwraiths were ... interested.'

'Yes.'

Bowman looked down at his lap, then: 'So I don't suppose you want to give me a clue?'

After a few seconds thinking about it, Lexar reached inside his jacket, pulled out a small pale object, and placed it on Bowman's desk.

'Shit, Bone Listener!'

'It's a young boy's hand. He was twelve years old, and his name was Samuel.'

All this, Lexar had learned from Listening to the boy-corpse's bones.

'You've been investigating a telephone company,' continued Lexar. 'What you've not realized is the special nature of their connecting lines, to carry the kind of signals they're transmitting.'

Bowman rubbed away the tears of pain.

'What special nature?'

'The main lines are formed from treated nerves.'

'My brother-in-law,' said Bowman, 'is an engineer. I happen to know that phone exchanges and major switchboards contain nerve-tissue lines. It's how they work.'

'But they wouldn't transmit the signals that you're concerned about.'

'So what's diff—?'

'The nerves were taken from a *living* person. A child. That's the first difference.'

The boy's pale hand lay on the desktop between them.

'And it takes a dark mage to carry out the procedure,' added Lexar. 'I mean, he has to be there in person.'

It took maybe five seconds for Bowman to stop blinking and focus on Lexar.

'Where did you find this?'

'In an Energy Authority complex.'

'Which one?'

'Westside.'

'And the mage has to be present?'

'He – or she – had to have been there yesterday, at least. That was when this boy, Samuel, died. His bones remember the process, Commander, and it was not a quick one.'

'Hades.'

'Yes. So what are you going to do?'

'I'm going to enlist Donal Riordan's help,' said Bowman, 'and take the fuckers down.'

'And I'll assist, however I can.'

'You already have. Thank you, Bone Listener.'

Lexar thought back to his conversation with Aldrevun, the old Bone Listener sitting on a bench who had somehow kicked a whole sequence of events into motion.

'Sometimes you have to step forwards,' he said, 'and try to make a difference.'

'That you do. I suspect Dr d'Alkernay would be proud of you.'

Lexar looked to one side, trying to blink away the moistness of his eyes.

Twenty-four

When Donal opened his eyes, he was in East Danklyn, and the steering-wheel in front of him moved by itself as the Vixen took a turning to the left. The woman beside him and the two zombies in the rear all reached over and touched him, just for a second, and withdrew.

'Thank you,' Donal said.

Outside, the shops were beginning to close. It was late evening, and here in East Danklyn there was no reason to open late. This was close to the city's edge, some eighteen miles from Donal's home in Darksan Tower, and already there were few pedestrians on the streets.

A small bank branch, its globular lights shining yellow on either side of its portico, caught his attention. He had money, and these three probably had little.

'Stop. Really. Please, Sis.'

The Vixen slowed, then pulled over. The doors remained shut.

'I'll be back in five minutes.'

As soon as the door clicked open, he slid out on to the sidewalk, and headed for the bank. Inside, there was only one person ahead of him at the single teller's station remaining open. Waiting, Donal had a moment's weakness in his muscles, and his eyes closed as he thought he was fainting.

'Sir?'

'No.' His eyes snapped open. 'I'm fine.'

I'm not.

He took control of his body.

Yes, I am.

The teller was free now, and beckoned Donal forward.

'I need to make a withdrawal,' Donal said.

'A large one?' The teller was standard human, his voice sympathetic. 'I understand.'

'Thank you.'

Donal used the white credit card, signed an authorization, and received a dark canvas bag containing the cash. When the transaction was over, he thanked the teller.

'I hope you find somewhere safe,' the teller said.

'Yes. Thanks again.'

As he left, he took three ninety-nine florin notes from the bag and put them in his pocket. The rest he carried over to the Vixen, whose driver's door remained open. He put the money bag on the seat.

'Take it,' he said to the woman inside.

'We can't—'

'Use it, before the city takes it from me. It's the only rational thing to do.'

'Yes. Good luck.'

The Vixen trembled when he placed his hand on the door.

'Get them to safety, and yourself.'

A soft note added itself to the engine's sound.

'Yes. I will,' he said.

He closed the door.

'Be well, Sis.'

The Vixen hesitated, even though the road was clear. Then she clunked her gears unnecessarily hard, and lurched forwards, accelerating, moving fast with her lights turned down low.

Look after yourself.

Donal turned away. He started off along the street in the opposite direction, looking back once, just as the Vixen turned out of sight, and then he carried on. Lights began to switch off in storefront windows, deepening the gloom of the street.

He had eighteen miles to walk. A taxi might come by, and he could always ask for directions to the nearest Pneumetro station, but he needed the time to himself.

I'm scared.

Perhaps he should have gone with the Vixen. But she had understood his need to remain.

That doesn't stop the fear.

Still, he walked on. After three blocks, he passed a sporting goods shop, its lights turned off, but its door open. A man in shirt sleeves was dragging a box labelled *For Collection* into the doorway.

'Are you the owner?' said Donal.

'Huh!' The man took two steps back. 'Who are you?'

Donal held out his detective's shield. Then he reached inside his pocket, and withdrew a ninety-nine florin note.

'Someone with money to spend, if that's OK with you.'

For a moment, the store owner looked uncertain. He glanced at a rack of metal spikeball bats inside the door. Then he nodded.

'Sure. Come on in.'

'Thank you.'

Once inside, the owner pulled down all the blinds before switching on the main lights.

'Whatever you need, Officer.'

Donal looked around the stacked shelves.

'You got any running suits?'

'Uh, sure. Any particular style?'

'Something in black.'

Twenty minutes later, he was jogging slowly along the near-deserted street. His running suit and shoes were black, as was the watchcap on his head, and the small backpack in which his ordinary clothes were tightly rolled up, along with the Magnus.

He staggered once, then continued.

Come on.

There had been a moment, getting changed in the store, when his balance had gone, and the store owner had looked concerned. But in seconds, Donal's equilibrium had returned.

Steady. You can do it.

He felt no tiredness, despite the part of him that wanted to lie down and sleep. It was an internal paradox, but this was not the time for intro-spection. This was a time to be getting on with things.

His pace picked up as his movement, the opposing swing of shoulders and hips, became more fluid. He leaned forward by a tiny further incre-ment, becoming conscious of the subtle change in the way his feet struck the ground.

'Hey, look at that.'

'What?'

'I thought I saw a zom—'

The voices came from a doorway, and Donal was already leaving it behind. There was little danger here.

Still, he turned left at the next corner, ran two blocks, and turned right, continuing parallel to his original route. His pace grew a little faster again, as he began to feel infinitesimally better with every step, as if running through some kind of emotional calculus, knitting his fractured self back together.

Just run.

Another twenty minutes, and he had left Lower Danklyn behind, and was entering Arachnia Halls. Wide spaces separated the hundred-foot-tall dark-grey stone spiders. Their splayed legs were hollow, along with their thoraxes and heads. In some of them, people lived, in warrens that were centuries old. Others were mercantile bazaars, filled with cheap goods and occasional valuable ones, the latter normally stolen. A small number of the spiders were cracked open, dark inside, and filled with a chill air that few people felt comfortable breathing.

Donal continued to run.

He was a shadow flitting through shadows, feeling good as he ran under the archway formed by one great spider-leg. From above came a low whistle, but he ignored it and ran on.

Farther along, near the end of this spider's body, a group of men spread out, blocking the way.

Shit.

He was a police officer, but he was no longer sure that counted for anything. For all he knew, during the past few busy hours, the city might already have declared zombie cops a thing of the past.

Donal slowed down.

Looking behind him, he saw more men filling the width of the walkway. There was only one thing to do. He continued on his current route.

'Here, little icicle.'

'That's right, lollipop. Come here.'

And ran faster, straight towards them.

'Ooh, this one looks eager.'

'Asking for it.'

'Well, he's gonna get—'

Then Donal turned right, running faster. The stone spider's swollen belly was overhead. Farther along, it reached the ground, forming a barrier Donal couldn't pass. But here he could continue to run, and did.

Faster.

Had he turned sooner, the men would have been able to intercept his run. By leaving it to the last moment before suddenly turning, he was leaving them behind. All of them were running after him. Light glinted off blades and glass-studded sticks. No guns, then.

Good.

He bore left and ran on past the spider, with the group following. Arachnia Halls was a large neighbourhood, and the next spider along was the first of many. When Donal estimated he had been running for a minute, he slowed down and looked back.

The pursuing men were strung out in a staggered line now, with the fittest in front. The leader, muscular and pounding hard as he ran, was only a few yards behind Donal.

Very good.

Donal dug in his heel, knee bending to absorb the impact, and thrust himself back. He turned, generating power from the waist, and the heel of his palm smashed into the big man's jaw, driven by his own momentum as much as Donal's power.

There was a crunch and the man was down, his face distorted, deeply unconscious.

Behind him came a second attacker, followed by too many to fight. Donal kicked at the man's knee, sidestepped, throwing an overhand left into the side of his neck, and was already running again without checking the effect of his punch.

Yes, faster.

He sped up.

That's it.

He ran faster than he thought was possible.

Across the dark interstitial space between spiders, he noted the terrain was uneven and hard to see. Behind him, he heard the pursuers slow down, then speed up once more. Perhaps they were entering unfamiliar ground, another gang's territory.

Donal leaped.

The jump fitted the rhythm of his run, and then he was near the first great stone leg of the next spider. He glanced back, saw the stumble and hesitation of the men behind him. They were looking for the wire fence that they'd seen him jump ... except there was no fence.

He grinned in the darkness, making his way over to the belly of the spider, where it touched the ground. Lowering himself on hands and knees, as if about to perform a press-up, Donal stretched himself out. Then, lying prone, he crossed his arms so that his black sleeves hid his hands, and turned his face towards the stone, away from his pursuers.

He listened carefully as they ran past. When they were gone, he rolled out of cover and on to his feet. Then he began to run once more.

Following the men.

They were strung out before him, and the last man was about to stop running, his chest heaving, and then he did come to a halt. He bent over, hands on knees, wheezing, staring at the ground. His face was in perfect position for a rising kick, and that's what Donal used, following with three curved punches to the neck as the man went down.

The next man was slowing, panting. Donal drew near, grabbed the back of the man's coat with both hands, and jerked. Then he hooked his leg in front of the man's shin, causing the bastard to smack face-first on to the tarmac, with Donal on his back.

Then Donal was on his feet, stamping down once, before springing into a sprinter's start. In front of him, another man looked round, calling, 'Are you all right back th—?'

Donal caught his sleeve, hook-punched him in the ear, and the man yelled. He spun around, throwing a punch of his own but with his fist glinting – *knife* – and Donal blocked with his forearm, while slamming his elbow through a short curve into the man's throat. He used his knee twice, three times, then pushed the falling man away.

He picked up the discarded blade, and threw it at the next man.

'Hey!'

The guy raised his arm to stop the spinning blade, and then Donal's shoulder hit him in the stomach. Donal clamped hard around the man's waist, knees bent, then launched himself upwards before letting go, peripherally watching the headfirst fall.

A clump of the guy's friends had come to a halt, and they turned around, raising their glass-shard-encrusted sticks and their blades, and Donal yelled as he ran straight at them.

'Shit!'

'Fucking—'

They scattered, running to all sides, except for one who stood frozen with his stick upraised. Donal ran into him, hitting in rhythm – *cross-hook-uppercut* – then pulled him around by his clothing and whipped in another three-punch combination – *rattat-tat* – and a five-punch, and then it was time to move.

There was another group of men ahead, so Donal ran to one side.

Good enough. Leave now.

And continued to run.

Viktor watched while the purple golem stamped on the ground surrounding the hole. Loose rubble broke free, spilling down. As the golem continued to work, the fallen rubble became a slope. Finally, the golem stopped, then took careful steps down the slope it had formed.

At the bottom, it squatted, hooked its broad arms under the cracked, wounded Phantasm, and stood slowly, powerfully upright. Leaning back to counteract the motorcycle's weight, it began to ascend the rubble slope. Twice, it slipped, and Viktor thought it would tumble down; but soon it was at ground level, ponderously carrying the Phantasm over to the silver truck.

Viktor followed.

Harald waited, his gaze fastened on the Phantasm, watching as the golem lowered the motorcycle into the truck. Inside, Alexa was already lying on a stretcher, her head enclosed in a web of white strapping encrusted with amber stones, over which Mage Kelvin was making hand-passes that caused the stones to glisten.

When Alexa was stable, Kelvin turned his attention to the Phantasm. He produced long silver rods out of nowhere, and laid them across the large crack in the motorcycle's carapace. Again from nowhere, he drew out a length of black cord and wrapped it in a strange configuration around the Phantasm.

'There.' He stood up inside the truck. 'That will hold them for now. Well done, golem.'

The golem was faceless save for a single horizontal yellow slit that served as an eye. It had no expression as it sat down in place, half filling the truck's interior. But Viktor thought back to the way it had stamped down to create the rubble slope, without being ordered specifically to do so. Mage Kelvin had said merely, 'Fetch the motorcycle.'

Tristopolis was becoming a harder place for non-humans to live in; but here was a type of being that perhaps, Viktor realized, never had been treated fairly.

'Nice work, Mage.'

'Thanks, Viktor. A spell in Mordanto' – Kelvin smiled – 'and they'll both be fine.'

'You'll be able to prove Alexa was ensorcelled?'

'It's already obvious. You'll have licensed mages swearing oaths to that effect, in front of journalists if you like.'

'Good.'

Kelvin looked down at Alexa. She had not been unconscious long enough to begin starving to death, but her emotional trauma might be profound.

'I'd like to know who did this to her.'

'Hard to tell,' growled Viktor. 'We suspect Cortindo, maybe Gelbthorne, maybe another of their friends that we don't know about.'

Beside him, Harald was sitting on the truck floor, his hands placed palm-down upon the wounded Phantasm. His face was expressionless.

'Cortindo,' said Kelvin. 'Malfax Cortindo.'

'You know him?'

'Of him. Well enough to know you'll need help.'

'What kind of help?'

Kelvin glanced at Alexa once more.

'The kind I can give you.'

Some five miles into his run, Donal was heading parallel to railroad tracks. Hundreds of stacked, empty freight carriages were all around, and it was dark. Only faint purplish light from the city on either side spilled into the shadowy environment.

Donal was a black shade running within darkness.

With a white shadow loping beside him.

'What—?'

~You are Donal Riordan.~

'Last time I checked.'

The white wolf was keeping pace.

~I'm sorry we could not help you more at City Hall.~

'What do you mean?'

~If you can mount a search of Möbius Park, you'll find remains among the trees.~

'Say what?'

Donal slowed the pace.

~The assassin you saw. His remains are there. I swear this by the Void.~

'No professional would run where ectoplasma wraiths are waiting.'

~He was hex-protected. We dealt with it.~

'We?'

~Myself and one of my comrades.~

'Comrades. In what army?'

~We have common enemies. You are not yet strong enough to join us.~

'Shit.'

~But you grow stronger with each step.~

They were running between two lanes of stacked freight containers.

'I'm hallucinating white wolves. Can't be a good sign.'

~That is funny.~

'What? A wolf with a sense of—'

Donal stumbled, and slowed to a stop.

'Shit.'

He was alone among the freight containers.

I'm insane.

No, I'm not.

He shook his head, then recommenced his run.

Commander Pel Bowman looked around his office, at the young Bone Listener, Lexar Pinderwin, who sat in a visitor's chair, and finally at the blue-and-white photographs of Andréa and the kids that stood on his desk. These were bad times, and his family's safety was paramount. But Andréa had told him last night that Arrhennius Vilnar's death demanded justice, and from what she had heard, it wasn't going to happen.

Bowman regretted inviting Lieutenant Zelashni to his house for drinks. They'd talked about Donal Riordan's sighting of what might have been a professional assassin clinging to the ceiling at City Hall, and the unlikelihood that the written-up report would ever see anything other than the inside of the folder it was contained in, buried in some cabinet in about-to-be-Commissioner Craigsen's office.

It hadn't been until Elleston Zelashni had gone that Andréa confessed she had been standing in the hallway outside his den.

'Arrhennius was good to us.'

'Yes. And my duty is to look after you.'

'Is that what the Colonel would say?'

The Colonel, long retired, was her father. He had been Pel Bowman's commanding officer over two decades before; and he had exemplified the ideals that Bowman aimed for: not just as a soldier, but as a man.

'If anything happens ... You'll go to him, won't you?'

'Pop will look after me. But you'll be fine.'

'Of course I will.'

Now, he stared at Lexar Pinderwin. Could he trust this young man – young Bone Listener – to carry on if he himself failed? It was a key question, of the sort Bowman had always been good at intuiting the answer to.

'Bone Listener Pinderwin, I have something I need to entrust you with. If something happens to me, I have some documents here that you will need to keep safe and very secret.'

'Yes.'

Bowman nodded. Then he got up, walked to the blank wall, and placed his hands in two precise spots. After a moment, a cross-shaped slit appeared, and the wall peeled back to reveal a safe. That opened with an ordinary code, and what Bowman pulled out was a stack of narrow folders fastened with manticore-gut straps.

He closed the safe, stepped back, and watched as the wall sealed up. Then he put the folders on his desk, picked up his briefcase, opened it, and tipped it upside-down over the waste-bin. He popped the folders inside the case, fastened it, and offered it to Lexar Pinderwin.

Lexar accepted it.

'I'll keep this safe. Is that all?'

'Someone needs to make use of the names listed in there. Names of allies. Show the documents to Donal Riordan, Harald Hammersen or Viktor Harman. They're all detectives you happen to know, right?'

'Yes. I also—'

'I left Alexa Ceerling's name off that list for a purpose, Bone Listener.'

'Oh.'

'If something happens to them, pick one of the people whose details you'll find in there. Use your own judgement. All right?'

'Yes.'

'Thank you for not trying to make cheery remarks about how everything will be fine.'

'No. I wouldn't, Commander.'

'Good. Now, I'd like you to come with me, if you would.'

'Of course. Um, is this the dangerous thing you're about to attempt?'

'It is, and right here in the building.'

Lexar looked down at the briefcase he was holding.

'Then I'll never be able to leave with this, will I?'

'Yes, you will. We're going to have someone with us, and she'll make sure you get clear.'

Bowman picked up a green callstone from his desk, and squeezed it. When he put the stone back down, it continued to glow for a second before growing dull once more.

'Who are we waiting for, Commander?'

'A friend. Her name is' – Bowman looked down, then up – 'Aggie.'

Then a bright-blue translucent form was rising through the floor.

You've found the key. Well done.

'No.'

Then you want me for something else. Not for a trip down below.

'No. Yes. That is what I need.'

I refuse.

Bowman rubbed his face.

'I've got to try now. What I heard an hour ago is, an emergency session of the City Council is in progress. They're going to pass a local version of the Vital Renewal Bill, whether it becomes a federal statute or not.'

'Hades,' said Lexar.

'I'm sorry, Gert— Aggie. I don't know what status freewraiths are going to have.' Bowman stared at the black telephone he'd received the call on, from a clerk in City Hall who used to feed information to Commissioner Vilnar. 'I *am* sure that zombies and other near-humans are going to be, um, disenfranchised.'

Interesting word.

261

'Yeah, sounds almost polite, doesn't it? It'll mean people – sorry, *non*-people – dragged from their homes, and Death knows what else.'

Bowman stared at his favourite photograph of Andréa, and touched the image of her lips with his fingertip.

'Let's go quickly,' he said.

I think you're wrong, but I'll do what you ask.

'Thank you.'

One fast descent through an elevator shaft, and they were inside a subterranean chamber in the deepest levels of HQ. Aggie's presence deflected a series of scanfields around which burning energies roiled, desperate to flare into the human continuum. Down here, ancient secrets and even forms of sentience unknown to the wider world were kept hidden, sometimes imprisoned, sometimes protected.

At the far end of the chamber stood a seventeen-sided door formed of blue metal, on which archaic equations composed from an extinct runic calculus were inscribed. The door looked newly finished, as if it had been installed yesterday.It had looked the same when Gertie – as Aggie now remembered – had first seen it, centuries ago.

'Commander Bowman,' said Lexar Pinderwin. 'I agree with Aggie's assessment of probabilities. Please don't do this.'

'I'm estimating the odds about the same way you are,' Bowman told him. 'I'm just coming to a different conclusion. It's not only about odds, it's about the cost of failing versus the cost of not even trying.'

'Whatever is in there, it's attuned to someone. I can sense that much.'

Astute, Bone Listener. The someone was Arrhennius Vilnar.

'Oh.'

Exactly.

Aggie was distracted by the Bone Listener. Suddenly, she diverted her attention back to Bowman, now standing with both hands flat against the blue, rune-inscribed door.

'I'm the designated successor of Commissioner Arrhennius Vilnar. If you scan me, you'll know the truth of—'

Bowman's corpse fell to the floor.

Twenty-five

Quicksilver rain was falling from the purple darkness as Donal ran the length of Avenue of the Basilisks. Otherwise called 1st Ave, it was a boulevard sided with ancient buildings whose gargoyles sometimes howled. They did so now.

He knew something was wrong as he neared Police HQ. Uniformed cops were gathered outside. An unmarked car, parked on the far side of the street, gunned its engine and pulled an illegal U-turn. Donal stared at the windshield, trying to see the occupants through the sliding glare on the hexiglass, then cancelled the evasive jump he'd been about to make.

Halting his run, he wiped silver rain from his face – no longer would he need his annual injection against the rain's adverse medical effects – and waited for the car to pull over. Then he opened the rear door and got in, still wearing his backpack.

Viktor was driving. Lexar was sitting up front beside him, arms wrapped tightly around a briefcase.

'What's up, guys?'

'You think it's good news?'

'Hardly.'

Lexar was shaking his head. Donal leaned over and touched him on the shoulder.

'Hang in there, Bone Listener. So tell me what's happening.'

Viktor grunted, pulling the car into the central lane. As he drove on, he gave a sideways nod towards Police HQ. There were angry faces among the uniformed officers standing on the steps.

'Craigsen's effectively Commissioner Craigsen, pending the legal swearing-in. All non-human officers are on suspension, supposedly temporary, and Bowman is dead. Bone Listener Pinderwin here was with him.'

'Shit. And you weren't?'

'I saw the Bone Listener standing on the street, and it turned out he was there for the same reason as me. To get hold of you, before you tried to get into HQ.'

'You think something might happen if I did?'

'I don't know. It might.'

Donal looked out at the familiar street rolling past. The buildings might remain the same, but the city was different now.

'What made you think I'd still be in Tristopolis? The Vixen is long gone.'

'If you snapped out of whatever happened to you, we knew you'd be back.' He glanced over his shoulder, at Donal's black running gear. 'Kinda thought you might use a taxi or something. I nearly let you run past us. Bone Listener Pinderwin has good eyes.'

'Lexar. I'm Lexar.'

'Viktor. So, we're going to Darksan Tower, to pick up Harald. We didn't know whether you'd go home, Donal, or to HQ.'

'Good thinking, my friend. So what's the news on Alexa?'

'We found her, and the Phantasm. Both in a bad way, both on the mend at Mordanto.'

'Is she under arrest?'

'We didn't tell anyone we'd found her. Until she comes round, it's best that way. Professor Steele—'

Mother.

No.

'—has taken care of the paperwork.'

'Any likelihood of her coming round soon?'

'Not according to Mage Kelvin. He came with us to help retrieve Alexa.'

'I vaguely remember him. The younger mage, right?'

'He's a good guy. He's also trying to make up for his little *faux pas*, mentioning the professor's name in front of you.'

'At least I found out.'

Viktor concentrated on the traffic for a moment. Then: 'We weren't going to say anything, because the professor said it might cause a profound reaction in you. Tell me she was wrong.'

'Point taken. But I'm OK now.' Donal leaned forward, between Viktor and Lexar. 'So what's in that briefcase?'

'Names, I think. Personnel dossiers. Commander Bowman gave them to me.'

'All right.'

'I think they belonged to Commissioner Vilnar.'

'Information on the Black Circle?'

'Maybe. There are also names of people to trust.'

Viktor turned on to 27th Avenue, saying: 'That might be more useful right now.'

'Yeah?' Donal sat back. 'I'm feeling a need to hunt the bastards down.'

'I can help,' said Lexar. 'That's kind of why Commander Bowman died. Because I brought matters to a head.'

'You found something?'

'The briefcase also contains the hand of a young boy. I severed the hand from his body. It's forensic evidence, but not so compelling if they have time to get rid of the remains.'

Donal shifted around, removing his backpack. It would have been easier to wait for the car to stop, but this gave him access to the Magnus.

'You want to explain that a bit more clearly?'

'There's a dark mage in the Westside Complex.' It was Viktor who answered. 'We've talked this through. Those new phones, they have to be routed through exchanges using children's nerves, or something.'

Donal remembered the engineers waiting near Finross's body, and the quicksilver birds descending.

'Not standard,' said Lexar. 'They removed the nerves while the boy was still living.'

'Shit.'

'But you don't just need technicians to do this. You need a mage to be present.'

'Cortindo.'

'Maybe.'

'An Illurian connection, and a dark mage inside the Energy Authority?' Donal thought they were finally discerning the shape of the opposition. 'It's Malfax Cortindo, all right.'

So much secrecy cocooned the Energy Authority, perhaps born of ordinary people's natural unwillingness to think about their activities, to let them get on with whatever they had to do.

'Tell me about Bowman,' Donal continued. 'What happened to him?'

Lexar's explanation lasted for the rest of the drive, until Viktor pulled up in front of Darksan Tower. He pointed.

'There's Harald.'

'OK.' Donal checked his watch: plenty of charge remaining. 'We could go to Mordanto, or up to my place. You say Alexa's not coming around any time soon?'

'Unlikely, they said.'

'So let's go up.'

As they got out of the car, Viktor gestured at it.

'What about this?'

'One of the doormen will park it for you.'

'Well, excuse me while I piss myself in excitement.'

'If you must.' Donal grinned. 'I'll get the butler to bring you a change of clothes.'

'Butler. Tell me you're joking.'

Harald was standing at the main doors, waiting for them.

'Come on up,' said Donal, 'and find out.'

An hour later, they were spread out in Donal's lounge. Dossiers were stacked in several loose piles on a wide, low table made of grey stone flecked with black and silver. Several open boxes of Fat'n'Sugar dough-nuts stood on other low tables, along with insulated snakehide cups of coffee. Harald had gone out to fetch them.

'Let's run through the categories, then.' Viktor pulled a dossier off the largest pile. 'Cops we can trust. Most of 'em, we already know.'

Harald pointed at the dossier in Viktor's hands.

'Adam Obsidian. Young guy. I've seen him training, gun range and gym. Excellent.'

Viktor looked at Donal.

'I don't think I've ever heard Harald call someone excellent.'

'Hmm. So, Harald,' asked Donal, 'just how would you rate us?'

Harald shook his head.

'Good answer,' growled Viktor. 'All right, here we have politicians we can go to for help. Maybe. But none of us know these people at all. And those' – he pointed – 'will help if we let them know that we know their secrets.'

'I've always wanted to be a blackmailer,' said Donal. He picked a dossier off another pile. 'Jo Serranto, journalist. I've met her.'

'She has an incisive writing style.' Viktor picked up his coffee. 'And a curvaceous ass.'

'What more could you want?' Donal remembered that the zombie Dr Thalveen had implied Serranto was a 'zombiefucker' – a term new to Donal, but not exactly hard to figure out.

Lexar was sitting in an armchair by himself, watching the three cops, frowning.

'You OK?' asked Donal.

'Sure. It's just … you take things so lightly. Or talk as if you do. I even understand why.'

'Can anybody spell "coping mechanism"?' said Viktor.

'We have our assets listed.' Harald gestured towards the files. 'Next we identify primary and secondary targets, and remember ORDER.'

'Observe,' Donal said for Lexar's benefit, 'reduce, decide, execute. Re-evaluate.'

Like every military acronym, it was short and simple. That was because the higher centres of the brain effectively shut down when bullets are taking off your comrades' heads. The ability to process any kind of logic at all under stress is what Donal had always found amazing.

'Oh, but' – Donal looked around the polished walls, the small expensive sculptures – 'we have another asset. I mean, real asset.'

'You're rich,' said Lexar. 'Even though you don't actually have a butler.'

'Exactly.'

'Although legislation could end that, in a matter of weeks. Take away your rights.'

'So in the meantime, just think how many bullets I can afford to buy.'

'OK.' Harald stood by the low table that held the files. 'We need plans of the Westside Complex, a timetable for contacting the cops we trust, and a briefing once our strategy is decided. Agreed?'

'Sure,' said Donal. 'As for the briefing, I believe it's my birthday tomorrow.'

'Er ...'

'Or something to celebrate, anyhow. So let's have a party.'

'A party?' said Lexar.

'Right here. Big one.'

'Ah.' Viktor smiled. 'Bring your own gun? Ammo supplied?'

'Exactly.'

For the first time tonight, Lexar's shoulder muscles released their tension.

'You guys are nuts, you know that?'

'Of course.'

'Why we became cops.'

'Party, party.'

'I mean, really insane.'

Kyushen stood inside the doorway of Sister Felice's room. She beckoned, and he came in and closed the door.

'Sit over there, Kyushen.'

'Um, sure.'

He took the hard-backed chair by the desk. Sister Felice was sitting on the single bed, her legs crossed and her spine upright. It was not a posture of invitation.

'The security locks on Records,' she said. 'They use encrypted hex codes, is that right?'

'Oh, no. Do you have any idea how many times people have a quiet word with me about this?'

'Why, Kyushen. I didn't know you were so popular.'

'And I've always refused to help.'

'That's because the other requests were for interview notes, personnel files on rivals, that kind of thing. I'm guessing here.'

Kyushen nodded, remembering that no Night Sister had ever asked him to do anything untoward. Not before tonight.

'This is related to the break-in, isn't it?'

'One patient is missing. Exactly one. Her name is Marnie Finross.'

'Oh, shit.'

'Anything we can dredge up on her, Lieutenant Riordan might be able to use.'

Kyushen formed a mental image of the security system, which he had in fact examined in the past, but never attempted to break. He visualized interlocking labyrinths, formed of yellow and blue light, that had to be rotated and translated in a sequence of transformations.

'It's not a five-minute job.'

'Wait here.' Sister Felice got up from the bed. 'I'm going to make a phone call.'

'I don't know whether—'

'Stay. Please.'

Kyushen began to feel shaky.

'All right,' he said.

After Sister Felice had slipped out, Kyushen turned to the small book-shelf over the desk. Not every book was familiar. He pulled out a heavy volume called *Sentenced to Sentience: an Evolutionary Fate*, and opened it to a chapter entitled 'Free Will is Inevitable'.

He looked up when Sister Felice returned. How much time had elapsed since her leaving, he could not have said. But the book's argument was compelling.

'You can borrow that, if you like.'

'Yes. Please.'

'And tomorrow, you and I are going to a party.' Sister Felice drew back the drape which concealed a clothes rail, extruded one claw, and hooked a hanger off the rail. 'Good enough, do you think?'

It was an elegant cream dress with a kind of bow beneath the bust.

'Er ...'

'It's purely business. You and I are invited to Lieutenant Riordan's place.'

'His home?'

'Sure. You think police officers don't have homes?'

'I never thought about it. I'm not sure I'm comfortable going to—'

'It really is business, Kyushen.' She replaced the dress on the rail. 'That's all.'

'Police business.'

'Even so.'

Kyushen looked at the book he was holding.

'I can borrow this?'

'Sure.'

'OK. Um ... Can I ask one other thing?'

He was sweating heavily, very aware of his skin sticking to the fabric of his shirt.

'If you like, Kyushen.'

'It's about ...' He blinked, swallowed, blinked several times more. 'Sister Lynkse.'

'Lynnie? What about her?'

'Is she ...?' This was really difficult. 'Is she ... seeing someone?'

There. He had finally said it. Now he waited for Sister Felice to snigger.

'I don't believe she is.'

'Oh.'

'You know, day after tomorrow, the musical society is putting on a little show.'

'I ... might have seen the notice. On the board.'

'Lynnie loves that sort of thing. She'll be there, on her own.'

'Ah.'

'I'll get you a ticket. And I'll make sure you sit together.'

Kyushen looked down at the book. He closed it carefully, and stood up.

'I ...'

'Good night, Kyushen.'

She was holding the door open for him.

'Yes. Um, good night.'

Then he was in the corridor, book in hand, and the door had closed behind him.

'I don't believe it,' he said.

269

A musical ... thing. Show. And he was going to be seated next to Sister Lynkse.

'Wow.'

He held up his borrowed *Sentenced to Sentience*, and realized he could not remember what page he was on. That was unprecedented.

'Oh, wow.'

Inside a large, near-ovoid chamber, a steel-enclosed bed stood, surrounded by shifting runes that glowed brighter when someone's gaze was turned on them. Mage Kelvin watched them, then directed his attention to the patient lying in the bed.

'H-hell-o.' Alexa Ceerling's eyes fluttered, then partially opened. 'Oh ...'

'My name is Finbar Kelvin, and you're safe.'

'Thank ... Oh. The ... Motor. Cycle.'

'I like motorcycles. The Phantasm is healing up.' Reflections from the runes played upon Kelvin's shaven scalp. 'And so are you.'

'I didn't ... The things I ... did.'

'Under compulsion. You must know that.'

'No. Yes.'

'Your friends tracked you down. I rescued you, in my silver magemobile.'

'Oh.'

'I'm joking. The others did the hard work.'

'Mage? There's a ... vault. In ... HQ.'

'In Police HQ?'

'You need to ... say. *Per. Vera. Veritas.*'

'A password?'

'Yes.'

'Tell ...'

But her voice was drifting off.

'That's fine.' Kelvin modulated his tone skilfully. 'And the images ... in your mind now ... of the things you were compelled to do ... grow vague ... and the colour fades ... as they grow ... distant and the feelings ... fade.'

Giving Alexa Ceerling amnesia – a limited amnesia, circumscribing every act she had committed under dark compulsion – was within Kelvin's ability to grant, and his powers did not compare to those of Professor Steele and the other seniors of Mordanto. But ethical standards dictated that they act only to dilute the emotional impact of those memories. Among other considerations, she would still be able to testify in court about what she had done.

270

Testify as a victim, not the criminal that the police department currently thought she was.

Kelvin watched her a while longer, then crossed the chamber to a desk. On it was a notepad bearing a phone number that he'd written down in response to an earlier call from Viktor Harman. Now, Kelvin picked up the desk phone – an ordinary black telephone – and spun the cogs to that number.

'Hello? Yes, Kelvin here. Alexa just woke up.'

He listened.

'Sure. She'll sleep now for a long time, fifteen hours or more. But she's turned a corner, and her mind is knitting back together. Yes.'

Then he listened again.

'I'm positive she will. But a party? Excuse me, but it doesn't sound like my kind of—'

He paused.

'Ah. I see. Right. Thank you.'

And he put the receiver down.

'A party.' He gestured, a flamboyant movement, and a brass knuckle-duster lay in his palm. 'Some kind of party.'

He curled his fingers inwards, as he twisted his hand palm-down, and the weapon was gone. In the bed, Alexa Ceerling groaned. Her eyelids fluttered, then she quietened once more.

'Perhaps Mage Cortindo will be there.' As Kelvin turned his hand over, a polished stiletto was in his grip. 'And perhaps we'll get to dance.'

Again, he twisted his hand and the weapon disappeared.

'Some kind of dance.'

Around Alexa's bed, the runes glowed steadily.

Twenty-six

The next night, at twenty-one o'clock, Sister Felice and Kyushen were in the back of a taxi, looking out through hissing quicksilver rain towards the entrance to Darksan Tower. Kyushen continued to watch outside, while Sister Felice counted florins from her purse and handed them to the driver.

Several hard-faced men and determined-looking women were approaching the place from opposite directions, carrying boxes tied with ribbon. One lean-faced guy with a scar running from crown to chin was holding a long bunch of black flowers.

'OK, Kyushen. Let's go.'

'Yes. I think we're not the first.'

'Are we fashionably not quite on time?'

Kyushen shrugged as he climbed out of the taxi. Sister Felice was wearing the cream-coloured dress, and it was far more elegant than he'd realized when he saw it draped from a hanger. If he'd known how to word an appropriate compliment, he'd have done so.

'I'm Kurt.' A uniformed doorman was smiling at them. 'You're expected. Floor 227.'

'Um, thanks.'

'You're very welcome.'

They entered the foyer, joined by some of the other men and women, and they all entered the same golden-walled lift. A curved grid of tiny studs appeared on the concave surface of the lift's interior, intriguing Kyushen. This was a defensive system, designed to skewer intruders. The mute wraith within the lift must have been briefed in advance by Donal, or it would not have held back.

A wide-shouldered man bumped into Kyushen as the lift halted. A long box wrapped in red ribbon was in his arms. It bore a tag that read: *Congratulations*.

'Sorry.'

'That's, er ...' Kyushen noted that the box was heavy and crumpled, containing something narrow. A tube appeared to be bursting through one corner. 'All right.'

Not so much a tube, as the business end of a rifle barrel.

'I guess we're all in a party mood,' said Sister Felice.

A short woman with black hair and calloused knuckles gave a soft laugh.

'*My* idea of fun.'

They stepped out into a twenty-foot high chamber. Black steel double doors stood open at the far end, revealing a wider room furnished in steel and black, with blue flames dancing on cups supported by helical stands. The apartment proper began with the room beyond that, through a doorway like a huge open mouth.

'Riordan lives here?' asked the man with the scarred face.

'It was Laura Steele's,' said the black-haired woman.

'Guess she didn't need the money, or she'd have rented it out to the Boreville Terrors.'

'Them, and all two of their supporters. Or has one of them died by now?'

'If you're talking about relegation to the Tertiary League, we was robbed in the—'

'Yeah, yeah.'

When they filed into the big lounge, everyone paused at the sight of twelve pale-faced zombies, all dressed in white, listening to Donal Riordan.

'—buses I've arranged,' he was saying. 'Be there at nine. Two bags per family, all pets in cages or on a leash.'

'Yes. Thank you.'

'And you've got the locations memorized?'

'Yes.'

'Then good luck to you all.'

The zombies headed for the lift then. Kyushen noticed that *Bertelloni's Bakery* was embroidered on the chest of each zombie's tunic. And it looked as if they had delivered a feast.

'Hey, Lieutenant.' The scarred man was unwrapping his heavy sniper rifle. 'It really is a party, then.'

'Yeah. You ready to do your party piece?'

'Tell me where and tell me when.'

'Typical man,' said the black-haired woman. 'Just point and aim.'

'At least I pee on what I'm aiming at.'

There were couches and comfortable chairs ranged around the large room. A long table bore savouries and sweet cakes, sparkling water and indigoberry juice and five jugs of coffee.

'No booze?'

'That's the other party.'

'*Other* party?'

'The celebration afterwards.'

'Ah. Got it.'

Kyushen saw a pale man watching him and Sister Felice. Pale skin, but not a zombie, and protuberant dark eyes: he looked like a Bone Listener.

'Hi.' The Bone Listener walked over to them. 'I'm Lexar Pinderwin.'

'Kyushen Jyu, and this is Sister Felice.'

They shook hands all round. Kyushen watched Sister Felice being careful to keep her claws retracted.

'Let's grab some plates, fill them up,' she said, 'and find a quiet corner. So we can watch these people in action.'

'Good idea,' said Lexar.

Kyushen thought that, in this company, he would rather stay silent unless someone asked him a direct technical question.

'Here's a technical question for you.' Sister Felice pointed at the buffet table.

'Uh.' Kyushen blinked several times, feeling off-balance. 'How did you—? What?'

'Is that indigoberry jam or purple caviar inside that pastry thing?'

'Um ...'

After a while, the food was finished. Some cops simply pushed their plates aside or put them on the floor, and forgot about them. Donal (who had drunk half a glass of water, and was satisfied) and Viktor brought out several easels. On the first, Donal propped a large scale map of Archon Borough, including the Arachnia Twistabout and colour-coded roads. Cops knew how to read such maps, with five or more levels depicted on one sheet. Viktor put up a plan view of the Westside Complex. On the remaining easels, he placed blueboards – they looked new – then he opened three boxes of yellow chalk.

At some point, Kyushen realized that a shaven-headed man was standing near his chair, although he had not seen the man enter. This wasn't a cop.

The man bowed to Kyushen, smiled, then turned his attention back to the briefing.

'McReady, Fleming, N'Gorbi.' Viktor wrote their names on one board. 'You're team one.'

'Can't we be team alpha?'

'Or charlie. I'd rather be charlie.'

'More like team dick.'

'Uh-huh.' Viktor pointed to the black-haired woman. 'Zarenski. You lead two. Take Obsidian and Walker.'

'All right.'

'Team three will be—'

The division of personnel continued. Viktor gave each team a primary objective, with no details yet, not until Donal had gone through more background. Then he called Lexar Pinderwin up to the Westside Complex plan, and asked him to point out the salient locations.

'The children's bodies' – Lexar pointed – 'I expect to be here, here and here.'

All around the room, expressions tightened. With all the jokes earlier, Kyushen had thought them flippant, although he knew medics who were as bad. Now every cop looked serious, and Kyushen swallowed. He wouldn't want these for enemies.

'Is that clear?' asked Lexar.

'No,' said the black-haired woman. 'I'm Ruth Zarenski, by the way. Could you be more specific about the route from the examination chamber?'

'Sure. The rooms off this corridor are used by osteoanalysts, whose primary job is to scan bones for—Well. Each room might be empty, or might have a dozen analysts working inside. The most likely possibility is—'

And so on, as several cops asked for clarifying detail. To each question, Lexar either gave a steady, logical answer or admitted that he didn't know.

'Good,' said Viktor finally. 'Thank you, Lexar. Donal, you want to go through the main insertion sequence?'

'Yeah. No smart remarks' – Donal nodded to the scar-faced man – 'about insertion, all right, Jacques?'

'We're all dicks here. I'll behave.'

'Good. So, the easy route from the Twistabout is going to be blocked. That leaves two—'

'How have you arranged that?'

'Sewage mains, bursting open right here. Team five, you get to be sewage workers, then pull in to enter the Complex from the tertiary insertion point.'

'Got it.'

'So the two routes will be the roads from Netherstands and West

Screams. If they're bringing in fresh bodies – I'm talking about tied-up or anaesthetized children – they'll have to use one of these roads. Kyushen, can we scan trucks as they pass by? For children inside?'

'I don't, er, see how. Not without a mage to help us.'

The shaven-headed man gave a tiny grin.

'All right. Let's come back to that. I'm going to ask each team to brainstorm your own plan, then we'll pool our thoughts. Any general questions first?'

'Yeah.' A young-looking cop with a square face raised his hand. 'Who is the enemy? Have all the workers been ensorcelled?'

'Good question, Adam. Lexar, you've been inside and worked out what the bastards are up to. What do you think?'

'Impossible to tell, but I think most of the workers are quite legitimate, and unaware of what's going on. Some of the analysts are definitely complicit, or else under deep compulsion.'

'OK,' said Donal. 'I poked around a few days back, and we agree. Any other questions?'

'What Bone Listener Pinderwin – Lexar, is it? – said about mages.' This was Ruth Zarenski. 'If we're up against a dark mage—'

'Then,' said the shaven-headed man, 'I'll do my best to hold him, while you do your thing.'

'And you are?'

'Everyone,' said Donal. 'Meet Mage Kelvin.'

'At your service.' Kelvin started to bow, then winked instead. 'It's going to be fun.'

'*Fun*,' muttered a hatchet-faced man at the rear.

'Any more questions' – Donal looked around the seated cops – 'before we separate into teams?'

'Just one. Where's Harald?'

'Harald who?' asked Viktor.

'Ha, ha.'

'Sergeant Hammersen,' said Donal, 'is playing politics. Because when this is over, we've our new commissioner and maybe City Hall to take down.'

'You're being, like, metaphorical?'

'Probably, if I knew what that meant. All right, everyone into your groups, refresh your coffee, and let's get brainstorming.'

Beside Kyushen, Sister Felice sighed. In the bright light of the room, the pupils of her eyes had tightened into vertical slits.

'What is it?' he asked.

'Nothing.' Sister Felice rubbed the back her hand along her face. 'He knows what he's doing, doesn't he?'

Even Kyushen had worked out that Lieutenant Donal Riordan was the one person in the room that Sister Felice couldn't look away from.

Harald stared around the pool room. The nine-sided, dark-grey tables stood in a circle, the balls arranged in neat triangles ready for play. No one was in the place besides himself and Captain Andrei Sandarov. The saloon below was busy, but tonight this room was unavailable to players.

'I'm a big believer' – Sandarov stroked his grey moustache – 'in the chain of command. It's how we keep order. It's discipline that keeps us straight, while criminal punks fail because they do not know how to coordinate and direct their efforts. Thank Fate.'

'Yes, sir.'

'And now we've got the official shit out of the way, you're going to hand me a way to stuff Craigsen, preferably before he's sworn in as commissioner. Or did I read your subtle hints incorrectly?'

'That's about what I was getting at.'

'So tell me how.'

'What if Captain Craigsen is getting support from Mayor Van Linder and his Unity Party cronies?'

'That's hardly news, Sergeant Hammersen.'

'And what if the UP politicos have already achieved similar rearrangements of personnel in the Energy Authority? For example' – Harald held up a folder, and extracted a sheet of paper covered with dense purple typescript – 'Director Braune, manoeuvred out of his job because he opposed links with their Illurian counterparts.'

'Energy Authority?'

'And the further link to the Illurian telephone company that's been running trial projects here in Tristopolis.' Harald produced two more typed sheets. 'Phones that can potentially ensorcel everyone who uses them.'

'Really?' Sandarov took the pages and ran his gaze down them, speed-reading. 'If I didn't know which task force you'd been assigned to for the past year, I'd think you were nuts.'

'Probably. Do you know how telephone switchboard circuits are made?'

'No, but I know what the main circuit lines have to be made from. That's why our Energy Authority has links to our phone company. I hope you're not trying to make this out as some kind of foreign conspiracy.'

'Not exactly.' Harald pulled out more pages. 'You'll know that we arrested Alderman Finross in Illurium, in Silvex City, on a cross-border warrant. Also, Lieutenant Riordan and myself attempted to take in Blanz, Cortindo, and Gelbthorne at the same time, but the three of them managed to translocate themselves, or whatever it is that mages do.'

'Riordan got Blanz in the end.'

'Not before Blanz killed Laura Steele.'

'Yes. I'm sorry about that. I mean, really sorry.'

Harald's voice went quiet as he said, 'I think you mean that, sir.'

Sandarov's face hardened.

'What are you implying?'

'Nothing more than that.'

'If you try to pressure me—'

'Sir, I know about your mother and father. If you don't feel comfortable helping us, we'll still keep their, ah, status to ourselves.'

For several seconds, Sandarov stared straight at Harald, saying nothing. Then he looked around the deserted pool room as if checking for eavesdroppers before releasing a long breath.

'They've been inside my house for months, afraid to go out. We picked up the signs early, and they sold their own place. Told their old neighbours that they were moving to the countryside, where resurrected folk are still welcome.'

That had been in one of the files. Sandarov's parents were zombies, resurrected together after a traffic accident three years ago.

'So here's the thing,' said Harald. 'The new phones require certain trunk lines to be made from what I guess you'd call high-grade nerves.'

'What does that mean?'

'The engineers take them from children.'

'That's—'

'When they're still alive.'

'Shit.' The last of Sandarov's defensiveness fell away. 'You mean that?'

'And it's happening here in Tristopolis.'

Sandarov scratched his face, almost tearing at the skin.

'Have you got any possible way of proving this?'

'We're working on that right now. Tomorrow, we're going to blow the thing wide open.'

'And if I can publicize the links to Craigsen ...'

'Maybe you'll be the new commissioner, not him.'

'Perhaps.' Sandarov walked to the nearest table, picked up the cue ball, then put it down. 'We said publicize. Did you mean that?'

'Uh-huh. You know Jo Serranto at the *Gazette*?'

'We've had our run-ins.'

'And if she gets hold of this story? Maybe with photographs?'

'In that case' – Sandarov smiled – 'it'll make the front page right the way across the Federation.'

'Then we'll have won.'

'Perhaps.' Sandarov's expression grew solemn once more. 'But Van Linder's going to be a hard man to beat. Remember, it's only by accident that he's taken over as mayor.'

'Not entirely by accident.'

'Yes, but it's not as if he planned Mayor Dancy's— He didn't, did he?'

'We think he did. We have reason to believe that if you ordered a forensic search of Möbius Park, you'll find traces of a professional assassin, not a resurrected person.'

'You mean the guys our officers killed—'

'Were set up. Ensorcelled. They had guns but they weren't the ones to take out the mayor or the commissioner.'

'Hades.'

'Proving a link to Van Linder, that I don't know about. But there has to be one. Otherwise it's a coincidence, of the kind that never happens.'

'That kind.'

'Exactly.'

'Then I'm with you,' said Sandarov. 'Because Mayor Dancy was the best thing that happened to this city for a long time, and if those bastards did for him, then I aim to return the favour. Deal?'

He held out his hand.

'Deal, sir.'

They shook, and Harald smiled.

At a quiet moment during the proceedings, Donal drew Mage Kelvin to one side. He intended to ask Kelvin what use a ripped-out eyeball might be.

'I'm uneasy,' Kelvin said.

'What about?'

'You think they'll be bringing in more children, but it seems like too much guesswork.'

'If we catch them with live captives, we blow the whole thing open. Analysing dead bodies with the nerves removed, that takes expert witnesses. Bone Listeners.'

'Ah. I understand. Non-humans are losing their jobs, and we expect a jury to take a Bone Listener's word that the nerves were removed pre mortem.'

'Yeah.' Donal's gaze drifted to the locked drawer containing Commissioner Vilnar's eyeball. 'Can you tell me exactly what you'd use an—?'

He stopped.

'What is it, Lieutenant?'

'Nothing. Just a little logic puzzle I wanted some advice on.'

Kelvin said, 'I'm good with puzzles.'

'I know.' Donal laughed, in a tone that caused several cops to look in his direction, frowning. 'But I think I've figured this one out.'

From the far corner, a voice said, 'And then we shoot the fuckers up. Hoo-ah.'

'Shit,' muttered a slight woman, not Ruth Zarenski.

'What's up, Nikola? Ovaries tightening up?'

'How'd you guess, peanut-balls?'

Close to Donal and Kelvin, Sister Felice blinked several times, and asked, 'Are they always like this?'

'Only when they're being friendly,' growled Viktor.

Kelvin smiled.

'Lieutenant Riordan, I don't suppose you're planning on going to HQ. Not before this ... operation, anyhow.'

'I'm on suspension, like every zombie.'

'Quite. Should you find yourself inside HQ, there's a certain vault, in the deepest levels, that Alexa Ceerling knows about. She accompanied—'

'The commissioner.'

'Right. There's a password: *Per Vera veritas*. I don't know what it means.'

'Arrhennius Vilnar's wife – widow – is called Vera.'

'Another innocent victim.' For a moment, a strange amber light seemed to circulate in Kelvin's eyes. Then they were normal again. 'It's as if injustice is filling up the world.'

'Maybe it always has.'

'Not everywhere, not all the time. Or humanity would never have survived.'

'Yes. You're all right, Mage Kelvin.'

'For a mage, you mean? Then you're OK, too, Lieutenant.'

Donal laughed again, and this time the glances that angled this way were accompanied with smiles, not frowns.

'For a black-hearted zombie that's no longer human? Thank you so much.'

'You're very welcome.'

They looked across the room, just as Adam Obsidian aimed a sniper rifle out the window and dry-fired it, snapping the action on an empty chamber. He handed the rifle back to the scar-faced man, whose name was Jacques McReady.

'Nice weapon.'

'Ain't she got the sweetest balance?'

Sister Felice walked over to Donal and Kelvin.

'You have the strangest friends, Donal Riordan.'

'Including yourself?' asked Kelvin.

'Quite possibly, Mage. Donal, we're wondering, Kyushen, Lexar and me, what use we can be tomorrow.'

'You're not coming into the Complex with us.'

Sister Felice's ears moved as her eyes narrowed.

'We know we're not combat-trained.'

'If you want to park nearby in a car or truck, and come in immediately afterwards to help, that would be great. In fact, I've got a woman I need to ring now, to see if she'll come along. You could take her.'

'What's her name?'

Donal noticed the slight extrusion of her claws.

'Serranto. She's a journalist, and I'm hoping she'll write it up, is all.'

'So. The authorities will try to bury the story.'

'The newspaper publishers aren't totally corrupt or scared. I hope.'

Sister Felice slowly blinked.

'What happens afterwards, Donal?'

'Step one: do what we have to do. Step two: find out if there *is* an afterwards.' Donal extended his fingers, counting. 'Step three: decide what to do next, if we're still around.'

'We?'

'All of us.' Donal gestured around the room. 'Everyone's risking something.'

'Oh. Um, I think I should go back and rescue Kyushen from your cop buddies.'

'Uh, OK.'

He watched her walk back across the room.

'I think you missed something there,' said Kelvin.

Donal shook his head.

'I'm not the person she thinks I am.'

But Kelvin's attention had shifted to the closed drawer that Donal had looked at earlier.

'You're certainly an intriguing individual, Lieutenant, with an interesting line in collectables. Was that the puzzle you were going to ask me about?'

'Maybe.'

'Then I guess that's your step three. If we survive tomorrow.'

'I'm glad you're with us, Mage.'

Around the room, the groups were growing quiet, and more and more cops were turning to look at Donal. The teams had finished their brainstorming, and every blueboard was covered in chalked lists and diagrams. It was time for the next stage.

Donal pitched his voice so it would carry, and called the group together.

Twenty-seven

Harald was in the parked truck, sitting up front, staring out at the spike-studded interior wall of the West Screams Tunnel. Behind him, in the body of the truck, waited two cops, Fleming and Roberson, plus the impassive Mage Kelvin, currently sitting cross-legged on a black mat. At the rear of the truck floated a kind of apparition: twisted lines of light, a distorted framework, rotating and slipping through geometric transformations that hurt to look at.

When Kelvin opened his eyes, he said to Harald, 'There's something approaching.'

'Another possible?'

'Exactly.'

There had been six previous 'possibles', each a false alarm, since taking up station here. Now, Kelvin slipped past Roberson – who was swallowing with nervousness despite the pump-action slivergun he held – and climbed into the passenger seat beside Harald.

'There's still not much traffic, Harald.'

'It's early.'

'I can't tell which vehicle— That one.'

Kelvin pointed at a small black milk float, its necrotonic motor whining as it passed, bearing its crates of yellow milk.

'Too small, isn't it?' Behind him, Roberson was looking out. 'If they've live prisoners aboard.'

'They're children,' said Kelvin. 'Stacked into a small place.'

'Children.'

'You knew that.'

'Yeah, but— Children.'

Roberson's face tightened as he pumped the slivergun's action.

'You've thirty seconds, Mage,' Harald was starting up the engine, 'and then I'm taking the truck in.'

'All right.' Kelvin was already climbing back into the rear, where the

283

shining illusion twisted and now began to moan. 'Just a moment.'

From his position in the truck's centre, Detective-Two Fleming said, 'I don't know how you've kept that thing manifested all this time, Mage. And kept a lookout as well.'

'I didn't.' Kelvin stopped in front of the apparition. 'That would've been impossible.'

'Then how's it—?'

'Professor Helena Steele,' said Kelvin, glancing mostly towards Harald, 'sends her regards.'

Then he stepped into the turning framework of light—

'Thanatos,' muttered Roberson.

—which pulled and distorted his body into elongated ribbons—

'Courageous bastard,' said Fleming.

—and out of existence.

'Hold tight,' called Harald.

Roberson grabbed the rear of the passenger seat. Fleming took hold of a stanchion. Both men stared at the evaporating illusion as it shrank to nothingness.

The truck lurched, as Harald took it through a swerving series of turns. Cones appeared to block off this tunnel completely, but team five had laid them so there was a chicane that could be navigated, but not at speed – at least, not by a normal driver.

Harald had the hair of an albino or an old man, the eyes of a poet, and the conversational disposition of a psychotherapist. None of those was the real Harald Hammersen. The ex-Marine was anything but normal.

Tyres screamed as he hauled the truck into another impossible turn.

Lexar climbed out of a different truck, parked on ground level beside a twisting highway that spiralled downwards from this point. He headed for the same iron doors that he'd used on his last visit. This time, when the doors opened and he went in to the short tunnel, he was followed by several people bent over beneath a dark-grey sheet of heavy fabric. They should have looked comical, scuttling in like that, but this was too serious a time to laugh.

When the inner doors pulled open, it was the same guards as before who greeted Lexar.

'Hello, Bone Listener. What's—?'

The dark-grey fabric was flung aside as three people leaped forward. The first was a dark-haired woman, Ruth Zerenski, and her heel took the bigger guard just under the heart as she thrust her kick from the hip.

Adam Obsidian whirled the other guard around bodily, whipped on a choke-hold, and squeezed, tucking his head down, closing his eyes, protecting them from the guard's darting fingers. Soon the strikes ceased, the body softening into limpness. Adam lowered him to the ground.

The third cop, O'Carnnel, stared at Ruth and Adam, and shook his head. He checked the slide action on his automatic. Shooting, he could deal with. This hand-to-hand shit was something else.

O'Carnnel noticed Adam's eyes shining as he looked at Ruth. Adam was young, an ex-Marine, and he stared at his team leader as if he was falling in love.

'Some people,' O'Carnnel muttered.

'What's that?' said Lexar.

'Nothing. Which way, Bone Listener?'

'Here.'

Lexar led them through the next tunnel, and they came out at the edge of the great pit. A bone-and-stone coach was waiting at the surface, ready to take them on the zig-zag ride down the pit wall.

O'Carnnel shook his head again, seeing how easily Adam Obsidian ran to enter the coach, taking up point with his Lucifer III sniper special held ready.

'Youngsters.' He noticed Lexar, probably the same age as Adam, staring at him. 'Oh, well. I'll try and keep up.'

He was the last one into the coach. As soon as he pulled the door shut, it shuddered and jolted its way into descent.

A guard called Malvern McGamma was head of the on-duty team behind the main entrance, reached by the Hypotown Expressway. He was in the big, iron-walled guardroom, staring at the distorting lens of the monitor. It showed the tunnel immediately before the huge, round, iron doors bearing a raised Skull-and-Ouroboros symbol taller than a truck.

McGamma touched a similar, smaller insignia on his tunic. The limousine he was seeing might or might not have been familiar, but when the rear window rolled down, he recognized the Very Important Passenger who looked out. The VIP stared straight into the glass eyes of the moving, metallic reptile that was looking at him from the ceiling, transmitting the image to McGamma's monitor.

'Open the Death-damned doors.' McGamma thumped the shoulder of his youngest team member. 'Come on.'

'But no one gave the—'

'For Death's sake, open the fuckers now!'

One of the other guards looked into the monitor.

'The mayor!'

They got busy with the levers. In a few moments, the great outer doors groaned and rolled into the slot in the wall. The limousine entered the Westside Complex. It drove through the shimmering aurora-like scanfields, through the inner doorway, and stopped in the tunnel just outside the guardroom.

'Oh, Hades,' muttered McGamma. 'Don't tell me there's a problem. Why couldn't this have waited another few minutes?'

Nine more minutes, and there would have been a change of shift. Barney Kilvarl would have had to deal with it, and more power to him.

Two guards pulled open the heavy armoured hatch of the guardroom. The familiar figure of Mayor Van Linder was standing there. Except that McGamma didn't remember Van Linder being that tall—

'Those are the door controls?' Van Linder asked.

'Yes, sir,' answered one of the juniors, called Laris.

'Wait a moment.' McGamma's hand went to his holstered firearm. 'Begging your pardon, but we need to—'

The mayor's features shimmered and shook.

'What the Hades?'

'Shit.'

And then a youngish, shaven-headed man was standing in the mayor's place, wearing the same suit. He smiled, and odd flecks of sapphire light appeared to circle his irises.

McGamma felt his eyelids begin to flutter.

'No . . .'

Then he slumped, grunted, and drifted into sleep.

Donal climbed out of the limo. He wore a black hexlar vest beneath his suit jacket, and carried a Lucifer VII assault rifle. He climbed up to a catwalk running along the wall. When he entered the guardroom, all the security guards were sprawled around the floor, and Mage Kelvin was working the door controls.

Donal was still thinking about the way that, several minutes earlier, a small, rotating cube of light – after floating gently in place inside the limo for hours – had suddenly expanded into Kelvin's form. In Illurium, Gelbthorne, Cortindo and Blanz had escaped by transporting themselves in similar fashion.

Cortindo. You're not getting away like that again.

Assuming it was Malfax Cortindo operating in the Westside Complex, and that he was somewhere on the premises now.

'Good,' said Kelvin. 'I've got the main doors reopening, without having to close the inner doors first.'

As Donal watched, the glowing auroras of the scanfields grew dimmer and more translucent, until he could no longer see them.

'Nice work, Mage.'

'Thank you.'

'I don't suppose you can sense—?'

'Oh, there's a dark mage here, all right.'

Donal stared at him for a moment, then said: 'Good.'

More cars and a truck pulled into the corridor outside the guardroom. Cops spilled out, Viktor and Harald among them. Everyone paused to look up at Donal, on the catwalk outside the guardroom.

'Yes,' he said. 'Do it.'

Eyes shone hard, chests expanded and contracted, nostrils flared, and mouths pulled back in a primordial expression: not a smile, but a predator's readiness to rend and tear.

Then the men and women moved, not needing to speak, each team heading for a designated hatch or doorway, into the depths of Westside Complex.

Team seven was only two men, Petrov and Arrowsmith, who had partnered each other on the streets for a little over two years. They moved down a winding bone staircase without a sound, weapons in hand. Three levels they descended, inside a dank shaft, meeting no one.

When they went through the door, they saw McReady and his team, entering through another hatch some fifty feet away. McReady nodded.

It was good luck that both routes were unguarded. Now they could go forward and—

Something moved overhead.

'The ceiling,' whispered someone.

Petrov tried to focus. The ceiling was bare stone, and nothing clung to it. The movement must have been an illusion.

Then a soft glow of white and red showed itself, and disappeared.

'Wraiths.' Petrov swung up his firearm. 'Ectoplasma wraiths.'

The cops ran.

'No!' shouted Petrov, firing round after round into the ceiling, shattering stones, with splinters flying. 'Bastards!'

He could not kill the wraiths, but he could buy his comrades time.

Arrowsmith was the last of the cops to reach the end of the corridor, immediately behind McReady. The others were already climbing down another stairway, to the next level.

He looked back.

'Petrov's gone,' said McReady. 'Don't even think about—'

But Arrowsmith was already running back.

'*Bastards!*' Petrov saw Arrowsmith return, just as the first wraith burned its way into his left shoulder. '*BASTARDS!*'

Both men emptied their weapons into the surroundings, knowing their silver-crossed bullets, passing through the wraiths, would cause some kind of distress, but nothing that could stop them. Then pain and fire was all the men knew, consuming their nerves, as their entire world became agony, and continued that way as the ectoplasma wraiths enveloped them.

The wraiths began to feed.

A balding guard stepped back from the doorway. Beyond him stretched a corridor leading to the osteoanalysis chambers.

'Good boy,' said Ruth. 'You'll keep quiet now, won't you? I can trust you, right?'

The guard stared at her, then nodded.

'You really shouldn't have hesitated,' she added.

'What? No, I—'

Her knee smashed into his inner thigh, buckling his leg as the muscles locked into paralysis. Then her descending hammer fist struck his carotid artery, and he was down.

Behind her, Adam Obsidian's mouth twitched.

'Nice.'

A blur of movement crossed the corridor, and more security guards came into view. These were armed.

'Shit.'

Ruth was down on one knee, firing, while Adam raised his Lucifer to his shoulder and shot six times. Behind them, two more cops, Gibson and Hayles from team four, took position and opened up.

Cracks of sound banged through the air, deafening, punching the ears. Then it stopped, leaving sickening silence.

The guards were down.

'Shit,' said Ruth again. 'We might have just killed some innocent men.'

But there was a groan behind her, and when she turned, she saw blood staining Gibson's chest.

'Not so innocent,' said Adam. 'Not now.'

Hayles was packing the wound from the medical kit that Gibson himself had been carrying.

'Stay with him,' Ruth told Hayles. And, to Adam: 'Obsidian, you're with me.'

'Yes, ma'am. I sure am.'

She waited, and in a moment, the two oldest cops, O'Carnnel and Gralinski, puffed into view.

'You two, secure the rooms after we've passed. You got snapcords, right?'

'Sure.' Gralinski held up a handful of the bright red cords.

'I got twenty,' said O'Carnnel.

'Good. Some of the analysts are innocent trainees, remember. Practically schoolkids. But make sure they can't move.'

'Got it.'

'OK.' Ruth nodded to Adam. 'Let's go.'

They advanced.

Donal's team passed through a vehicle bay that contained seven trucks in addition to the small black milk float. The milk crates, along with the metal bed they had lain on, were stacked to one side. A hollow compartment was revealed in the float, from which a faint smell rose. At least one of the missing captives had urinated while enclosed inside.

An engineer walked into their path and stopped, blinking.

'Police.' Donal moved his Lucifer rifle from port-arms to loosely aiming above the guy's head. 'Hold out your hands.'

A female detective called Johanssen pulled out a snapcord restraint. At that, the engineer's eyes narrowed, focusing on Donal's weapon, and Donal whipped the rifle through a vertical half-circle, shattering the man's jaw, dropping him.

'Thanks for saving us the time.' Donal looked back at Kelvin. 'You sensing his location yet?'

'No. But he is here.'

'OK. We're going through—'

'Aah!' Kelvin's eyes squeezed shut. 'Fuck. *Fuck*.'

It was not the kind of language Donal expected to hear from a mage. Wasn't there some kind of incantation for him to use in defence?

But Kelvin was already on his knees, and trickles of blood appeared from his eyes.

'Hades, Mage. What can I do?'

'Donal ... Pit. Reactor piles. Round ... platform.'

'That's where the bastard is?'

'Yes ...'

Kelvin was on the floor, on forearms and knees, trying to push himself upright.

'Fuck ...'

Then he was sprawled, fists clenched as he continued to struggle, rivulets of bloods across his face.

'Right.' Donal hefted his rifle. 'Fight him as much as you can, Mage.'

He moved into the next hallway at a lope.

'Fuck ...' faded behind him.

Then he was inside a big, white-tiled chamber where children lay on slabs. The boys wore knee-length dark-grey shorts and cheap shirts, the girls wore dark-grey skirts and blouses, and they all looked asleep. At the far end of the room, a woman wearing a lab coat was bent over what looked like an open-topped aquarium, lacking water but filled with rustling silver things that crawled across each other.

The woman's face went pale as she saw Donal.

Behind Donal, Johanssen muttered, 'Shit.'

Two more cops, Kaligan and Dorse, entered and looked at the children. Their features hardened. As they looked, a boy's eyelids opened half-way, and in a drowsy voice he asked, 'Are you my new daddy?'

Orphans. The clothing had changed little since Donal's day.

'They—' The woman swallowed. 'They've got no one. It's a kindness to ... to ...'

'From an orphanage, right?'

'Y-Yes ...'

'Just like me,' said Donal, putting his rifle down on the floor.

'N—'

He took hold of the woman's clothing at neck and thigh, and dropped into a squat. As her weight toppled, he boosted himself upwards, and threw her at the open-topped tank. She was heavier than he'd thought, and she landed on the edge, one hand going into the seething mass of silver to save herself from toppling further.

Then she screamed, as the neural scorpions got to work.

'Help—'

'You've got a nerve,' said Donal, retrieving his rifle.

He would have been willing to stay and watch the mass of scorpions draw out her living neurons, but there was work to do. Kelvin might already be dead.

'You three, get the children clear.'

'Lieutenant.'

There was a door at the end of the chamber. Donal kicked it open and ran through.

Harald's team went down beneath a bolt of black sheet lighting that smashed its horizontal way at waist height along the corridor. Some peripheral cue caused Harald to drop just before the darkness sheared through three torsos and left them screaming, cut in half. There were two figures standing at the corridor's far end, their outlines partly visible.

'I hate mages.' Prone, Harald took aim.

Then his head was filled with images of swirling red-and-black skies, of immense views over plunging chasms where lava boiled and spat.

'Illusion.'

Harald closed his eyes, focused on the hallucinated images, memorized them, and opened his eyes once more. The stone floor was hard beneath his chest, and he noted how it sucked heat from his skin, in contrast to the blazing heat of the imaginary lava he was not really suspended over.

The vision was bright, but every Marine underwent trance-training, and all he had to pick out were the tiny differences from the images he'd seen with his eyes shut and the traces of reality he saw now.

'There,' he said.

And squeezed the trigger four times: *crack-crack, crack-crack.*

Two mages dropped.

Harald went back to his dying comrades. One was already unconscious, the others still aware that their lower bodies had been sliced off, that they were entering the final seconds of their lives.

He took hold of their hands, and began to intone the words of the Last Induction, bringing rapid anaesthesia, dropping them fast into the calmness of the Death Trance, to face the end.

When it was over, he retrieved weapons and stood up. His eyes were gentle as a poet's. His pale-skinned hands, each holding an assault rifle by its pistol grip, were steady.

His breathing was even as he strode forward.

As he passed the corpses, he noted how young they had been. Apprentice mages, devoting themselves to the wrong side.

Now they were nothing but reactor fuel.

Two minutes later, he was approaching the sound of protracted gunfire. He rounded a corner. Six men in Energy Authority uniforms – their backs to Harald – were firing at two figures Harald instantly recognized: Ruth Zarenski and Adam Obsidian. Adam was already down.

Battlefield ethics also formed part of Marine training. The six men showed the slack expressions of parazombies, so they were firing under someone else's volition – but they were still firing.

Harald's bullets tore through their spines.

*

291

In the room where he had fallen, Mage Kelvin lay prone and still. Then his fists clenched, and he groaned, aware of the salt-sweet blood in his mouth, the eruption of hot blood inside him, the bursting of capillaries around his eyes.

But he was still fighting.

Alone, rifle at the ready, Donal came out on to the stone landing that he remembered, overlooking the great caverns containing the reactor piles. In front of him, a long walkway stretched, ending in a seven-sided platform. Beyond that was the vastness of the caverns.

When Donal had been here before, that platform was where the dignitaries stood, looking out over the rows of massive reactors, experiencing the dark shimmering resonance that filled the air, even for those who were not especially sensitive.

Now, a single man in a dark suit stood there, looking out, his back to Donal.

He didn't look like Malfax Cortindo.

Mages can alter their appearance.

Beyond the man stood two convex glass screens, with transparent cables linking them to a floating area of twisting light and darkness: a portal through spacetime, as Kelvin had used earlier. Whoever this man was, he had to be a mage.

Donal stepped into the open, to the near end of the walkway, and raised the rifle, tucked the hard butt into his shoulder, and aimed. Then the man turned, and Donal wavered.

Mayor Van Linder smiled at him.

Twenty-eight

Dead parazombies lay face down, but Harald had already checked they were no threat. Instead, he concentrated on checking Adam Obsidian's wounds. The hole through Adam's thigh was serious, pumping hot blood. With Adam's own help, Harald tied off a tourniquet, and checked it for tightness. Then he got to his feet, and beckoned Ruth Zarenski.

'Down there' – he pointed along the corridor – 'is where they tip the bodies on to the trucks, and wheel 'em to the reactors.'

'So we can get out to the caverns. What about Obsidian?'

'We always leave our men behind.'

It was a Marine dictum: sooner abandon a man than a platoon, a platoon than a battalion, a battalion than a regiment. Despite the pain he was fighting, Adam looked up at Harald and grinned.

'Fuck 'em and die, brother.'

Harald gave a gentle smile.

'Fuck 'em and die.'

Every Marine knew how to invoke the Suicide Trance if it came to that. But Adam was going to live, provided he got medical help in time.

Provided they didn't screw up the operation.

Donal still held his rifle, but he had not fired. Mayor Van Linder spread his arms wide. Behind him, on the circular platform, images shifted in the two curved glass screens.

Cortindo.

One of the screens showed the revenant Malfax Cortindo, the other a dark-haired woman it took several seconds to recognize: Marnie Finross. Donal had seen her only in Commissioner Vilnar's office, with silvery cables attaching her eyes to the surveillance system.

Van Linder chuckled as easily if he were in an elegant club, mixing with business people and political supporters.

'I find it amusing,' he said, gesturing to his own face, 'that your young friend Kelvin used these exact features to get you inside.'

'Keep laughing, fuckface.' Donal kept the rifle aimed.

Pull the trigger.

But he couldn't. Van Linder was amused without a hint of nervousness. Something had to be wrong with Donal's simple plan.

'Poor Kelvin. He's suffering, you know. I thought I might reconfigure his neural patterns, bring him over to our side, but he resists so nicely.'

Van Linder reached inside his pocket, and pulled out what looked like a pendant. With his thumbnail, he drew out something like a fragile, three-dimensional snowflake coloured amber. It might have been spun sugar, so easily broken now Van Linder had removed it from its protection.

'If you try to harm me,' said Van Linder, 'I'll drop this or crush it in a muscular spasm. Call it a deadman switch.'

'So what?'

Beyond the platform loomed the rows of reactor piles. Could Van Linder have set up some device to trigger an explosion?

'So nothing just yet. Oh, but what's this?'

Donal lowered his Lucifer VII and looked down to his right. The landing he stood on was set into a virtual cliff, one side of the main cavern. Further down, a long walkway was set into the rock, but open to the cavern. Two figures were running along it: Harald and Ruth.

They were nearing the detachable section under which a large freight car could stand, ready to receive a fresh load of processed bones for the reactor piles. But the freight car was standing off to one side, and Harald and Ruth were walking on thin metal hanging above a fatal drop.

'And this is such a pretty device.'

In Van Linder's hand, the amber snowflake began to glow.

He's been bluffing.

Donal brought the rifle back up, just as a metallic squeal sounded, and the walkway down below tipped through ninety degrees, spilling Harald and Ruth into space.

Yellow light flared.

Donal did not fire.

It's a stasis field.

He lowered his rifle once more.

'That's right, Donal Riordan. Because you value their lives, don't you?'

Van Linder was projecting the field, a long yellow cone of light, down towards the collapsed walkway, holding Harald and Ruth suspended in mid-air. The field softened to a scarcely visible amber overlay of the image beyond: hard stone, and a long drop to the cavern floor, where metal rails and scattered equipment lay ready to break any human bodies that might fall on to them.

'If it flares up once more,' continued Van Linder, 'I'm afraid that means time has begun to flow inside the field again, entropy breaking the symmetry. Or do you have any idea what I'm talking about, Riordan?'

'It's an illusion. You couldn't have known they'd be there.'

He meant Harald and Ruth, their limbs outstretched, hanging above the fatal drop.

'Oh, but I did. Kelvin's mind held such a bright picture of your plans. It was a pleasure to tear it out of him. He really does squeal prettily inside.'

Donal squatted down, laid his rifle on the flagstones, and stood up.

'Why this trickery, Van Linder? If you're so powerful, you'd have just killed us.'

'I'm going to, of course. And the city will be outraged, at a zombie-led attack on the Energy Authority itself.' Van Linder gestured towards the dark space containing the reactors. 'People hate to think about how these things work, but threaten them with a life of no warmth, no transport, and no food in the shops— That's all we need.'

'Go fuck yourself.'

Behind Van Linder, the image of Malfax Cortindo moved, distorted by the convex glass.

'*Kill him now.*' Cortindo's voice came from a speaker below the glass.

'Oh, but I think I'll make him love me first.'

Then Van Linder's features grew liquid, rippled as if shaken, dissolving and shivering into a new configuration, a face that Donal recognized.

'Gelbthorne.'

'The real Van Linder died last night. Before that, he did in fact dream of becoming Mayor of Tristopolis with our help.' He looked at the fragile amber snowflake on his palm. 'I like to think I'm keeping the spirit of our bargain.'

Then he stared at Donal.

No.

Stared, with eyes that seemed to shine with a pale, icy blueness that Donal could not turn away from.

Close your eyes.

Donal tried.

Can't.

Gelbthorne's gaze was everything, encompassing the world. All the anger Donal had, that he had *used*, was useless, his strength abandoned, despite the memories of orphanage and suffering, the things that had happened to Laura, to the children here. None of it mattered as trance enveloped him.

Donal was lost.

Kelvin groaned, his face against the hard floor, smearing his own blood, knowing he had failed and cost everyone their lives. For Donal, the price was even worse.

Adam sat slumped against a stone wall, his rifle in his lap, his chin down on his chest, feeling cold with blood-loss. The ache in his leg was distant, held at bay by trance. His clothes were sticky and stained with red.

'Yo, soldier. You taking a nap down there?'

The voice was gravely.

'Hey ...'

Big hands helped Adam to his feet.

'You got a job to do, my friend. One that our mage friends don't know about.'

Gelbthorne's soft, deep voice, uttered in a rhythm to match the neural activity of Donal's mind – Donal knew that, somehow – became everything there was, and everything there had ever been, filling the universe that Donal inhabited. All the old, bad feelings became ephemera that he could let go of. Peacefulness, now, was the way of surrender. Gelbthorne asked the final, pivotal question.

'Will you obey me now, in everything?'

Donal opened his mouth—

A massive explosion blew out the wall beneath the stasis field, spilling a thousand, two thousand corpses into a ghoulish scree slope, formed of tangled lifeless limbs and staring faces of the dead.

From his vantage point on the cavern floor, where he stood with a heavy grey hexzooka in hand, Viktor judged the angle, noting how the corpses lay beneath the suspended, floating figures of Harald and Ruth.

'Good work, young Adam,' he murmured.

Then he swung the hexzooka to his shoulder, raised his aim to the platform high above, and pulled the trigger.

'Shit.'

His aim was perfect. Stone and dust burst from the platform, as Gelbthorne's bloodied figure fell. But Viktor had felt the hot exhaust blast go across his back, and he knew without looking that his leather coat was ruined.

'Bastard.'

—and said, *'No!'*

Donal's right hand whipped inside his jacket and came out with his Magnus. He followed Gelbthorne's fall from the walkway with rapid aim, firing shot after shot, silver-crossed chitin-piercing rounds tearing into the bastard's body as he dropped to the stone floor.

Already mutilated from the hexzooka round's blast, Gelbthorne took every hit from Donal, and smashed skull-first on to flagstones some eighty feet below.

Almost certainly, any one of those factors would have killed him. But Donal grinned when he realized that Big Viktor was taking no chances.

A second round from the hexzooka blew Gelbthorne's body into shredded fragments and hot red vapour.

Donal turned around. On the half-destroyed platform, the screen that had displayed Marnie Finross's image was gone. The other, though cracked, showed Cortindo, his mouth moving in a curse Donal could not decipher. Then that screen toppled, fell down to the cavern floor, and smashed apart into a white spray of shards.

'Got the fuckers,' Donal said.

Twenty-nine

When Viktor pulled Harald and Ruth from the pile of corpses, they were bruised and sore, having been tangled on top of each other. They helped each other to stand upright on the cavern floor.

'After that,' said Ruth, 'we have to get married.'

'Er ...' Harald looked straight in her eyes, and swallowed.

Then Ruth swallowed.

Viktor looked up at the ruined wall. There was a gap through which Adam Obsidian, bomb trigger in hand, was visible. Adam looked at Harald and Ruth, and his expression shut down.

'Good man,' Viktor called, then looked up at the high walkway. 'You OK, Donal?'

'Oh, yeah. Can you see any phones down there?'

'None in sight. I'll go look.'

'And I'll do the same up here.'

It took less than five minutes to make the calls they needed. When help began to arrive, the various teams were already regrouping. Mage Kelvin was under sedation, wrapped in a blanket that Fleming had found.

When Jo Serranto came – with a police escort, and written orders from Captain Sandarov granting her entry to the Complex – she was accompanied by a photographer plus a white-skinned man in a black coat: Dr Thalveen. Donal smiled. Thalveen gave an impassive nod.

The term *zombiefucker* hung unspoken between them.

'This is amazing,' Serranto was saying. 'Get a shot of the body from over there. And another close-up.'

Gelbthorne's features, in death, were a blurred composite of his own face and Van Linder's.

'"Mayor Replaced by Dark Mage." What a headline.'

To one of the uniformed cops, staring around the damaged premises and the slope formed of spilled corpses, Donal said, 'You guys got a spare ride? I need to get to HQ.'

The biggest man spat.

'Wish I'd been here with you, Lieutenant. And yeah, Captain Sandarov said, come in when you want. Reinstated.'

'That's good of him.'

At approximately the same moment, Captain Craigsen paused in the letter he was writing to the mayor's office, accepting the offered post of Commissioner of Police. He looked up at the door to his office, reading the reversed gold lettering that gave his rank, imagining 'Captain' replaced by 'Commissioner'. Of course, when it happened, he wouldn't stay here: he would need a suitably imposing office, new furniture, and perhaps that blonde female clerk from Surveillance to be his secretary.

Bulky shapes in uniform were standing outside the door. One of them opened it.

'Haven't you heard of knocking?' said Craigsen. 'Why don't you go back out and—'

Behind the uniforms, a lieutenant named Higgs waved a sheet of paper.

'This is a warrant for your arrest, Craigsen. You are charged with twelve counts of child kidnapping, more counts to follow, with accomplice to homicide on the same additional counts.'

Craigsen could only stare as Higgs came in.

'Further, conspiracy to commit political assassination, complicity in ensorcelment without victim's consent, eight known counts with more to follow, and additional charges to be appended once you are incarcerated.' Higgs lowered the paper. 'Also, Captain Sandarov sends his regards, and says fuck you.'

'No.'

But Craigsen scarcely struggled as the uniforms hauled him from his chair and snapped on the cuffs.

'And if I may say something else, sir.' Higgs held up his hand, and the officers held Craigsen in place. 'You're very careless as regards health and safety. This floor is highly polished, and someone could slip, you know.'

'What—?'

Higgs ripped an uppercut punch that started low, about knee-height, and rammed into Craigsen's groin. Craigsen folded over, his chin coming up, and Higgs smashed his knee into his face.

'Take this piece of shit to the cells.'

'You got it, Lieutenant.'

Higgs stared into the outer office. There, officers turned away, suddenly busy with paperwork. Higgs nodded. They understood.

When it came to Craigsen's resisting arrest, none of them would have seen a thing.

It was too soon for the city's mood to have changed. Several pedestrians, seeing a zombie in the back of a police cruiser, grinned or cursed with an upraised finger. Donal did not react.

At HQ, they dropped him off in front, and he climbed the steps between two groups of deathwolves whom he did not know. When he went into the huge foyer, he found an outlined rectangle on the floor where Eduardo's granite block had stood. Sooty marks scraped in the direction of the exit. Some twenty uniformed and plainclothes officers stood around.

'What happened?' Donal asked a grim-eyed detective.

'Bastards took Eduardo away, don't know where.'

'Hades.'

'But we'll find out, Loot. Like we heard you got Alexa Ceerling back safe. Good work.'

'Yeah. Thanks.'

So it was a beginning. Donal was almost smiling as he reached the lift shafts, paused in front of number 7 – still empty – then took another, and asked the wraith to take him deep into the vaults.

It descended without a word, carrying Donal in an impersonal grip.

Soon he was standing in front of a seventeen-sided door on which runic equations burned and glowed. To reach the chamber, he had passed through scanfields that *hurt*, causing him to dry-vomit and stumble, but they had allowed him to enter.

'*Per Vera veritas*,' he said.

Equations shifted and rearranged themselves, matrices reformed, and graphs assumed new configurations. The door appeared to pulse, but did not open.

Blue brightness grew on the floor behind him.

Don't do it, lover.

The wraith that billowed over Donal was big, shining with energy.

'That sounds like the old Gertie. But I know you're not.'

Aggie's form twisted in the air.

No. I know, as Gertie and Xalia knew, how dangerous hypergeometric vaults can be.

'Yes.'

Commander Bowman dropped dead right where you're standing. He collapsed mid-breath.

'Good job I don't breathe.'

This is not a joke.

'I've given it the password.'

It takes more than that. The vault is attuned to—

'Commissioner Vilnar, I know. It'll be all right, Gert— Aggie.'

Donal stepped forward and placed both pale hands upon the door.

No!

But the door was opening, and the energies that blazed beyond had not destroyed him.

'You want to give a hint here? On how to work it?'

For a moment, sapphire brilliance flared through Aggie's wraith form.

Hold a question in your mind. Damn you!

'All right.'

Donal stepped forward, into coruscating light.

No ...

And screamed with pain.

As he awoke, he groaned, trying to hold on to the memory of what he had experienced. He failed. White light and pain were all he could re-member ...

'Donal?'

...along with the dry facts answering the question he had posed.

'He's coming round. Good work, Aggie.'

Good work would have been stopping the silly bastard before he went in.

Harald and Viktor were standing over him. They were in an outer chamber of the vaults, outside the agitated scanfields.

'There's something ... ugh ... Give me a hand will you?' Donal, supine, raised one arm, and Viktor tugged him to his feet. 'Thanks.'

'You OK to walk?'

'Yeah.'

'Then let's get out of this place.'

Donal began to feel better as they moved. When they reached the bank of lift shafts – number 7 being empty still – he had a thought.

'Let's go up to the gun range. Get some extra advice from Brian.'

'Is this relevant?' growled Viktor.

'Marginally. We could get the information from a few phone calls.'

'Perhaps,' said Harald, 'we should check that Brian's doing all right.'

Donal remembered the marks on the foyer floor where Eduardo's granite block had stood.

'Gert— Aggie?' He looked at the empty opening of shaft 7. 'Could you take us all up at once?'

Certainly. You'll have to hold each other's hands, and sing the national anthem. You can do that, can't you?

"Course we can,' said Harald. 'See you up there.'

He stepped into shaft 9, and whisked upwards, out of sight. Viktor looked at Donal, shook his head, and took number 10.

My shaft is still empty, lover. Are you desperate for a ride?

'I'd like that. You're not going to work the elevator gig any more, are you?'

Very insightful. You and I have a lot in common, zombie man.

Her bright form enveloped him, carried him into the shaft, and began to ascend. Her partially materialized grip was all around him.

'I'm still mostly Donal. You're still mostly Gertie.'

Don't be too sure, darling.

'That's the way Gertie always talked to Donal.'

They rose for a time in silence, slowly. Then they came to a halt, floating in mid-shaft, and odd fluorescent sparkles danced across Aggie's wraith form.

Perhaps there are things that the other part of me always wanted to say to the other part of you.

While Donal was trying to parse the sense of that, Aggie shot upwards, carried him out into the reception chamber of the firing range, whirled around, glowing, then flew up into the ceiling and was gone.

Donal stared at the blank stonework.

'What was that about?' asked Viktor.

'Um ... Nothing. Is Brian there?'

'Harald's talking to him round the back. He's fine.'

They walked through, past the trays of target sheets and the shelves of ammunition, into the storage room that still served duty as Brian's bedroom. Brian and Harald were drinking purple tea from tin cups.

'Hey, Lieutenant.'

'Brian. You've been OK here?'

'Kept my head down. And I've got a lot of friends.' Brian gestured to a bookcase whose shelves contained handguns. 'To keep me company.'

'Things are going to get better in the city,' said Donal. 'Soon.'

'Sandarov will move fast.' Harald picked up a .39 Zak, checked the balance, and replaced it. 'He's motivated.'

'Captain Sandarov?' Brian's skin went a shade darker blue. 'He treats me all right.'

'Commissioner Sandarov, if things go the way they should.' Donal looked at the handguns. 'Is that a GA over there?'

'Sure. You want to take a look?'

Donal picked up the handgun, checked the sword-blade logo embossed on the grip, and showed the weapon sideways-on to the others.

'Gladius Armaments. I used a smaller-calibre version a few weeks back.'

'Those Illurians build robust weapons,' said Brian. 'Clean design. You can drop 'em in mud and they'll still fire.'

'And GA? Where are they based?'

'Illurium, like I said. Oh ... Aurex City.'

'Silvex City, I've been to.'

'Aurex is a long way away, Lieutenant. It's almost terminatorial. You wouldn't want to be outdoors in a place like that.'

'I'll wear a hat.'

Viktor's basso profundo growl was almost too deep to hear. 'You want to tell us what's going on?'

'I kept a simple question in mind,' said Donal, 'when I went into the vault. Really simple.'

'And?'

'Who is Marnie Finross?'

'Laura arrested her. You were there when they executed her uncle.'

'Uh-huh. So if the alderman was her uncle, who are her parents? Why didn't anyone even try to find out? And why is she important enough to break out of a secure facility?'

'Huh.'

'Her father's name is Brax Finross.' Donal put the GA handgun back on the shelf. 'And he's—'

'The head of Gladius Armaments,' said Brian. 'I got a picture of him somewhere. An interview in an old copy of *Trigger Monthly*.'

'Good man. Anything else you've got on GA will be useful.' Donal picked up another gun, a polished dark-red Stigmatix, checked the action, and put it back. 'The Old Man was investigating something else in connection with GA. To do with weapons.'

'What was it?' asked Harald.

'I don't know. I had a peripheral sense of it, I guess you'd say. The vault ... it gives you links from the information you've asked about, and you can follow them partway. Then it fades.'

'Fades into pain?'

'Yeah. How could you tell?'

'Donal, if you'd seen your face when you were lying there outside that Death-damned vault, you wouldn't need to ask.'

'Oh.'

Just then, the floor began to sparkle and swirl with light. Aggie rose up through it, and hung in the air, glowing and billowing.

There's something I need to know, lover.

Donal glanced at Harald, Viktor and Brian, and wondered what they were thinking.

'What about, Aggie?'

Exactly how you attuned yourself to the vault.

'That ... was a gift from the Old Man.' Donal unknotted his tie, and got to work on his shirt buttons. 'I wouldn't do this if I weren't among friends.'

I'm not saying anything.

'Right.' He pressed into his chest, and pulled the flap open. 'See?'

Something nestled in the cavity, against his black, beating heart. Donal reached in and drew out the eyeball.

'Like I said, a gift.' With his other hand, he sealed up his chest opening. 'He tore it right out of his own eye socket, when he was lying there shot.'

'Thanatos,' growled Viktor.

You won't need it again. The vault knows you now.

'I guess.'

The thought of entering again was dreadful. Donal knew he would not be able to manage the ordeal soon.

Then can I have it? Call it a keepsake.

'What? Oh—'

Donal looked down at his hand, then reached out.

Thank you. Arrhennius was my friend.

Aggie's bright form enveloped Donal's hand. When she drifted back, Commissioner Vilnar's eyeball was gone.

Be careful, Donal. I don't want to lose you too.

'Of course I'll—'

But Aggie was already sinking down through the floor.

Seven big uniformed cops, with weapons drawn, stepped from seven elevator shafts simultaneously into a grey-carpeted lobby. Two of them went to the female officer behind the desk, one clasping a hand over her mouth, while the other used snapcords to bind her wrists.

Seven more cops stepped through, and this time one of them was Captain Sandarov. They took several paces forwards, then stopped. None of the cops spoke. Sandarov looked at the glowing sign that hung below the ceiling.

~CUSTOMER RELATIONSHIP BUREAU~

A white-haired woman stepped into the lobby, accompanied by three shaven-headed men. She looked at Sandarov.

'We're ready, Captain.'

'Thank you, Professor. Let's do it.'

They poured through the entry door, into the open office space of the call centre.

'*No!*' One of the call handlers was very quick, leaping from his chair. 'Get—'

A uniformed cop whipped an elbow into the man's mouth, knocking him back across his desk. The others brought their weapons to bear.

Professor Steele reached over to the fallen man's indigo phone, took hold of the receiver cord between both hands, and lowered her chin, eyes squeezed shut. A gunshot cracked at the far end of the room, but she kept her concentration.

White lightning sizzled down the cord from her hands. It sped across the connections, spread out around the room as every telephone blazed with white. Call handlers cried as they threw the phones aside, falling back.

Another call handler whipped a knife out, but a heavy boot took him below the ribs, straight into the bladder, then a hard elbow rammed into the back of his neck, and he was out of it.

Sandarov was biting his lip. The call handlers were trained cops, and victims of ensorcelment. He didn't want any casualties – but if any occurred, it would be among the call handlers and not his own team, or the mages.

Or perhaps the mages had no need of his protection. The three shaven-headed men were standing back-to-back, forming an outward-facing triangle, and like Professor Steele they were closing their eyes, slipping into whatever altered state allowed them to manipulate thaumaturgic energies.

A mesmeric droning filled the air.

Even Sandarov felt unsteady, although the effect was targeted, specifically not aimed at him or his officers. He turned, checking the room.

Everywhere, call handlers were slumping in their chairs or slipping to the ground.

'Very nicely done,' said Sandarov.

The victims were asleep.

Two big black helicopters rose from an airfield outside Fortinium. Their triple-bladed rotors chopped the dark sky. Inside the holds, the noise was loud, and it would have been hard for the passengers to speak, had they wanted to.

Both choppers contained rows of dark-suited men and women, their expressions grim, concentrating. Each of them held a map of Tristopolis, with the telephone exchanges belonging to Central Resonator Systems, Exc. marked in purple. None of them needed the maps any longer, having finished creating eidetic memory-images. They were clear on what they had to do.

They were federal spellbinders.

When Donal walked into Surveillance, followed by Harald and Viktor, the atmosphere was disorganized. Some of the officers stared into their monitors as normal, others were arguing with each other. Rob Helborne stood with his arms crossed, not even trying to calm things down. When he saw Donal, he walked over quickly.

'Are you all right?'

'Sure,' said Donal. 'Why do you ask?'

'Look at it.' Helborne gestured around the screens. 'Tristopolis is going nuts. Craigsen's under arrest, there are cops pulling busloads of zombies off the streets, other cops preventing them. It's got to calm down soon, or we'll end up with chaos.'

'Are the newspapers being delivered?'

'Uh ... As far as I know.'

If Jo Serranto had lived up to her promises, there would be some interesting headlines on the late edition. It should kill the zombie-baiting. At least, Donal hoped it would.

Captain Sandarov entered the room, accompanied by three of his uniformed cops. He nodded to Donal, and walked past him to the iron portal leading to what had been Commissioner Vilnar's office. Sandarov stood there quietly, waiting.

'It won't open for him,' said Helborne.

'Probably not.' Donal nodded to Harald and Viktor. 'That's why we're here.'

When Donal approached, the portal pulled open, and stayed that way as Harald, Viktor and Sandarov passed through. The inner door opened.

No ciliaserpents rustled around the doorway, and when they stepped inside the room, it was almost bare of furniture. The few items remaining were insensate, ordinary chairs and cabinets. One of the cabinets bore a label: *Commissioner's Eyes Only*.

'I don't think I'll touch that,' said Sandarov, 'until it's official.'

'Wise idea.' Donal noted the emptiness of the room, and wished he hadn't come. 'How definite is your appointment?'

'I talked to Councillors Brownstone and Camberg. One of them will almost certainly be the next mayor. They've both agreed to support me.'

'Good. Sir, I need to go to Illurium. I've already booked a flight to Silvex City.'

Sandarov stared at the wall, as though he could see through it to Surveillance.

'Things are still uncertain. Not just for resurrected people on the streets. There are Unity Party supporters everywhere, and things could well get worse over the next few days, not better. Travelling is not safe.'

'Yeah. Did you talk to the feds?'

'Spellbinders are on their way. I had a rather unsettling phone conversation with their commanding officer.'

Harald smiled.

'They're unusual people.'

'That they are.'

The commissioner's black telephone was on the bare floor at the far end of the room. Donal walked over and picked it up. He looked at Sandarov.

'Go ahead, Lieutenant.'

'Sir.' Donal spun the cogs. 'Hi, international operator? Yeah, Illurium, please. Police Central, Silvex City.'

He waited.

'Hello,' he continued when a wraith answered. 'Inspector Temesin, please. My name's Donal Riordan.'

But when the extension rang, the gruff voice that picked up wasn't Temesin's.

'Just tell him I rang,' said Donal. 'Please.'

He put the receiver down.

'I still don't think you should fly to Illurium,' Sandarov said. 'I know for a fact there are UP members among airport security.'

'I know. That's why I'm not flying. But if anyone anticipates my going to Illurium, they'll find my booking for the fifteen o'clock flight from Tempelgard, the day after tomorrow.'

'Maybe they'll expect the misdirection.'

'Nothing lost if they do.'

'I guess not. You'll have exactly the legal status of a tourist in Illurium. I hope your friend there can help.'

'Yeah ...' Donal stared down at the phone. 'Somehow, I think of Temesin as Commissioner Vilnar's friend. But that doesn't make logical sense, does it?'

'I've no idea.' Sandarov looked at Harald and Viktor. 'You two, stay with me for a while. Donal, good luck.'

'Thank you, sir.'

Sandarov held out his hand, and Donal shook it.

Then Harald likewise offered his hand. Viktor raised his eyebrows, and Donal could understand why. Within the team, wishing someone luck was usually a punch to the upper arm or a sarcastic remark about their ancestry.

'Take it easy, Harald.'

'Good luck, Donal.'

As Donal left, he made sure to turn so that neither Viktor nor Sandarov could see his right hand, nor the small, hard object that Harald had passed to him.

Something powerful.

Yes, I feel it.

He clenched his fist hard as he walked from the Old Man's office, which seemed already to be a relic of the past, losing focus in memory. He wondered whether he would ever return to this place, and whether it would matter if he failed.

Laura.

It's all right. Everything is fine.

His grip tightened further.

Not while Cortindo lives.

Thirty

Two days later, Donal was swimming naked through black seawater, with a small pack strapped to his chest. Behind him was the diminishing outline of a rusted grey trawler, whose legitimate function of fishing for barbhydra and tigersquid was only part of what the hard-faced crew got up to.

A shot sounded, flat across the waves. Whether it was intended for him, Donal could not tell. On that vessel, it could have meant anything.

He continued to swim.

The trawler was one of a small fleet owned by One-Hand Krohl, a graduate of the same orphanage that Donal had survived. No model citizen, Krohl had helped Donal on occasion. But Donal had known better than to trust he would reach Port Sinstra intact, just because he was on Krohl's boat.

Soon, he could make out skeletal cranes outlined against the indigo, near-black sky. Had it not been for ripples of phosphorescence deep below, he would have been content in the quiet waters. As it was, he held the thought of his destination strongly in his mind, nothing but that, allowing his body to swim.

Some time over an hour later, a concrete dock loomed in front of him. Swimming, his hand missed a rusted ladder, and he hit a rung face-first, before grabbing hold. He hung there for a few seconds, then hauled himself up.

He was exhausted, but in a good way, with the same triumph he got from completing a long run. But this wasn't training.

Get into cover.

It was easy enough, among the stacks of freight containers, to find shadows where even a pale zombie's skin could not be seen. There, he slipped off his pack, and pulled out the first waterproof membrane-sac, and tore it open, revealing a large towel.

Soon he had dried off and dressed, a long dark overcoat covering his

309

suit. The backpack and torn membranes, he rolled up and stuffed into a waste can as he walked past. No one challenged his presence on the dock.

Under his arm, the Magnus was dry and intact, giving comfort in strange surroundings.

To leave the dock area, he had to climb a tall wire fence. He did it carefully, taking his time, trying to keep his clothes untorn. He might have to interact in civilized company, without a chance to re-equip. The fanged wire at the top wriggled at Donal's approach, but it stilled when he placed his hands on it. All along the fence, the topmost coils grew limp. Someone might notice, but Donal held on for as long as he could, replenishing his energy.

Then he went over the top, scaled down, and reached a deserted road. Wasteground lay beyond it, but further on were lights and ordinary-looking tenements. Donal set off walking.

He had some Illurian currency from his previous visit. When he reached the houses, he retrieved eight- and ten-sided coins from his pocket, and looked for a phone booth.

Finding one, he went inside, spun the wheels to a memorized number, and shovelled in coins. He asked for Inspector Temesin.

'One moment.'

Outside, a white lizard stopped on the sidewalk, looked up at Donal, then scuttled on into darkness.

'Temesin.'

'This is—'

'I know who it is. And I've cleared the board to help you. With you around, I'm going to get a promotion or fired, maybe dead. Better than being bored.'

'You're expecting me?'

'Yeah. Where are you now?'

'I'm in Illurium.' This was a moment for trust. 'Port Sinstra.'

'You can catch a train to Silvex City.'

'That's not my final destination.'

'I have two air tickets to Aurex City, and friends there who can help. What, you think I'm an amateur?'

'Obviously not.'

'So let's take a trip. It'll be fun, except everyone in Aurex City thinks Silvecians are country bumpkins.'

'You mean you aren't?'

'Shit, yes. We just don't like them pucker-asses telling us, is all.'

Donal laughed.

'So, listen. Do you know your measurements?'

'Say what?'

'*Clothes. Shoes. Like that.*'

'Oh.'

Having been measured for bespoke suits in the Janaval, Donal knew the numbers exactly, and recited them now.

'Is this for a disguise?' he added. 'Do I get a false nose?'

'*Ring me when you arrive.*'

The line buzzed.

Donal went out, and walked along streets towards the obvious centre of town. By the time he reached the main railway station, the first services were beginning to run. He bought his ticket, and stood on a near-empty open-air platform, watching a winged sea-lizard hovering overhead, facing into the wind, until it spotted a family of dark moths and descended to feed.

He wondered at Temesin's knowledge of what was going on, and his own conviction that Temesin had known the Commissioner, although there was no logical basis for that belief.

Since the vault.

'Ah,' he said to no one at all.

I've felt that way since the vault.

It was one of the peripheral pieces of information lodged in his mind since that ordeal. Since he'd been through pain to get it, he hoped the information was accurate.

The train that pulled in was long, polished burgundy and yellow, and looked as Donal had expected except that all four locomotives – two in front, two at the rear – and every carriage bore wheels set into the roof, with no obvious purpose, in addition to the usual wheels underneath.

When he got on board, he found a comfortable window seat. Few people were travelling this early, but of those who were, just over half had skin that was stippled with prickles, scaled, or even feathered. Whatever faults Illurium might have, prejudice against non-humans wasn't one of them.

An Illurian telephone company – or power company – would have no inherent reason to support anti-zombie legislation in another country. So why had they been operating not just covertly, but with links to the Unity Party in Tristopolis, and perhaps in other Federation cities?

Perhaps it was just a fault line in Tristopolitan politics. If the culture had been different, the companies – or certain people in those companies – would have looked for a different way to generate instability: not for commercial reasons, but because the Black Circle was behind them, with its own destructive agenda.

Incomplete reasoning.

The logic seemed to curve in on itself, leaving a gap. He thought of busloads of zombies, driven to the Outer Counties by shitkicker cops. What the Hades had been happening there?

Perhaps I should have stayed to—

'Is this seat taken?'

'No. Please, sit.'

The woman was pretty, her eyes bright and her glossed lips parted, as if permanently. She smiled at Donal.

Donal closed his eyes.

He allowed himself to drift as the train began to move. Still with his eyes shut, he smiled as he heard a faint 'Hmmph,' and the sounds of someone getting up to find another seat.

After a while he opened his eyes. Outside, bands of blackness crossed the indigo sky, an effect that Donal had never seen before. Things would change as the train neared Silvex City.

He settled in place, feeling relaxed, knowing there were hours to go before the Glass Planes became visible.

Overhead, the sky was a solid black in which yellow stars were visible. Underneath, the ground was about to drop away, by thousands of feet, as the train approached the Maximal Scarp.

The edge of the drop appeared to run on for ever. Donal leaned against the glass. Here and there, narrow curved lines reached out across the gap.

'Oh, shit.' It was the young woman who'd moved seats. 'I hate this part.'

Someone else began muttering prayers, or possibly curses.

The train edged forwards.

After a time, clunking sounds rocked the carriage. When Donal looked downwards through the window, there was nothing but air, and a tiny landscape far below.

Craning his head, he could not quite make out the overhead rail they were now travelling under. But off in the distance, miles away, another brightly lit train was making a similar journey, crawling beneath the five-hundred-mile curve of the rail, currently downwards. At some point, it would arc upwards, beginning its ascent.

It was awe-inspiring. It was frightening. But eventually, Donal got used to the view. So did most of the other passengers, judging by the amount of business the steward did, serving from his refreshments trolley. Or perhaps that was due to the small bottles of hard liquor he sold.

A long time passed before Donal could make out the Glass Planes. When he did, awe returned.

The gigantic planes were horizontal, stacked hundreds of feet apart, supported by titanic glass columns. How many square miles each plane stretched for, Donal did not know; but each was capable of supporting a city in its own right.

Despite Temesin's joke about country bumpkins, Silvex City was vast. Donal watched the glistening city grow larger, trying to ignore the increasing groans from the locomotives dragging the train up the steepest section of the overhead track.

There were many competing theories, held by different churches and academicians, about the origins of the Glass Panes. One major church taught that the Planes were a natural phenomenon, though how natural processes might produce regularly spaced glass squares on such a scale was beyond Donal's comprehension.

Splendid lighting made the buildings even grander than they already were.

'At last,' sighed the young woman.

The overhead track straightened out, and the train crawled level above the glass ground, on the final stretch. Impatient passengers were already pulling down luggage from overhead racks.

Soon enough, they pulled in to Terminal Station.

Temesin had grown a moustache.

He was waiting – narrow-shouldered, expensive moleskin coat, unlit cigarette in his thin-lipped mouth – to meet Donal, at the top of the diamond ramp ascending from the platform. They shook hands. Then Temesin led the way across the magnificent concourse, to the first escalator, formed of levitating glass steps, that bore them up to the airport level.

Temesin stopped in front of a coffee shop that Donal remembered from last time.

'Tell me,' said Temesin, 'that I look dashing.'

'Uh, sure. Like always.'

'Fuck off.'

'I should act like something's different?'

'Definitely not. You want coffee?'

'Mind you, if I had a pet caterpillar, I'd keep it at home, feed it on black cabbage, whatever. Carrying it around on your upper lip, that's a bit obsessive.'

'I take it that's a no for coffee.'

But Donal noticed, as they crossed the polished concourse floor, following the signs for restrooms, that Temesin made no return wisecracks about changes in Donal's appearance; and that was more than a point in Temesin's favour.

Last time they had met, Donal had been alive.

Inside the men's room, Temesin and Donal stood by the sinks waiting while the sole other occupant washed his hands, gave them a sidelong look, and picked up his case without drying his hands. He walked out quickly.

'I'm glad I don't live here,' said Donal. 'And that you don't have a reputation to care about.'

'Maybe my wife will stop bitching about my salary, and just divorce me.'

'So how much do we need?' Donal reached for his wallet. 'I've got plenty of dinars, and I can change more florins.'

'Pay me for the airfare,' said Temesin. 'Later. Four seventy-six for the both of us.'

'I can afford to pay for more than—'

'Just the airfare. Right now, I need you to gimme your gun, because I am a law enforcement officer who's allowed to carry firearms on board, and you're not.'

'You want the shoulder rig, I'll have to take my coat and jacket off.'

'Hades, you want I should turn my back?'

'And promise not to peek.'

On board the aircraft, Temesin insisted that Donal sit by the window.

'I might need to take a pee.'

'I'll try not to get excited if you squeeze past me.'

'Honestly, I don't—'

'And take these.' Temesin was holding out a pair of shades. 'For later.'

Donal took the dark glasses.

'For wearing *outside*?'

'You got it.'

'That is so fucking insane.'

'I know. And Aurex City isn't even on the Lightside.'

As they neared the end of the flight, Temesin pointed across Donal to the window. Along the horizon lay a greenish blue glow, a colour of sky that Donal had never seen before. He remembered his lessons in the orphanage with Sister Mary-Anne, but this was real, a reminder that the Earth was a giant sphere floating in space.

'That's the terminator?'

'Carry on going in that direction, and the whole sky's the same as over Aurex City.'

'I can't imagine what that is.'

'You'll see it soon enough.'

Twenty minutes later, the engines changed pitch, causing Donal to tense. Then the aeroplane banked right, and forward of the plane, everything was bright.

'Hades.'

A brilliant white heptagon of light shone in the sky, surrounded by blueness, tapering off to purple, then indigo.

No one else on board the plane seemed shocked.

'It's incredible,' whispered Donal. 'Beautiful.'

'Put the shades on,' said Temesin. 'And don't stare at it, or you'll go blind.'

'Huh.' Donal looked at him. 'Is that like what the nuns used to tell me, about keeping my hands above the covers?'

'No, it's literally true. On the Lightside, you can go blind in seconds.'

'But how do people get around?'

'By not looking directly up at the Sun. Or in Aurex City, not at the Mirror. You look at everything else, but not that.'

Donal turned to the window once more.

'How can they not look? It's amazing.'

'Come on.' Temesin leaned across him, and pulled down the blind. 'You'll get used to it, once we land.'

'Impossible.'

Then there was a whine as the undercarriage descended, and they began their approach. Donal looked around the aircraft. Light shone through the windows on both sides now. He raised the blind a little, and saw a landscape rushing past beneath: purple fields, a silver river, then the speeding greyness of the runway.

The plane bumped three times as it slowed, and then it was taxiing into place.

'I guess we're still alive,' said Donal.

It was an ill-phrased remark for a zombie to make, but Temesin just nodded.

'Wait'll you see. If I wasn't such a sophisticate, even I might be impressed with this place.'

After waiting for most of the other passengers to disembark, they walked to the exit, and Donal stepped through on to the top step. The movable stairs were locked in place, quite steady, but he felt unbalanced. The sky was so bright, it looked vast, and he felt as if he were going to topple.

'Steady.' Temesin held his shoulder. 'Take a deep breath.'

I don't need to breathe.

But Donal followed Temesin's advice, shaking his head as he looked across the runway and terminal buildings once more. He began to descend the steps, one hand on the rail for balance.

Then they headed with the other passengers to Arrivals. Apparently, two people travelling without proper luggage were not suspicious when one of them was a police officer. Security personnel waved Donal and Temesin through. In seconds, Donal was staring around the interior of a glass-sided building that shone with the light.

But the amazing thing was, the light came from outside.

From the *sky*.

'You're wrong,' said Donal. 'I'll not get used to this.'

'Yeah, you will. Come on. The taxis are this way.'

They were different, like everything else. Every cab was mostly iridescent blue, yet unique. Some shaded towards metallic green at the edges, others towards red. The drivers smiled politely, and spoke with soft cultured voices.

Donal was definitely not in Tristopolis.

The first driver, standing on the sidewalk next to his cab, said something, but Donal wasn't paying attention.

'Flixton Lawns,' answered Temesin. 'Is that OK?'

'My pleasure, sir. Please do climb inside.'

The driver held open the rear door, and Temesin got in. Donal paused, glanced obliquely up at the heptagon of white light high in the sky, and shook his head. He climbed in beside Temesin.

'The Mirror's held up by Aurecian mages, right?'

'Sure. Reflects light that would otherwise miss the Earth, and directs it down.'

'I can't imagine any other city that could manage that.'

The driver got in and started the engine. A green glass partition divided his compartment from the rear, where Donal and Temesin sat.

'There probably isn't one,' said Temesin. 'They say Aurecian mages are the best. Weird, but brilliant.'

Donal lowered his voice, as the taxi turned on to a wide white boulevard.

'And you think the Black Circle is legitimate here?'

'No.' For the first time, Temesin sounded offended. 'I definitely do not.'

'That's bad news,' said Donal.

Temesin's long face twisted into a strange expression.

'How can you say that?'

'Because anyone who can hide their activities from mages capable of *that*' – Donal pointed towards the sky – 'is even better than I thought.'

'Shit.'

'Yeah.'

Outside, the surroundings changed to clean, lovely suburbs with crisp blue lawns and shell-like houses. Prosperous-looking people were washing cars, chatting to each other, wearing dark glasses against the pervasive glare, smiling often.

Inside the taxi, neither Donal nor Temesin felt like talking.

A pink path led to a front door that opened before they knocked. A stocky man stood there squinting, and he was a cop. Donal knew it immediately.

'Temesin, you old bastard. And you must be Riordan. I'm Hayes.'

'Good to meet you.'

It was strange for Donal to remove dark glasses when *entering* a house. It was strange for the world outside to be bright and the interiors to be dim, inverting normal reality.

'Through there, the front lounge.' Hayes pointed, a blunt-fingered gesture, revealing the thickness of his wrist.

Four other cops were sitting there, in ordinary clothes. Three were human, while the cop in the biggest armchair had a shiny, dark-blue exoskeleton and white globes for eyes. He clacked his mandibles at Donal.

'That's Brint,' said Hayes. 'Best man in the department. The other reprobates are Fredrix, Atlong, and Shelbin.'

Fredrix was blond, Atlong dark, and Shelbin had close-cropped grey hair.

'Hey.'

'Hey.'

There were maps, diagrams and brown bottles everywhere. This was a cop's house, with an off-the-books briefing session under way.

'Is that beer you guys have there?' said Donal.

'Sure.'

Alcohol had no effect on zombies, but social activities strengthened teams, so Donal took a beer and found a seat. Temesin did likewise. Hayes found the half-finished beer he'd put down to answer the door.

'This little meeting is costing me a fortune,' he told Temesin. 'I hope you're properly Death-damned grateful.'

'You want beer money?'

'It ain't the booze, old buddy, it's the wife and three daughters and a whole day out shopping.'

But Donal was looking at the nearest purpleprint schematic lying on the carpet. The complicated diagram was labelled with a version number, date, and other technical descriptions, along with: *Gladius Armaments Exc., Site Alpha, Building 7*.

'You guys been investigating Brax Finross?'

'Could be,' said Hayes. 'Temesin, you ain't briefed him for shit, have ya?'

'I thought I'd leave it to an expert.'

'Well, I can understand that.'

'I don't suppose you *know* any experts?'

Atlong and Shelbin laughed, Fredrix smiled, and Brint clacked his mandibles once more.

'Ha. Ha. OK, Riordan, we got us an infiltration exercise set up here, and one of us locals *might* get through, but you'll definitely pass the scans.'

'Scans. You're talking about the main GA site.'

'Sure. You got the motivation to take the fuckers down, and you'll get through the scanfields cos of who you are, so it's what you might call ironic, don't you think?'

'Fuckin' A,' said Shelbin.

Donal looked at Temesin, who was putting a cigarette in his mouth.

'Am I missing something here?'

'Sure.' When Temesin lit a match, a silvery membrane slipped down from the ceiling, forming a column that enclosed Temesin and the chair on which he sat. 'Why do you think GA is encouraging zombie-killing inside the Federation? Because you know it's beginning.'

Donal had already worked out that prejudice against non-humans was absent here.

'Tell me.'

'"Zombie bones are wild",' said Fredrix. 'It's what they say inside Gladius.'

Reactor piles were unknown in Illurium, or at least in Silvex City where Donal had been before. He remembered the cabled children in the Power Centres.

And he remembered standing by the graveside while men lowered Laura's coffin into the ground. Because she had been spared the fate of ordinary humans.

'You can't use zombie bones for fuel,' said Donal.

'That's right.' Atlong had been silent, observing. Now, his voice was deep and certain. 'A kind of feedback sets up, sends the necroflux to uncontrollable levels.'

'GA don't build power stations,' said Shelbin. 'They make weapons.'

'Weapons?'

'Weapons.' Temesin sucked his cigarette, then blew out smoke. It billowed upwards, trapped inside the membranous column surrounding him. 'Resurrected bones make shit-hot energy projectors.'

Donal remembered the books he used to get from Peat's store.

'You're kidding me. Death-rays? That's impossible.'

'Yeah?' Temesin pointed to the window. 'You wanna look up in the sky and tell me what's impossible?'

'Shit.'

'Speaking of which …' Hayes burped. 'Bathroom break. Back in a minute.'

Brint made a gesture with his foreclaws that Donal couldn't decipher.

'Same to you,' said Hayes.

Thirty-one

While Hayes was gone, the others got into general chitchat about spike-ball teams. Donal picked up the purpleprint schematics and sat down, working his way through the diagrams, just letting his gaze follow the structural lines, *feeling* the patterns in his mind.

From upstairs, he thought he heard Hayes muttering to someone, but no reply. Talking to himself.

'Temesin?' Donal held up a purpleprint. 'How much of this did Commissioner Vilnar know?'

'A lot.'

'And is there anything specific I should know, but don't?'

'Probably.'

'And you're going to carry on being this helpful?'

'*Yes*,' said Fredrix and Shelbin together.

'Someone shoot me now,' said Donal. 'Please.'

'Later.' Atlong pulled a small-scale map towards him, then held it up. 'Delivery convoys travel along this road, GA personnel with military escort. Remember, Gladius Armaments is a bona fide arms manufacturer, with government contracts.'

'So don't go stealing any military secrets,' said Fredrix.

Brint made a scratching sound from some portion of his exoskeleton.

'Then why are you doing this?' said Donal. 'You're cops, not government. If Brax Finross's company is developing nasty new weapons for your country, shouldn't you be on his side?'

'Using resurrected people's bones' – Temesin puffed out blue smoke, and it billowed upwards in the membranous column – 'is illegal. There are no contracts to research, develop or manufacture such weaponry.'

'That might be the official line, but—'

'It's also the *internal* policy,' said Temesin, 'of military high command and civilian government. Really.'

So they had contacts that were highly placed, if Temesin knew what he was talking about. Donal wondered about those contacts, and whether he himself was some kind of traitor to the Federation by working with these people.

And if the Vital Renewal Bill is passed?

This was insane.

I'll be a non-person. A thing.

He had to trust his observations and his logic.

'Tell me more about the convoys, Atlong.'

'We've already got our own people among the GA workers, and the military will cooperate.'

'This isn't as off the books as it looks, is it?'

'That depends on how you look at it.' Hayes had re-entered the lounge. 'Discounting the fact that if we screw up, we'll get disowned and fired, jailed or killed, it's kind of official ... almost. Nearly.'

'So tell me about the convoy.'

'Well, the one tomorrow,' said Atlong, 'will be the first that we've interfered with.'

'So if I mess things up, you've lost your chance?'

'Uh-huh. Please do it right.'

Fredrix yawned, and Donal realized that it was getting late.

'Hayes? What time's your family coming back?'

'Tomorrow, late. Staying with my sister-in-law. You and Temesin can billet here tonight.'

Donal nodded, noting the use of *billet*. Hayes was ex-military, and so were the others, almost certainly.

'Detailed briefing coming up?'

'Sure. Let me get the coffee on, first.'

'One thing,' said Donal. 'You've been watching the GA place. Any sightings of Malfax Cortindo?'

'That bastard. Yeah, he comes and goes, not to any schedule we've determined.'

'So if I go in, he might not be there? They don't need his presence all the time?'

'That's right.'

'Does that imply,' asked Donal, 'that Brax Finross is a mage in his own right?'

Brint hissed and splayed his claws.

Donal looked at Hayes.

'That means, "Fucked if we know."'

'Oh.'

'Feel secure. You're among professionals.'

Climbing the stairs afterwards, Donal noticed a pair of heavy, curved dark-blue shades lying on a small table. For a moment, they caught his attention, then he shook his head, forgetting about them. He carried on to the front room, where Hayes had said he could stay. Temesin was going to use the middle daughter's bedroom.

'You might need this.' Temesin held out a small black spiked device. 'It's an adapter.'

'Thanks.'

Donal went into the room, closed the door, and looked around. On the bed which he wasn't going to use, someone had laid out a dark form-fitting jumpsuit and a pair of combat boots. That was good.

He went to the window and looked out. Brightness filled the exterior world. A few glistening cars – iridescent purple, some gold and bronze – still crawled along the street, but most people were indoors and settling down to sleep.

The adapter fitted a wall socket. Donal stripped above the waist, and opened his chest cavity. His narrow power cord connected the adapter to his heart socket.

He pulled on the dark glasses that Temesin had given him.

I hope he gets some sleep.

Had Donal been alive, needing sleep, he'd have found it difficult to close his eyes in this place. As it was, he left the drapes open, and stood unmoving at the window, staring out at the sunlit night.

Not sunlit. Mirror-lit.

Close enough.

He watched the world, and felt his energy build.

Several minutes later and two thousand miles away, at the edge of Black Iron Forest, a convoy of camouflage-painted trucks mixed in with black-painted buses came to a halt. The buses had the insignia of several different police departments on them, but Major Walvern grouped them together in his mind under the name of *Rectalfuck County PD*.

The drivers weren't the asswipe cops who'd made the roundups. They were Walvern's men, and therefore trusted.

'*Sheila*,' he muttered.

'Sir?'

'Nothing, Lieutenant. Carry on.'

'Yes, sir.'

Troops jumped down from the army trucks first, surrounding the com-mandeered police buses. Then the bus doors open, and the white-faced passengers began to descend. They stared at the clearing beyond, unable to help themselves.

It would have been poetic, or something, for the zombies to dig their own graves. However, Major Walvern's orders had been clear: swiftness was a priority. That was why teams from the Engineering Corps had already dug five long pits in the clearing. Soil was heaped up on the black grass, but it was not exactly bodies that the soil would cover up.

A translucent block of soapy gel stood at the side of each pit. Across each block, metal netting stretched, held tautly in place with iron pegs. The arrangement was precise. Walvern called them zombie-strainers. The grass around the blocks was already dying.

The first squad of soldiers had already led six captives to stand against a gel block. The squad leader looked to Lieutenant Davix, who in turn looked to Major Walvern. Walvern nodded.

Most of the squad raised rifles, preparing to aim, under orders to fire head-shots only. Other soldiers were taking hold of long, insulated poles, ready to push the zombies into the acid gel block.

The flesh would go straight through, while the metal netting would catch the valuable bones.

Walvern bit his lower lip, aware of the blood that sprang from the puncture, not caring.

It had been seven whole years since he had returned from leave to find that Sheila, silly bitch, had not only got herself killed in an accident, but resurrected. At night, the thing that mocked the memory of her stood sleepless, laughing at him. Dealing with the abomination had been the most courageous, empowering act of his life.

No one would ever find that body.

'*Bitch,*' he muttered now.

He raised his hand. A downward chop, and more monstrosities would be removed from the world.

'Ready ...'

His teeth were stained with his own blood.

In her tiny apartment in Lower Halls, old Mrs Westrason woke up when the phone rang. Although it was late, she smiled at the sound, and climbed out of her bed with an agility she had thought long lost. She padded into the sitting-room, and picked up the indigo receiver.

'Hello? Yes, of course.'

She smiled again.

'I'm feeling *wonderful*. And at my age, too.'

Then she listened.

'Why not? I've got carving knives in the kitchen, and oil I can put in a bottle. Will someone light the wick for me, when I need it? Oh, thank you.'

Some part of her was aware that perhaps two thousand similar conversations were taking place in Tristopolis. The thought made her feel warm and comfortable inside.

'Oh, zombies. Yes, marvellous. How many would you like me to kill?'

She bent her head forward, listening carefully.

The glossy, vast apartment took up the entire 227th floor of Darksan Tower. In the main lounge, Harald and Ruth Zarenski sat together. There were sounds from the kitchen.

'Guys? I can't find any food.'

Harald shook his head, got up, and went to look. Brian was looking inside metal cupboards, finding bare shelves.

'Donal and Laura weren't the world's best home-makers,' said Harald. 'But check the pantry to your right.'

'Oh, OK.' Brian's blue skin grew a little paler as he opened the pantry door. 'Stasis field. And some cheese inside that might be, what, prehistoric?'

The phones – there were seven extensions scattered around the apartment – rang. Ruth picked up the receiver – the black receiver – close to her.

'Really? Of course. Please send them up.'

Brian and Harald looked at each other. Then Ruth reached the kitchen doorway.

'Cops are coming,' she said.

'Death damn it,' muttered Brian. *'We're* cops, aren't we?'

'Just make yourself fucking scarce.'

There was a chime, warning that the lift was about to reach their lobby.

'Move it,' said Harald.

In his office, Captain Sandarov sat alone at his desk, waiting for the call. He reached into his desk drawer, pulled out the blue-and-white photograph of his resurrected parents who had been hidden for so long, and propped it in place, in full view.

Whatever happened tonight, he would live or die by his principles.

A sergeant called Royle, with a grey moustache and a stone expression, led the team of uniforms into the apartment. The men spread out through the elegant rooms.

'What are you looking for, Sergeant?' asked Ruth.

'Non-humans, ma'am, as I'm sure you're aware.'

'You won't find any here,' said Harald. 'Not in our home.'

'This place' – Royle gestured at the gleaming lounge and sneered – 'is due to be possessed by the city, I think you'll find.'

'No.' Ruth took hold of Harald's hand. 'We bought this apartment from Riordan, when he was still legal owner. *We're* the owners now, not the city, and with papers to prove it.'

'Huh.'

Royle turned and stomped through the room. His skin grew darker with increased blood pressure as his men, one by one, reported failure.

'Come on,' he said finally.

After the cops had left in the elevator, Ruth continued to hold Harald's hand. Neither of them said anything.

Then the chime sounded again, and the elevator door re-opened. Royle came back in.

'Forgot something.'

He went in and out of every room, some twice, before deciding that no non-human had crept out of a hiding-place. His skin a little more normal-hued, but still looking angry, he stomped back to the anteroom, got into the lift, and told it to descend.

Harald went to a shield-shaped mirror on the corridor wall, rapped it, and pulled it open. Beyond was a vertical shaft, and a luminescent green-grey ladder to which Brian was clinging, his arms wrapped tightly, swallowing often.

'Safe for now,' said Harald.

As soon as it rang, Sandarov ripped the receiver from the hook.

'Yes … Oh. Yes, Mayor Camberg. Congratulations, sir. Tristopolis needs you.'

He listened a while more, then grinned.

'Definitely. Yes. Right away.'

Quietly, he put the phone down. Then he stood up, punched his right fist into the air, and yelled, '*YES!*'

Although it was late, a handful of detectives were working in the outer room. One of them opened Sandarov's door.

'Captain? Is everything all right?'

'Not exactly.'

'Sir?'

'I'm not exactly Captain any longer.'

'What?' The detective frowned, then said, 'Really?'

'Yes, really.'

A grin stretched across the detective's face, almost as wide as Sandarov's.

'Congratulations, Commissioner Sandarov.'

'Thank you very much.'

The fortified chamber was deep below ground, surrounded by solid stone, guarded by pentagonal steel doors several feet thick. Inside, on stepped tiers, consoles stood in rows, festooned with cables and switches. Hundreds of indigo-uniformed men with empty eye sockets sat at the consoles. Each man wore an indigo headset, and whispered sounds that no ordinary human throat could have uttered. Their voices were chaotic overlays, and only their own trained senses – trained in the crucible of agony – could separate out the meanings. Each man was conducting up to thirteen conversations simultaneously, with different words transmitted down different lines, to different people.

'Yes, Mrs Westrason, take your sharpest knives now and—'

'You will feel good as you kill—'

'That's right, all the zombies—'

The massive doors blew inwards, spilling the eyeless men from their seats. They turned, although they surely could not see, to face the dark-suited men and women pouring into the chamber.

'Special Agent Hall,' called one of the newcomers. 'Federal spellbinder. Raise your hands, you are all—'

The eyeless men snarled, clenching their fists in unison, and blackness swept from their eyes in a torrent, whirling into a massive vortex, heading for the spellbinders.

Then sapphire lightning exploded across the room.

'—dead,' finished Hall.

Eyeless corpses wearing indigo uniforms sprawled everywhere. None of the dark-suited men or women smiled or showed other emotion.

They were federal spellbinders.

Mrs Westrason clucked, stared at the dead receiver in her hand, and put it down. Then she blinked sleepily at the room.

'I'm going back to bed,' she said.

Major Walvern's hand was still upraised when he saw white movement among the dense trees of Black Iron Forest. He could not have said what held him back from making the final gesture.

The zombies lined up against the execution pit, the others still to be herded from the buses, the soldiers about to fire — everyone stopped still, and waited.

And then they came, white and silent, out of cover.

'Sweet Hades,' muttered someone.

The white wolves took up position in front of the zombies, and turned to face the soldiers.

'Oh, shit.'

There was a thud as a rifle fell to the ground. Then a cacophony of thumps and rattles accompanied the mass dropping of weapons. Almost simultaneously, every soldier jerked into a run and fled, heading in all directions apart from their vehicles, all training forgotten. Even Lieutenant Davix was sprinting down the road.

Only Major Walvern stood in place.

'*Sheila*,' he whispered.

The white wolves advanced on him.

Donal took off his shades, and turned over his wrist. His watch-face showed a solid disc of black, indicating full power. He disconnected the cord, checked his chest cavity, and smiled.

'Time,' he said.

He sealed the cavity up.

Thirty-two

Black beetlehovers, the size of houses, hung in the air overhead, the beat of their wings a deep, subsonic vibration that shook the guts of every person on the ground. Even Donal was affected, but he was able to push the feelings into some imaginary distance, to oblivion.

Feeling warm in his dark jumpsuit, he drank cool water from a flask, preparing himself. His physiological processes still utilised water. While he rarely needed to eat, or drink anything but occasional H_2O, he deliberately hallucinated now that he was drinking strong coffee, remembering the taste, building it up on his tongue, with that cleansing, warm feeling of caffeine-high sweeping up and down through his body.

Temesin was frowning, perhaps trying to work out whether someone had laced the water with stimulants. Donal felt himself grow sharper, stand taller, because the strong imagined experience had produced *exactly* the neurochemical effect of the real thing.

Being a zombie had its advantages.

'I'm ready,' he said.

'All right.'

They walked up a sloping embankment that was covered in blue grass, and reached the straight white road where the military convoy had halted. In the middle of the convoy were two huge silver trucks, without insignia. They were the Gladius Armaments vehicles, transporting weapons components, and advertising would have been inappropriate. Right now, they weren't exactly anonymous, with military trucks fore and aft, and the beetlehovers overhead.

One of the beetlehovers descended, so that Donal could just make out a silhouette of the pilot, through the convex black-glass 'eyes' across which reflected sunlight slid. Heavy automatic cannons were slung beneath the buzzing wings.

'It would be a lot easier,' said Donal, 'if you guys just blasted your way inside.'

'We will.' Hayes approached, carrying what looked like a black stave. 'Here's the flare. I'm going to fit it here, on this external rack.'

The lead silver truck had a section for equipment on the rear of the cab. Hayes pushed the stave-like flare into clips, fastening it vertically in place.

Donal glanced at the military trucks. Most of the soldiers were out of sight. The others – big muscular men, short lean men (the majority) and fit-looking women, all of them intelligent and hard-eyed – gave Donal confidence. Hayes had said that the normal escort would have been from an ordinary regiment; but today, the troops were special forces.

'It flares silver,' Hayes said now, tapping the stave. 'It's a different colour from anything built by GA.'

'Good.'

Fleming and Atlong were fitting a metal ladder on to the side of the truck. Fleming climbed up first, walked along the flat spine of the truck, and got to work on a hatch.

'Where's Brint?' asked Hayes.

'Here he is.'

Brint was ascending the blue-grass embankment, his mandibles working without sound, his forelimbs held high. He wore a garish yellow sleeveless shirt over his chitinous torso. The shirt was unbuttoned, swinging open, revealing twin rows of bulbous sacs, each twice the size of a human fist.

'He's in a cheerful mood,' said Hayes. 'OK, Donal. Up you get.'

Donal climbed the ladder, and stood up on the flat strip that ran the length of the silver cargo trailer. Fleming had already worked the hatch open and pulled it right back.

'We don't have much time,' he said, 'before the little bastards try to climb up.'

'Let me see.'

Donal peered into the open hatch. Down inside, thousands of small black armoured creatures – stingers – were scuttling across equipment crates. They were part of the security system that GA used to protect their freight. Any one of the stingers could kill a man.

'Pleasant little fuckers,' muttered Fleming. 'Sooner you than me, Riordan.'

'I'm not going to enjoy this, am I?'

'I doubt it. And here comes Brint, ready to do his thing.'

'Oh, shit.'

From the ground, Hayes called up: 'Remember, the convoy will hang around as long as possible on site, and if they leave before you send up the signal, they'll travel *really* slowly.'

Donal nodded, understanding that the message was to move carefully, taking his time, not to be seen before he found the evidence that he, more than anyone else, should be able to track down.

Zombie bones.

It occurred to him that he hadn't asked how GA had managed to get the bones on site if possessing them was illegal. Obviously, they weren't transported in a convoy like this. But there was no more time for questions, because Brint had discarded his loud shirt and was advancing along the top of the trailer, his forelimbs spread, the rows of sacs on his blue-black torso beginning to pulse.

'Oh, fuck.'

'Keep your mouth shut.' Fleming was pulling on gauntlets. 'I mean, *tightly* shut. And your eyes.'

'Try not to die,' Temesin called from road level. 'I want you to see me get promoted, or get your ass kicked if I don't.'

Thank you so much.

There was no time for a sarcastic comeback, because pink viscous fluid was spurting from the nozzles opening across Brint's torso. It played up and down, hardening on contact. When it hit his face, Donal felt the impact, aware that it had already covered his nostrils, sealing them up.

This was another reason why a zombie was an ideal candidate for infiltrating the premises. From what Donal had seen, the local special forces were all standard human. Without special equipment – maybe detectable equipment – it was impossible to breathe inside this cocoon.

Then he was being manhandled, feeling the dizzying sensation of being lowered on some kind of rope – extruded from Brint's glands? – into the trailer. He felt a thud along the side of his leg as he swung into something, then solidness below his feet, and finally a gentle tipping until he was lying horizontally on the floor.

A distant clang was the sound of the hatch shutting.

As he lay in the moving truck, he reviewed the schematics in his mind, bringing them to life as three-dimensional images through which he moved, going through the possibilities. It was most likely that the truck would stop in the cargo bay of Building 3, and that the illegal weapons Donal sought would be in Building 17, home to GA's Private Projects Section and to the apartment that Brax Finross lived in whenever he was on the premises.

If Marnie Finross or Malfax Cortindo were here, that was almost certainly where they would be.

Remember.

Oh, yes.

Should Donal succeed, Hayes had promised that legalities would be arranged in retrospect, so that Donal would have entered the country on a visa he did not in fact possess, with a cross-border warrant that did not yet exist, tracking the escaped criminal Marnie Finross whom the Illurian authorities were honour-bound to extradite. During these explanations, Temesin had silently smiled, perhaps guessing Donal's true plans.

The truck jolted, then slowed.

Donal intended to fire off a signal flare, so that the Illurian military could sort out their own mess. But he wasn't going to do it as soon as he sensed zombie bones. He had a dark mage to deal with first.

Cortindo, I hope you're here.

Now, the truck was moving on, more steadily than before. From inside his cocoon, the sounds were too distant to make out, but Donal guessed that the convoy had passed through the gates, and was now inside the GA facility.

It was a huge place, and it would be some minutes yet before the truck reached the designated cargo bay. Donal went back to reviewing his mental model of the site.

Brax Finross may be a dark mage, too.

So, two targets, not one.

And with Marnie Finross, that made three. If Donal could take them down one at a time, he would, but he didn't think that likely.

There was exactly one solution that appealed to him. Had the cocoon not been tight against his face, he would have smiled. For he was entering an armaments facility, and not even a Black Circle mage could survive an explosion.

He remembered facing off against Malfax Cortindo, back when he, Donal, was a living being and Diva Maria daLivnova had been beside him, desperate for protection. Cortindo's words, his mesmeric abilities, had made Donal pause long enough for the Diva to die.

Not again.

No.

This time, there would be no discussion, no questioning, no legal warning, no arrest procedure. If dark mages saw him coming, they would stop him, and failure would be total.

'Try not to die,' Temesin had said, but that was unimportant.

Donal mentally put aside the imagined schematics, because he had a much simpler visualization to construct in his zombie mind, the image that would draw him forward, give him impetus to get through whatever faced him, to carry out one clearly pictured objective.

Kill every dark mage on site, at the same time, and fast.

Almost there.

The truck halted.

He felt the pattering of insectile legs across his protective cocoon. They would be leaving via a small opening, now unsealed, at the side of the trailer, called back to the nest by some pheromonal signal. In moments, responding to the same airborne molecules, Donal's cocoon began to evaporate.

There was a clang, signalling the lowering of the trailer's hitherto-sealed rear end. Donal sat up, shredding lumps of pink cocoon sliding from his jumpsuit. Wisps of pink vapour rose from the remnants, mingling with the purple mist entering the trailer.

This was another security measure, deadly even to a zombie if they were stupid enough to inhale. Donal made sure not to breathe as he brushed off the remaining unevaporated fragments of pink stuff, crept past equipment crates, and looked out of the trailer's rear opening.

He was in a cargo bay with no people, just two big trailers and an open channel down which the last few stingers were scuttling. His feet made minimal sound as he dropped to the stone floor, then made his way around to the front of the truck, and unclipped the long, stave-like signal flare.

Then he made his way to the door where he expected people to enter. He waited, listening, sensing no one outside. If it was locked, he would have to wait until someone came, or try to crawl out through the channel that the stingers had used.

The door opened when he pushed.

A passageway stretched left and right. In front was an emergency exit, theoretically set to sound a banshee alarm when opened. But someone had used a security key to detach the banshee's cage from the alarm circuit, probably the same person who had propped open the door with a fire extinguisher, and was standing outside now, smoking.

Donal would have smiled, but his emotions were so shut down that his facial muscles scarcely moved. Stave-like flare in both hands – the Magnus was inside his jumpsuit, but he did not want to fire it, not even here, where the sounds of weapon-testing were common – he took cross-steps to the doorway, peeked out, drew back.

Only one man, pacing up and down.

Listen.

With concentration, he could tell where the man was, when he turned, when he neared the doorway once more.

Now.

Donal lunged into the open, slamming the flare forward like a lance into the man's throat.

One down.

He left the body behind, jogging into the open, heading for the next building.

Trucks drove across the flat white ground surrounding the scattered facility. Donal moved when the angles were right, trotting alongside three buildings in succession, sprinting across the open sunlit gaps – Mirror-lit – when no one seemed to be observing.

Next was Building 11, also labelled Power Hall on the schematics Donal had seen but they had shown little interior detail. It rose high, with blue metallic walls formed of riveted sheets, and when he drew close he saw a window, some fifteen feet above the ground, that someone had left partly open.

He did not intend to enter. But there was an engine sound from around the corner. This side of the building was in shadow, but not enough to hide a person from a jeep full of sentries. Donal laid the dark, stave-like flare on the ground, flat against the wall, hoping that the shadows would be enough to conceal it, at least. Then he took hold of two rivet-heads on the wall, and began to haul himself upwards.

The window was tricky, but he pulled and tugged, and then he was through the opening. He crouched on the inner sill. It was one of a series along this corridor, where the walls were painted pale blue. Here, Donal could detect no sounds of people.

Outside, at ground level, the vehicle – it was a jeep – came into view, moving slowly. Donal jumped down from the window, and moved further into the corridor.

There was a side passage, and what looked like a balcony beyond, overlooking some internal space. There were no indications of people up here.

He advanced. When he reached the railed metal balcony, he looked out at rows of big vats, rising higher than he was, almost to the ceiling. From this balcony, metal steps led up to catwalks running over the vats. Other stairs led down to ground level.

Donal climbed.

No one was in sight as he found himself on a catwalk, looking down on the vats from above. Every vat was capped, so that it was impossible to see inside. There were inspection hatches, but Donal had no time to work on opening one up, to see inside a vat.

He trotted along the catwalk, to the far end. There was another balcony, and a sheer wall, but Donal knew from his memorized plans that this was the midpoint of the building. Leaning over the edge, he could make out a sign, formed of what looked like beaten gold in a giant cursive script, fastened against the wall below.

PALACE OF QUEENS.

It seemed a strange decoration for such industrial surroundings.

A passage led onwards, and Donal took it. Steps descended to the right, and he took them, wanting to get back to ground level. Then he stopped.

He was about to enter a chamber in which a bare-shouldered woman lay on a metal bed. Only her head and bare shoulders were visible, the rest disappearing through a yellow-draped opening in the wall. But it wasn't the strange set-up that halted Donal.

It was the expression in her eyes when she saw him.

'Oh,' the woman said. 'Please.'

She knew he was an intruder. She had to.

'Kill me, sir. Please kill me.'

'I won't hurt you.'

Donal entered the room, walked closer.

'I want you to—' She stopped, then looked at the drapes below her chin. 'Open it.'

He was afraid, but he did what she said.

Don't look.

You must.

There was no way of shutting the image out of his mind once he had seen it. Beyond the opening in the wall, the woman's nude body continued on ... and on ... and on, swollen into vastness, enough to fill a huge vat. It was her womb that was bigger than a truck, than several trucks, where the skin had been pulled back and opened, leaving a permeable transparent membrane through which workers could reach, tending the unborn.

The thousands of embryos she was nurturing.

Children.

For the Power Centres.

Donal turned away from the abomination.

'I had a husband,' the woman said. 'A normal life, before—'

Tears welled up.

But there were so many workers down there, reaching into the womb where umbilical cords sprouted like tendrils. If something happened to the woman, they would realize immediately.

'I can't,' whispered Donal.

'P-Please.'

'I can't risk it.'

'No ...'

He walked away from her, found an exit to steps leading downwards, and descended. He was at ground level, and he could go left or right. It was an easy choice.

It was awful.

As he climbed back up the steps, he undid his jumpsuit enough to pull out the Magnus. When he reached the woman, he was calm inside, his decision made. Wishing Harald were here with his superior expertise, Donal stopped, and crouched down beside the woman.

He touched her forehead.

'Remember a time,' he murmured, 'when you were with your husband, and everything was all right.'

'Yes ...'

She closed her eyes, and Donal talked her through the stages of strengthening the memory, making it more vivid, reliving it.

'Let everything become richer, clearer ...'

The bang was loud when he pulled the trigger. Fragments of her brain spattered across his face.

He wiped them off as he got moving.

Two minutes later, he burst through an emergency exit. Its banshee alarm went off, but it was drowned by the already-wailing cacophony of alarms triggered by the woman's death. This was the Palace of Queens, and one of the queens was down.

In the open, he ran around the outer corner, and saw a puzzled man holding the stave-flare in his hands. He was turning it and hefting its weight.

'I can tell you what it is,' called Donal.

'What?'

Donal's palm-heel smacked into the guy's forehead, then he ripped the stave from the man's opening grasp, and whipped a shin-kick into the man's thigh. The man fell, followed by a downward thrust from Donal's stave, and a soft crunch.

'The end of your world,' said Donal.

Stave-flare held horizontally in one hand, he set off into the open, heading straight for Building 17, knowing that if Hayes and the others had guessed wrongly, there would be no time left to look elsewhere. Donal would have failed.

'Hey.'

Glancing back, Donal saw two men, neither of them armed. There was a sense of other people exiting the Palace of Queens behind them.

Run fast.

He turned towards Building 17, and began to speed up.

Run faster.

For years he had used this discipline to give him strength to face life, running the catacombs, sometimes ten miles, sometimes longer, pushing himself. Now, with his resurrected existence likely to end, he could meet Death with a kind of physical joy, almost as if true, warm-blooded life were his again for the final moments.

A rifle shot banged out behind him.

Building 17 was only feet away.

Rifle fire cracked once more.

Shit.

Then he kicked the door open and was through.

Got it.

And he was in the right place.

Do you hear the bones?

In the name of Hades, this was it. Dark resonance washed back and forth, sweeping through him.

Do you feel us howl?

Do you hear us suffer?

He hefted the stave-flare in his left hand, the Magnus in his right.

'I certainly do,' he said.

It was a vast, silver, airy hangar-like space, its arched metal ceiling very high. At ground level, Donal walked past row upon row of field-guns that did not fire shells, but instead contained resonance cavities filled with zombie bones whose agony screamed in Donal's mind, burned every nerve, but not enough to stop him.

There were hundreds of field-guns or cannons, half of them painted in the Illurian national colours of red and yellow, the others silver and purple, bearing the Salamander-and-Eagle design that Donal knew so well, the symbol of the Federation. Gladius Armaments was an arms manufacturer. Of course it would sell to both sides in any war.

Beyond the field-guns lay a mostly empty space. On a raised platform, a giant energy projector stood, about the size of a truck, its casing removed to reveal the intricate steel components surrounding the resonance cavity itself. From here, Donal could feel the tortured chaos inside the cavity.

It's as powerful as all the other weapons put together.

I know.

Something like a huge silver kite hung in the air, levitating, unsupported by anything that Donal could see ... until he noticed two figures standing beyond the energy projector, their hands upraised. As they gestured, the floating kite-mirror adjusted angle.

'Cortindo.' Even from here, Donal recognized the revenant mage. 'You fucker.'

The other man was Brax Finross.

So he is a dark mage.

The two mages directed the floating mirror to the angle they wanted. Then the huge projector hummed, and spat a white, coruscating beam straight at the mirror. The reflected beam angled downwards, blasting a huge pit. Then the beam cut out.

'Hades,' muttered Donal.

Solid floor – solid ground – had been replaced by a deep pit with blackened walls.

'It's all about geometry,' said a woman's voice beside him. 'Along with rather impressive control, don't you think?'

A blue-haired woman was standing three paces away. As Donal stared, her hair changed colour to scarlet.

'Eyes,' he said. 'Or should I call you Marnie?'

'Call me anything you like. So here's the bit you can remember in oblivion. We can hit Tristopolis from here, by floating that mirror high enough, and aiming the projector just right.'

'Shit.'

'Before that happens, some of these babies' – she gestured to the silver-and-purple field-gun projectors – 'are going to open up on civilian targets in Aurex City. And we even have some dead Federation soldiers in storage, ready to be found near the projectors. Isn't that clever? The rest of the weapons, we'll sell to a Federation desperate to defend itself when Illurium declares war.'

'Fuck off,' said Donal.

He raised his Magnus and pulled the trigger.

'Oops,' said Marnie Finross.

Dust spilled from the weapon. Whether it was the bullets or the firing mechanism that had crumbled into nothing, Donal could not tell.

'My father' – black flecks moved across Marnie Finross's eyes – 'has been teaching me some things.'

'Like when to shut the fuck up?'

'Little man, it's time for you to—'

With his thumb, Donal pressed the firing-stud on the stave-flare. Silver fire burst forwards, tearing a hole through Marnie Finross's stomach. Then he whipped the hot flare through a vertical arc, snapping her head back, and threw the flare aside.

Fast, now.

Very, very fast.

He ran for the truck-sized projector.

It was Brax Finross who screamed, 'What have you *done*?'

The floating mirror wobbled. Malfax Cortindo, strange highlights rippling across his rebuilt skin, groaned as he fought to keep the levitation going, then threw his hands down. The mirror slid edge-first through the air and struck the ground.

By that time, Donal was climbing up the side of the big projector. Black waves of suffering pulsed through the air, agonizing now that he was this close to the cavity filled with aligned zombie bones.

At least the lack of casing meant he had finger- and toeholds, helping him to climb.

It hurts.

Not for long.

And then he was at the top, hauling himself into place. There was an inspection cover, but he ripped it off as he stood up. He balanced, one foot on either side of a deep opening into the projector's dark heart. Inside, pure pain screamed back and forth, in standing waves of suffering: harmonics of torture, the wavelength of death.

Malfax Cortindo's face was a rippling mess, not quite rebuilt, certainly not finished to make him look near-human. It was a long procedure, creating a revenant from a long-dead corpse, long after resurrection to zombiehood was no longer possible.

Too bad.

Pity he won't live to suffer longer.

'You,' said Cortindo. 'Riordan.'

Brax Finross was staring across at Marnie Finross's corpse. Then he looked up at Donal.

'I'm going to kill you,' he said. 'And it will hurt, for a long time before the end.'

'You can't.'

'Why—?'

This is it.

Yes, my love.

'I'm already dead,' said Donal.

Then he put his feet together, and dropped inside the cavity.

Into the middle of undead zombie bones, carefully positioned.

Into agony.

Thirty-three

Without the floating mirror to reflect it, the ravening white beam of energy burst through the wall of Building 17, across an expanse of flat white ground, and tore into a warehouse full of conventional high explosive. The detonation was immense.

From the military convoy five miles away, where Hayes stood atop a truck with binoculars in hand, the rising column of flame and sooty black smoke was appallingly visible.

'Oh, shit,' he said.

Beside him, Temesin was silent, staring downward.

It took two minutes to get the convoy into motion, heading back to Gladius Armaments, pouring on the speed. By the time the vehicles reached the site, GA personnel had already thrown the gates open, welcoming the soldiers as rescuers.

Less than ten minutes after the explosion, Temesin and Hayes were with the special forces team that burst into Building 17. The first body they found was a ruined corpse of a scarlet-haired woman.

'Marnie Finross,' said Temesin.

Next, they found two dead men. One was a revenant, obvious from the rippled skin, whose legs and torso were intact, ending abruptly below the shoulders.

'Cortindo.' Hayes kicked at the corpse. 'Must've stood in front of the beam.'

'Bad idea.' Temesin crouched over another man. 'And this'll be Brax Finross.'

'I wonder what killed him?'

A foot-wide triangular fragment of metal had buried itself inside Finross's skull.

'Yeah, I wonder. Where the Hades is Riordan?'

All around, the special forces troopers were fanning out, working their way along the rows of zombie-bone weapons, laying demolition charges.

'Sir?' One of the soldiers had climbed on top of the big energy projector. He stood there now, an explosives pack in hand, staring down.
'You'd better come up.'

In the end, it took two more soldiers, in addition to Hayes and Temesin,
to haul Donal Riordan's body out of the resonance cavity.

'Shit. Ah, shit.'

'Let's get him out of here, before they blow the building.'

'Ah, shit.'

The soldiers were gentle, carrying the body.

Thirty-four

Some two hundred mourners came to Donal's funeral. They stood around the opened double grave, and watched as pallbearers – Harald and Viktor on one side, Kresham and the glowing form of Aggie on the other – carried the coffin from the black ambulance.

Gravediggers, using black ropes, lowered the coffin into place, then walked away to a discreet distance, waiting for the rituals to finish.

Commissioner Sandarov said some words. So did Harald, before returning to stand beside Ruth, who hugged his arm as she cried. Viktor's deep voice became a croak, unable to finish what he'd intended to say.

Brian stood alongside Eagle Dawkins from the firing-range. When the gathering of mourners finally began to break up, Dawkins muttered something about sightseers. He'd been at Laura Steele's funeral as well, and there had been only a handful of people to watch her burial in the same grave where Donal had joined her. Suddenly, though, it was politically expedient to bid farewell to a symbol of tolerance and reunification, as the streets of Tristopolis became safe once more.

Yesterday in Fortinium, the Senate had voted against the Unity Party's Vital Renewal Bill, by a massive majority.

One by one, couple by couple, group by group, people drifted away, heading back to the various cars and taxis that waited for them. Jo Serranto and Dr Thalveen left just after Commissioner Sandarov. Soon, there were few people remaining. Shaven-headed Kelvin stood with Alexa Ceerling, neither of them strictly well enough to be out of Mordanto Hospital. Professor Helena Steele remained close to them, her face a mask without expression; but she required her driver, André, to help her when she finally walked back to her limousine.

And then there were three people left beside the open grave. Kyushen Jyu and Sister Lynkse held hands tightly, as they had throughout the burial ceremony. Sister Felice, arms crossed, stood apart from them.

'You two go now,' she said finally.

'We can wait.'

'No, Lynnie. Take Kyushen home.'

'I ... All right. See you later.'

'See you.'

When they had gone, Sister Felice stepped back, and waved to the gravediggers. They came over.

'We can wait a while longer, ma'am.'

'No, go ahead.'

'Ma'am.'

She watched them shovel dark earth into place, filling the hole. She watched them smooth the soil on the surface. And she watched them leave the graveyard, so that she was alone. There were no lights nearby, and the sky was dark purple as always. Darkness shrouded the headstones.

She stood and watched nothing move, nothing make a sound, nothing live any more.

'Oh, Donal.'

Something glinted red off to her left, then again to her right.

'He'd be glad you came.'

One by one, the cats drew near, until they were sitting, perhaps a hundred of them, in a circle around Donal's grave. For a long time they sat, silent and without movement, while Sister Felice held herself still. Then the cats turned and slipped away into darkness.

A single small cat, little more than a kitten, remained.

'Hey.' Sister Felice squatted down. 'Spike? That's a good name.'

She held out her hands, the cat jumped into them, and she stood up. Cradling the cat, who drifted quickly into sleep, she remained standing in place.

After some unknown time, she realized a man was standing beside her.

'Who are you?' she asked.

The man was tall and thin. Despite the darkness, he wore peculiar, curved, heavy-looking dark-blue shades.

'My name is Lamis.' His voice was sepulchral. 'People forget about me.'

He looked down at the grave for a minute, maybe two, then turned and left.

After a while, Sister Felice, turned and stared at a spot of ground beside her, frowning as if trying to remember something. Then she shook her head, and looked down at the little cat still cradled in her arms.

'Come on, sleepy Spike. You're coming home with me.'

Then she was gone, and the graveyard was silent.

Thirty-five

Fifty days later, beneath the heavy soil, the blackwood coffin was still intact. Paid for by the Aurex City Police Department, it would not dissolve for months, perhaps years. Eventually, it *would* disintegrate, allowing the worms and insects who crawled through the soil finally to feast.

Inside the coffin, Donal, too, lay intact.

Then a bright amber light filled the interior, and he gasped. His body jerked, and he clawed open his shirt, pulled open his chest cavity, and ripped out the pendant producing the searing, blinding light.

Inside glowed the snowflake, the stasis generator that Harald had retrieved in the Westside Complex, and handed to Donal via a handshake. Nothing had changed inside its field: no entropy, no physical process, no time passing since he'd dropped inside the weapon cavity.

He sucked a breath in, his nerves alive with pain.

Now, the amber light was fading, as the stasis field began to dissipate. For a few seconds, Donal had illumination to see where he was. He pressed his fingers against the satin lining, felt the hard wood beyond, and understood everything.

'Oh, fuck.'

Acknowledgments

As always, love and thanks to Yvonne, whose guidance and encouragement grow wiser and more elegant through the years.

Boundless gratitude to Simon Spanton, editor without equal. (I'd say *nonpareil*, but that would be showing off.) The theme and direction of this book derive from two sentences that Simon uttered over lunch in London's Chinatown. Or perhaps it took three sentences ...

Heartfelt thanks to Gillian Redfearn and Jon Weir, and the rest of the Gollancz crew. And isn't the cover art gorgeous?

Ta lots to Chris Hill for early feedback on the book. Cheers, mate!

To John Richard Parker – always – I'm honoured that you're my agent and friend.

And to Paul McKenna, for trance-figuring so many while spelling out the difference, endless thanks.